She lay waiting for sle... quarrels that had rocked the house. The hard words she had spoken to Olivia came back to her, and she flinched, wishing that she had bitten her tongue out before saying such things.

But once spoken they couldn't be denied. Annis was quite certain in her own mind that she had stumbled on the real reason for Olivia's determination to make the best marriage she could — a better marriage than her sister's. Olivia wouldn't settle for anything less than a larger house than this house, a husband wealthier than Douglas, a social position higher than the position Annis held.

But there were few opportunities in Greenock for a penniless young woman to marry out of her class. Better by far to grasp the one hand that was being held out to her, as Annis had done. She herself, slipping at last into the deep soft blackness of sleep, would have been happy indeed to hear that a man such as Gideon Brenner had asked permission to court her.

If, of course, she had been unmarried. If she had been free. If, if, if . . .

If only, whispered a tiny voice deep in the core of her being; if only she had been Olivia.

Also by Evelyn Hood

The Damask Days
A Stranger to the Town
The Silken Thread
A Matter of Mischief

A Pride
of Sisters

Evelyn Hood

HEADLINE

Copyright © 1991 Evelyn Hood

The right of Evelyn Hood to be identified as the Author of the
Work has been asserted by her in accordance with the
Copyright, Designs and Patents Act 1988.

First published in Great Britain in 1991
by HEADLINE BOOK PUBLISHING PLC

First published in paperback in 1991
by HEADLINE BOOK PUBLISHING PLC

10 9 8 7 6 5 4 3 2

All rights reserved. No part of this publication may be
reproduced, stored in a retrieval system, or transmitted, in any
form or by any means without the prior written permission of
the publisher, nor be otherwise circulated in any form of
binding or cover other than that in which it is published and
without a similar condition being imposed on the subsequent
purchaser.

All characters in this publication are fictitious and any
resemblance to real persons, living or dead, is purely
coincidental.

ISBN 0 7472 3473 6

Typeset by Medcalf Type Ltd, Bicester, Oxon

Printed and bound by
HarperCollins Manufacturing, Glasgow

HEADLINE BOOK PUBLISHING PLC
Headline House
79 Great Titchfield Street
London W1P 7FN

This book is dedicated with gratitude
to my dear friend WENDY REID, who has shared the
bad times and rejoiced generously in the good times.

1

The *Grace and Charity* came sweeping up the southern reaches of the Firth of Clyde on a bright clear April day in 1872 with all the dash and splendour of a superb showman. Men and women with business to see to in the busy Greenock docks, local people and seamen whose ships had put in to unload cargo and take on new goods, stopped what they were doing to watch the American-built clipper glide into port for the first time.

But one person was missing. Despite the fact that she had been impatiently awaiting the clipper's arrival, Annis Moncrieff, wife of the *Grace and Charity*'s new owner, was busy dealing with the day's marketing, weaving her way along the busy narrow footpaths and wishing that her sister Olivia would stop carping on about the blessed length of plum-coloured ribbon she needed to trim one of her gowns.

'Now that all the grand Glasgow folks are building their summer houses not half a mile up the hill from this very spot you'd think the drapers would be getting in more stock, not less!' Olivia complained as she impatiently butted her way through the oncoming pedestrians, whisking the full skirts of her fine green gown above shapely ankles to save the hem from a dirty puddle.

'I thought that the deep red ribbon was fine, myself,'

Annis offered placatingly, but her elder sister merely gave her a sidelong hazel glare from beneath sweeping lashes and said, 'Not at all, it was quite, quite wrong! Now I shall have to take the train to Glasgow. Life would be so much easier,' she added as they turned into Cathcart Square, 'if it wasn't necessary to make over my old dresses. But I've no choice, of course, since Papa saw fit to ruin us all before he . . .'

At those final words the irritation that had been simmering in Annis ever since she had trailed out of the last draper's shop in her sister's imperious wake suddenly surfaced, unbidden and unexpected.

'Olivia Kerr . . . if you're about to berate Papa once again for leaving us without any money you might as well save your breath, for I don't want to hear it!'

Olivia's lovely face went blank with shock under the attack, then flushed like a rose. 'How dare you speak to me in that fashion! Just because you found yourself a wealthy husband . . .'

The injustice of the remark hit home. 'I did not find Douglas, as you well know! He found me!'

'How very fortunate for you,' Olivia sneered, low-voiced, aware of the passers-by and the need for decorum that had been drilled into the two Kerr girls from the moment of birth. 'At least it saves you from the vexation of having to look for trifles such as plum ribbon so that you can make over dresses only fit for the ragbag.'

'Ragbag?' They had stopped, and were standing almost nose to nose now in a quiet little corner, quarrelling in fierce whispers. 'Your dresses are all very fine indeed. For myself, I would have settled quite happily for the red ribbon!'

'That,' said Olivia stiffly, 'is because you have a poor

sense of fashion. I should — we should — have had money of our own.' She would have said more, but a glance from Annis caused her to bite back the words.

'Papa is dead, Olivia. Let him rest in peace.' Realizing that a few of the people hurrying by had turned to look inquisitively at them, Annis put a hand on her sister's arm and added, forcing her own anger back, 'And don't let's quarrel.'

Olivia tossed her head. 'If we're having a quarrel it's not of my making,' she said haughtily, and swept off the kerb and across the square, stepping aside to prevent her hem being contaminated by an elderly beggar who was sitting close by the entrance to the White Hart Inn with his back to its stone wall, playing a penny whistle. Beside him lay a threadbare greasy cap with two halfpennies in it.

The man instinctively scrambled his feet out of the way as Olivia swept by. Annis, already suffering the first pangs of guilt for rounding on her sister, stopped and dipped a hand into the small purse hanging from her wrist. She took out a penny, hesitated, put it back and selected a sixpence. It glittered as it fell into the cap. The man stared, then took the whistle from between his lips and stammered out his thanks, the words falling over each other.

Olivia, who had turned her head in time to see the glint of the coin as it fell, said accusingly, 'You'll bankrupt Douglas as well as Papa at that rate!' and marched into the flesher's, trying and failing to gain entry before a solidly built elderly matron clutching a huge basket.

The two of them fretted together for a clumsy moment in the doorway before the older woman, using her basket as a battering ram, won the tussle.

Annis bit down hard on her lower lip. That final shot in the small battle had been most unfair. It was Olivia, the favoured older daughter, who had been encouraged to spend her father's money while he had it. Annis, who knew that she had disappointed her father at birth by surviving when her twin, a boy, had died, had never in her life been given anything other than her due by George Kerr, nor had she asked it.

But she had already unwittingly started one quarrel and she didn't want to start another, particularly in front of the flesher, so she said no more as she followed her sister into the shop.

They had a long silent wait while the elderly woman ahead of them bought one item after another, then took her time to decide between beef and mutton for her husband's evening meal.

Annis shifted from one neatly shod foot to the other and wondered when she would ever learn to be a nicer person, less impatient and less critical of others. Part of her was shocked by her own sudden and quite unexpected attack on her sister. She had learned at a very early age to suppress the quick words that all too easily jumped to her lips, and had learned so successfully that people tended to look on her as placid and submissive. But on this particular day, when she had awakened with the disturbing feeling that life had tucked her into a neat little box and passed her by, Olivia's griping about poor Papa was more than she could swallow.

Outside, spurred by the friendly wink of the silver sixpence in the cap by his side, the beggar launched into a cheerful reel. The thin thread of his music unrolled itself through the doorway and twined about Annis, lifting her out of her gloomy thoughts.

Subtly, subconsciously, her restless shifting took on the rhythm of the music.

'Can you not be at peace?' Olivia eventually snapped under her breath. Annis blinked and hurriedly stilled her feet on the sawdust-covered floor.

The customer being served decided on mutton. Money changed hands, the parcel of meat was popped into a huge basket, and a final flurry of courtesies volleyed back and forth across the counter. Then the flesher, wiping his hands on the front of his apron, was bowing and smiling at Annis and Olivia as though they were the most important people he had seen that morning.

'Mistress Moncrieff . . . Miss Kerr. Good morning to you, ladies. What can I do for you?'

His eyes automatically rested on Olivia as he asked the question. Olivia was a mature and confident twenty-one years old, whereas Annis, despite the gold marriage ring on her finger, often looked more than three years the junior.

It was Annis, however, who replied, resting her basket on the counter, studying the meat on display with a knowledgable eye.

'I'm looking for a nice piece of roast, Mr McMillan. Not as much fat as the last order you sent round, if you please.'

He had the grace to redden slightly under her pleasant smile. More than one tradesman who thought to take financial advantage of recently wed little Mrs Moncrieff had found out his error. Despite her youth Annis was much more experienced in the ways of running a house than her sister. Olivia had never been greatly interested in domestic affairs; Annis, tired of a succession of unsuitable housekeepers, dusty rooms and unappetizing meals, had taken over responsibility for the running of her widowed father's house at the age of fourteen and had dealt with it efficiently.

Until the terrible day, just over a year earlier, when she had gone into his room and found him dead on his bed, an empty laudanum bottle by his side. What had happened was horribly clear and Annis still woke in the night at times, shaking with the memory of that moment. She worked hard, all the time, to erase it from her memory.

Now it was Olivia's turn to shift from foot to foot as her sister and the flesher discussed the merits and faults of the selection hurriedly laid out before Annis. She had just settled on a suitable piece of roast and was counting the money out when a young lad raced past the shop calling to his friends, 'The Yankee ship's coming in!'

Annis's head jerked up and the coins spilled from her fingers, missing the flesher's outstretched hand and clattering noisily on to the counter. She swung round on her sister, face alight. 'Did you hear that? It must be the *Grace and Charity* arrived early from Boston!'

All thought of that evening's supper vanished from her mind. Determined to reach the quay in time to see Douglas's new ship coming in, she gathered up her skirts and ran from the shop, along the footpath, round the corner and into the narrow length of East Quay Lane, following hard on the heels of the boy and his companions, skipping dexterously over puddles and skirting groups of chattering people and piles of refuse.

She reached the end of the lane, rounded the corner into Custom House Quay, and came to a sudden stop, grey eyes wide with admiration at the magnificent sight before her.

Although she was being towed by a steam tug which

fussed along at her bows, the clipper's master had left on as much canvas as he dared in order to make her first entry to her new port impressive. The fresh breeze bellied out the sails sufficiently to make it appear that the *Grace and Charity* was moving ahead under her own wind-power, the Red Ensign streamed from her taffrail where until recently the Stars and Stripes had fluttered and, in spite of the long haul from Boston and the rusty travel-streaks on her black hull, her brasswork gleamed under the sun. There was a freshness and neatness about her that spoke of a smart crew and a good shipmaster's firm hand.

Even without the topgallants and royals and skysails set, the clipper's rigging was impressive, looming high above that of the barques and brigantines and schooners already in the harbour, stretching towards the blue April sky. Seamen scrambled up her three masts and along her rigging, loosening the sails and gathering them up, hand over hand, as the clipper slid smoothly towards her berth. The boatswain's mate called out orders in a sing-song chant that was taken up by the men balancing easily on the rat-lines as they worked, apparently oblivious to the great drop between themselves and the deck far below. Annis Moncrieff was transfixed.

'Annis!' Olivia burst out of the lane behind her. 'What a way to behave, rushing out of the shop like that — and you a married woman too! I swear I didn't know what to say to Mr McMillan when you just left him standing there—'

'Look.' Annis's voice was only just above a whisper. 'Look at her. Have you ever seen anything as beautiful?'

Olivia looked, and shrugged. To her, a ship was a ship. The busy Greenock quays were always full of them, and she had never found them particularly interesting. Her eyes were elsewhere.

'There's Douglas.' Olivia pointed to a group of men some distance in front of them, near the stretch where the incoming ship would berth. Douglas Moncrieff stood in their midst, hatless, his fair hair ruffled by the breeze.

By his side was his shirt-sleeved clerk, brought from his high desk to gape as unreservedly at the clipper as his employer. Everyone had been waiting for the arrival of the *Grace and Charity*, and everyone wanted to see her berth. Although American ships called regularly at the thriving harbour, this was the first to be bought by a local shipowner.

'Come away before he sees you,' Olivia's voice was sharp with disapproval. 'You know he doesn't like you coming down to the quay — and neither do I,' she added, peering anxiously at the sleeve of her stylish green dress as a grubby little boy, scampering forward to gaze up at the clipper, brushed past her. 'It's a nasty, dirty place!'

'Bother what Douglas likes,' his wife said with a toss of her bonneted head. 'I'd not miss this for a thousand Douglases!'

The men poised fore and aft on the clipper's deck held coiled lines ready in their hands. On dry land, other men eased their way through the crowd of onlookers and hurried along the edge of the quay, ready to catch the lines. At that moment Douglas Moncrieff turned his head and saw his wife and sister-in-law. On any other day a shadow of disapproval would have darkened his long face, for like Olivia he didn't consider the waterfront with its noise and its riff-raff and its salty language to be a fitting place for the women beneath his protection, and he had forbidden Annis on more than one occasion to

visit it. But today things were different. Today his fine
new ship was coming home after making excellent time
from America, and Douglas was bursting with pride and
eager for his young bride to share in it.

'Annis, my dear! And Olivia . . . ' He stepped away
from the group of men, holding out his hand, a
welcoming smile on his bearded face.

Annis went to him eagerly, anxious to be in the
forefront of the crowd, thanking the Fates for the fact
that, in an effort to chase away her early morning
depression, she had decided to put on her pretty blue
striped silk dress and brown lace-trimmed mantle.

Olivia trailed behind reluctantly. Word of the new
arrival had travelled, and more people were crowding on
to the quay to see the American ship.

'Well, my dear, what do you think?'

'Douglas, she's beautiful!'

His brown eyes, normally serious and guarded,
sparkled with pleasure as he looked at the oncoming
vessel. 'Aye, she's every bit as fine as the agent promised.
The sight of her should stop their carping about me
buying a foreign ship, eh?' He glanced smugly about the
vast quay, dominated by the handsome pillared Custom
House, then nudged his wife and said with a chuckle,
'There's Jem Moncrieff . . . will you look at the envy
in the man's face!'

Annis followed his gaze and saw her husband's
kinsman standing some distance away. Jem was a
shipbuilder, but in a small way, for he was a man who
had not been overburdened by good fortune. There had
been some who said that when the best of Douglas
Moncrieff's three ships went down it would have been
an act of kindness for him to order its replacement from

Jem instead of buying from America. Secretly Annis agreed with them. But because of a family quarrel that had flared many years before, Douglas had refused to consider giving business to his cousin.

Jem bowed slightly as he turned and saw husband and wife standing not far away. Douglas inclined his head in a stiff, dismissive nod, but Annis smiled at the man before turning back to watch as the tug cast off from the clipper, the tall ship's lines were thrown ashore and claimed by the waiting men, and the *Grace and Charity's* shapely, graceful length slid into place with scarcely a bump. The pilot, who had boarded earlier to bring the clipper into her berth, stood well forward, his mouth curving in a satisfied smile as his charge nudged the quay, a matter of yards from where the new owner and his wife watched.

Annis tipped her head back at the risk of losing her pretty straw hat to see the men scrambling along the rat-lines with as much ease as if they were walking in the street. The sight made her dizzy. She clutched at Douglas's arm for a moment and hurriedly turned her attention back to the deck, where she caught sight of the ship's master for the first time.

He stood on the poop deck aft, tall and steady on spread feet, fists resting on his hips and chin tilted as he watched the men in the rigging complete their work. After a moment his dark head dipped in a brief, firm nod of satisfaction and he turned to rest both hands on the railing before him while he scanned the quay.

His eyes studied the upturned faces, the top hats and caps and bonnets and parasols, the children and the horses and carts, the barrels of sugar for the big local refinery being unloaded from a sailing ship in the next berth. He took it all in unhurriedly; the warehouses and offices, the crowded roofs of the town beyond, the green tree-packed hills above and beyond that. Then he nodded again with the air of a man who has faced a possible adversary, sized him up, and felt confidently able to throw down a challenge.

Fascinated, Annis continued to stare. There was something about this man that caught and held her full attention. His clothes fitted him like a second skin — a green cravat at his throat, a snowy white shirt, a brown frock coat over buff trousers that were tucked into high leather boots. He must have found time, as the *Grace and Charity* moved up into the mouth of the River Clyde, to visit his cabin and change for his meeting with the good people of Greenock.

His eyes met hers, travelled on, and stopped. Annis saw the tautening of his weather-browned features, the lift of his brows. He had seen Olivia.

'Look, Annis,' her sister said at that moment. 'That woman on the deck, isn't that the maidservant who ran away from Papa's house without as much as a word?'

Annis dragged her gaze away from the shipmaster and looked at the main deck below him, where a woman stood surveying the quay. She was plainly dressed in dark clothing, but there was something about the set of her head, the twist of her pale mouth as she surveyed the crowd on the quay, that caught her attention.

'Adeline? I do believe it is! What's she doing aboard?'

'Travelling with the captain, presumably. Impertinent hussy!' Olivia said under her breath, her lovely face suddenly hard with resentment. 'Making off without so much as a word of explanation, let alone a day's notice, then turning up out of the blue again! And on your own husband's new ship, too! I do declare that she—'

'Come along, my dear,' Douglas broke in, one hand curling beneath his wife's elbow, impatient to set foot on his new acquisition.

Annis willingly allowed herself to be bustled on board, along the gangplank that had just been run into place, and on to a freshly holystoned deck as white as a houseproud woman's kitchen table. The man who had caught and held her attention earlier was stepping easily down to the main deck and moving towards them, his hand outstretched to Douglas.

'Mr Moncrieff?' The drawling American accent was strange to their ears. 'Gideon Brenner, sir. I'm pleased to be able to hand over your new ship. And a fine vessel she is too.'

Annis could see he was every inch a sea-traveller. His firm-jawed face, broad across the cheekbones, was tanned by continual exposure to all weathers, his eyes were as green and as clear as the deep waters and his black hair had a strong curl to it that gave it a windblown look.

Annis knew now why he had fascinated her from the first moment she caught sight of him. Had she been the male child her father had hoped for, this was just the sort of man she would have wanted to become.

'Mr Brenner.' Douglas acknowledged the shipmaster crisply. 'You'd a good passage?'

'A very good passage, sir.' There was no acknowledgement of Douglas's slightly condescending note in Brenner's reply. Moncrieff was accustomed to using that tone towards his employees and accustomed to being treated deferentially. But Gideon Brenner spoke to him calmly and confidently, as though to an equal.

'How was your crew?'

12

The American gave a shrug of his broad shoulders. 'They gave a good account of themselves once the trouble-makers were identified and dealt with. There was one man' — suddenly his eyes took on the chill and colour of ice — 'who tried my patience until I . . . showed him the error of his ways.'

'I trust, sir, that you didn't use the lash on him,' Douglas said at once. 'I've heard that the Americans are over-quick to flog men, but that sort of treatment has no place aboard a Scottish ship.'

Brenner's eyes suddenly blazed, but he answered with controlled civility. 'I've never had need of the lash on any ship under my command, Mr Moncrieff. My own two fists suffice.' Then he added dryly, 'I wouldn't have allowed him on board but for the fact that he claimed to have worked on your ships before. I'd advise you never to let him work on one again. The man's a trouble-maker, a wastrel by the name of McNair. D'you know him?'

'I have three ships, Captain. I can scarcely be expected to know the name of every seaman aboard them.' Then Douglas remembered, belatedly, that he was not alone. 'Annis, my dear, let me introduce Mr Brenner. My wife, sir. And this is my sister-in-law, Miss Kerr.'

'Your servant, Mrs Moncrieff. And yours, Miss Kerr.'

'Oh Lord,' Annis thought, watching Brenner's gaze linger on Olivia's face, 'he can't take his eyes off her.' And she was at once furious with herself for the slight surge of envy twingeing within her heart. She already had a husband — a very good husband at that. And of course the man found Olivia attractive. With her proud bearing, thick-lashed hazel eyes, shining dark brown hair and oval face, her sister was a striking beauty. She was, and always had been, far more beautiful than Annis, with her small

13

face, grey eyes and rebellious hair the colour of a beech hedge in autumn, could ever hope to be.

Not that Annis needed to be beautiful, she told herself, for she already had a husband — a very good husband at that. The thoughts squirrelled around inside her head as her sister gave a polite little nod, acknowledging the American. Then Olivia's elbow brushed Annis's in the faintest of nudges as the woman who had been at the rail moved boldly forward to stand beside the young shipmaster.

He acknowledged her presence immediately. 'Mrs Fraser, ma'am. Mr Moncrieff, permit me to introduce Mrs Fraser, wife of the mate of the *Columbine*.'

'Wife?' There was the faintest disbelieving question mark in Olivia's clear voice, and the woman's sharp-featured face flushed, although her eyes refused to lower their gaze. Adeline had always been one to look people straight in the eye, Annis recalled.

'I wed Walter Fraser in Boston, Miss Olivia.'

'Indeed?'

Brenner's green gaze swung from one face to the other. 'You already know each other?'

'Mrs Fraser, as you call her, was a maidservant in my father's house.' Olivia spoke each word as though it was a droplet of iced water. 'Until a year ago, when she saw fit to disappear without a word of explanation.'

Adeline moved a step nearer to the American, as though seeking his protection. 'I had the chance of a passage to Boston. Walter and I were married there.'

'And now that the *Columbine* has gone down' — Brenner seemed quite unruffled by the small domestic storm that threatened to break about his head — 'Mrs Fraser is widowed, and quite destitute. So I offered her passage back home.'

He removed his eyes from Olivia's stormy face and fixed them on Douglas. 'I believe, sir, that there's still some payment owing to her late husband. I promised her that I would take up the matter with you.'

'Very well,' Douglas spoke impatiently, interested only in his new ship. 'Let her call in at the office tomorrow morning and my clerk will settle up with her.'

'You've got somewhere to go until then?' Brenner asked the woman.

'My cousin will give me a bed for the night. Thank you, sir — for all your kindness.' She put a hand on his arm, shooting a sly sidelong look at Olivia from under lids that were suddenly, surprisingly, lowered demurely.

'Tell one of the men to carry your box on to the quay,' he said, and she slipped away without another word.

'Where are you going to lay your own head, Mr Brenner?' Annis asked after Adeline had disappeared.

'No doubt there are plenty of rooming houses, ma'am.'

'Aye, you'll find that the town's not short of good accommodation,' Douglas told him, adding, 'You'll dine with us tonight?'

Brenner glanced at Olivia, then said, 'Thank you, sir, I'd be happy to accept.'

'I'm sure we can offer you something better than the sort of fare you've had during the journey. Eh, my dear?'

'Yes indeed. We're going to have a nice piece of beef tonight, and there's plenty for — ' Annis stopped, suddenly remembering that the evening's roast was still sitting on the slab in the flesher's shop where she had left it in her headlong dash to watch the clipper coming in. Or had Mr McMillan, thinking that she had lost interest, already sold it to someone else?

She realized that everyone was looking at her: Douglas

15

inquiringly, Gideon Brenner with a twist of amusement at one corner of his mouth, as though those far-sighted eyes of his had reached into her mind, and Olivia accusingly.

'Well now, Olivia,' she found her voice again, 'We must go at once and see to that roast if there's to be any supper tonight.'

'Yes,' her sister agreed dryly, pleased enough to get away from the boring ship and its boring master. 'We must.'

2

The dining room of Douglas Moncrieff's villa in Low Gourock Road was a dark cavern only dimly lit by the gas brackets on one wall. In winter the chamber was cheered to some extent by a good fire in the large hearth, but on summer evenings, when the hearth lay empty, it was dismally dull.

Not long after her marriage some three months earlier Annis had unearthed several beautiful silver candlesticks from the depths of a cupboard, filled them with candles and set them along the length of the huge solid teak table to brighten the room during evening meals.

Douglas had indulgently given the move his approval, though his sister Tib, who had always shared the family home with him and had no intention of making other plans now that he had a wife, made it plain that she considered it to be a waste of good candles and an unseemly show of vanity into the bargain. She had announced firmly when the silverware first appeared that she had no intention of polishing it, then sniffed when Annis cheerfully assured her that she herself would take on the task.

In actual fact Douglas approved far more of the candles than anyone realized. It delighted him to see his new wife seated at the other end of the table, her face brushed with dancing gold light that made the most of her grey eyes, those eyes that had an amazing ability to reflect pinpoints of flame in their depths and take on tawny and emerald hues. Like many young matrons she had discarded the custom of wearing a lace cap indoors, and the candlelight picked out fiery bronze highlights in her rich auburn hair.

The reflection of the small flames, continually moving in the drafts that plagued the old house, softly stroked her smooth neck and throat and shoulders and subtly highlighted the warm inviting valley between the upper curves of her young breasts. Tonight, at his request, she wore the bronze watered silk dress he had recently had made for her, its shimmering colour complimenting her hair and her creamy skin.

A hardheaded businessman, Moncrieff had had no time for women until the day he had suddenly become aware of Annis Kerr, his neighbour's daughter, as she went to and fro past his house, her shopping basket over her arm, her face so alight with the pleasure of being alive.

Child though she was at the time, each sight of her had caused a strange fluttering pain in the region of Douglas's heart. He had started watching out for her, revelling secretly in each glimpse. As time passed and he saw a pattern to her comings and goings he began to contrive to meet her in the street whenever possible so that he could lift his hat to her and wish her a good morning or a good afternoon. For four years he had watched her growing up from gawky adolescence to graceful womanhood. For four years he had nursed his feelings for her, never daring to believe that one day he might experience the pleasure of gazing down the length of his own table at her and knowing that she belonged to him alone.

But his chance had come. George Kerr, a respected town merchant, had taken on an untrustworthy partner and joined him in an ambitious venture that would, if it had succeeded, have made them both very wealthy. Instead it failed, and George Kerr had killed himself rather than face the town as a bankrupt.

The Moncrieffs had known George Kerr only as a neighbour, for neither household cared much for social gatherings: although they were both local businessmen Douglas and George Kerr had met only occasionally. When rumours of the older man's rash investment and financial troubles had first reached Douglas's ears he had dismissed the man as an incompetent fool who should have known better.

When George Kerr died, Douglas's first reaction was anger against the man who had taken the easy way out of his difficulties and left Annis and her sister to cope as best they could on their own. Then it had dawned on him that now they were in need of a champion.

Going against his own astute business sense for the first time in his life, he had used his own money to pay the most pressing of Kerr's debts, thus gaining Annis's gratitude. Then, flying in the face of Tib's fierce opposition, he had offered his protection to the two young women left destitute by their father's foolishness. To his regret, he realized that he could scarcely offer aid to the younger sister without including the older sister. Olivia's stiff-necked pride had always intimidated him, and he was one of the few men in Greenock unmoved by her beauty, preferring instead Annis's gentleness. Finally, after a clumsy, trembling courtship, he had achieved his dream and won Annis as his wife.

He knew when he proposed to her that sheer gratitude played a large part in her acceptance. But that didn't matter, for he loved her with a passion that filled every waking moment. But thanks to his upbringing as a God-fearing Scottish Presbyterian he lived in continual fear that such love, such joy in the possession of another human being must surely be sinful, and bring about its own punishment in due time.

'Aye . . . she looks a damned sight better to a man's eyes than our Tib ever could.' The thought came to him automatically, as it always did when he sat opposite his own wife at his own table. On his right, his sister held herself aloof from the conversation, giving her attention totally to her soup, which she sipped in tiny drops, scarcely parting her thin lips to allow the spoon entry. Isabella Moncrieff, known for all of her life as Tib, had never been a pretty woman. Like Douglas, she had the long Moncrieff face and brown eyes and in her case her eyes were small and sharp, and so was her nose. Her hair was almost fawn in colour, scraped back tightly from a thin bony face. It was covered tonight, as always, with a black lace cap. She rarely smiled; when she did, it was fleetingly, and only with her mouth. Tib was thirty-five, and had embraced middle age and spinsterhood at least ten years earlier. Since the death of her parents shortly after her thirtieth birthday she dressed at all times in black bombazine.

The serving-woman came in to clear the soup bowls away. As Annis gave a peal of laughter at something that Gideon Brenner had said, a faint frown drew Douglas's thick fair brows together. There was altogether too much merriment going on at that end of the table. It had perhaps been foolish of him to sit the American between Annis and his nephew Robert, opposite Olivia. It left Douglas himself and Tib sitting at the other end of the table like two old crows at a wake. The comparison might fit Tib but by God, Douglas told himself, it wasn't for him!

Great platters of potatoes and greens were placed on the table, then the servant brought in the roast that, fortunately, Mr McMillan the flesher had kept for Annis after her precipitous dash from his shop that afternoon.

Carving it with deft, experienced strokes of the knife, Douglas took possession of the situation. 'So you were pleased with the performance my new ship gave on her way here, Mr Brenner?' he asked his guest at the other end of the table.

'I'm always pleased with the *Grace and Charity*, sir. She and I are old friends – she was built in my father's yard. I can safely say,' the young man added without wasting time on false modesty, 'that she came from the best yard in New England.'

Annis beamed at his confident reply, enjoying his company. It wasn't often that the Moncrieffs had such a lively visitor. Tonight he wore a black cravat and a green coat that matched his eyes. His hair had been firmly subdued with a brush and the crisply curling tips were touched with gold in the candlelight. He brought a breath of fresh air into the gloomy house. She had never in her life met a man so – she searched for the right word, and could only come up with 'complete'. Gideon Brenner was self-possessed from the top of his head to the tips of his toes.

'Did you see her being built?' Robert Moncrieff, Douglas's nephew, was asking with interest. At fifteen he was still gawky and long-limbed, but he showed promise of being a fine-looking young man in three or four years' time.

'Indeed I did. I was much the same age as yourself when her keel was laid. I attended her launching, then I sailed in her for a handful of voyages as mate – I was employed by the man who had commissioned her.'

'Did your father not want you to go into the shipbuilding business with him?' Annis asked, glancing covertly at Robert.

Brenner's green eyes turned on Annis. 'He left the choice to me.'

Robert, who had been born to follow his father and uncle into the shipbuilding business, gave a small, involuntary sigh of envy.

'If you don't know how to behave at the table, Robert,' snapped Tib, rolling the first letter of the name on her tongue so viciously that she almost managed to turn it into a weapon, 'you may go to your room.'

The tips of poor Robert's ears crimsoned and he muttered an apology to the tablecloth. His aunt, who never missed the opportunity to humiliate the boy, opened her mouth to deliver another reprimand, but Gideon Brenner, raising his voice slightly, talked on without seeming to notice any interruption, and Tib, thwarted, subsided.

'For a while I was torn between building and sailing, Mrs Moncrieff. But in the end I followed my elder brother into a life on shipboard.'

'You're surely young to be a shipmaster,' Douglas remarked bluntly. The implied criticism slid off the American's shoulders like rain from a water-bird's feathers.

'I was fortunate to get my first command in my twenty-sixth year, seven years ago. America breeds the best seamen.' It was a flat statement free of any false modesty and Brenner didn't even trouble to look in Tib's direction when she gave an audible sniff.

Annis, who for years had enjoyed keeping her father's household accounts, busily added twenty-five and seven, and came up with the astonishing realization that at thirty-two years of age Gideon Brenner was one year older than Douglas. The thought took her aback. She knew, of course, that she herself was thirteen years younger than her husband, but somehow he had always seemed even older to her, in the same age-group as her own father. Certainly much older than this lithe, relaxed, easy-moving newcomer.

She looked along the length of the table at Douglas with a critical gaze that took in his heavy-lidded eyes and the slightly stooped shoulders of a man who had spent most of his working life indoors, bent over a desk. But the difference between himself and the American shipmaster didn't stop there. There was the look of an elderly man about Douglas's pursed mouth, the precise, almost fussy way he moved, as though afraid to let his limbs relax and swing naturally.

Only thirty-one, Annis mused again. A sudden compassion for Douglas swept over her. She had wanted to restore his vanished youth to him, but there seemed no way to do it — not while he lived in this gloomy house with Tib. If only they had moved to another home when they got married. Perhaps things would have been different then.

Thoughts of the man Douglas could be scattered as Brenner addressed a question to her and she was jolted back to her duties as hostess.

During the rest of the meal Gideon Brenner, urged on by Annis and Robert, talked about the tea trade and the huge American clippers that swung between America and China, using the winds and the tides to make their way across the seas. They hung on every word, and almost against his will Douglas became just as fascinated.

But Olivia and Tib remained silent, keeping themselves

23

steadfastly outside the spell that the young seaman's drawling voice cast around the table.

Supper was long over and the candles almost burned down before the party stirred themselves at Tib's impatient bidding and went into the Moncrieff's gloomy parlour where they sat, surrounded by furniture still arranged just as Douglas's parents had placed it almost forty years before. As Douglas poured brandy for himself and his guest, Tib, without reference to Annis, took charge of the delicate tea-cups on the small table by the fireplace and dispensed tea to the women.

Robert, too young for brandy and scornfully determined that he was certainly too old for tea, declined a cup and asked Brenner if his father was still building clippers.

A sudden frown drew the shipmaster's brows together. 'My father's yard's closed down now, and the harbours are filled with good ships lying idle. Thanks to our Government's short-sighted policies the days when the American clippers ruled the oceans are over.'

'They say that now steam's been introduced and the new Suez Canal's open the days of all sailing ships are numbered,' Robert pointed out, and his uncle gave a scornful bark of laughter.

'We'll not see that in my lifetime, or in yours, I'll be bound. Confounded kettle bottoms!'

'Steam's unreliable,' Annis agreed, eager to become part of the conversation. Ships and their travels interested her far more than buying ribbons and worrying about whether the furniture and the silver needed polishing. 'Engines can break down or even explode. And a steam cargo ship has to give up far too much space to carrying coal.'

'Besides,' Robert agreed with growing enthusiasm, 'a steam-powered ship can't begin to match the beauty of a sailing ship.'

'So you hope to make the sea your career, as I did?'

Robert's face, long and fair in the Moncrieff mould, but with more vitality to the brown eyes than his uncle and aunt had, lit up. He hitched himself to the edge of his chair and began, 'I'd be more interested in designing ships than—'

'Robert,' said Douglas crisply, 'is going to join my office when he finishes his schooling.'

'But I—'

'He will be of great help to me in the business. The business,' Douglas reminded the boy coolly, 'that he will inherit one day. It was your own father's wish, boy, and mine too.'

Annis's heart ached as she saw the light fade from Robert's eyes. He was only four years younger than she was herself, and their relationship was more that of brother and sister than nephew and aunt. Orphaned too young to remember either of his parents, raised by his grandmother's and then Tib's iron rule from babyhood, the boy had never really had a chance to enjoy childhood. He too had learned early to subdue his true feelings, but Annis had managed to break down the barrier he put up against the world, and he trusted her. She was the only person who knew of his desire to go to art school, the only person who had ever seen the portfolio of drawings and sketches hidden in his room which included several beautiful drawings of the Greenock harbours and the ships that called there, as well as some precisely detailed ships designs. And only Annis knew of the secret friendship between Robert and Jem Moncrieff, the shipbuilder, and

25

Robert's wish to work one day, in some capacity, with Jem rather than with Douglas. Annis bit her lip in distress at Robert's humiliation.

'I agree that there's still a great need for sailing ships.' Gideon Brenner's strange but attractive drawl filled the awkward silence that had fallen. 'And I hope you're right, sir, and that nothing will change in our lifetimes.'

'You may be certain of it. The yards on the Clyde are turning out more sailed ships than ever before. As well as steam-powered vessels,' Douglas added carelessly.

'That's why I offered to bring the *Grace and Charity* over when your agent put the word about that he was looking for a reputable master. There's nothing for me in America now that the best of our clippers are confined to port, or to short-haul voyages. This is where the future lies – Britain.'

Brenner's steady square hand put his glass down, his voice gathering new enthusiasm. 'It's my intention to settle here, at least for the time being. I hope, sir, that you will consider me as a possible shipmaster for your new ship.'

The suggestion was made so baldly that Tib gasped audibly and Douglas was taken aback.

Annis realized that her mouth had fallen open, and hurriedly closed it again. The American's sudden introduction of business matters into the drawing-room, his bold attempt to force a swift decision from Douglas, was altogether wrong in Greenock society, and she would not have been surprised to hear her husband ordering the impertinent young man from his house. And yet she felt her pulse flutter and excitement drew her upright in her chair, her tea-cup forgotten. How refreshing it was to meet someone so out of the ordinary, so different. So un-Scottish.

'Well, I . . .' Douglas started to say.

'You lost the master as well as the crew when the *Columbine* foundered. As I understand it from your agent the *Grace and Charity* is her replacement. And unless you've already taken on a new master for her . . .'

'You haven't, have you, Uncle? Surely Mr Brenner would be—'

'Robert!' This time the name fairly ripped from his Aunt Tib's tongue. Like a man tearing off a false beard, Annis thought, surprised by one of the irreverent thoughts that popped into her mind from time to time. 'Don't be impertinent!'

The boy bit his lip and colour rushed into his face once again.

'It's true that I haven't replaced Coombes as yet,' Douglas said slowly, sheer astonishment seeming to have a mellowing effect on him. 'But what about your personal commitments, Mr Brenner? Family ties at home. A wife, perhaps?'

'I have no wife, sir, nor ever did.' Gideon Brenner cast a look at Olivia, who sat silently opposite, the only person in the room unmoved by his daring. She returned the glance coolly. 'I certainly like what I've seen so far of Greenock. My interest in shipbuilding's still well to the fore, and as you say, the yards here are busy. I might eventually invest in one of them.'

Douglas's brows rose. 'You've money behind you, then?'

'Not much, but I hope to make it grow.'

'My shipmasters don't make a fortune, young man, let me tell you that here and now.'

'There are other ways of turning a penny to advantage. For instance, the cargo of pitch-pine that your man had

27

secured for the *Columbine* didn't take up all the *Grace and Charity*'s hold. I don't think,' said Brenner, a slightly smug smile curling his mouth, 'that he realized just how much an American-built clipper, even a small vessel, can carry, so I used my own money to buy some cotton and had it brought aboard.'

'Did you indeed?'

Annis's mouth was dry. Gideon Brenner had surely gone too far now, she thought in despair. He had come into her life — their lives — like an unexpected and most refreshing sea-breeze and she would have welcomed the opportunity to see and hear more of him. But Douglas, one of the most successful and respected merchants in Greenock, hated to be crossed. Douglas Moncrieff's captains all knew that his word was law, and that nobody but himself made use of his ships.

'Be just a little meek,' she silently implored the American, staring down at her cooling tea, afraid that if she looked up Tib's sharp eyes might read her thoughts. 'Give Douglas the respect due to him and then perhaps he might allow you to stay among us.'

But Brenner, still serene and apparently unaware of the heightened tension in the room, was saying, 'I did, sir. And I believe I can sell it here for a fair profit.'

'The proceeds of any cargo on my brother's ship belong to him,' Tib said sharply, in the same voice she had used to reprimand her nephew. Spots of angry colour blossomed in her pale cheeks and her brown eyes snapped at the visitor.

'With respect, ma'am, cargo that I paid for and commissioned myself belongs to me. And so does any profit I may make from it, apart, of course, from the shipowner's commission, which I fully intend to pay.'

A frown knotted Douglas's brow. 'My agent knew full well that he should have added more ballast to trim her if the cargo was small. Or he could have cast about and found additional goods.'

'To my mind it's a criminal waste to add extra ballast instead of filling the holds,' Brenner told him curtly, his own voice now taking a brisk businesslike tone to match Douglas's. 'That ship sits better in the water when her holds are full. She's built to carry cargo, not to sail in ballast. And as I understood it, sir, your instructions were to get your cargo to Greenock as soon as possible. You'd already lost valuable time when the *Columbine* went down. Seeking additional cargo would have delayed us.'

'But you, Mr Brenner, just happened to know where you could lay your hands on some cotton.' Olivia, deceptively demure in a creamy dress with dark brown trimming the colour of her hair, spoke for the first time.

The sarcasm wasn't lost on Brenner. Looking up, Annis saw him acknowledge her sister with a faint amused curl of the mouth and a slight bow. 'As it happens, Miss Olivia, I did. It's not unusual, sir, for a master to invest in some cargo of his own if there's room for it. As far as I know it's permitted everywhere.'

'Nevertheless it's not a custom that I encourage.' Douglas's voice was cold.

'Then you stand alone, sir.'

'But surely, Douglas,' Annis said swiftly, 'if Mr Brenner knew nothing of your preferences . . .'

For a long moment shipowner and shipmaster faced each other, neither prepared to back down. Then, recalling that he was the host, and Brenner a guest from a far country, Douglas relaxed and gave a slight shrug of the shoulders.

'Of course you're right, my dear. Brenner wasn't to know, though my agent certainly did,' he added with an edge to his voice that boded no good for the unfortunate agent. 'We'll say no more about it. You'll have another glass of brandy?'

'Thank you, sir, I will. And you'll consider my application?'

'You still want to work for me, even though you know you'll not be allowed to make yourself rich by adding your cargo in with mine?'

Brenner lifted one shoulder in a slight gesture of resignation. 'If, in future, I choose to put my money into goods that I think might sell in other ports, someone else's ships will carry them. Although to my mind it would be a pity for you to lose your commission as the shipowner.'

'I can do without it well enough . . . the little it will be.' Douglas raised his glass to the light and admired the colour of the fine brandy within it; brandy brought to Greenock from France in one of his own ships.

'I'll be putting the clipper into the graving dock to have her refitted and painted. It'll be a while before she goes out again. A while before she needs a shipmaster.'

'I've enough money to keep me until you make up your mind, Mr Moncrieff, and a fancy to make Greenock's acquaintance. Should you decide against me there are no doubt ships aplenty in the harbours here where a good deep-sea man can find a berth. But as you'll know yourself it's advisable,' Gideon Brenner added blandly, 'to have the ship's master on hand while she's in the graving dock, to see that the work's carried out in the owner's best interests.'

Douglas rubbed a hand thoughtfully over his beard. 'I'd

no thought of taking an American shipmaster as well as an American ship.'

Pride coloured the young man's high cheekbones and made his green eyes glitter. 'You must be aware that my country's produced the best sailors in the western world.'

'So you've already told us, Mr Brenner,' Olivia reminded him.

'In the past, sir, in the past. It's Britain that's taken the lead now.' It was Douglas's turn to be smug.

'That,' said Gideon Brenner crisply, 'is why I've come to Britain. But my country's failure to maintain her commercial fleet as she should doesn't detract from the excellent training I've had.'

Douglas cleared his throat, took another mouthful of brandy, savoured it and swallowed it.

Then he said, 'Come to the harbour office tomorrow morning and we'll have a talk .'

'What d'you make of Mr Gideon Brenner?' he wanted to know a few hours later when he and his wife were alone in the privacy of their bedchamber.

Annis unfastened her pearl earrings, took off the matching bracelet, and laid them all carefully in the handsome jewel box her husband had given her as a wedding present. Then she reached to the nape of her neck to loose the catch of the double-stringed necklace.

Beyond her own reflection in the mirror she could see the handsome tapestry screen in the corner of the room. A cravat was tossed over the top of it as she watched, followed by a collar, then a shirt.

Douglas Moncrieff had never, since early babyhood, been seen naked by a woman. He always dressed and undressed behind the screen. Annis thought it strange and more than a little ironic that she hadn't once seen the body that her own body and hands knew so well and so intimately in the dark, beneath the blankets of their marriage bed.

'I found him somewhat outspoken.' She chose her words carefully, anxious not to antagonize her husband. 'But then, he knows nothing of our customs. No doubt he'll learn quickly — if he stays here. Do you think you will employ him as the *Grace and Charity*'s master?'

Douglas's trousers joined the row of clothing draped over the screen. 'I don't know. I'll decide tomorrow, when I've got a better idea of the measure of the man. He's altogether too sure of himself for my liking.'

'Is he correct when he claims that Americans make the best sailors?' She knew well enough that he was, but it was important to defer to Douglas as the expert in such matters.

Whatever his other faults, Douglas Moncrieff was a fair man. 'Aye, he is, though more conceited that he had cause to be. The British seamen are almost as good.'

'I believe he's made up his mind to stay in Greenock whether you take him on or not.' She slipped deftly out of her bronze silk gown and her petticoat as she talked. 'If you don't take him on there are no doubt others who will.'

The wire frame that had puffed out her skirt a little at the back was unfastened and put aside.

'I'd realized that. But that business about the cotton . . .'

Douglas had always made it his policy not to take on a partner or to allow anyone to become closely involved in his business. He claimed that he had seen too many businesses ruined through partners falling out. Annis, the memory of the way her own father was bankrupted and driven to suicide through the misdeeds of the wrong partner still achingly clear in her mind, could only agree with him.

'He had no way of knowing your views, Douglas,' she pointed out, discarding her chemise. 'He knows the *Grace and Charity* well, and he's probably right when he says that her holds need to be filled.'

'I intend to find out for myself tomorrow just how much her holds can take.'

There was a silence, during which she slipped her nightgown over her head, feeling its folds cool and fresh on her skin, then took off her drawers and stockings. She began to gather up her scattered clothes and put them neatly away in the huge dark wardrobe. Douglas's parents had hung their clothes in that wardrobe and slept in the bed she was about to step into. Annis knew it pleased Douglas to know that he was following in their footsteps, but as she gazed around she longed to make her own footsteps, leave her own mark on life.

'From now on,' she heard Douglas promise grimly, 'there won't be a spare inch for Mr Gideon Brenner to fill. I'll see to that.'

'So you intend to take him on?' She discovered that she was holding her breath, and let it out in a long, silent sigh that stirred the clothes in the gloomy depths of the wardrobe. Gently, soundlessly, she closed the door, wondering why she was so eager on Gideon Brenner's behalf. Was it for Olivia's sake, because the young American clearly admired her? Or was it because Annis herself had become so bored with her life that she yearned for new company?

'Coombes was a good man. I need someone just as able

to replace him. Mebbe I'll give Brenner the chance to show his worth. But he'll have to give me my place as owner of the clipper or he goes — I promise you that.'

Douglas came out from behind the screen, sedately covered from throat to strong muscular calves in a night-shirt. His hair and his short neat beard had been ruffled during his disrobing, giving him an unexpectedly boyish look that touched Annis's heart.

She smiled at him through the mirror as she sat down again and withdrew the bronzed slides that had drawn her hair back from her face. Neither of the Kerr sisters had ever had to resort to frezettes and scalpettes, the popular hair-pieces that women of fashion added to their coiffures. They were both blessed with thick, healthy hair, although Olivia, as usual, was more blessed than Annis, having hair as straight as a waterfall. Annis's russet tresses were so obstinately curly that she kept them quite short, though long enough to be pinned up in the evenings and pinned back during the day, though never harshly like Tib's.

'Let me do that,' Douglas said, and she lowered her arms as he came to stand behind her. When all the pins had been removed carefully and deposited in the flowered china dish on the dressing table he picked up her hairbrush and started work. She smiled again as she watched him through the mirror. If the men who worked for Douglas Moncrieff only knew that one of his greatest pleasures lay in brushing his wife's hair as gently and thoroughly as any lady's maid their eyes would pop. But nobody else knew of it, not even Tib. Nobody but Annis. It was an intimate secret to be shared only between husband and wife, she thought with pleasure.

'What d'you think of the ship's name?' he asked, his hands and eyes intent on his work.

'I like it.'

'I'd had it in mind to change it, but I'm not so sure now. There's a good Biblical ring to it. Traders would trust a man who owns a ship with such a name. D'you not think so?'

'I do.'

'Brenner seemed quite interested in your sister,' Douglas said thoughtfully as he worked. Her hair crackled as the brush lifted it, ran through it, then released it in soft glowing curls.

'Olivia's beautiful. Any man would find it hard to keep his eyes from her.' Annis said the words lightly enough, but as she spoke she realized for the first time since her marriage that for her the excitement and romance of a new face, the thrill at the interest in a stranger's eyes, was over. Until that day, that moment, it had never occurred to her. She felt a slight surge of panic at the thought. She was four months away from her nineteenth birthday. Her life had scarcely begun, yet already an important part of it was over, gone for good.

'Olivia's looks are well enough.' Her husband's voice was dismissive. 'But she's altogether too vain, too aware of her beauty. Not like you, my own darling . . .'

The brush was laid down and his hands landed on her shoulders, easing her from her chair, turning her face to him. 'You have no idea of your own charms, have you?'

She looked up into his face and recognized the heat in his eyes with a mixture of affection and dismay. Affection because she loved her husband and wanted to please him at all times; and dismay because tonight she was tired and there was a lot to think about. Tonight she had hoped to lie peacefully in the darkness before sleep came washing over her, picturing again the magnificence of the clipper

35

ship as she came into her berth, the sight of her young master on the poop-deck, his watchful gaze on the crew in the rigging.

'No, Douglas,' she said obediently, hating herself for letting the childish note creep into her voice. It was a game that Douglas never tired of playing, a game that she was fast outgrowing but he, it seemed, never would.

'My little innocent,' he said. 'My innocent little girl . . .'

She stood before him meekly, submissively, as his fingers fumbled with the tie-strings of her gown. The feminine, frilled and beribboned nightwear she had carefully stitched during the exciting months of her betrothal lay discarded in a deep drawer in the tallboy, interleaved with bags of lavender. Douglas preferred his wife to wear plain childish gowns. She hated them, for they made her seem even younger than she was.

The last tie-string gave way beneath his touch and the gown was pushed back to the curve of her shoulders, where it lost its purchase and slid with a soft rustle to pool about her small, shapely bare feet. Although he refused to be seen naked Douglas had no such scruples where Annis was concerned.

'My . . . own . . . little . . . innocent . . .' he whispered, and slid to his knees before her in homage.

Annis breathed out the faintest sigh and gently stroked the head that was now pressed hard into the soft, flat silkiness of her belly.

3

Annis perched precariously on an upper-storey window-sill at the front of the house, clutching the wooden window sash with one hand and buffing the outside of the glass to stainless perfection with a duster clutched in the other.

She had chosen a time when Tib was out marketing and the roadway was quiet. She had also taken the precaution of covering her plain dark blue housedress with a huge apron and tucking her hair into a white cap so that anyone who happened to glance up from the footpath would assume that she was one of the servants.

Douglas would have been horrified if he had known that his wife undertook such menial and dangerous tasks as cleaning her own upstairs windows, but as Annis never felt that the two serving-women could polish the panes properly, and as her healthy young body clamoured for some form of exercise, she had got into the way of seeing to the windows herself when there was nobody around to tattle on her.

It was a clear, fresh morning with very little wind disturbing the leaves of the neat shrubs that lined either side of the front garden path some distance below her. She rested for a moment and turned her head to look across the road to where she could see the Clyde between two of the houses opposite. The tiny pinpoints of sunlight glancing from the tips of small waves made her blink. On the other side of the Firth, above the neat little town of Helensburgh, soft green hills reached to touch the sky.

A tug hurried across the slice of water between the stone house walls, a compact little beetle of a vessel trailing smoke from its squat funnel. It disappeared, and after a moment its tow came into view, a top-masted schooner very like the vessel that Douglas used for trading along the rivers and inlets and bays of the crumpled and creased west Scottish coastline. The schooner called in at the islands and the remote coastal communities virtually shut off from the land behind them because of poor roads.

Sunlight warmed Annis's face and head. She pulled the restrictive cap off to let the breeze riffle through her hair, her mind still on the schooner and its travels. The shallow-draught vessel could be run right up on to the beach in remote coastal areas and its cargo unloaded into horses and carts. Then the schooner's crew rowed the anchor out into deep water, dropped it there, rejoined the vessel and warped her off the beach by tramping round the capstan, winding in the anchor cable and thus easing the ship towards her sunken anchor. When they had refloated her in deeper water they ran her sails up and turned her bows further north, towards the next small community. On a day such as today, Annis envied the crew. If only she had been the boy that Papa had wanted, she might have seen all those things, not just dreamt of them.

The sound of brisk footsteps on the pavement below brought her out of her pleasant daydream and, glancing down, her anchoring hand almost lost its grip on the window frame as she recognized Gideon Brenner marching along the pavement, clearly bound for his employer's house.

Her gasp of horror couldn't have reached his ears, but the sudden flurry of movement at the window as she tossed her cap and duster into the room beyond and began to squirm in after them may have attracted his attention.

Eeling her way off the sill, she caught a glimpse of his uplifted face as he turned in at the gate and began to ascend the flight of steps that led from the roadway up to the garden. Then her feet were on the bedroom carpet and she was flying across to the mirror above the wash-stand, unfastening her apron as she went and thanking her lucky stars that she had almost finished the windows before she was interrupted; otherwise the bucket of water on the bedroom floor would have been poised on the sill and she would probably have tipped it over in her hurry, dowsing either the garden or the bedroom floor.

The door-knocker rattled as she threw the apron aside and plunged her arms, bare to the elbow, into water that had been poured into the basin in readiness earlier. Annis, who had counted on the steep flight of steps from gate to path to give her a few precious minutes before his arrival gave a sharp 'Tut!' of annoyance under her breath as she scrubbed her hands. Douglas always took the steps with slow deliberation, arriving at the door slightly red in the face and short of breath, but Brenner, young and fit, accustomed to climbing about the rigging of tall ships, had scaled those steps with ease.

She dried her hands and arms and was rolling her sleeves down when a glance in the mirror showed that there was a dusty smear across one cheek where her face had brushed against the window-frame as she wriggled into the room. This time her lips shaped a stronger word as her newly-dried hands plunged back into the water. On occasions such as this, when she was particularly hard-pressed, Annis found a certain guilty satisfaction in silently using one of the graphic words that dropped frequently from the lips of Greenock's world-wise seafarers.

'Ma'am . . .' As was her wont, the little housemaid burst into the room with scarcely time to tap at the door. Her headlong entry into the room infuriated Tib, but Annis, who had come into the house as Douglas's bride at much the same time as Janet had arrived, liked the girl and was untroubled by her mannerisms.

'Ma'am, Captain Brenner's come to call.'

'I know, I know. Drat the man, choosing this time of day! Take the pail of water and the cloth downstairs, Janet.' Annis's hands flew as she spoke, scrubbing at her face until the dusty smear was replaced by a glowing red mark, rolling her sleeves down and fastening her cuffs, smoothing her dress and her hair in a flurry of continuous movement. 'And tell Betty to make some tea.'

'I'll make it myself,' Janet offered willingly, scooping up the pail and cloth. 'Cook's busy with the pastry for tonight, ma'am, and it's more than my life's worth to ask her to stop, as you know.'

'Very well . . .' Annis ran her eyes over her mirrored image and wished that she had had time to change into a prettier gown. The wish was no sooner in her head than it was pushed out again. It wasn't seemly for a married woman to think of dressing herself up for another man's eyes. But there was an air of sophistication about Gideon Brenner, who must in his travels have seen beautiful and elegant women all over the world, that made Annis want to present herself in the best light possible.

'Remember to heat the pot well and let the water boil before you pour it on to—'

'—the tea-leaves, ma'am,' Janet gabbled along with her, and hurried from the room, the dirty water in the pail slopping to and fro and almost spilling over on to the linoleum.

Gideon Brenner, hands tucked behind his back, was inspecting the pictures on the parlour wall when Annis arrived in the doorway. Her nostrils quivered appreciatively at the scent of fresh salty air that he had brought into the dim room. His very presence there seemed to light the place up. He swung round as she stepped into the room. 'Ah. I'm afraid I've called at an inopportune moment, Mrs Moncrieff.'

'No, indeed.'

'I'd not be over-pleased myself if I was summoned down from the rigging to attend to a visitor,' he said with a faint smile.

'The rigging?' She couldn't for the life of her see why he should have launched so precipitately into tales of shipboard life.

He pointed one long finger towards the ceiling. 'Your upper windows. As I came along the road I saw that you were cleaning them. Not many women have a good head for heights. I admire you, ma'am.'

Colour rushed to her face. 'Captain Brenner, your praise belongs with my maidservant, not with me.'

'Your maidservant? But I was certain that it was you that I—'

'Not at all!' Agitation sharpened her voice to such an extent that she sounded to her own ears like a positive harpy. The heat increased in her face until she knew that she must be poppy-red. 'Not at all,' she repeated more gently. 'A lady does not perch on her own window-sill and clean her own windows, I can assure you.'

There was a short pause, then, 'Ah,' said Gideon Brenner again as understanding dawned. 'You're quite right of course. I must have been mistaken. My apologies, ma'am.'

'Not at all, Captain Brenner. Will you take a chair?'

For a moment he looked at her blankly. Realizing that he had been thrown by her Scottish choice of phrase she indicated a nearby chair, and with a third 'Ah!' he moved to it, and sat down.

'I hope you've found Greenock to your liking?'

'Indeed, ma'am. An interesting town with a thriving waterfront.'

'Have you been to the graving dock to see the *Grace and Charity*?'

'I've just come from there. She's looking very handsome. I like the mock portholes that the Scottish clippers have. They look well on her.'

'When do you hope to take her out to sea again?'

'In seven to ten days, if that's your husband's wish.'

'I'm sure it will be. Douglas hates to see one of his ships lying idle.'

'On that we're of the same mind.'

Knuckles rapped on the door, then it opened. 'The tea, ma'am.'

Brenner began to rise. 'I had no intention of—'

'I always take tea at this time in the morning, Captain Brenner,' Annis lied easily as Janet put the tray on a small table nearby.

He subsided, and watched as she poured the tea. To her bent head he said thoughtfully, 'It strikes me as odd that . . .'

'Yes, Captain Brenner?'

She looked up to see that there was a faint glint of amusement in his eyes, the shadow of a curl about the corners of his well-shaped mouth as he rose to take the tea-cup from her. 'It strikes me as odd that your maidservant has brown hair. I could have sworn the young woman cleaning your windows had hair of a bronze shade. Much like yours.'

The blush threatened to rise again and was subdued by sheer strength of will. 'As I said earlier, you were mistaken sir.'

'It seems that I must have been, ma'am.' He tasted his tea and then, to her relief, changed the subject. 'I wondered if perhaps young Robert might be home.'

Annis, who was quite convinced that he had called in the hope of seeing Olivia, felt her eyebrows rise slightly. 'He's in school this morning. My husband is in his office, and my sister-in-law is seeing to the marketing.' She let a little silence draw out between them, fragile as a spider's web, before she relented and added, 'As for my sister Olivia, she has taken the train to Glasgow to buy some ribbon.'

'Oh.' The flat finality of the word, the slight shadow that crossed his face, told her that he had indeed hoped to come across Olivia. Then the shadow disappeared and he said firmly, 'I believe there's to be a dance in the town next Saturday evening. I wondered if perhaps your sister . . .'

'If you're referring to the Assembly Ball at the White Hart Inn, we'll all be there. Douglas and Olivia and myself, that is. Why don't you accompany us?' It was a daring move on her part, but she knew that in the two weeks since making Brenner his new shipmaster Douglas

43

had had no further cause for complaint, and had begun to thaw towards the American. Brenner had been at the house for a second evening meal, and had conducted himself admirably. Besides, Douglas, who felt duty-bound to attend the occasional social event in the town, disliked having to escort two women and would no doubt welcome a partner for Olivia.

Brenner grinned broadly in his relief. 'Thank you, ma'am, I'd be honoured. I've heard about the Scottish dances and I'd like to sample them for myself.'

'You'll do that, Captain Brenner, never fear. The Scots may get the name of being dour, but we do know how to enjoy a dance.'

'I can't say that I've found your countrymen to be . . . dour, as you put it.' He put the cup and saucer aside, stood up, dipped a brown hand into one of the pockets in his tailcoat, then held something out to her.

'I brought this for your nephew. Perhaps you would give it to him.'

She took the object from him. It was cool and smooth to the touch, and surprisingly heavy; a walrus tusk that some seaman had painstakingly carved with the likeness of a clipper ship not dissimilar to the *Grace and Charity*. She rode proudly on tossing waves, while in the distance whales spouted and a flying fish arced from the water to be held forever in mid flight, sharply outlined on the ivory.

'It's beautiful!'

'The whaler who carved it gave it to me himself when I was much the same age as Robert.'

'Then surely you must keep it.'

He shook his head. 'It's served its turn with me. It kept me company while I was working my way up in

44

command, and now it's time for me to pass it on to someone else with his future before him.'

'Robert,' Annis reminded him gently, putting the tusk down beside the tea-tray, 'is to make his career on land, not at sea.'

'That's not what the boy wants, Mrs Moncrieff.'

'It's the life that was planned for him by his father before he was a month old, as I understand it. I'm afraid that neither Robert nor I — nor you — can change it.'

'You would if you could?'

She carefully folded a pleat in her skirt, keeping herself busy so that she didn't have to look up at the man seated opposite.

'I had a twin, Captain Brenner, a brother who died within a few minutes of his birth. I've wished over and over again that he had been the survivor, or that I had been the boy. If I had been I would have gone to sea.'

'Would you indeed?'

'I can understand Robert's feelings,' she said, then looked up, straight into his intent green eyes. 'But I cannot change plans that were made for him long ago. It would be cruel to encourage him to go against his dead father's wishes. My husband would never permit that to happen.'

'Robert doesn't strike me as a candidate for an office. I've met him more than once at Jem Moncrieff's yard. He's at home there.'

Alarm sharpened her voice. 'I trust you've not said a word to my husband about Robert and Jem?'

'No. Nor will I. I gather from Jem that an old family squabble comes between himself and Mr Moncrieff. It sometimes seems to me that families, people who share the same flesh and blood,' said Gideon Brenner coolly, 'can cause more trouble than enemies.'

'Are you speaking from experience?'

'No, from observance. I'm thankful that my own family has always maintained close and affectionate bonds.'

'And yet you're content to turn your back on your own folk and seek your future in Scotland?'

'The closer the bonds, Mrs Moncrieff, the further they stretch. Distance can do nothing to harm true affection and respect.'

'You're a most fortunate man.' Annis spoke from the heart.

'You don't come from a large family yourself?'

She emptied her cup, set it down, then lifted the teapot inquiringly. When he shook his head, she busied herself refilling her own cup so that she didn't have to meet that direct gaze. 'My mother died at my birth, together with my brother. My father' — she forced herself to steady her voice — 'my father killed himself just over a year ago. His business had failed.'

She knew Olivia would have been furious if she had heard her. Her sister always spoke to others of her father as though he had been taken by a fatal illness. Annis preferred to face the truth: she was used to shocked reactions, to embarrassed silences and sudden withdrawals. But Gideon Brenner only said, 'I'm sorry. It must have been a great shock to you and your sister.'

Annis looked up at him, grateful. 'Yes, it was. But Douglas was very kind. He saw to everything on our behalf.' Then she changed the subject. 'Captain Brenner, do you know how the *Grace and Charity* came to be so named?'

'She's called after two sisters born in Boston more than a hundred years ago. Born within the same hour, died within the same year; as like each other, I've heard, as reflections in a looking-glass, and every bit as close as sisters should be.'

Annis bit her lip and her fingers twined round each other in her lap. She would have given all she possessed to be able to say that she and Olivia were close. But all that she had was not enough.

'When they grew into womanhood Grace married a childhood friend and Charity became the wife of an Englishman who had made her acquaintance while he was in Boston on business. He settled there, and the two sisters were able to continue seeing each other almost as often as before.' Brenner got to his feet and unhurriedly began to pace the carpet as he spoke, for all the world as though he was on the deck of a ship. As she watched him Annis found her imagination caught and held by the story he was unfolding, the story of two loving sisters very unlike herself and Olivia.

'Then came the Revolutionary War — America's bid for independence from Britain,' he explained, seeing her puzzled frown, 'and Grace and Charity found that marriage had placed them on separate sides. Charity's husband took her at once to England, and from that day on the sisters never saw each other again, nor communicated with each other.'

'Charity never went back home?'

'Oh yes, she went back home. Her husband died, and when the war was ended she returned to Boston. But Grace never forgave her sister for turning her back on America during the war and Charity never forgave Grace for her criticism. They lived in the same city, not far from each other, both widowed young and both childless. They died in their nineties without ever having made up their

47

quarrel. When their great-nephew commissioned the clipper years after their deaths he gave it both their names so that at last they would be reunited.' He stopped pacing, coming to rest before the screened fireplace.

'What a romantic story!'

'On the contrary,' said Gideon Brenner, his voice suddenly crisp. 'I see it as the tale of silly women too wrapped up in selfish pride to see an inch in front of their noses.'

She blinked at him, feeling as though he had just thrown a cup of cold water in her face, then said, just as crisply, 'Indeed?'

'Indeed, Mrs Moncrieff. My own mother was a member of Boston society when she met and married my father. I know how stiff-necked pride can make those people. I thank God, though,' he added with a softening of his voice and expression, 'that she was also blessed with more common sense than the sisters Grace and Charity.'

'I think it's a delightful story. I'm even more pleased by my husband's decision not to give the clipper a new name.'

'I would have expected him to prefer something more . . . Scottish.'

'He thinks that Grace and Charity are good biblical words. It might be best,' she added thoughtfully, realizing all at once that Douglas would scarcely look kindly on the true reason behind the ship's name, 'if we said nothing to him of the sisters' story.'

Then she coloured as it came to her that in a short space of time the two of them had united to keep not one but two secrets from her husband. Three, if she counted the window-washing. She stared at him, feeling guilty.

Suddenly the door opened and Tib Moncrieff stood framed in the doorway, her sharp brown eyes taking in the scene.

Brenner sketched a slight bow and Annis bounced to her feet, scooping up the walrus tusk and holding it out to her husband's sister. 'Captain Brenner called to leave this for Robert. He got it from a whaler. Robert will be delighted, don't you think?'

She was gabbling, but she couldn't help it. Tib had a way of making her feel like a child caught in the act of some naughtiness.

'I was about to leave,' Brenner said blandly. 'Thank you for your hospitality, Mrs Moncrieff.'

The older woman's eyes scarcely took time to rest on the ivory piece that was held out for her inspection. With a dry, grudging, 'Good morning, Captain Brenner,' she stepped back to let the visitor go past her into the hall.

He did so unhurriedly, dwarfing her thin figure. Annis followed him, feeling the blast of Tib's disapproval as she, too, went by. She took the American's hat from the stand and held it out to him, then opened the door.

'I'm sure Robert will want to thank you himself.'

'I expect I'll see him down by the harbour some time. Until Saturday evening . . .' he said, and then he was gone. Annis closed the door and went back into the parlour where Tib, her mouth a disapproving wrinkle-edged button, was inspecting the tray.

'Would you like a cup of tea, Tib? It's still hot.'

The woman wagged her head vigorously from side to side. 'With the cost of tea these days I'd feel downright sinful drinking it at this time in the morning! What did that young man say about Saturday evening?'

'I've invited him to attend the Assembly Ball at the White Hart Inn with us.'

Tib sniffed. 'I doubt if my brother will approve of one of his employees making merry as if he was an equal.'

Annis held on to her temper. 'I don't think Douglas will object. After all, Captain Brenner is a stranger in Greenock, far from his own folk. We must make him feel welcome.'

'The colonials are pushy enough without being encouraged,' said Tib, and swept out on her way to the kitchen to harangue the servants. Annis, snubbed and deserted, only just refrained from letting the point of her tongue slip out from between her teeth. Instead she muttered under her breath, 'Snibby Tib!' Then she caught sight of herself in the mirror by the door, and grinned at her reflection. Childish though the nickname was, it always helped to break up the frustration that she suffered each time she was bested by Tib.

As he descended the steep flight of steps down to the road Gideon Brenner pondered the enigma that was Douglas Moncrieff's young wife.

She was a strange little creature. At first he had thought that she had no more life in her than a rag doll, but this morning he had discovered another, livelier side to her nature. He wondered with amusement if Moncrieff might live to rue the day he took that seemingly biddable young woman to wife.

Then Annis Moncrieff faded from his mind, to be replaced by a picture of her sister. Now there was a woman!

Brenner's blood warmed at the very thought of Olivia. He repeated her name over and over again in his mind, shaped it silently with his lips. From the first moment he had seen her, standing below him on the quay, he had been strongly attracted to Olivia Kerr. He was certain that there was a passion in her, burning beneath the cool exterior, held in check but there for an astute man to recognize.

She would take a deal of wooing, but he was quite certain that she would be worth the effort. It was clear to see that she was bored and frustrated by the life she led in her brother-in-law's household. An ambitious young shipmaster could do a sight worse for himself than take Olivia Kerr to wife.

He had done right to come to Scotland, he was certain of that, hard though it had been to leave his homeland and his family. But he knew well enough that his homeland had little now to offer a man determined to spend his working life aboard sailing ships, and as to family — if his mother had had her way he would have found himself married within the year to one of those Bostonian society beauties he had just spoken of so scathingly to Annis Moncrieff.

Of all her four children, Gideon's looks and bearing were most like those of his mother's family. Because of this, and the fact that he was her youngest, he had always been her favourite and she had disapproved of his decision to go to sea rather than work with his father in the shipyard, where he would be safe on dry land.

When places on board sailing ships became hard to find she had determined to marry her younger son, who had all the confidence needed to mingle with society people, to the daughter of one of her dearest friends. The young woman's father was extremely wealthy and a place would certainly be available in his engineering empire for a suitable son-in-law.

But Gideon would have none of it, nor would he consider going to sea in a steam-ship, as his brother had done. The opportunity to take the *Grace and Charity*, a ship he had loved since the days when he had watched her taking shape on the stocks in the shipyard, to Scotland had come at just the right time for him.

He stepped into the gutter to make way for a fat woman who took up the full width of the footpath as she sailed along, aflutter with ribbons. Grey-haired though she was, she simpered and blushed as the young man who had moved aside for her smiled and bowed her on her way.

Gideon stepped back on to the footpath again. He had no objection to making his fortune, but not through a society marriage to a rich man's daughter. He wanted to have more control over his own destiny than that. It occurred to him that marriage to Olivia Kerr, as well as being an infinitely desirable prospect, would make him brother-in-law to Douglas Moncrieff, with, no doubt, the prospect of becoming more involved in the business himself.

He thought of the coming Saturday and of dancing with Olivia, her rounded body near his, the scent of her hair in his nostrils. His steps quickened as he strode towards the harbour and the clipper ship that was now his to command.

4

Much to Tib's annoyance Douglas approved of his wife's invitation to the young shipmaster. But Olivia was furious.

'I don't know what possessed you, Annis! He'll only stare at me with those eyes of his that look right through me. He'll expect me to dance with him!'

'I can think of worse fates than dancing with Gideon Brenner,' Annis commented, and her sister glared.

'It's easy for you to say that. You've got Douglas. That — that sailor,' she said scathingly, unable to think of a more insulting word, 'will no doubt look on himself as my partner for the evening!'

'There are plenty of pretty young women in the town for him to dance with.'

'Then you'd best introduce him to them as soon as we get there in the hope that he'll leave me in peace.'

'Olivia, what's wrong with Captain Brenner?'

'For one thing, he's an American. For another, he's only a shipmaster and as poor as a church mouse. I've a good mind,' said Olivia, 'to plead a headache and stay home.'

'As you please.' Annis could afford to take the threat calmly, knowing as she did that her sister would never miss a town Assembly Ball and the opportunity it gave her to outdress the other women and run her hazel eyes over the menfolk. Although there was a great deal of poverty in Greenock there was also money. In past years some large houses had been built on the outskirts of the town by wealthy manufacturers from Paisley and Glasgow. They and their guests often attended the local soirées if they were in residence at the time. It was from their ranks, Annis knew, that Olivia hoped one day to recruit a suitable husband.

There was a pause, then Olivia said, her voice heavy with accusation, 'You realize, I hope, that you've quite ruined the entire evening for me!'

Annis bit her lip to hold back a sharp retort and watched her sister flounce up to her room. Olivia's vanity angered her at times — perhaps because it was justified. All her life, Olivia had been beautiful. Their father had been proud of that beauty, always urging her to spend money on herself even though they never went anywhere. When the sisters went out together few men had passed them without a second or a third glance at Olivia. Annis, on the other hand, had attracted notice from nobody but Douglas.

She caught herself up sharply. Not only was Douglas the best and most considerate husband any woman could wish for, but he had chosen her, not her sister. She was much more fortunate than Olivia — yet it would have been very pleasant if, just once in her life, she had been able to assume, as Olivia had, that a man as exciting and as handsome as Gideon Brenner would want to partner her at a ball.

Tib refused, as usual, to attend the Assembly Ball. Robert would have gone willingly, but his aunt and uncle both felt that he was still too young, so he was forced to stay at home.

Going into his room before the carriage arrived to take Douglas and the womenfolk to the inn, Annis found the boy lying on his stomach on the floor, sketching.

She had rapped lightly on the door; as she went in there was a scuffle as Robert tried to hide his sketch-pad under a school-book. He looked up, his face flushed with guilt, then grinned and let his breath out in a sigh of relief. 'It's only you.'

'What are you drawing?' The slightly hooped skirts of her pale green ball-gown wouldn't allow her to kneel beside him. Instead, she seated herself carefully, gracefully, on a low chair and held out her hand. He gave her the pad and waited solemnly for her opinion. As always, the drawing was skilfully executed with bold confident strokes and painstaking attention to detail.

'Is it a new design?'

'It's a small schooner that Jem's about to put on to his stocks at the yard. I wanted to show him how he could modify the deck plan to allow for more space.'

Although he made his money by building commissioned ships, Jem Moncrieff made it a rule to have a small vessel on the stocks in a corner of his shipyard at all times. In the event of a slump in business his men worked on this ship instead of being laid off. As each 'shipyard' vessel was completed a buyer was found for it and Jem then started on another.

'Will he use your plan?'

'I think so,' Robert said happily, then sat up on his heels and studied his uncle's young wife with open admiration. 'You look beautiful.'

She glowed with pleasure and smoothed the skirt of

the new gown Douglas had bought for the occasion. 'You should see Olivia.'

'Bother Olivia,' said Robert.

'You don't think it's too fancy for a married woman, do you?'

The dress was made of very pale green tulle with lace flounces of deeper green at the low square neck and on the hem of the skirt. The bodice was tight, following and emphasizing the curves of her body. Lace ruffles sweeping down from the waist at the front to the frilled hem at the back led the eye to a small frothy train. A dark green bow in the small of Annis's back accentuated her slim waist.

'I think it's going to be the finest gown in the place,' Robert said with touching sincerity, and added as she rose and turned slowly before him 'The cut of it suits your shape well.'

For a shocked moment she blinked, then erupted in a flurry of giggles as his young face slowly crimsoned. 'There speaks a ship designer!'

Then she added hurriedly as an impatient masculine voice called from below. 'I must go.'

'You look like a princess,' he called after in an attempt to soften his earlier comment. She turned at the door and blew him a kiss.

The carriage had arrived and the front door lay open to the soft balmy June evening. Olivia and Douglas both waited in the hall with Tib. Three pair of eyes watched Annis accusingly as she hurried down the staircase.

Olivia, too, had been invited to choose a new dress for the occasion, but unlike Annis she had scorned the Greenock seamstresses and had travelled to Glasgow, where she bought a ready-made gown in one of the big new department stores.

Annis had to admit that it put her own gown in the shadows. If Annis looked like a princess, Olivia was a queen. But then, she reminded herself firmly, Olivia was unmarried and therefore it made sense for her to give greater attention to her appearance. Annis only had her husband to please, and Douglas, who had as always been consulted at every step of the way during the making of her dress, was delighted with the result.

Her sister was dressed in a gold silken gown trimmed with scarlet rosettes. They were scattered extravagantly over the full trained skirt and along the edge of a skintight bodice that plunged to show the upper curves of her full breasts to advantage. The front of the skirt, following the latest fashion, was quite flat, and a bold cluster of scarlet ribbons was fastened over the bustle at the back. Scarlet ribbons also edged a frilled overskirt and the bottom of the underskirt.

Both women wore soft white leather shoes and white stockings. Annis's shoes were decorated with small green rosettes and her stockings were plain, while Olivia's shoes had a row of scarlet bows from instep to toe, and her stockings were embroidered with glittering gold thread.

It took some time to fit Olivia and her beautiful dress into the hired carriage to her own satisfaction, and by the time it was done Douglas's mouth had begun to look distinctly thin. But at last they were all in and the coachman shook the reins and clicked his tongue at his patient horse.

Cathcart Square was thronged with carriages of all descriptions and loud with the clatter of shod hooves and the yells and whistles of the drivers and grooms. From the open windows of the White Hart Inn music floated out to the ears of the ragged children and adults who had come flocking to stare at the more fortunate townspeople who could afford to go inside and take part in the evening's celebrations. Some of the gentlemen descending from their carriages tossed a few coins to the children, who scrambled on the ground for them, fighting fiercely with each other, and though Annis tried to persuade Douglas to find some change he refused outright.

'It shames me to think that the visitors to our town should see local children groping in the gutter for pennies as though they were beggars,' he said, disgust curling his lip.

'They are beggars, poor mites,' Annis said, but he pretended not to hear her as he climbed down and offered his hand to her and then to Olivia.

Gideon Brenner stepped forward to greet them, sweeping a top hat from his head as he came towards his employer's party. He was impeccably dressed tonight in a white frilled shirt with a green satin waistcoat embroidered in peacock colours with iridescent threads. His trousers were fawn, his jacket deep blue. Beside him, Annis noticed, Douglas looked elderly and crowlike in his dark coat and trousers. Her husband's cravat, too, was dark, whereas Brenner's was blue and patterned with small green leaves. With a bow, he offered his arm to Olivia, who had no option but to place her gloved hand into the crook of his elbow. Douglas drew his wife's hand through his arm and they followed the others.

As the small party reached the door of the hotel Annis happened to look to the side, to where a group of the poorer townsfolk were clustered near the door like moths jostling near a flame. Her gaze was met and returned by a pair of bold eyes in a sharp face framed by a shawl.

Annis hesitated, and for a brief moment she and

Adeline Fraser, the former servant who had returned to Greenock on board the *Grace and Charity*, stared at each other. Then Annis, urged on by Douglas's arm, turned away and stepped through the door into a world of lights and laughter and music.

As Annis had said to Gideon Brenner, the Scots knew how to enjoy a dance. By the time the evening was half over the more sedate southern dances had been discarded in favour of strathspeys and reels, and the musicians had begun to earn their money in earnest.

Even the most prim and proper guest took to the floor, though after a few rousing dances the older people began to settle themselves in chairs by the walls, content to play their part by tapping their feet or clapping their hands.

Douglas soon joined them but when Annis accompanied him, disappointed but dutiful, he pushed her gently back towards the dance-floor.

'On you go . . . enjoy yourself.' He smiled at her indulgently.

She didn't stop to argue. Circles of six were being summoned for the Dashing White Sergeant, and for once the ladies didn't have to wait to be sought out by gentlemen before they went on to the floor. She joined the nearest circle and quite by chance found herself standing beside Jem Moncrieff, handsome in a coat the colour of milky coffee, with a brown cravat tucked in at the neck. Swiftly, nervously, she glanced over her shoulder at Douglas and saw that he was half-turned away, talking to someone. He hadn't yet noticed that she stood beside his despised cousin. She would have moved, but the circle was formed and it was too late. Besides, it would have been a cruel snub to Jem, who was grinning down at her.

'You look bonny, Annis. Is Robert not here? I know he was hoping to come along.'

'Douglas and Tib said he was too young.'

'Ach!' Jem's exclamation succinctly said everything he thought about Douglas and Tib. 'The laddie's close to being a man. He should have been brought along. Douglas is altogether too strict with him. And with you,' she thought she heard him add, then, 'You've not been down to the yard for a week or two.'

'Tib's busy turning the whole house out and having it cleaned from top to bottom, so I've not had a minute,' she said ruefully. She loved her visits to Jem's boatyard, but they could only be undertaken when neither Tib nor Douglas was about to ask where she was going, or where she had been. If Douglas knew that she and Robert visited his cousin there was no telling what he might do.

The music struck up, Jem seized her hand in his own warm strong clasp, and off they went, circling eight slip steps to the left and eight to the right, with no time or breath left for conversation. Jem danced well, Annis thought as the circle broke into two lines of three and she and her husband's cousin set to each other then linked arms and spun round in a circle. He was light on his feet and had a natural grace and a feel for the rhythm.

He was a kindly man too. She knew that his wife had died in childbirth some twenty years before when Jem was scarcely out of his teens. She thought it a great pity that he had never married again, and wondered, for the umpteenth time, what had happened in the past to set Douglas so hard against the man. She had made the mistake of asking her husband that question once, in the early days of their marriage when she had had some notion of bringing the two cousins together again. His reaction had been so swift, so angry, that she had never dared ask him again. And she wouldn't dream of asking Jem. If he had wanted her to know he would have told her during the few conversations they had managed to have since she joined the Moncrieff family.

The three of them, Jem and Annis and the woman on Jem's other side, linked hands and danced towards the other three in their original circle. Then they dipped back, advanced again. Jem's fingers loosed as they slipped between the other dancers then clasped hers again as they moved on to meet three more and start the circle afresh.

At one time, on their journey round the dance floor, she and Jem passed Douglas, who managed to convey in one twist of his mouth both his pleasure at seeing her and his displeasure at seeing her with Jem. On another occasion they met up with a trio that included Olivia and Gideon Brenner. The American was doing his best to follow the pattern of the dance, not a whit bothered by the amusement the Scots were enjoying at his expense.

Olivia, more hampered than Annis by the style of her gown, and forced to twitch the train out of Brenner's way at almost every step, was unsmiling, her full mouth tight with irritation. Annis beamed at her and was rewarded with a look that came close to being murderous.

During the interval Olivia disappeared to an upstairs room that had been set aside for the ladies, muttering something about repairing a small tear in her skirt. Douglas watched her go, a frown tucking itself between his brows.

'Your sister seems to be wallowing in a fit of temper, my dear.' He always spoke of Olivia as 'your sister' when he was displeased with her.

'She doesn't care for this style of dancing,' Annis said, and he snorted through his thin straight nose.

'It seems to me that there's a lot Olivia doesn't care for. She's too pernickety by half. God help the man that takes her for wife, though the sooner she finds him the better I'll be pleased.'

Olivia, easing her way through the crush of folk who were now standing on the dance floor, had come face to face with Gideon, carrying two glasses of lemonade. He said something to her and she snapped back a brief reply before moving on. For a moment he stood looking after her, then came across to the Moncrieffs.

'I brought some lemonade for Miss Olivia, but it appears that she doesn't care for it.'

He stood helplessly, looking at the glasses he held, not quite sure what to do next. Annis saved him by holding out her hand. 'I, on the other hand, have a weakness for it. If you have no objection, Captain Brenner, I would enjoy a second glass. It's very hot in here.'

He handed her one of the glasses with a relieved smile and sipped at the other.

'I thought you'd be drinking spirits,' Douglas said bluntly.

'I enjoy a drink as much as the next man, sir. But I'm particularly thirsty tonight.'

Several people drifted up to them, mainly in search of an invitation to the American who had apparently decided to make his home among them. While Douglas and Brenner talked to the menfolk Annis was caught up in the feminine chatter about dresses and recipes and servant trouble.

It was a relief to her when the musicians struck up again and everyone scattered to find partners for the next dance.

'Strip the Willow!' Annis caught Douglas's hand. 'We must go on the floor for this!'

He shook his head. 'It's altogether too energetic for me, my dear.'

'Please, Douglas!'

'Perhaps Captain Brenner will oblige you. After all, he's eager to learn our dances.'

The shipmaster, who had been looking in vain for Olivia, gave his full attention to his employer's wife. 'Indeed, Mrs Moncrieff, I would be delighted.'

'I'll warrant you may not be delighted for long,' Annis heard Douglas say dryly as she and Brenner moved on to the dance floor. She looked back over a lacy shoulder and shook her head reprovingly at him. He answered her look with a surprisingly youthful grin that broadened by the minute once the music began and the shipmaster found himself caught up in the most intricate dance of the evening.

Helpless with laughter, Annis and the other people in the set pushed him bodily through the steps. Every time he caught the nearest woman by the hands and began to swing her round he was met by a breathless chorus of 'No . . . not her . . . not now! The next one!'

'This isn't a dance, Mrs Moncrieff, it's a form of torture,' he panted when he finally caught up with his partner at the end of the double row of dancers.

'Nonsense, Captain Brenner, you're doing very well.' She caught his hands, spun him round, pushed him towards the nearest woman. 'That way . . .'

'You mean we've not finished our part?' he asked in horror as he was caught up by determined hands, whisked round, and pushed towards his next partner, a well-built woman who grabbed at him enthusiastically.

Annis was laughing so much that she could scarcely go through the dance herself. Her feet scarcely seemed to touch the floor and she felt younger than she had felt for a long time, young and carefree.

When the music finished at last and the dancers scattered, Brenner said breathlessly, 'That's unfortunate – I was just beginning to get the way of it.'

She pushed a lock of hair from her eyes and shook her head. 'I don't believe you were, but you made a very good try.'

'To my way of thinking it's a lot easier to reef in a sail in a gale than to perform a Scottish dance properly.' He laughed, his eyes sparkling like emeralds.

Although his face was almost grim in repose, laughter came easily to Gideon Brenner, Annis thought. She wished that Douglas had the same ability. True, when he smiled or laughed his whole face was younger, but that happened all too seldom. Glancing at the corner where he sat she wondered in despair if she would ever find a way to bring real happiness to the man who had honoured her by choosing her for his wife. All she had to give him in return was her love and loyalty. They were his, but at times it seemed to her that they were not enough. Turning back to Gideon Brenner, amusement still lighting his features, she was suddenly envious of Olivia, who had the opportunity, should she care to take it, of winning this man for her own.

As though reading her mind he looked over her head, his gaze searching the crowd. 'Your sister hasn't appeared yet,' he said, then all at once, quietly, 'Mrs Moncrieff, I hope you won't take this amiss but I find myself drawn most strongly to Miss Olivia. You know her better than anyone. Do you think that she herself might . . .?'

'My sister has a very strong will of her own, Captain Brenner.'

'I know that,' he said with open admiration. 'I'd not have her any other way. I'll soon be going to sea again; do you think that you could perhaps talk to your sister on my behalf while I'm gone?'

Annis felt sorry for the man. Was there any sense in explaining to him that Olivia needed nobody, least of all her young sister?

'I'll try,' she said weakly.

'Thank you, ma'am. And now,' he said formally, 'I'd best return you to your husband.'

Olivia didn't reappear until the evening was almost over, when she arrived in time to be claimed by Brenner for the final dance. Watching her, noting the way she held herself aloof from her partner, Annis again felt sorry for Gideon Brenner.

'It's a fine evening,' the young shipmaster said later, as the four of them forged their way through the crowds and stepped outside into cool fresh darkness spangled by carriage lamps and hand-held torches. 'I would be happy to escort you if you care to walk home, Miss Olivia.'

'We could all walk back,' Douglas suggested, and Annis agreed eagerly, in no hurry to return to the gloomy Moncrieff house. Olivia looked down her pretty nose and said that speaking for herself she was tired and had no intention of catching a chill after being in the warmth of the hall.

To Annis's disappointment, and, she saw by the downward turn of his mouth and the darkening of his eyes, to Brenner's, it was finally agreed after some mild wrangling that the Moncrieffs and Olivia would return home the way they came — by carriage.

The shipmaster took his leave of them, then turned and walked into the darkness, wishing that Olivia walked by his side, her hand resting on his arm. He knew well enough that she had gone out of her way to snub him all evening, but that didn't bother him. It was rarely that Gideon Brenner was rejected by a woman, and to him it merely showed that Olivia had fire and pride and was all the more worth the winning. She would come to him eventually, his own natural pride told him that. He strode on, wild Scottish music still ringing in his head, his inner eye recalling in every detail how lovely she had looked in her gold and scarlet ball gown.

The *Grace and Charity* sailed for South America two weeks later. In the last few days before she left, Gideon Brenner had been a frequent visitor to the house in Low Gourock Road. Annis and Robert welcomed the breath of fresh air the shipmaster brought into the house, and the stories he had to tell of America and his career aboard the sailing ships.

Tib had continued to look down her long nose at the American, and Olivia all but ignored him, although on the evening before the clipper sailed, when Brenner dined with his employer's family, he had managed to coax her into walking in the garden with him before he left.

They were only out for a few minutes when they reappeared, Olivia announcing that it was too cold to be out of doors. Brenner said nothing, but the slight hardening at the corners of his mouth and the frown tucked between his brows made Annis wonder if he was beginning to find her sister's reluctance tiresome.

Annis would dearly have liked to go down to the quay to see the clipper, with the Moncrieff house flag at her mainmast, leave on her first voyage for her new owner. But Douglas would of course be there, and Douglas wouldn't approve of her presence.

Instead, stifled by the dark house and longing to get into the sunshine, she pointed out to Tib that the pantry supply of eggs was low, and offered to go to one of the farms on the hills above Greenock and Gourock to fetch more. Clearly happy to get the house to herself, Tib agreed, and Annis went off shortly after breakfast, taking Robert with her.

When they had been taken on a tour of the farmyard and given a glass of buttermilk each and had settled the eggs carefully on a bed of grass in the basket, the two of them set off on the homeward journey, dawdling along, reluctant to go back to the house too soon on such a lovely July day.

They stepped off the narrow path to admire a great clump of golden broom, and Annis nodded her satisfaction as she studied a thicket of bramble bushes nearby.

'I'll remember where they are. We'll gather in a good crop of brambles from them in the autumn.'

'Good,' said Robert, who loved home-made bramble jelly.

Near to the brambles a burn bubbled and chattered down the hillside. Through the crystal water could be seen stones smoothed by its passage over the years and washed to pale browns and fawns and greys. Here and there an underwater weed bowed its fronds to the occasional leaf and twig that swirled busily past it. A small natural waterfall had been created by a sudden steep drop, the tumbling water gouging out a deep pool just below it. At that point the slope of the hill shelved briefly to form a natural soft seat.

The sun burrowed through all the layers of Annis's clothes. Even the breeze that whisked at her skirt was warm. The sparkle and the cool musical babble of the water on that hot day was more than she could bear. On an impulse she placed the basket gently on a flat stone, turned her back on Robert, who was tossing twigs into the stream and watching them tumble over the waterfall, and slipped off her shoes and stockings.

'Let's dunk our feet before we walk down to the town.'

Robert hesitated, reddening self-consciously.

'Come on,' she urged, lowering herself until she was sitting on the grassy bank, turning to squint up at him, her eyes dazzled by sunlight. 'Who's to see us except a few birds?'

Then she gasped as her naked feet plunged into the pool. The icy coldness of the water numbed her and took her breath away for an instant before a delicious refreshing tingle started in her toes. Tentatively she raised one foot clear of the water, then dipped it back again. Ripples caught and curved about her ankles, tickling the smooth skin.

Watching her, Robert's mind was made up. In a moment his shoes and stockings were tossed aside and his pale bony feet were plunged into the water beside hers.

'I haven't done this for years and years,' Annis said in wonder at herself, as they sat side by side, swinging their legs.

'If I ever become Prime Minster I'm going to decree that everyone should be made to dip their feet in a burn at least once a year,' Robert announced.

'Your Aunt Tib as well?'

The thought made them giggle like the conspirators they were, but even so he insisted, 'Everyone, even the fat wifies and the old men. It's a shame to think that we live so near to all this without making the most of it when we can.'

'Mmm,' Annis agreed, lifting her face to the sun.

They sat in a companionable silence for a while, cooled by the water and drowsing gently in the sun's warmth, listening to the burn and the birds and the bees bumbling among the bright yellow broom. Their feet, his long and bony, hers small and neat, shimmered up at them from beneath the burn's crystal surface.

Below them the hugger-mugger of roofs and streets that made up the town was partly hidden by the rest of the hill. Annis could just see the docks and the masts and spars of the ships moored there. Beyond the masts the river itself was seething with traffic.

'Robert,' she asked suddenly, struck by a thought, 'what time do you make it?'

'Hmm?' Robert, lying back on the grass now with his hands tucked behind his head, opened one eye, marked the sun's position, and said lazily, 'About an hour to noon.'

'Already?'

'We've got plenty of time,' he said, but she was leaning forward, paying no heed to him, her eyes scanning the river intently. They found what they sought.

'Look.'

'What is it?'

'Just look!'

He sat upright with some reluctance and followed the line of her slim pointing finger. His face lit up.

'It's the *Grace and Charity*. I'd forgotten that she was going out this morning.'

'So had I – almost,' said Annis, straining her eyes,

eager to see as many details of the vessel as she could.

The clipper was standing out in the river, her elegant bows pointing towards the west, where the mouth of the Clyde opened into the sea. Her sails were all set, the canvas on the foremast and mizzen filling out before the breeze. Her mainmast was backed, the yards turned so that the sails they carried lay against the wind, acting as a brake, holding the ship back to ensure that she made slow headway in the busy waters. Most sailing shipmasters used tugs to take their vessels to the open sea, but Gideon Brenner had scorned such an idea. He clearly knew how to handle the clipper, even in the enclosed and crowded firth, although Annis knew Douglas would be watching anxiously at that moment, terrified lest his precious clipper come to grief.

Tugs and fishing boats, small brigantines and schooners and ketches and yawls fussed through the water like so many beetles as the huge beautiful clipper, her white sails dazzling in the sun, towering high above the river traffic, glided through their midst like a queen passing through massed ranks of her subjects.

'Think of it, Robert,' Annis said, her mind's eye recalling clearly the route she had traced on the globe in Douglas's study. 'Out into the Atlantic Ocean, down past the Portuguese coast, through the Doldrums and then south and south until she can drive round Cape Horn. Then it's into the South Pacific and along the South American shore to Valparaiso.' The very name of the place had an alien beauty to it.

'You wish you were on board, don't you?' said Robert quietly.

'Of course I do. Don't you? One day you will, Robert. One day you'll be old enough to do anything you like.'

'One day,' said Robert bleakly, 'I'll own the company.'

'And when that day comes you'll be your own master.'

'No. I'll own the company, but it will own me. I'll mebbe sail aboard one of my own ships now and then as my uncle does, but only to do business and make more money.'

The bitterness in his young voice was strong enough to drag Annis's eyes away from the magnificent sight of the *Grace and Charity*, now heading towards the stubby finger of land that thrust into the river between Greenock and Gourock. 'You'll be your own master,' she said again, insistently. 'You'll be able to do anything you want then.'

'Even sell it?'

The thought of such a thing took her breath away. The family business was Douglas's whole life. Selling it would be a terrible betrayal, even after his death. But there was such misery in the brown eyes watching her, such wretched anticipation of her outrage, that she swallowed, then said evenly, 'Even that . . . if it's what you want when the time comes.'

Astonishment replaced the misery. 'You'd not mind?'

'Why should I mind? What has it got to do with me?'

'You're Uncle Douglas's wife. You'd surely want me to see his company carried on.'

Annis reached out and touched the boy's cheek with the tip of one finger. 'I want you to be happy, Robert. What do I care for the business if it makes you unhappy?'

'I'm not cut out for office work, Annis.' The words were wrenched from the depths of Robert's soul. 'If I had the freedom to choose I'd sell every stick and stone of it. Except perhaps . . .'

He looked beyond her, to where the clipper was beating

her way down river to catch the breeze. 'Except perhaps the *Grace and Charity*. But everything else.' His laugh was a bit shaky, and Annis dearly wished that she could take him into her arms and give him a reassuring hug. But the Moncrieffs frowned on emotional displays, and Robert would probably fall headlong into the pool with the shock of it if she as much as put an arm about his shoulders.

'If Uncle Douglas and Aunt Tib could hear what I'm saying they'd swear that I'm not a true Moncrieff.'

'What would you do with yourself if you sold the business?'

'Give the money to Jem,' Robert said, his eyes hot and defiant. 'He needs it and he deserves it. He's a Moncrieff too and he should have had some share of the money my grandfather left. He didn't get a penny, did you know that? My father and Uncle Douglas should have given him his share, for he was as much a grandson as they were. If I was free I'd go into partnership with him and design fine boats for him to build, and be damned to what folk might think of me for betraying my grandfather and my father and my uncle.' He finished on a defiant note, then, suddenly guilty, he asked, 'You'll not tell him — them — what I've said?'

'If you don't tell them about me sitting here like a wanton hussy with my bare feet in a burn when I should be doing the housework.'

He laughed, then said, glancing down at the guilty feet, 'Your toes are like little pearls. I didn't know that feet could be so small and so lovely.'

Pleasure and embarrassment brought an added flush to her face, already glowing with sun and fresh air. She kicked at the water, setting up a glittering spray. 'Och, Robert! That's a daft-like thing to say!'

'It's not,' he defended himself. 'They're like little white birds. Come to think of it, that's what you remind me of at times. A wee bird in a cage where it doesn't belong.'

'And where else would I be?'

Robert's wide mouth turned in a ready smile. 'There,' he said, indicating the clipper, now closing on the outcrop of land that would soon hide her from sight. 'On board that ship on your way to the Americas and adventure.'

'That's for men, not women. Women,' said Annis, keeping her voice cheerful, 'aren't allowed to have adventures. They've got more important things to do. Now come along, or your Aunt Tib will be fretting about us.'

He sighed, but got to his feet obediently. His hand, large and warm and bony as his feet, reached down to help her up.

As they left the little burn behind and started down the slope towards the town, Robert said thoughtfully, 'I'd really like it, Annis, if Uncle Douglas had a son to leave the business to. Then I'd not have to feel guilty about wanting to do other things. I hope you'll give him a son.'

She pretended to be navigating some tricky tussocks of grass, so that her face was hidden from him. More than once, feeling that perhaps the restlessness in her would go away if she had a baby to think about, she had said wistfully to Douglas that they should think about starting their own family. But each time he had brushed the idea aside, telling her that there was plenty of time, that his little girl was far too young to burden herself with child-bearing and child-rearing.

Now she said carefully to his nephew, 'If Douglas and I had a son — when we have a son — the business will be divided between you.'

'I'd feel a lot happier if there was someone else to inherit. Someone who'd mebbe care as much about it as my grandfather and my father and Uncle Douglas.' His voice was heavy with the burden of his future responsibilities and Annis's heart went out to him as she longed to lighten his load. Yet she was helpless.

She could just see the *Grace and Charity*'s topgallants now. The ship's hull and the lower part of her masts were hidden behind the land as she passed Gourock. Soon the *Grace and Charity* would be completely out of sight, well on her way to the open sea where she belonged, a white-winged bird, free to skim across the oceans, far from Greenock.

As she stood watching the ship move away from her, Annis felt very lonely.

5

'How dare he!' Olivia's voice, usually carefully modulated, was shrill with fury and disbelief. She stood in the middle of the parlour floor, facing her brother-in-law, her lovely face flushed to a poppy red.

'I see nothing wrong with Captain Brenner's request—'

'Nothing wrong?' Olivia almost shrieked. 'Nothing wrong? Am I to be bought and sold with as much consideration as a — a harlot?'

'Guard your tongue, madam!' Douglas's voice rang out over an outraged gasp from Tib, an avid spectator. His cheekbones had also taken on an ominous colour.

'I am not an animal to be bought and sold in the cattle market!'

Annis, trying to look as though she was intent on her embroidery, wished passionately that she had been allowed to approach her sister when the two of them were alone. But Douglas, head of the household, had told her in the privacy of their bedchamber that he would see to the matter. It was time, he had said, that Olivia had a household of her own and it was his duty to lead her in the right direction.

Annis had to agree to a certain extent with Olivia. Douglas's idea of leading a woman in the right direction had a lot to do with the rough and ready bullying of a cowherd. But she knew full well that interference on her part at this stage would only make things worse.

Tib, seated as usual on an upright uncomfortable chair, had no such scruples. Douglas's business was her business, and now her hard voice added itself to the storm that was already raging. 'My brother has your best interests at heart, Olivia. You should heed what he has to say to you.'

'I don't wish to hear anything that he has to say to me!' Olivia rounded on her new adversary with a swish of skirts. 'How dare that — that colonial upstart ask for my hand! And how dare your brother listen to such a—'

'Captain Brenner has not asked for your hand. He has asked if he might call on you when he comes back from his present trip, and I have agreed.'

'Indeed, sir? But I have not agreed! And I will not agree — not ever!'

'Marriage doesn't come into it as yet. It will be a full year before Brenner's in a position to take a wife, but in the meantime—'

'I refuse to entertain Captain Brenner or any thought of a future with him,' Olivia said through set teeth. 'I will not, ever, lower myself to marry a man of his class!'

'It seems to me that you're setting your sights far too high,' Tibs said dryly, and Douglas nodded.

Olivia's voice cracked like a whip across the space between brother and sister. 'I find it strange that a woman who has never in her life, to my knowledge, attracted the attentions of a cabin boy, let alone a shipmaster, can be so critical of others.'

Tib sucked in her breath with a sharp malevolent hiss and her sallow face was suddenly blotched with ugly red spots. The sewing in her hands slithered from her lap to the floor as her fingers curled into ugly hooked claws.

'You impertinent hussy!'

For a moment Annis, appalled, her own sewing discarded as she jumped to her feet, thought that the two women were going to attack each other. But Douglas, his face dark with anger, growled 'Tib!' and his sister subsided. He turned, furious, to Olivia.

'You'll apologize for that, miss!'

In answer Olivia marched to the door and threw it open. Then she turned, head high. 'I'll not be courted by Gideon Brenner, and you can tell him so when he comes sailing back into Greenock!'

'By then,' her brother-in-law said icily, 'you may well be singing a different tune. It's time you were wed and tamed.'

As the door began to swing to behind Olivia, he added vehemently, 'Was ever a man more hag-ridden than I am!'

'Douglas!' Annis protested as the door closed behind her sister, not with a slam as she had expected, but with a chilly quiet click that told her that Olivia had heard the final remark.

He had the grace to look slightly embarrassed as he came over to take her hands in his. 'I wasn't referring to you, my dear. Nor to Tib,' he added hurriedly, a shade too late.

The blotches on his sister's face had spread until they almost, but not quite, met in an all-covering blush. The result was patchy and most unattractive. The end of her sharp nose twitched with rage, and one hand was clapped dramatically to her thin flat chest as she flopped clumsily against the high back of her chair.

'Smelling salts . . .' she whispered.

77

'Brandy would do you more good.' Douglas went to the small table and poured out a generous glassful.

'Get me my smelling salts!' Tib protested in a stronger voice, glaring at his back. Annis hurried to fetch the salts from the small cloth bag that was never far from Tib's hand. Swiftly she uncorked the bottle and waved it beneath her sister-in-law's nose.

As Tib coughed and choked, Douglas drank the brandy in one mouthful and refilled the glass. 'You'd best get to your bed, Tib,' he said shortly.

'Yes, indeed you should,' Annis added anxiously. 'I'll help you.'

Despite Tib's display of the vapours, the hand that pushed Annis away was strong. 'I'll see to myself,' Tib snapped, adding as she got to her feet, 'Since nobody else in this house sees fit to defend me, I must needs see to myself!'

'I should go with her,' Annis said as the door closed for the second time, leaving husband and wife alone.

'Leave her. Once Tib's got it into her head to act the martyr there's no stopping her. Life in this house,' said Douglas gloomily, 'is going to be well nigh unbearable for the next day or two, with those two at each other's throats like a pair of fighting cats.'

He emptied the brandy glass again, then added, 'Since the evening's spoiled, we might as well do as the rest of the household has done, and go to bed.'

In the bedroom, while they were undressing, he said from behind his screen, 'You must talk to your sister, Annis. I see no reason why she should turn her nose up at the thought of Brenner as a husband. She's so pernickety that nobody else dares offer for her, and the good Lord knows I've no wish to keep her under my roof for the rest of her life. Persuade her.'

Annis slipped her nightgown over her head. 'She won't listen to me.'

'Make her listen,' said Douglas. 'She'll have to learn that she's putting far too high a price on herself. Brenner's a man who'll make his own way in life, I've no doubt of that. Go and talk to her now, before she gets the chance to rally her arguments . . . but don't take long.'

Olivia, in a beribboned gown far prettier than any that Annis owned, was sitting before her looking glass, dragging a stiff-bristled brush through her long, silky dark brown hair. She cast one angry look at her sister then went back to her work without a word.

When their father's house had been sold to offset some of his business debts and the sisters had moved into the Moncrieff house, Olivia had been given a small back bedroom, adjoining Robert's room. Douglas and his young bride had the large master bedroom at the front, with Tib in the next room . . . too close for Annis's comfort. The two maids slept in the attic.

Olivia's room, as always, overflowed with clothes. The tall narrow chest of drawers and the gloomy wardrobe weren't enough for the gowns and skirts and blouses and petticoats and jackets that she bought or made for herself as the fashions changed. They hung from the hook on the back of the door and from hangers suspended on the outside of the packed wardrobe.

The clothes Olivia had just taken off were draped carelessly over the only chair in the room, waiting for Janet to pick them up in the morning and either put them away or launder them. As the mistress of the house, though in name only, Annis had the right to expect the servants to look after her in this way, but she could never bring herself to it. Olivia, however, had no such scruples. In her view servants were paid to save others trouble, and she wouldn't have dreamed of hanging up her own clothes.

Annis perched on the arm of the chair and said, after her sister had allowed a cool silence to lengthen between them, 'Olivia, Douglas only has your interests at heart.'

'My interests?' Olivia asked with brittle amusement. 'My interests, you say?' She jerked the brush in a strong sweep from roots to feathery ends and her hair crackled. Then she said, 'Your husband, you silly little fool, has no interests in mind but his own.'

'That's most unfair! Douglas has given us both a good home. What would have become of us if he hadn't come to our rescue when Papa . . . Papa . . .'

'When Papa selfishly took his own life and left us unprotected, impoverished, at the mercy of the world?' Olivia's arm didn't stop wielding the brush. Her furious eyes met Annis's in the mirror. 'If I'd been left to my own devices I'd have fared better in the world than I'm faring now, I can assure you of that. Marriage with a colonial shipmaster, indeed! How dare Douglas think that he can drag me down that way?'

Annis's fists clenched until she could feel the fingernails digging in to her soft palms. 'Douglas is a good man, with the welfare of everyone in this house at heart.'

The brush went down and Olivia swung round to face her sister. 'Loving, obedient little Annis, ' she mocked. 'So grateful to Douglas for rescuing her and marrying her that she's turned into his little pet lap-dog with not a thought of her own in her head.'

Annis swallowed hard and tried to concentrate on the matter in hand. 'I fail to see why you should be so hard on Gideon Brenner. I'll warrant that in another year half the unmarried women in this town will have their eyes on him.'

'And at least one of the married women?' Olivia asked silkily. 'I have a feeling, little sister, that if the shoe was on the other foot you'd not be averse to being thrown into his arms. But not for me, for I've no wish to warm a seaman's bed!'

'If the shoe was on the other foot,' Annis said slowly, beginning to see the light, 'You'd be Mistress Moncrieff, not me. Is that what you wanted, Olivia?'

Crimson flamed in her sister's cheeks. Her hair hung in a silken sheet about a face that was even more beautiful than usual in its anger. 'Me . . . want a dull dry stick like Douglas?'

'I'm not talking about Douglas,' said Annis, her voice gathering strength as she surged on. 'I'm talking about being Mistress Moncrieff, wife of a man who's looked up to in the town. That's what's been sticking in your throat these past months, isn't it?'

Olivia's fingers curled round the hairbrush, gripping the tortoiseshell handles until her knuckles were bone-white.

When she lifted her arm Annis flinched involuntarily, half-expecting the brush to be used against her as a weapon.

Instead, Olivia sank white teeth deep into her lower lip, gained control with an effort, and swung back to the mirror.

'Run off to your middle-class husband, little sister. We've nothing to talk about.'

81

Annis stood up, went to the door, then turned. 'You're a fool, Olivia. You're waiting for the Fates to shower you with riches . . . but Douglas is right when he says that you've waited long enough. If you've got any sense in you at all you'll settle for the love of a man who's mebbe too good for you after all.'

Out in the passageway, with the solid timbers of Olivia's closed door between her and her sister, her knees suddenly gave way. She leaned against the dully flowered wall for a few moments and realized that her heart was thumping so wildly that it threatened to tear itself loose from its moorings and jump into her throat. Olivia and she had never in their lives had such a vicious quarrel. Annis had never in her life answered her elder sister back, or been so cruel. But Olivia, too, had been cruel. She had said unforgivable things about Douglas, the man who had rescued her from poverty and given her a home. That was what Annis found hard to bear.

A large tear slid from each eye. Then Douglas's irritated voice, muffled by the bedclothes, called her name.

She ran a sleeved arm over her face to blot the tears away, and went into the room she shared with him.

'No need to ask how you did,' he said sourly as she slipped her robe from her shoulders and climbed into bed. 'I'll wager half the street could hear the two of you squalling like a pair of cats. I swear, Annis, I don't know what's to be made of that sister of yours. If Brenner doesn't tame her soon whether she likes it or no, you'll be wearing widow's weeds by the time the next twelve-month's out! Turn the lamp out, for pity's sake.'

She did as she was told and he reached for her in the darkness, Olivia mercifully forgotten for the moment. A few minutes later Douglas gave a sudden shuddering sigh and rolled away from her. Annis lay quietly for another fifteen minutes or so, until she was certain that he was in a deep sated sleep, then rose as she always did and poured water from the ewer into the basin. Then, working by the dim light of the moon shining in at the window, she kilted her nightgown round her waist and bathed the stickiness from her belly and thighs. She could never settle to sleep after Douglas's loving without cleaning herself. She emptied the basin into the slop pail beneath the wash-stand then slipped back into bed. Douglas murmured something in his sleep and threw one heavy arm across her waist.

She lay waiting for sleep, trying not to think of the quarrels that had rocked the house. The hard words she had spoken to Olivia came back to her, and she flinched, wishing that she had bitten her tongue out before saying such things.

But once spoken they couldn't be denied. She was quite certain in her own mind now that she had stumbled on the real reason for Olivia's determination to make the best marriage she could — a better marriage than her sister's. Olivia wouldn't settle for anything less than a larger house than this house, a husband wealthier than Douglas, a social position higher than the position Annis held.

She recalled her sister's cold antagonism during the months before her marriage, the way Olivia had refused to become involved in buying Annis's wedding dress, the terrible day Annis timidly approached her and asked for help with the problem that had been burning in her mind ever since she had agreed to marry Douglas.

The motherless sisters had been raised by a man so

steeped in the Scottish philosophy of 'keeping himself to himself' that nobody was ever invited to his house and his daughters had been discouraged from making their own friends. Because of their father's belief that he and his family were at least one degree above everyone else they had been educated by a series of governesses instead of attending the local school. Never having had a mother or an older relation to advise her, or even a school friend to gossip and speculate with in secret, Annis found herself facing marriage with no knowledge whatsoever of a wife's duties, other than the obvious tasks of running a household.

Douglas had been the saving of the two sisters. With the house about to be sold from beneath their feet, no relatives to turn to and no money of their own, they had been at their wit's end. There had been no question of turning him down and in any case Annis, bewildered and frightened, was filled to overflowing with gratitude for this man who had singled her out from all other women, the first person to ever want her for herself. But then had come the terrible dilemma. Married people shared a bed, she knew that. And married people had children. But she had no idea what they actually did together when alone in the privacy of their bedroom, or how their children came to be conceived. As the wedding day grew nearer her anxiety turned to dry-mouthed, heart-fluttering panic. Finally, in an agony of embarrassment, she turned to her only hope — Olivia.

'How on earth should I know?' her sister demanded to know when Annis, after several false starts, finally stumbled out her question.

'I thought that perhaps . . .' Annis, beet-red, twisted her fingers tightly together.

'You're the one who's getting married, not me. I had supposed that you knew all about it. Douglas surely isn't marrying a complete fool. If he is,' said Olivia bitingly, 'he must be a fool himself!'

As a result of her ignorance and her sister's sharp tongue Annis's wedding day had been the most miserable day of her life. She had gone through the ceremony in a state of dread, convinced that when he discovered what a nincompoop he had married Douglas would immediately change his mind and regret ever having proposed.

When at last they were alone in their bedchamber for the first time she burst into tears and sobbed out the whole shameful story of her complete ignorance into Douglas's comforting shoulder. And instead of being shocked he had been delighted, assuring her, as he dried her eyes with his own handkerchief, that it was a man's pleasure and his duty to instruct his wife, not hers to know everything beforehand.

After that he had gently and tenderly undressed her and tucked her into bed before going behind the screen and undressing himself. Then he had blown out the lamp and joined her between the sheets where, still gentle and tender, he had taught her the duties of a married woman.

It hadn't been so terrible after all. She was so grateful to him that she was eager to make him happy. Although when he had kissed her and assured her that she was the most willing and adorable wife a man could wish for, then fallen asleep, she lay awake, strangely restless and somehow dissatisfied with the wife's role in the intimacies of marriage.

But it wasn't seemly for a wife to have such thoughts. Since that night she had been a dutiful student, quick to learn and eager to please, for Douglas told her that it was imperative that a woman should satisfy her husband and make him happy, and that she intended to do, always.

Her thoughts drifted back to Olivia. There were few opportunities in Greenock for a penniless young woman to marry out of her class. Better by far to grasp the one hand that was being held out to her, as Annis had done. She herself, slipping at last into the deep soft blackness of sleep, would have been happy indeed to hear that a man such as Gideon Brenner had asked permission to court her.

If, of course, she had been unmarried. If she had been free. If, if, if . . .

If only, whispered a tiny voice deep in the core of her being; if only she had been Olivia.

The atmosphere in the Moncrieff house was quite unbearable for the next few days. Olivia spoke to nobody, and was scarcely to be seen.

In the mornings she waited upstairs until Douglas had breakfasted and left the house before she came down. Egged on by Tib, he had announced that anyone who didn't come to the table by the time the grandfather clock in the hall struck eight o'clock would go without breakfast. It made no difference to Olivia, who rustled downstairs as soon as she heard the front door closing behind him, seized the morning newspaper he had left by his plate, and retired to her room.

In the evenings she sat at the supper table like a spectre at a feast, refusing to be drawn even by Tib's malicious jibes. She wasn't eating enough to keep body and soul together. Annis, worried about her, took food to her room when Tib was out of the house, but Olivia merely looked up from the newspaper, stared coldly and refused whatever she was offered.

Every one of Annis's overtures was spurned. So, too, was Douglas's attempt to heal the breach on the second evening. Enraged as he had been with his wife's sister he couldn't keep his anger simmering indefinitely. But when he tried to speak normally to Olivia, as though there had been no quarrel between them, she answered briefly then retired to the privacy of her own thoughts.

'It's even worse than her carping or her bursts of temper,' he complained bitterly to his wife. 'Damn it, the woman makes me feel uncomfortable in my own house!'

Robert, who had been in bed when the quarrel first erupted, had heard the bare details of it the next day from Annis.

'I can't see what her objection is,' he said flatly. 'To my mind Captain Brenner and Jem are the two finest men in Greenock.' Then he reddened and blurted out hastily, 'Next to Uncle Douglas, of course.'

The maidservants crept about the house and were happy to obey Olivia's orders to keep out of her room. The only member of the household who revelled in the situation was Tib, still waiting for her apology. She carried an air of wounded self-righteousness about with her as flamboyantly as if she had been brandishing it on a long stick, and delighted in sweeping out of the parlour the moment Olivia entered it, or talking at the table as though Olivia's chair was empty. Even though Olivia didn't even seem to notice the snubs, Tib obviously enjoyed delivering them.

Annis began to feel as though she had aged three years in as many days. The house was claustrophobic whether or not Olivia and Douglas were in it. She often thought longingly of the *Grace and Charity*, racing over the sea with the fresh wind in her sails and the water breaking at her bows and her young shipmaster walking her decks, tall and straight — and no doubt thinking of Olivia and his return to Greenock. Poor Gideon Brenner!

On the morning of the fourth day Olivia left the house before anyone else was about, apart from the servants.

Annis, hearing the front door open then close, looked out of the bedroom window and saw her sister start down the steps to the pavement, dressed in a neat brown travelling mantle over a blue dress, with her favourite hat, a smart little beribboned straw bonnet, perched becomingly on the back of her head.

Her gasp of horror brought Douglas to her side. 'What's amiss?' He peered over her shoulder.

'It's Olivia . . . oh Douglas!' She caught at his arm, panic in her heart. 'She's left home!'

'Don't be ridiculous!' His voice was dismissive. 'Your sister is merely going out for some fresh air. Why should you think she's running away?'

'I — I don't know.' She felt very young and very stupid. Douglas was right, of course, but the ominous cloud that had been wrapped about Olivia since their quarrel had made Annis so uneasy that she was more than ready to jump to foolish conclusions.

Douglas peered out again to where Olivia, straight-backed and with never a turn of her head towards the house, had negotiated the flight of steps. She paused for a second on the pavement and the onlookers saw her shoulders twitch as though she was shrugging off the house's atmosphere and bracing herself for the day ahead. Then she walked briskly in the direction of the town.

'Olivia would never leave unless she had somewhere better to go.' Douglas said as he turned from the window. 'And if that had happened she'd be crowing about it from the very chimney pots. In any case, she's not taken as much as a change of clothing. She'll be back . . . more's the pity.'

Annis, hurriedly buttoning up her neat cream housework blouse and tucking it into the waistband of her plain green skirt, scarcely heard him. As soon as she was decent enough to be seen she ran downstairs to where Janet, dutiful to the orders of the grandfather clock, which had just chimed to mark half past seven, was carrying the teapot into the dining room.

'Janet, do you know where Miss Olivia's gone?'

'To the railway station, ma'am, and not a mouthful would she take before she left.' The little maid settled the teapot into its crocheted nest and turned it so that the handle would be close to Tib's hand once she had taken her usual place at the table. Then she carefully pulled the crocheted matching cover over it to keep its contents hot. 'She said that if anyone cared to ask I was to tell them that she's taking the train to Glasgow' — she paused to draw breath, then finished in a rush — 'and won't be back until tonight, ma'am.'

They were all at supper when Olivia arrived home. Annis, who had been on edge all day, half-rose from her chair when she heard the front door open, but Douglas stopped her with a quiet, 'Finish your soup, my dear. No doubt your sister will join us when she's a mind to.'

'She's too late for her broth,' Tib said swiftly. 'And if she doesn't watch herself she'll be too late for her meat too.'

To Tib's obvious disappointment, Olivia timed her entry perfectly, arriving just before Janet carried in the main course.

Then she waited until the little maid had scurried from the room before calmly announcing that she had obtained a position as a governess and would be leaving Greenock in four days' time.

Even Tib put down her fork and gaped. Olivia, well pleased with the reaction she had got, proceeded to cut her meat into very small precise squares.

'A governess!' Tib rallied almost at once, and managed to load the word with derision.

'Why not? Papa always insisted that we had the best governesses ourselves, so I'm well educated. I shall be earning my own money, and no longer a burden on poor Douglas,' Olivia added sweetly.

Douglas squirmed, then asked, with an attempt to regain his place as the head of the household, 'Who are your employers? Do I know them?'

'I doubt very much if they would know you, Douglas,' his sister-in-law said sweepingly, nose in the air. 'Mr Stobo is in the banking business. A well-respected man, with a charming wife.'

Robert, always hungry, picked up his fork and began to eat stolidly, uninterested in the details.

'How did you come to hear of the Stobos?' Douglas persisted.

'They advertised in the newspapers. I wrote to Mrs Stobo and today, at her invitation, I called on her at her Glasgow home. The matter was decided within an hour of our meeting.'

'So you'll be going to live in Glasgow, Olivia?' Annis fought hard to keep her disappointment from showing.

Difficult though Olivia was to live with, she would be sadly missed, by her sister, at least. 'I hope that your duties will allow you to come down to Greenock often.'

Olivia tossed a triumphant little smile across the table. 'I doubt that, Annis, since Mr Stobo is about to take up a position as bank manager in Australia.'

For a moment Annis felt as though the world had rocked on its axis. She clutched at the table's edge for support and heard Douglas say incredulously, 'Australia?'

This time even Robert put down his fork. Olivia helped herself to salt, delighted with the effect her news had had on them.

'We sail for Melbourne in ten days' time. I do declare, Annis, that this is the most savoury piece of meat Mr McMillan has ever sold across his counter. How clever of you to choose it.'

'Australia! Olivia, it's so far away!'

'On the other side of the world, I believe. As far away from that dreadful sister-in-law of yours as anyone can get.'

A large sea-trunk, specially bought for the trip, stood in the middle of the room. Olivia, sorting and folding clothes in readiness for her departure, still radiated the calm pleasure she had shown the night before when she announced her imminent departure.

Sitting on the bed, helplessly watching the relentless preparations, Annis found herself remembering the pretty little ormulu clock her father had kept on his parlour mantelpiece. Annis had loved it, but it had been sold when the house was disposed of. There was no place for it in the Moncrieff house.

She wondered, confusedly, why she should think of the

clock at that moment, then realized that it was because her sister, like the clock, seemed to be encased in glass, untouchable and unreachable.

'But . . . Australia! Why should you want to go there? Why not Glasgow or Edinburgh?' Somewhere, she wanted to say, close enough for me to see you now and again. But such pleas would only bounce off the hard transparent shell encasing Olivia.

'I'm going to Australia because that is where Mr Stobo's new business is.'

'But you say that you despise colonials: why go and live among them?'

Olivia threw a frosty glance at her sister. 'Living among them doesn't make me one of them,' she pointed out pityingly. 'I'm British — and I understand that the continent's filling with professional and business people from this country. It's no longer a land for convicts and cannibals, you know. There are cities and universities and great businesses there. And Mrs Stobo tells me there's a fine social life.'

Olivia's hands stilled for a moment; her eyes looked beyond Annis, beyond the bedroom wall, to the other side of the world. 'Opportunities to meet people I could never meet here,' she finished scornfully, carefully settling the skirt she had folded into the trunk and reaching for a petticoat.

She held it up, studied it with her head on one side, then tossed it aside and picked up another garment.

'That petticoat's not good enough . . . you can have it if you want it. Or you can give it to one of the maids.'

'Won't you be lonely, going so far on your own?'

'Lonely? I shall have the Stobos for company, and their two little girls. And I intend to make a great many new friends. I believe,' said Olivia crushingly, 'that the Australians care little for the silly conventions and stuffiness that hamper the folk in Scotland.'

It had to be said. Annis couldn't leave it unsaid. 'I shall miss you.'

'I doubt that. After all, you've got Douglas. You've got everything you want,' her sister replied with carefully honed cruelty. 'And soon I shall have everything I want too.'

Olivia left Greenock on a damp, drizzling day at the end of May. Annis and Douglas accompanied her to the station in Cathcart Street, where the three of them loitered awkwardly on the platform for a long five minutes before it was time for Olivia to board the train.

Olivia had added a touch of sophistication to her brown travelling mantle and bought a new bonnet. It was a smart little blue frilled hat that perched over her forehead, with a froth of deeper blue lace running down the back of her head to culminate in a velvet bow tied beneath a severe chignon that added to her remote beauty.

Now that she had finally taken her own future into her hands, Olivia's normal air of poised confidence had increased even more; it seemed to Annis that her sister, never as close to her as she would have liked, had already become a stranger.

Douglas had done his duty with his usual thoroughness, taking a day from his own work to travel to Glasgow to make certain Olivia's new employer was all that she had claimed, a respectable banker taking over his new duties as manager of his company's Melbourne branch. Now he and his sister-in-law could find nothing else to say to one another. Annis, who had so much to say, was struck dumb by Olivia's cool, remote gaze.

When the time came for her departure Olivia offered an elegantly gloved hand to Douglas, dropped a light kiss on Annis's cheek, then stepped into the carriage. The guard blew his whistle, Olivia gave one last wave, then withdrew her head into the carriage, and was gone.

For a few moments the Moncreiffs stood watching the train puff its way out of the station before Douglas said with obvious relief, 'Well, that's that,' and took his wife's arm.

'Perhaps now,' he added as they walked out of the handsome station which looked, from the street, more like a mansion than a railway depot, 'the house will get back to normal. I can't say I'm sorry to say goodbye to Olivia. I cannot understand how two sisters raised in the same household could be so unlike each other. I'll find a cab for you.'

'I'll walk home.'

'You'll get wet and catch a chill.'

'No, I shall be quite all right.' Annis opened her umbrella as they stepped into the street. 'I have some shopping to do on the way.'

It was a relief when they reached the building where his offices were situated and he left her to walk on alone. Despite her claim to have shopping to do she passed all the shops without so much as a glance in their windows.

As she walked, matching her step to the persistent despondent tapping of raindrops on the umbrella, she thought only of Olivia, now travelling farther from her with every minute. At the realization that they might never see each other again, tears stung her eyes. The sisters had never, to Annis's great sorrow, been close, but

Olivia had always been there. Now that she had gone Annis felt as though she stood alone.

She sniffed back the tears and tried to count her blessings. Tib was swiftly dismissed, for not even the wildest imagination could picture her as a friend and confidante. Robert was very dear to her, but she couldn't over-burden him with her need for companionship. He must be allowed to develop and strengthen his own character in preparation for the difficult road he must walk in his struggle to live his own life in his own way.

There was Jem — at the thought of him Annis smiled without realizing it. Dear, gentle Jem, who never complained when she and Robert stole into his boatyard for secret visits, but made them both very welcome. Next to Robert, Jem was her closest friend, always willing to listen to what she had to say. And there was Douglas. Surely, Annis fretted, walking faster, her husband should be the only company a woman needed or wanted? Was it right for a wife to feel so lonely? Was their relationship as perfect as it should be, and if not, was the fault hers? With no woman friends of her own, either married or single, it was hard to know what marriage should be like. The few romantic novels she had read as a girl gave the picture of marriage as a wonderful, exhilarating state, but then, romantic novels were a little like fairy-tales and couldn't be used as a yardstick.

In any case, there was no true substitute for a sister. Recalling Gideon Brenner's story of how the clipper ship came to be named the *Grace and Charity*, Annis thought how terrible it was that two sisters should live apart and die apart because of pride. And yet she was beginning to understand how it could happen.

Lost in her thoughts, she had almost passed her own

front gate before she realized she was home. She shook her umbrella vigorously and left it in the stone porch to dry, letting herself in at the front door. The oppressive gloom of the house enfolded her in its embrace as soon as she closed the stained-glass door behind her. She shivered, realizing that for the first time in her life she was without Olivia. Panic welled up in her, and she had to use all her strength to force it down.

Upstairs, she found Janet at work in the room that had been Olivia's. The bed had been stripped and the little maid was down on her hands and knees, vigorously polishing the linoleum. Her face, already pink with exertion, took on added colour when she saw Annis standing in the doorway.

'Miss Tib told me to get this room cleared before I did anything else, ma'am.' Her voice was apologetic. Annis understood why; Tib was ostentatiously clearing the house of Olivia's presence as quickly as she could. But there was nothing Annis or Janet could do about that, and the room would have had to be put to rights sooner or later.

'That's all right, Janet.'

'And she says there are clothes to be sorted and put out as soon as possible.'

The wardrobe and the large drawer beneath it were filled with garments that Olivia hadn't considered good enough for her new life. Annis began to take gowns and skirts and blouses and jackets from their hangers, laying them on the bed. From the big drawer came corsets and drawers, stockings and petticoats and ribbons.

'Take what you want,' Olivia had said carelessly, 'and send the rest to the old clothes shops. There are plenty folk in Greenock who'll be glad of them. For myself, I've done with them for ever.'

Annis began to fold each item, laying them in neat piles. She would take nothing for herself; the hurt of losing her sister was so great in her that she couldn't bear the thought of seeing any of those clothes, so distinctively Olivia's, hanging in her own wardrobe.

'Janet, when you've finished your work you can parcel these things and take them to one of the clothing shops.'

'Yes ma'am.' The little maid sat back on her heels, wiping the back of one wrist over her forehead. 'She had some lovely things, Miss Olivia.'

'Would you like to choose something for yourself before you make up the parcels?'

Astonishment leapt into the girl's brown eyes, followed by hope, then delight. 'Oh ma'am! I couldn't!'

'Why not? I'm sure Miss Olivia would be very pleased if you did,' Annis lied.

Janet scrambled to her feet and came to the bed, reaching out a small rough hand to touch the flounced yellow skirt of one of Olivia's plainest gowns. 'I always liked that one. Do you think . . .?'

The yellow dress had looked superb against Olivia's rich dark beauty. Looking from it to the maidservant, Annis saw that the bright gown would leach what little colour there was in Janet's face and do nothing for her lank pale brown hair. She almost suggested the blue gown instead, then looked again at the girl's eyes, suddenly vivid with excitement and hope, and said, 'Take it, by all means. And some underclothes and stockings to go with it.'

'Oh, ma'am! It's more beautiful than anything I've ever owned!' Janet breathed the words in a stunned whisper. 'Wait till I walk out in that dress! Wait till . . .'

She stopped suddenly, colouring, and Annis asked, 'D'you have a young man, Janet?'

Pride and happiness lit up the plain little face, bringing to it a beauty that had never touched Janet before. 'Yes ma'am . . . a carter, he is. I only just started walking out with him. I've never had a sweetheart before and it's . . . oh, it's lovely to have someone of my own at last!'

When she had dealt with all the clothes and put mothballs into the wardrobe and drawers Annis left the girl busily polishing the bedstead, now and again running a proudly possessive eye over the yellow gown. She knew that the little maidservant, who came from a squalid one-roomed house in East Quay Lane where any money that came in was as often as not drunk away by her parents, could be trusted to take only what she had been invited to take before parcelling everything else up.

In the downstairs hall she paused before the mirror to tidy her hair and to stare hard at her neat, calm face for a moment. Her grey eyes stared back at her from beneath softly arched brows, mute and unquestioning. To please her father and, later, to please Douglas, Annis had worked hard at cultivating a look of calm, expressionless repose; it never did for a woman to look sulky or lively or, heaven forbid, clever or secretly amused.

She wondered briefly if, in those early days of loving Douglas, she had looked as radiant as Janet had when she spoke of her carter. She couldn't remember.

6

The *Grace and Charity* came up river under tow early on a cold November afternoon, her mainsail and foresail up to keep her under easy command in the crowded waters, her upper royals and topsails furled, men strung along her yards in readiness for docking orders.

As the long slender bowsprit, then the sleek hull, emerged from the winter fog that had held her in a clammy grip during the passage up river from the mouth of the Clyde, Gideon Brenner, in his usual place on the poop deck, cast a satisfied glance at the busy scene before him at Custom House Quay. The last time the clipper had docked here he had been a stranger, eyeing Greenock with a certain amount of apprehension. This time he was returning to the place where he now lived, bringing back a shipload of goods for his employer.

And tonight, he hoped, he'd have his feet under Douglas Moncrieff's table with perhaps the chance to talk privately with Olivia afterwards. He had no way of knowing when his next trip was to be, but he expected it to be soon. There was little sense in letting a fine vessel like the *Grace and Charity* lie idle in port for long, and he anticipated having only a short while in which to start courting Moncrieff's beautiful sister-in-law.

Another two voyages and he would be in a position

to rent a small house and ask formally for Olivia's hand in marriage. He was sure that he had done the right thing in approaching Moncrieff and letting him know of his interest in the man's sister-in-law. He had realized quickly that his employer found Olivia's presence in his own household onerous, and as he had expected, his voiced hope of marriage with her had been well received.

Moncrieff was a useful ally — and no doubt he would be grateful to the man who whisked Olivia off to a home of her own. Grateful enough, Gideon mused, to offer a partnership. And by this time Olivia herself would possibly be beginning to mellow towards him. Yes, in another two voyages, or three at the most, he could well be sailing back to his own home and his own wife.

The thought brought a smile to his lips as the tug drew its towering charge into position slowly and with practised ease. Lines were thrown ashore, the tug cast off and withdrew, and the men aloft on the yards drew the stiff canvas sails up, hand over hand, and secured them with gaskets as the clipper slid into her berth with scarcely a ripple of disturbed water.

When Gideon had satisfied himself that all was in order he went ashore, leaving the ship in the capable hands of his mate, and made his way to his employer's offices in Cathcart Square.

The fog, clustered in the narrow space between high wet stone walls, tried to wrap itself about him. He strode on, breaking clear again and again of its clutching white fingers, glad of his warm broadcloth coat.

The door to the inner office was fast closed and the hum of voices could be heard from behind it.

'Mr Moncrieff's talking with Captain Barclay,' Beaton,

the senior of the two clerks told him. 'Take a seat, Captain.'

Gideon ignored the upright chair set against one wall for visitors and strolled to the small window overlooking the square. The fog seemed happiest in the narrow side lanes — in the broad square it contented itself with tossing floating chiffon scarves about the pedestrians.

Although it was a chilly day the usual beggar, dressed in little more than rags, was sitting against the wall of the White Hart Inn playing his penny whistle. The square was busy, and those who could afford warm clothes were well wrapped up. There were plenty, though, wearing thin clothing, their hands and legs and faces mottled with cold.

The murmur of voices droned to a standstill. The inner door opened and Thomas Barclay, captain of the Moncrieff coastal schooner, came out and nodded recognition at Gideon.

'Good passage, Brenner?'

'Fair enough. Yourself?'

'Could have been worse . . . but *he* doesnae think so,' the Scotsman whispered, jerking his head towards the office. 'Ye'll tak' a drink wi' me the night? God knows I need yin!'

Gideon hesitated, thinking of his plans for that evening, picturing himself seated opposite Olivia in the Moncrieff dining room.

'If ye're free, ye ken whaur tae find me,' the other shipmaster said, and went on his way as the senior clerk put his head round Douglas Moncrieff's door to announce Gideon's arrival.

'Mr Moncrieff says will you go in, Captain,' the man said, and Gideon stepped past him.

He could see at first glance that Douglas Moncrieff was in an ill humour. He was riffling through a snowstorm of papers that covered his desk.

'Confounded schooner!' he said as Gideon walked in. 'The fool of a captain let almost every sail blow out in a sudden squall. She came back into harbour flaunting the spare set, and now there's new sails to be bought before she can go out again. The fool must think I'm made of money. Well?'

Gideon laid down the *Grace and Charity*'s papers, adding to the pile before Moncrieff, and thanked his good fortune that he was a seaman and not a landlubber to be drowned in paperwork.

'A good voyage, sir, with nothing unforeseen to report.'

'Hm.' Moncrieff scanned the lists. 'Nitrates, copper ore, and beans. They're unloading into the warehouses now?'

'Aye, sir. I had to take on extra ballast, for the clipper's holds could have carried more. If the decision had been mine,' he added carefully, 'I'd have taken her up the coast to Portland and bought timber.'

'You would, would you? Still out to line your own pockets at my expense, Brenner?'

Gideon swallowed down his anger and met the other man's eyes with a straight look. 'No, sir, I'd have bought in your name. We could have filled the holds and lashed a good amount of it on the deck as well. It wouldn't have added many more days on to our voyage, and as it was we made good time there and back.'

'Then why in damnation didn't you go for the timber, man?'

Gideon began to see his hopes of a supper invitation

slipping away. He had been rash to even broach the subject. 'Because you gave me to understand that I was only the shipmaster, sir, to do as I was told and no more.'

Douglas Moncrieff pondered for a moment, running a hand through his beard. Then he said, 'There's always a margin for some clear thinking, young man. You should have gone for the timber.'

'I'll remember that in future, Mr Moncrieff.'

'Aye, you do that. Tell Beaton on the way out to get the crew's money ready. You can collect your own payment from him now. And your bonus for making good time,' Moncrieff added a trifle grudgingly. 'It would have been a better bonus if you'd brought the timber as well. Think on, Mr Brenner.'

'Sir . . .' Gideon persisted as his employer bent over his work, signalling that the meeting was at end.

The fair head was lifted sharply. 'Well? What is it now?'

'Miss Olivia, sir. If you recall, before I sailed you were good enough to give me permission to . . .'

'Olivia? Man, she's long gone.'

Gideon's mouth, open to shape the next word, gaped foolishly for a moment. Then he said, 'She's . . . gone?'

'Flew up in a rage when I mentioned your intentions,' Douglas Moncrieff said flatly. He had had a bad day. Tib had been particularly tiresome that morning and a contract he had been counting on had been snatched from beneath his very nose by a competitor.

The loss of the schooner's sails had been the last straw, and he was in no mood to break the news of Olivia's departure gently to the man on the other side of the desk.

'It seems that my wife's sister expects life to present

103

her with something better than a shipmaster, Captain Brenner. And when I told her she should be grateful for your interest she upped and found herself a position with a family on their way to a new life in Australia. Good fortune to the poor souls who've taken her on. That'll be all, Mr Brenner. Your work may be finished for the moment, but mine's still to do.'

Gideon collected his money and left the office in a daze. The decision to visit Low Gourock Road and seek confirmation from Olivia's sister came to his mind without conscious thought and it wasn't until he found himself opening the gate and going up the steps to the path that he even knew he had made such a decision.

Impatiently, he rattled the door-knocker and when the little maid came to the door he demanded to see Mrs Moncrieff so curtly that the girl's eyes opened wide and she went scurrying off in a panic, leaving him to pace the hall, oblivious in his anger and despair to the sweet summery scent that filled the air about him that November day.

Tib, having turned the entire house upside down that morning with a bout of waspish temper, had developed a headache and retired to her room. Annis had taken advantage of the sudden peace to go out to the back garden to rake up the wet leaves that covered the paths and the tiny lawn.

The gloomy wintry weather made the garden a sad place. Only the roses survived, mainly the hardier yellow bushes, obstinately budding and blooming, tiny coloured lanterns doing their best to light up the short grey days. The elderly man who tended the Moncrieff garden on three days of each week usually pruned the roses early in November, ruthlessly chopping down the late blooms and buds. This year rheumatism had chopped him down, and Douglas hadn't yet had time to find a replacement. On an impulse Annis had armed herself with a pair of secateurs and thick gloves and begun pruning the bushes herself, carefully putting every bud and every opened flower worth keeping into a basket and mourning over the blossoms that were too old and weather-bitten to be saved.

Thorns caught at her gloved hands, her jacket, her skirt, but she patiently untangled herself each time and worked on, oblivious to the cold, enjoying her task. When she had finished she gathered up the unwanted stems and put them in a pile at the far end of the garden, then took her basket indoors and started working on the flowers. There were far too many of them for even the largest vase in the house, so she burrowed in the cupboard beneath the stairs and brought out a brightly patterned china container originally intended to hold a large plant pot. She set it on a table in the front hall, then filled it with tepid water.

When the roses were arranged to her satisfaction she stepped back to study them, and knew that her work had been worth the effort. Nestling among glossy rich leaves, the sun-bright yellows, with here and there a crimson or palest pink head, gave a glow to the hall, echoing and emphasizing the muted colours in the stained glass of the front door.

The soft chiming of the grandfather clock reminded her of the time. It was unlikely that anyone would make an afternoon call, but Tib, following on her own mother's customs, always insisted that someone should be ready to receive visitors, just in case. Dutifully obedient to the rules that had been imposed on the household before her own birth, Annis went up to her room where she washed, changed into a pale fawn afternoon gown sprigged with bunches of tiny gold and pink flowers, and brushed her hair until the tips of each curl shone, pleased with the colour her work in the garden had brought to her face.

Since Olivia had left Douglas had remarked more than once on his wife's pallor. Annis suspected that the only ailment she suffered from was boredom, lack of fresh air, and premature ageing. If it hadn't been for Robert's welcome presence in the house she was sure she would have settled by now into middle age along with Douglas and his sister. The difference in her appearance after only a short while working outside in the cold bracing air proved her point. It was a pity, she thought, allowing herself some vanity for once, that there would be no callers to see how well some colour in her cheeks became her.

She was pinning her hair back when the door-knocker rattled. Within a few moments Janet appeared at the bedroom door, her eyes large with apprehension.

'If you please, ma'am, it's that Captain Brenner and I don't think he'd like it if I tried to send him away.'

A throb of excitement pulsed through Annis. She hadn't realized that the *Grace and Charity* was due to return quite so soon from South America. Then the excitement was obliterated by a sensation in her stomach, as though she had just swallowed a stone. She would have to tell him about Olivia.

'Why should you send him away, Janet? Show him into the parlour.'

She smoothed her hand over her dress, gave a final pat to the lacy frill at her throat, and ran downstairs, stopping at the parlour door to take a deep breath and smooth her dress again.

'Captain Brenner, this is a pleasant surprise,' she began as she entered. 'My husband didn't tell me that the *Grace and*—'

'Is it true?'

He had been pacing the room, his back to her as she entered. As soon as he swung round she saw that his eyes were blazing, his anger seemed to fill the room. His dark hair was ruffled, as though his fingers had been raked through it again and again. Annis's own fingers lost their strength and fell from the door-handle. There was no need to ask what he was talking about.

'Yes, it's true.'

'Australia!' The word was forced out from between set teeth. 'Why in God's name did she have to go there?'

She moved to a chair and sat down, folding her hands in her lap. 'Because the family who have employed her are going there.'

'But why did she have to seek employment at all, when—' He broke off and continued his pacing. 'No need to ask the question. From what your husband tells me, Mrs Moncrieff, Olivia chose to go to the other end of the world rather than submit to my attentions.'

Annis, appalled at the open misery on the young American's face, began to rise, then sank back into her chair, snapping an angry little thought in Douglas's direction. Why couldn't the man have shown some compassion?

'I – I'm sure that . . .'

'I beg of you, ma'am, don't be kind to me! I would find that even less bearable than your sister's actions!'

For a moment she was baffled, then swift anger took

hold of her. 'Allow me to speak in my own parlour, Captain Brenner.'

He stopped in his pacing and looked fully at her, seeing her properly for the first time since her entrance. Then he said, 'My apologies, ma'am. I've behaved badly. I'll go at once.'

'Captain . . .' she stopped him as he was about to leave the room. 'In my opinion my sister doesn't yet know what she wants out of life.'

His face tightened and his eyes blazed emerald fire at her. 'Obviously, ma'am, she doesn't want me,' he said curtly, and was gone, almost knocking Janet down in the hallway. He pushed past the little maid and stormed out of the house before Janet, in a flurry of confusion, could open the front door for him.

'Oh, ma'am . . .' she squawked faintly, helplessly.

'It's all right, Janet,' Annis soothed. 'Get back to your work now.'

When the maid had returned to the kitchen Annis found herself pacing the carpet just as Brenner had done earlier. Now that she was alone she was free to recall that moment when the compulsion to rise from her chair and go to him, to touch him, smooth the misery from his face — to hold him — had been so strong that she had to force herself to ignore it. She stopped before the oval mirror and stared at her reflection, then turned away swiftly, reluctant to meet her own eyes. In that moment she had known a strength of feeling that no married woman should feel for any man other than her husband. The feeling was still with her. She put a hand to her mouth to stop its quivering, then forced herself to sit down again, pick up her sewing, concentrate her mind on polishing the silver, on the joint she planned to buy for tomorrow night's meal. Anything, rather than Gideon Brenner and the storm that was raging within her.

Tib arrived downstairs a few moments later, announcing as she walked into the parlour that she for one would not strain her back picking up fallen petals when the roses in the hallway began to cast.

'And the Lord only knows what beasties you've carried into the house in these flowers,' she added. 'Did I hear someone at the door earlier? Did we have a visitor?'

'No,' said Annis, staring wearily down at her embroidery. 'Nobody at all.'

Gideon's anger at the blow Fate had dealt him was still smouldering when the day drew to a close.

The *Grace and Charity*'s unloading had begun, and would continue on the morrow. Only after it was completed could the decks be scrubbed and the tackle all stowed away. There was nothing for her master to do for the moment.

He left the harbour and made his way to Rue-end Street, to one of the public houses frequented by the seafaring men who lived in Greenock as well as those calling in temporarily.

It was early and the low-roofed place was fairly quiet. Some of his own crew members were already in, but after one look at his black expression they contented themselves with brief nods of recognition and left him to find a table in a dark corner.

He ordered food and beer, then changed his mind and bawled at the retreating servant to bring a bottle of whisky instead of the beer. When it arrived he poured himself a glassful, downed it, refilled the glass. He was quite unaware of the people around him. His thoughts were filled with Olivia: no woman had ever treated Gideon Brenner so harshly before and he found it hard to accept that she had really gone beyond his reach. Not, he corrected himself, beyond his reach. He was a seaman – he could, and would, take the *Grace and Charity* to Australia, seek Olivia out, bring her back. He would make Douglas Moncrieff see that it was only sensible to make full use of a good ship like the *Grace and Charity*. He would persuade the man to start trading with Australia. Others had made their fortunes in that way, why not Moncrieff?

The one thing he would not do, Gideon swore to himself, filling his glass again, was to turn tail and run for home. No doubt the Boston heiress was still there – or another like her. No, he would stay in Scotland, make his fortune, seek out Olivia and win her. He would show them all that Gideon Brenner was not to be spurned!

When Captain Barclay arrived an hour later the plate of food, scarcely tasted and now cold and congealed, had been pushed to one side and the whisky bottle was half empty. The schooner master, clutching his own bottle and a glass, pulled out a stool and dropped on to it beside Brenner.

'The devil take this toothache,' he grunted, pounding at one side of his jaw with a huge fist. 'It only ever troubles me ashore. Never a twinge o' it when we're afloat, but on land there's naethin' can shift it but strong drink.'

Gideon found it hard to focus on the man's face. It swam before him, then divided into two. He wasn't certain which face was real. 'Get it pulled,' he said indistinctly, and the man grinned, showing a ragged selection of rotten teeth and gaps.

'I'd as soon tend tae it in my own way. Wi' your permission, Brenner, we'll feenish your bottle then start on mine.' He sloshed whisky into his glass and swilled it noisily round the aggravating tooth before swallowing. With a gusty sigh of pleasure and relief he refilled the glass.

'Here's tae Moncrieff an' his mean soul. His father was a fine businessman, an' his brother an' a'. It's a peety they're baith gone, for this yin . . . this Douglas Moncrieff I'm talking' aboot . . . he's no' the match o' either o' them. Damnation tae his black heart!'

Gideon had settled into a misty stupor, but the mention of the Moncrieff name re-awakened his misery with a twinge as near to toothache as anything else. He refilled his own glass and raised it.

'Here's damnation to women,' he mumbled, and drank deeply.

Brenner stayed in the public house, matching drink for drink with Barclay, until the place closed and they were ousted by the landlord.

Outside, Barclay turned his coat collar up, swore at the bitter wind knifing along the street, then lurched off. Although his lodgings were near Barclay's, Gideon turned in the opposite direction with some thought of taking a look at the *Grace and Charity* before going back to his cheerless room. He had intended, during this stay on land, to find somewhere else to live, a place that would be fit for Olivia.

The thought brought a sour taste to his mouth, and he spat into the gutter then suddenly, unexpectedly, found himself bumping into a house wall. His legs seemed to have been loaned out to someone else; they refused to do his bidding and carry him in a straight line, choosing

111

instead to straggle all over the footpath and even into the gutter.

He came up against a lamp-post and wrapped one long arm about it for support while he tried to get his legs and body used to the idea of being together again.

'Good evening, Captain Brenner.' The voice was soft and clear, pleasant to the ear.

Gideon squinted into the shadows beyond the small circle of gaslight. 'Who'sat?'

'Only me.' A woman joined him in the pool of light. 'D'ye not remember me, sir?'

A shawl was wound tightly about her head and the upper part of her body to protect her from the wind that blew her skirts against her legs, but even in his fuddled state he recognized the pale, sharp-featured face.

'Mrs Fraser,' he said, letting go the lamp-post so that he could sketch a bow.

'Just so, Captain.' She caught his arm deftly as the wall threatened to take another run at him, and looped him around the lamp-post again.

'I heard that the *Grace and Charity* was back. It must have been a good voyage . . . I see you've been celebrating.'

He started to say 'Celebrating!', but the word got tangled in his lips and tongue and refused to come out properly. So he gave up and said instead, 'You're out late tonight.'

'Visiting a friend. I'm on my way back to my sister's house . . . she lives not far from here. Would you care to come in for some supper, Captain Brenner?'

So there was someone in this godforsaken town willing to offer hospitality to a homecoming seafarer after all. 'I would, ma'am. Thankee.'

'It's this way. Your arm, if you please, Captain,' said Adeline Fraser demurely, taking his free arm and draping it about her shoulders so that she could support him.

Linked closely together, weaving from one side of the footpath to the other, they walked out of the lamplight and into the darkness.

Gideon Brenner woke to a grey dawn and a thumping headache. When he tried to move he found that he was pinned to the mattress beneath him and his left arm seemed to have disappeared.

He prised his eyes open and realized that he wasn't in the master's cabin aboard the *Grace and Charity*, or in the small room he had rented in Greenock. He was in a shabby little apartment he had never seen before. Wallpaper peeled off the wall by the bed, and what was still in place was black with dampness and spotted with mould.

Slowly, fighting the pain that stretched from above his eyebrows to the back of his neck, he turned his head to the left to find out what had happened to his arm, and looked into Adeline Fraser's face, on the pillow next to his.

'What . . .?'

She opened her eyes at once, moving from sleep to waking with ease, smiling at him. 'Good morning, Captain. Did you sleep well?'

'I've no knowledge of that. Where is this place?'

She shifted in the bed and he realized that she had been lying on his arm. 'My sister's house. D'you not remember meeting me last night and coming back here for supper?'

He did, but only vaguely. He tried to moisten his lips

with his tongue, then said thickly, 'I'm as dry as a piece of salt beef.'

'I'll fetch you some water.' She pushed back the blanket that covered them and got up from the bed. Once her warm body was removed the chill morning air stung Gideon's skin, helping to clear his head.

A table in one corner of the shabby room held a cracked china jug and some cups. Rubbing life back into his numbed left arm, Gideon watched as Adeline Fraser poured water from the jug, moving with unself-conscious grace.

She was naked, and her dark tangled hair hung down her back. Dressed, she had given the impression of being thin and angular, but in fact her body was womanly, with firm, pear-shaped buttocks and a neat waist.

When she brought the cup of water to him and bent over the bed, he saw that her breasts were full, firm and dusky-nippled. Her skin smelled of sweat and musky warmth.

'Here.' Apparently oblivious to the cold that goose-pimpled her body, she sat on the edge of the bed to watch as he pulled himself up then drank thirstily. Then she took the empty cup back and put it on the floor. She stretched, and Gideon's eyes followed the smooth movement of muscles beneath her skin, the lifting and tautening of her breasts and buttocks. 'I'd best get dressed. You'll want to be on your way, I suppose.'

He was naked too. He felt a stirring beneath the bedclothes as he watched her. 'What time is it?'

She listened, head cocked to one side, then said, 'Early. My sister's bairns aren't up and about yet.'

'Come back to bed, then.'

She smiled, a long, slow smile, keeping her mouth

closed over her bad teeth. 'You want me to, Captain?'

'Why not? I don't remember what happened last night. Remind me.'

He reached up to take her hands and draw her down towards him. She laughed as she turned the blanket back and climbed in beside him. Her breasts were cool and soft against his chest; her body moulded itself willingly to his.

Gideon thought of Olivia. Others would know what she had missed through her pig-headedness, he thought, as he took Adeline Fraser's mouth in a kiss. Damn Olivia Kerr and all her cold-hearted, selfish breed to eternity. Give him a warm, willing woman any day.

7

Mrs Stobo's character seemed to change with every mile she travelled from Scotland. And it wasn't a change for the better, as far as Olivia was concerned.

Her employer's wife took to her cabin with the first fair-sized wave, and stayed there during most of the journey. This meant that Olivia, not in the least bit affected by the motion of the vessel beneath her feet, was in sole charge of the two Stobo children, with scarcely any time to herself. What little time there was, was spent caring for Mrs Stobo.

Even the still, balmy days in the Doldrums did nothing for the banker's wife. She ignored Olivia's suggestions that some fresh air would do her good and shut her ears to her children's pleas to come and see the flying fish and the porpoises gambolling around the ship. And she utterly refused to become involved in the ceremony to mark the crossing of the Equator.

Much to her own surprise Olivia enjoyed the voyage — apart from the need to be with the children all the time. She liked the sensation of freedom that filled her now that she had left Greenock and Douglas Moncrieff's house behind once and for all. She looked forward to her new life in a new country, and she even joined in the fun of the Equator crossing, laughing and applauding as

Neptune and his assistants shaved then ducked the male passengers. Among them was Mr Stobo, who turned out to be more outgoing than his wife.

It was Melbourne that put the finishing touches to the change in Mrs Stobo. In Glasgow she had intimated to her well-educated, ladylike governess that she would be looked on as a member of the family, but once they had put the sea voyage behind them and arrived in the smart verandahed villa in South Yarra, a suitable suburb for a bank manager, Olivia found herself abruptly relegated to the position of one of the servants.

Furious though she was, she could do nothing about it. Mrs Stobo had swiftly discovered that Melbourne was the largest and most sophisticated of Australia's cities, a place where she could establish herself on a higher social scale than she had enjoyed at home. And on that scale, governesses were not companions, let alone friends.

While Mr Stobo worked at the bank and his wife entertained new acquaintances and made social calls, Olivia escorted Martha and Ruth Stobo to the outdoor swimming baths at Saint Kilda, where they splashily learned to swim while she sat watching, bored and yearning for some interesting company. After the swimming lessons the three of them strolled down the fine esplanade overlooking the vast land-encircled sea that was Port Philip Bay, or took the omnibus to one of the beautiful parks or to the museum.

At night the Stobos attended the opera or the theatre or a concert in Melbourne's Town Hall, leaving Olivia behind to put the children to bed, then amuse herself as best she may.

There were other governesses and nursery-maids in the area; within a few weeks Olivia had met them all, for the bank manager's offspring were soon invited to all the children's parties in the district. But they were lumpish, dull young women, unambitious and content with their lot, and Olivia immediately decided that she would rather be lonely than join them on their off-duty ploys.

Instead she whiled away the warm, flower-scented evenings reading in her room, walking round the lovely garden that surrounded the villa, or lying on her bed beneath the mosquito net, cursing the impetuous decision that had led her to the Stobos' door.

She also wrote long letters to Annis, letters filled with details of concerts and dances that she had supposedly attended, of a social life far beyond anything that Greenock had had to offer. No matter how bored or unhappy she might be, Olivia had no intention of letting her young sister suspect for one instant that in coming to Australia she had only exchanged one prison for another.

She had been in Melbourne for a month when Mr Stobo decided to hold a dinner party. His wife flew into a panic and, for want of a close friend and confidante, summoned the governess to listen to her worries.

'Twenty people! I've never had so many folk in my house in my life. We didn't entertain on a grand scale in Glasgow,' she confessed, too worried to care about what she said. In Glasgow her husband had only been an assistant manager; he wasn't expected to entertain clients.

'I could advise you.'

Jean Stobo started at the governess. 'You?'

'My father held dinner parties for his business colleagues on several occasions,' Olivia lied coolly. 'Naturally, I acted as his hostess.' George Kerr had never once invited anyone into his home. If he had, Annis would have been expected to provide the meal. But the last governess employed to teach the Kerr girls had once worked for a minor title and Olivia, anxious to develop her social knowledge, had listened for hours to the woman's reminiscences, coaxing her to go over each detail again and again. She hadn't forgotten a single word.

Mrs Stobo's pale blue eyes had taken on a hopeful gleam, 'Then perhaps you could . . .'

Olivia smiled sweetly on her. 'Of course I will,' she said.

As the dinner party date approached there was a battle of wills between employer and governess. Olivia had every intention of being present at the dinner she had so carefully planned and supervised, but Mrs Stobo disagreed.

On the day itself, however, word came that the daughter of one of Mr Stobo's most important clients had succumbed to a migraine, and Olivia had to be brought in to make up the numbers. Triumph flowered in her heart as she placed a card bearing her own name on the immaculate table.

Mrs Stobo, fighting a rearguard action, insisted on inspecting the gown that Olivia planned to wear.

'Just to make sure that it's suitable for the occasion, my dear,' she said, marching into her governess's room without bothering to knock on the door.

For this occasion, which she looked upon as her long-awaited entry into Melbourne society, Olivia had selected the pale gold silken gown trimmed with scarlet rosettes that she had bought for the ball in the White Hart Inn in Greenock.

Jean Stobo took one look at it, carefully spread out on the bed, and shook her head so violently that her soft pouchy cheeks quivered. 'Oh my dear girl, that's quite unsuitable! Much too elaborate for a governess. You must have something more suitable, surely . . .'

To Olivia's fury the woman swept open the door of her narrow little wardrobe and pawed her way through the few gowns hanging inside. She selected one, a demure dark green dress, and tossed it on to the bed beside the rejected gown.

'That's much better. More suited to your station, don't you think?'

'That,' Olivia pointed out with the faintest curl of a lip, 'is a day dress.'

Jean Stobo flushed, then rallied. 'But very pretty, and quite suitable for someone in your . . . position, my dear. I'll expect to see you wearing this one at my dinner party.'

When she was alone again Olivia glared at the closed door, then picked up the green gown and eyed it thoughtfully. She had no choice but to wear it, but there were ways of improving a plain gown, and Olivia had learned them all, particularly in the dark days after her father's death when she had had to live on Douglas Moncrieff's charity.

She riffled her way through a drawer she'd filled with ribbons and pieces of lace, and soon found what she wanted.

Because she had to put the children to bed before she could begin to dress for the evening, she was late in presenting herself to the assembled company, which suited her plans admirably. As the carriage carrying the final guests drew up, she studied herself in the dressing-table mirror, and was pleased with the result.

The lace inset at the neck of the gown had been removed to reveal her smooth creamy throat and the tops of her full breasts. The low square neck was edged now with small bright yellow bows, and a further row of bows ran down the front of the skirt. A light green frill, ruthlessly ripped from another dress, decorated the hem.

Her glossy dark brown hair was secured on the top of her head by mother-of-pearl combs, while the ends fell in ringlets below the nape of her slender neck. She wore pearl studs in her ears and a single strand pearl necklace clasped her throat.

The pearls were genuine, a gift from her father, a memento of the days when there had been plenty of money and both Olivia and her father had assumed that a glittering future lay before her as the pampered wife of some wealthy man. Throughout the time of poverty following his death she had steadfastly refused to sell or pawn the jewels; not because of any sentimental attachment, but because she knew that one day she would need them. That day had come.

She eyed herself critically, then nodded in satisfaction. Her skin, lightly dusted with gold from the Australian sun, had a peach-like bloom to it. Her hair and her eyes shone, and the deep green gown set off her looks just as a cluster of dark leaves would set off a perfect crimson rose.

The verandah that skirted the entire house was empty when she stepped on to it. The double doors to the large parlour were ajar and the murmur of voices could be heard from behind them. Boldly, knowing full well that the governess would be expected to slip unobtrusively in through the gap in the doors, Olivia swept them wide and paused in the doorway. To her gratification heads turned and the buzz of conversation faltered then died. Olivia had time to notice that Mr Stobo's jaw had dropped and he was staring at her like an idiot before Mrs Stobo, plump and matronly and over-dressed in deep blue silk, detached herself from a small group and came darting towards the door, her eyes blank with shock for a moment then hardening into dawning, frustrated anger.

'Come in, my dear . . . no need to be shy,' she fluted, her voice trembling with suppressed rage; then she said to the roomful of staring guests, 'This is the children's governess. I thought it would be pleasant for the girl to join us.'

'The pleasure,' said an elderly man who had come hot on her heels to the door, 'is all ours.'

There were little cries of appreciation from the ladies when the party was ushered into the dining room where the table waited for them in all its splendour. Mrs Stobo accepted a flurry of compliments with a gracious smile that remained pinned firmly on her round face throughout the meal that Olivia had planned on her behalf. Later, when the ladies had retired to the parlour, she said pointedly, 'Miss Kerr, you may pour coffee.'

Olivia did so, handing the small cups round, well aware that as far as the women were concerned she was a threat. They banded together, giving her sidelong glances, fluttering and clucking together like birds in a henhouse.

Sitting apart and sipping at her coffee, she went over the guest list in her mind. Unfortunately there didn't seem to be anyone of interest on it. Almost every man invited was married, and it was not part of Olivia's plan to become involved with a man who already belonged to another woman.

There was only one bachelor, the reason why she was present to make up the numbers. No doubt, she thought with amusement, there had been some plan to link him with the young woman who was languishing at home with a migraine. She was welcome to him as far as Olivia was concerned. He was lean and tall, heavily tanned and dark-haired: good-looking in a way, she acknowledged to herself, but Olivia had never been one to put looks before other considerations. He wore his formal clothes with an air of awkward discomfort that irritated her and she had quickly discovered during dinner that he was quite impossible when it came to conversation. He concentrated on his food and she gladly left him to it. She took him to be a clerk in Mr Stobo's bank.

When the men came into the room, flushed with brandy and smelling of tobacco smoke, John Mundy was among the group that gravitated towards the corner where Olivia sat alone. Like a startled rabbit Jean Stobo jumped to her feet and squeaked, 'Miss Kerr, fetch a jug of lemonade and a tray of glasses. I'm sure everyone must be thirsty.'

'Surely one of your servants could do that,' the man who had been the first to greet Olivia protested, and his wife said sweetly, but with a cutting edge to her voice, 'Precisely, dear, that's what Mrs Stobo means.'

Olivia hid her fury beneath lowered lids and a small, polite smile. One day, she thought as she went duti-fully to the kitchen, one day I shall have more money than any of them. And then let them look out for themselves!

For the rest of the evening she was kept busy pouring glasses of lemonade and passing plates of confectionery and arranging chairs so that they could all sit and listen to one of the wives playing the piano badly, and without sincerity.

Bowing to the passion that the people of Melbourne had for music, the Stobos had bought the piano from one of the best stores in Bourke Street and Mrs Stobo had announced that she would teach her children to play it. Her own knowledge of music was poor, and Martha and Ruth, spoiled as they were, quickly lost interest with the lessons and refused to continue them.

Mrs Stobo, who had become as bored with the notion as the children but was determined that they should be able to play for guests, then decreed that Olivia should teach them the simple beginnings before a qualified teacher was brought in. It was a decision that she regretted when it was discovered the governess was an accomplished pianist.

When the polite smattering of applause ended and the pianist had smirkingly retired to her seat, Mr Stobo called for Olivia to play. His wife shot him a glance that would have crushed him if he hadn't been busy drawing Olivia forward and placing the chair for her.

The usual buzz of conversation faltered and stilled as she began to play. When she finished and turned to acknowledge the applause, led by a delighted Mr Stobo, she saw that his wife's mouth had taken on the lines of a mantrap.

For the rest of the evening, John Mundy, the inarticulate bachelor, followed her around like a shadow, backing off nervously whenever she happened to catch his eye. She ignored him, and was almost relieved when a maidservant came scurrying in to report that Miss Ruth had had a nightmare and wouldn't stop crying.

'My poor baby! Miss Kerr, see to her. And don't leave

her,' Mrs Stobo added firmly as her governess obediently put down her glass of lemonade and walked towards the door.

On the following morning Mr Stobo left for the bank earlier than usual. Mrs Stobo stayed in bed until noon then had a light lunch and announced that she was taking the children to an afternoon concert in the Town Hall.

'You needn't accompany us, Miss Kerr,' she said coldly. 'I'm sure you can find something to do while we're gone. Martha's tarlatan dress is getting too short for her; it needs letting down.'

It was too hot for sewing. Once the family were well out of the way Olivia took a chair and a book out into the garden at the rear of the house and settled herself beneath the shade of a tree.

She had only read a few pages when one of the maids came scurrying out.

'If you please, miss, there's a Mr Mundy come calling.'

'Tell him that Mrs Stobo's not at home.'

'I did, miss, but, when I said you was at home, he asked to see you,' the girl persisted, short-lashed lids blinking over pale blue eyes. Jean Stobo had found her maid-servants from among young women who had travelled out to Australia from Britain in search of a new life. Many of them found it quickly, in the shape of men who had also emigrated to make their fortunes. Those who were left to take up domestic service were usually plain and lacking in intelligence. This particular girl had sandy coloured skin and sandy coloured hair, and an annoying way of shuffling from one foot to another when she should have been standing still.

'Oh very well, since you've told him that I'm here,'

Olivia said ungraciously, and a moment later John Mundy was with her, refusing the chair that the maid had brought out for him, preferring to pace the lawn, fiddle with the bushes, and stand before Olivia so that she was forced to tip her head back to look up at him, shielding her eyes from the sun with one hand each time. He shifted from one foot to the other just as the maid had done.

He wore a short grey jacket with matching waistcoat and trousers. The clothes were of good quality and on any other man they might have looked elegant. But as before, he looked uncomfortable and awkward as though unused to being dressed so well. His body was like a whip, wiry and with an air of suppressed energy about it. Above a dark beard and moustache his eyes were keen, with a humorous glint to them when he smiled, which was rarely.

'You, er, ever go to a show in Melbourne?' he asked hesitantly after ten minutes of small talk from Olivia, which he'd answered by a few muttered words here and there.

'Show?' For a moment she thought that he was talking about the fairs that occasionally visited Greenock in the summer, with their pig races and swing-boats.

'Concerts.' He cleared his throat nervously. 'The Theatre Royal in Bourke Street has a good French musical comedy running at the moment.'

His blue eyes removed themselves from a roaming study of the house and garden and fastened on her face. She realized with amused anger that the impertinent jackass was actually about to invite her to attend the theatre with him.

'I never attend concerts, Mr Mundy,' she said crushingly. 'I have far too many important things to do during my free time.'

127

His face fell, and she watched without a shred of sympathy before rising to her feet. 'In fact, I have some letters that must be written this afternoon, and the sun has given me a slight headache . . .'

Mercifully, he took the hint and left, red-faced with confusion, apologizing again and again for having troubled her. When he had gone she swept into the house and scolded the servant who had admitted that she was at home without asking her permission first. Then, discovering to her annoyance that she had indeed developed a headache, she dabbed some Eau de Nil on her temples and lay down on her bed in a thorough temper.

How dared John Mundy, with his clumsy Australian accent and his hopeless manners, think that she, Olivia Kerr, would accompany him to anything as vulgar as a French musical comedy? It would never occur to the likes of him to invite her to the Opera House right across the street from the theatre. Not that she would have agreed to go to the opera with him. She wouldn't attend any occasion on the arm of such an uncouth man. She'd have been as well staying in Scotland and accepting Gideon Brenner's courtship.

There *must* be more refined men in Australia, wealthy men, unmarried men, Olivia thought with frustration. If only she could find out how to meet them!

The maidservant, in revenge for Olivia's scolding, told Mrs Stobo when she arrived home that there had been a caller. Mrs Stobo, in turn, scolded her governess for her lack of hospitality.

'To think that the poor man came all the way out from the town and you didn't offer him as much as a glass of lemonade! You should have entertained him until I arrived home . . . you knew I wouldn't be long.'

'I had a headache,' Olivia said icily. 'And to the best of my understanding, entertaining your guests is not a part of my duties.'

Jean Stobo's face, flushed with the heat of the day, reddened further. 'Your duties, Miss, are whatever I consider them to be. As for headaches, I would be grateful if you could suffer them in your own time, not in mine. Mr Mundy's father happens to be one of my husband's major clients and he has every right to expect his son to be received with consideration when he's kind enough to call.'

'Mr Mundy's father?' The remnants of Olivia's headache vanished with the shock of the revelation. The inarticulate, clumsy young man who had gazed at her hopefully and invited her to attend the theatre with him didn't strike her as the son of a wealthy family.

'Of course . . . why else would we have invited him to dine with us, you foolish girl? The Mundys own a million acres of land . . . thousands of head of sheep, not to mention opal mines. I don't know what my husband will say when he hears how discourteously that poor man was treated!'

But if Mr Stobo was ever told of John Mundy's visit he didn't let it bother him. From the evening of the dinner party he treated his children's governess, formerly invisible as far as he was concerned, with new interest, passing the time of day with her if they happened to meet in the house or garden, making more frequent visits than before to the room set aside as a nursery, complimenting Olivia on her good work and lingering to talk to her until his wife's raised voice calling his name dragged him reluctantly back to her side.

After the dinner party the gulf between employer and

governess widened. Mrs Stobo did her best to relegate Olivia to the level of a common servant, asking her to carry out small household duties planned as subtle downward steps. But Olivia refused to give in to her employer and, although she realized that it would be wise to look around for other employment, she hadn't done anything about it when, not much more than two months after her arrival in Melbourne, she received a rude, if not totally unexpected, shock.

Martha, who had her mother's podgy looks and arrogance, had been quick to sense and make use of the gulf between Mrs Stobo and the governess. She became more and more impertinent towards Olivia who, as she didn't even care for children, found her behaviour insufferable. However, until she found more suitable employment elsewhere she knew that she had no option but to suffer in silence.

She did so, until the day when she returned from a walk with Ruth to find that Martha, who had stayed at home because of an imagined sore toe, had raided her room and tried on all her clothes, spilling a glass of lemonade down the front of the green gown.

Mrs Stobo, brought from her room by Martha's shrill screams, arrived to see Olivia standing over her daughter, hazel eyes blazing. Martha was still swathed in the gown, which was soaked and stained down the front. The pearl earrings clung uncertainly to her ear-lobes and the necklace was balanced on top of her head like a crown.

As soon as Martha saw her mother she lunged towards her, tripping over the gown's trailing skirt. There was a nasty ripping sound and she fell over, to be scooped up into her mother's arms.

'Darling girl, what's wrong?'

'She hit me!' Martha roared. One hand, swathed in green silk, indicated Olivia.

'She did, she did . . . she slapped Martha's face,' Ruth chimed in, jumping up and down excitedly.

'How could you!'

'I will not have your undisciplined children rooting through my belongings!'

Jean Stobo's round face turned purple with rage. 'You are dismissed,' she shouted above her elder daughter's roars. 'You'll take a week's—'

Olivia raised her own voice so that it topped Mrs Stobo's and even Martha's. 'I will not be dismissed, Mrs Stobo. I resign from this moment. I'll pack my things and send for my trunk when I'm settled elsewhere.' Then she asked icily as the other woman turned away, 'Before you leave the room, would you please return my pearls?'

With a trembling hand Jean Stobo unclipped the earrings, whipped the necklace from her daughter's head, and handed them over. Then she began to unfasten the buttons on the front of the gown Martha was wearing over her own clothes.

'Martha may keep the gown. I've no desire to have it now that she's ruined it.'

Mrs Stobo's hand was unpleasantly sticky from the lemonade. She realized that the fresh white lacy blouse she had just put on must also be stained and sticky from contact with Martha, now snuffling in her arms and clinging tightly. She realized, too, that until she found another governess — a plain mousy governess who always did as she was told — the children would be her sole responsibility.

She returned to her own room, with Ruth trailing behind her, and burst into self-pitying tears.

*   *   *

Shaking with anger, Olivia packed all her belongings into the sea-trunk that had been bought in Greenock, then left the Stobo household with a small bag, all that she could carry.

She caught the omnibus which passed by the end of the road and travelled into the town to find somewhere to stay. Her first impulse, while she was still in the grip of her self-righteous rage, was to go to one of the fine hotels where she would be pampered and treated like a lady instead of a servant.

But common sense told her that the money she had managed to save from her salary might have to last for some time, so she found a respectable but inexpensive rooming house in Little Flinders Street and surveyed her small domain there with grim pleasure. It was only large enough for a single bed, a wardrobe, a small chest of drawers which also served as a writing desk, and a chair. There was scarcely room to take three steps in any direction, and normally Olivia would have looked down her nose at it. But at least this room was free of Martha and Ruth and their domineering mother. At first she felt triumphant, carried along on the crest of her indignation. She had demonstrated to Jean Stobo that she was not a servant to be treated as the odious woman chose. Then as night approached she began to realize that she was alone and almost penniless on a vast continent far from her home. There was nobody to care about what happened to her, nobody to turn to. A lump formed in her throat and she found herself thinking of the house in Greenock and wanting Annis with a longing she had never known before. She sat down and wrote a long letter to her sister, pouring out all her fears and loneliness.

It helped a little. In bed later she cried into her flat, hard pillow before finally falling into a sleep shot through with dreams of Greenock.

On the following morning, with the sunshine sparkling outside, Olivia felt better, and angry with herself for having been so weak. She tore up the letter to Annis, then went out and tried two employment agencies, leaving in disdain when she discovered that they expected her to go into domestic service.

'If you were dismissed you've little chance of getting another post as a governess,' the blunt Dundee woman at the third agency told her.

'I resigned,' Olivia insisted coolly.

'Will they give you good references?' the woman asked, then as Olivia bit her lip, she went on, 'There's folk pouring into the place from back home, plenty of them looking for more than they'll get.'

'Surely there's a place for a well-educated lady?'

The woman looked sceptical. 'There's little call for lady's maids or governesses as far as I'm concerned, lassie.'

Olivia trudged round the other agencies and studied the newspapers. There were few offers that she cared to take, and when she did apply for them the fact that she had no references told against her. Mrs Stobo held the references Olivia had obtained from Greenock people, and a curt note requesting them had not so far resulted in a reply. Whatever happened, Olivia vowed to herself, she would not go back to that house to ask for them.

Three days after her angry exit from the Stobo household she had begun to realize that finding work wasn't going to be as easy as she had thought.

In the privacy of her room she counted her money out

carefully into small piles and decided that she could hold out for one more week. If nothing had happened by then she would either have to swallow her pride and apply for a domestic position or use the money that was left to pay for her return fare to Greenock.

She had no doubt at all that if she did admit defeat and go back to her sister's house Douglas Moncrieff would insist on dictating her next move, which would probably be marriage to Gideon Brenner. Douglas certainly would not want to see her back in his house for good, any more than Olivia herself wanted it.

Her despondency swept back in a black cloud, bringing homesickness with it. This time, though, she refused to give way to tears. Rather than face the Moncrieffs and admit defeat, she would accept a position in domestic service for the time being. But only if she had no other option.

She hadn't written to Annis in the few days since leaving the Stobos. After counting her money and making her decision she drew the single chair up to the chest of drawers, opened the battered brass inkwell, and dipped her pen into it.

'Dear Annis,' she wrote, then paused, chewing at her lower lip. Once or twice the pen dipped towards the page, and each time her hand stilled. Any news given to Annis would be passed on to Douglas and Tib. Olivia straightened her shoulders. She would not have the Moncrieffs, Annis included, pitying her or gloating over her misfortune.

She dipped her pen into the dusty inkwell and carefully wrote, 'I expect that you're suffering cold winter weather in Greenock just now. Here, it is warm and sunny and most pleasant. I have just taken the children on a visit to the Museum, where there is an absorbing exhibition of the wools and leathers on which a large part of the Australian economy is based . . .'

The landlady's voice corkscrewed up the narrow stairway, yelling, 'Miss Kerr!' for all the world as though she was selling coal in the back streets of Greenock.

'Yes?' Olivia inquired irritably from the small landing.

'A visitor. In the parlour,' the woman announced, then the door leading to her own quarters at the back of the house opened and shut.

Puzzled, Olivia went downstairs. To her astonishment John Mundy, in the grey suit he had worn when she last saw him in the dazzling sunshine of the Stobos' garden, was pacing the tiny gloomy parlour. He swung round when she entered and said without wasting time on any greetings, 'Stobo told me you'd been dismissed.'

Much to her surprise, her first reaction at seeing him had been one of overwhelming relief. He was a slightly familiar face, and after three days of seeing only strangers and talking to nobody but the women in the employment agencies it was good to see someone she knew. But his blunt words angered her. 'I left Mr Stobo's employment of my own accord,' she corrected him coolly. 'How did you know where to find me?'

'I called at all the shipping offices and the employment agencies. Didn't know if you'd be heading for home or staying. One of the agencies gave me this address.'

'They had no right to—'

'I didn't give them the chance to think about that,' said Mundy flatly. 'I wanted to see you.'

'If you assume that because of my changed circumstances I'd now be happy to attend the theatre with you, Mr Mundy, the answer is still no.'

'Wasn't going to ask you that. The thing is' — his big hands, clutching his hat, turning its brim round and round — 'I'm heading for home on Thursday. It's time I was getting back to the sheep station. I want you to come with me.'

She glared at him, 'I presume that this is the result of your discovery that I've been visiting the agencies. Let me assure you, Mr Mundy, that I am not interested in going into domestic service. And if I was, it would certainly not be on a sheep station.'

'Confound it, woman, not as a servant,' John Mundy said impatiently. Today he was different, more positive than before. 'My father's got as many of those as he needs. As my wife.'

She gaped at him, at a loss for words. He stared back, his face above the dark moustache and beard suddenly colouring until it almost glowed red in the dim room.

When she found her voice again Olivia said weakly, 'But . . . we scarcely know each other!'

'That was why I invited you to the theatre the other day. Where I live there's little chance of taking time to court a woman. I knew from the first minute I set eyes on you that you were the one I wanted and I've not got time for any of the usual folderols.'

'But you can't just . . .'

'I've already done it. What d'you say? I must head for home on Thursday, with or without you.' He hesitated, then added gruffly, 'I'm hoping that it'll be with you.'

Olivia drew a deep breath and linked her hands to stop them from shaking. She recalled what Jean Stobo had said about the Mundys and their million-acre sheep station with its opal mines. The bank's largest clients.

'My father's got as many servants as he needs,' John Mundy had said.

All at once Olivia felt as though she had just found the gates of Heaven, after a lifetime of searching. This was what she had longed for, what she desperately needed at that very moment . . . a wealthy man who wanted to marry her. She looked at him with new eyes. He was certainly presentable. Only a fool would turn him down, and Olivia certainly wasn't a fool.

Relief settled over her like a soft warm cloak as she said a trifle shakily, 'Thank you, Mr . . . John. I'd be happy to be your wife.'

He gave a long relieved sigh then grinned widely. He looked almost handsome when he smiled. 'I appreciate it. It's . . . that's really good of you,' he said, then added, as though cautiously testing the name on his tongue, 'Olivia.'

As he seemed content to just stand there, grinning at her, she asked delicately, 'Will we be married here, or at your home?'

He jerked out of his dream. 'Oh . . . here, before we leave. I'll make the arrangements right away. I'm staying at the Oriental Hotel in Collins Street. You'd better move in there until we leave for Vanduara. In a room of your own until the wedding,' he added hastily, the colour beginning to surge into his face again. 'It'll be more comfortable for you. I'll send someone round within the hour to collect you and your luggage.'

'My trunk is still in South Yarra. There's no room for it here.'

'I'll have it brought to the hotel.' Now that he had something to organize he had taken on a masterful air that was new to her. 'I'd best get started. See you at the hotel later, then.'

'Yes.'

He went to the door, hesitated, came back and put his hands on her shoulders. Then he leaned forward.

Olivia braced herself, lifting her head and offering her lips to him. His kiss was chaste and awkward and his beard scratched her chin. Then he released her and blundered from the room.

When he had gone Olivia went slowly upstairs and closed the door of her little room. She began to pack her belongings, carefully folding each garment and putting it into her small suitcase. All at once she pictured Mrs Stobo's face when she heard that her former governess was to become the wife of her husband's wealthiest client. The son of the wealthiest client, she corrected herself, then repeated the words slowly, savouring each one.

She caught sight of herself in the fly-spotted mirror set into the wardrobe door and saw that she was smiling broadly.

And why not? An hour ago she had been facing a life of domestic service, or Douglas's scorn. Now she was on her way to one of Melbourne's best hotels and about to marry into a wealthy family.

She sat down on the bed and deliberately conjured him into her mind, thinking of the lean brown face and the lithe, muscular body. A faint tremor ran through her at the thought of sharing her life and bed with the man, and she stood up abruptly and went on with her packing.

She felt nothing for John Mundy, but that didn't bother her, for romantic love had never seemed to Olivia to be important. Nor had physical attraction. John Mundy would find her a dutiful wife as far as the intimacies of marriage were concerned – within reason. The man was shy and awkward; clearly he knew little of women and therefore he would be easily controlled, she thought with relief. His hesitant kiss had told her all she needed to know. She could deal with this marriage and she would be well compensated, financially. After all, Annis claimed to love Douglas, and Olivia was quite certain that Annis wasn't nearly as happy as she, Olivia, intended to be with John.

Her letter-pad still lay on the chest of drawers. Olivia couldn't resist taking time to tear off the page she had begun to her sister, crumple it, and throw it into the waste-paper basket. Then she dipped her pen into the inkwell and started afresh. This time, she thought triumphantly, she had no need to cover up the truth. This time she had news indeed for Annis, and Douglas, and disapproving, dried-up Tib Moncrieff.

'Dear Annis, I have wonderful news for you. I am to be married within the next few days. After the wedding John and I will travel into the country, where his family own a million acres of land . . .'

They were married by the minister of the Scottish church in Melbourne a few days later, with one of John's business colleagues and his wife as witnesses and guests. With the last of her savings Olivia had brought a cream silk dress, embroidered with blue flowers and trimmed with blue ribbons, for the occasion.

The ceremony was over very quickly, and to Olivia's disappointment the witnesses excused themselves as soon as they left the church.

'I thought we might all have had supper together,' she said as she and John walked back to the hotel.

'I wanted us to have supper alone,' he said, and paid no heed when she pouted a little.

Before returning to the hotel they went to the French musical comedy that she had so scathingly turned down before. Olivia's protests that she would rather have attended something more serious were ignored.

'I like this show,' said John as they settled into their seats.

'You've seen it before?'

'Several times, but this is my last chance.'

It was, as Olivia had expected, vulgar. The women were scarcely decent, the jokes bawdy, the music loud and the voices harsh. But John — and the rest of the audience — clearly loved it. Olivia watched the antics on stage with little interest, the fingers of her right hand constantly caressing her new wedding ring, and made up for her disappointment over his refusal to take her to a proper wedding supper by pleasurably picturing what a to-do there was going to be in the Moncrieff household when the letter bearing the news of her marriage arrived.

Douglas would be speechless, she thought; Tib would go patchy red . . . and how envious Annis would be! This made a mockery of her sister's ridiculous accusation about Olivia's own jealousy. She would not have married Douglas Moncrieff if he had gone down on his knees and begged her, in spite of his wealth. Oh yes, she had shown them all that she was indeed worthy of someone far better than Douglas. Within weeks of arriving in Australia she had made a far better marriage than her sister's.

By the time they arrived back at the hotel she was hungry, and looking forward to some food, but as she made for the supper room John put a hand underneath her elbow and steered her firmly towards the stairs.

'We'll eat alone in our room,' he said and marched

her upstairs, ignoring her protests. She had looked forward to dining in public with everyone admiring her fine gown and aware of the gold band that now sat snugly on her finger, and tomorrow they were leaving for the sheep station.

Worse was to come. Instead of ordering the meal as she had expected, John took her into his arms as soon as the door of the room had closed behind them. This time his kiss was hard and strong, and when Olivia, her tender skin chafed by his beard, tried to pull back, his arms tightened about her.

When he finally released her it was only to fumble with the buttons of her dress.

'John!'

'We're married, aren't we?' A button refused to slip through the buttonhole and he tugged at it. It parted company with the dress and rattled to the floor.

'Stop it!'

'You can sew it on again . . . you can sew 'em all on again,' he said recklessly, and pulled the bodice apart with a great cascading of buttons.

There was no denying him. With his wedding ring safely on her finger the quiet, shy young man had turned into a husband set on consummating their marriage without further ado.

Within minutes their clothes were scattered all over the room and the two of them, naked as the day they were born, were on the bed.

In the days following John's proposal Olivia had given some thought to their wedding night. She had once heard the female body described as the sacred temple of womanhood, a phrase which had pleased her. She had pictured his hesitation, his trembling gratitude as she

141

permitted him access to her own sacred temple. But the reality was far from the picture in her mind.

Instead of shy hesitation when confronted with her nakedness, John Mundy said with enthusiasm, 'Yes, Livvy – oh, yes!' then proceeded to fondle and use her in ways that she could not have thought of in her wildest imaginings.

'John!' she protested breathlessly, but his head was buried between her breasts and he was too busy to pay any heed.

Now that his own clothes had been shed she could see that his body was indeed lean and muscular, and tanned an even brown all over apart from a creamy smooth belt of skin over his buttocks and thighs and groin. When he moved to lie beside her and drew her into his arms so that they touched from lips to toes the sensation of his smooth warm skin sliding easily over hers was not, Olivia realized, unpleasant. Nor was the smell of him – a smell of soap and warmth underlaid by something deeper and musky.

'Livvy . . .' He breathed the word into her ear, his lips tickling the lobe, then blew gently. Olivia's whole body shivered, then shivered again as he ran his tongue along the lobe of her ear then down over her neck and shoulder to her breast. To her astonishment she felt her body responding to him, nipples tautening, one leg bending at the knee and sliding slowly up over his hard strong thigh.

When he finally entered her the sharp stab of pain made her cry out, but the deep-seated throb of pleasure that followed it almost immediately turned the cry to a moan. As his eager body moved against her she heard herself moaning again, a sound that was almost lost under the sound of John's own cries. She heard the bedsprings squeaking a protest and wondered for a moment if the people in the adjoining rooms could hear them.

Then she stopped caring about other people, clutching at John, moving with him, feeling excitement building within her, until he gave one final yell and collapsed on to her before rolling away to lie by her side, panting for breath. His body glistened with sweat and his damp hair lay over his forehead. For a while there was no sound but their swift breathing. Finally he said, 'You're some woman, Livvy.'

'I bought such a pretty night-dress.'

'You can wear it later.' He stretched and yawned, then raised himself on one elbow and looked down at her with a look that was enough to send a well-brought-up young lady into a blush from her tousled head to the tips of her bare toes.

'Livvy . . .'

'My name is Olivia.' She tried to collect her dignity about her again but it was difficult.

'Livvy . . .' he said again, reaching for her, the light of battle in his eyes once more.

'I'm hungry!'

'So am I,' said her husband, moving to straddle her. 'You can eat later . . . before we go to bed.'

8

'You cannot mean to put Janet out of the house! It's . . . it's a cruel and unchristian thing to do!'

But soft words and pleading, even from his beloved wife, had no effect at all on Douglas Moncrieff. Nor did her angry outburst. 'If anyone is being unchristian, my dear,' he said in an icy voice, 'it is the girl. I will not have servant girls giving birth to bastards on my premises. She must go!'

Annis was appalled at his reaction. Janet had come to her in tears that morning, asking for her help. She was with child, she'd sobbed, by the carter she'd been walking out with: the man, Annis realized ruefully, Janet had been so eager to impress with Olivia's old dress. Without a second thought Annis had assured the girl there would be no question of her losing her position with them. It seemed now she had been very wrong.

'The man has left her, Douglas,' she protested. 'He's disappeared to Glasgow, and her parents might not take her back.'

'I see no reason why not, drunken louts that they both are, no better than their daughter. We should never have taken her into service in the first place.'

'If they reject her where is there for her to go?'

'She should have thought of that months ago. Tib,'

he added to his sister, 'give her what money's due and see that she leaves the house at once.'

'Give me the money and I'll tell her.' It was the least Annis could do.

'Indeed not, my dear, she would only take further advantage of your tender heart. Tib's more used to this sort of domestic unpleasantness.'

Douglas Moncrieff rose swiftly from his chair and took both Annis's hands into his as Tib went silently from the parlour.

'But I promised Janet . . .'

'You had no right to promise the girl anything, Annis,' Douglas said. 'You must know that.'

'To treat a good servant so harshly . . . ' The words choked in Annis's throat and she swallowed hard to keep back the tears that wanted to overflow.

Douglas's hands tightened. He drew her towards him and into his arms. 'My love, what else can I do? A man must be master in his own house. Would you have the whole town thinking that Douglas Moncrieff's gone soft in the head, willing to fill his house with sinful lassies and their illegitimate bairns?'

For the first time Annis fully realized that those with money were those with power. She, who would gladly have given what she could to Janet, knew she was as impoverished as the little maidservant, for everything she wore or ate or touched belonged to Douglas. She wished now, as Olivia had always wished, that their father had been able to leave them a little money.

She made a final bid. 'You could give her a little extra money so that she could perhaps rent a room for herself.'

'I already support the Poorhouse and the Asylum most generously,' Douglas was saying. 'If she ends up there, as she probably will, she'll benefit from me indirectly, I can assure you. Now come and sit down beside the fire.' He drew her to the couch, where they sat down together, his arm protectively around her waist.

Douglas's clothes, Douglas's food, Douglas's wife, Annis thought as the ball of his thumb moved slowly back and forth over the gold ring that he had placed on the third finger of her left hand. She had been proud and happy to receive and to wear that ring, but tonight she had the absurd feeling that the little gold circlet was getting heavier and tighter, clamping itself to her finger, yet at the same time growing, circling about her chest, pulling her down into the darkness where she couldn't catch her breath properly.

She threw out her free hand and gripped the arm of the couch, feeling it solid and yet strangely spongy and flexible beneath her touch. From far away as she gasped for air she heard Douglas say her name, then repeat it with rising anxiety. Something that smelled sharp and pungent caused her paralysed lungs to inflate sharply, sucking air. The darkness released her, and through streaming eyes she saw that she was back in the parlour, with Tib's little sal volatile bottle being waved under her nose.

Choking over its bitterness Annis pushed it away and sat upright, coughing.

'Annis.'

'She's fine, Douglas,' Tib said sharply, and her dry hard voice did more than anything else to bring Annis back to her senses.

'I'm quite all right . . . ' She was shaking uncontrollably, her teeth chattering. 'I just felt a little f—faint for a moment.'

'That's the girl's fault,' her husband fumed. 'You're not used to such unpleasantness. I've a good mind to chase after her and —'

'Douglas, please!' Annis pulled herself together. 'I'm perfectly well, but if you'll excuse me I'll retire early tonight,' she added, knowing that he would insist on accompanying her instead of running after poor Janet and causing even more misery in her life, if that was possible.

In the privacy of their bedroom he undressed her gently, without his usual hot-eyed excitement, and slipped her night-gown over her head, tying the ribbons carefully.

Despite her anger, love for him warmed her heart as she watched him work over her, his brown eyes soft with concern. Then she remembered Janet and wondered how any man could be so harsh to one woman, yet so tender to another. At the thought her pleasure in his tenderness dimmed a little.

When she was in bed, luxuriating in the warmth that hours of pre-heating with a warming-pan had given to the sheets, the shaking ebbed away, leaving her feeling very weak, as though convalescing from a long illness.

Douglas, retiring behind his screen as usual, said anxiously, 'I must leave the house quite early tomorrow morning, but I want you to promise me that if you're still unwell you'll stay in bed and tell Tib to fetch the doctor.'

'I'll be perfectly all right in the morning. It was just a passing thing!' For the first time that day a pleasurable thought struck her and she said sleepily from the nest of pillows, 'Wouldn't it be fine, Douglas, if it turned out that I was expecting a child?'

There was a moment's silence before he said briskly,

'If you ask me, your fainting fit was all the fault of that serving-girl. She had no right to run to you with her problems instead of confessing at once to Tib then leaving the house.'

'But Douglas . . .'

'Not another word on the subject. It's upset you enough.' He came from behind the screen, and she watched him as he made certain that the door and windows were closed, then turned the gas lights out one by one, tall and reassuring in his long, voluminous night-shirt.

Then he slipped into bed beside her, dropped a kiss on her brow, and removed himself to his own side of the bed, leaving her alone.

'I want us to have a child of our own soon, Douglas,' she said into the bleak darkness, the thought of Janet's forthcoming ordeal still haunting her.

His voice floated across the width of the bed to her, 'You're too young for that. There's plenty of time yet. Plenty of time. Go to sleep, my dear.'

Each time she went into the town she saw women of her own age and younger with children in their arms, many of them wrapped in the shawls that their mothers wore, so that mother and baby were bound together in a cocooned world, their bodies warming each other. Even Janet would have the comfort of a child, would have something of her own, whatever the circumstances.

If *she* had a child, she thought, closing her eyes against the darkness of the room, the loneliness that had been growing since Olivia's departure would be eased. A child would need her, love her, never criticize her and find her wanting. A child would fill her days and perhaps bridge the space that was opening slowly but surely between herself and Douglas. He didn't seem to be aware of it, but it was there.

Then sleep fled as she wriggled her toes in the warmth. She remembered that it was Janet who had warmed the bed. Her eyes opened. Where was the girl now? It was certain that she wasn't in a warm cosy bed, well protected from the sleety December wind gusting around the town. She had failed the girl miserably. The tears that Annis had managed to hold back during the scene in the parlour flowed down her cheeks and on to the pillow. She had promised to do all she could to help her yet she had been forced to break that promise. She wept silently for herself and for Janet, and for a way of life that had little regard for the wishes of both maids and mistresses.

Drying her face on the sheet, listening to Douglas's breathing move into an even rhythm that told of guilt-free sleep, she wished that he had put his arm about her instead of turning away. She thought of snuggling up to the warmth of his body, then decided that she might disturb him. Although she longed for comfort she had no desire, tonight, for love-making.

Douglas coughed and turned over without waking. The feeling of great loneliness that had been growing swept over Annis. She wondered if she would be able to put her trust in him again.

Since the day Gideon Brenner called to find out if Olivia had really left Greenock, he had taken to visiting the house whenever the *Grace and Charity* was in harbour.

He found trifling excuses for each occasion, bringing with him a delicate hand-painted ostrich egg for Robert, a sandalwood fan, also beautifully painted, for Annis, cigars for Douglas, a black shawl, received with grudging, tight-lipped thanks, for Tib.

'A sailing man calls in at many ports,' he said lightly each time gifts were handed over. 'It's a pleasure to buy curios for the people back home.'

She wasn't daft enough to believe him. She knew that his real reason for calling on her was to seek news of Olivia. But without being aware of it he helped to banish some of the emptiness in her life and she didn't want his visits to stop.

Tib resented the sight of him in what she still considered to be her parlour, wasting time and drinking her tea. Douglas, when told of the visits, agreed with his sister.

'The other captains in my employ don't call at my house,' he told Annis, a frown between his brows. 'I see no reason why Brenner should . . . other than the occasions when I see fit to invite him.'

'He's a newcomer to Greenock, Douglas, and far from his own home. Surely there's nothing wrong in making a stranger welcome.'

'He's been here long enough to have made friends other than ourselves,' her husband grumbled. But it was true that Brenner's visits were few and far between because of the time he spent at sea, so Douglas let the matter drop, with a parting shot. 'Besides, Olivia's gone and it's time he realized that.'

'Something's worrying you,' Brenner said, when he called a few days later, adding quickly, 'Has something happened to your sister?'

Annis wondered, with more than a touch of exasperation, why his thoughts must always fly to Olivia. There was more to worry about than her.

'As far as I know Olivia's fine. I had a letter from her

the other day. It's not her I'm concerned for, but Janet, our maidservant.'

'She looked well enough to me when she answered the door.'

'That,' explained Annis with just a trace of exasperation tingeing her voice, 'is Celia, the new maid. I'm talking about our former maid.'

'Ah,' said Gideon, then, to her surprise, 'Tell me.'

She gaped at him, then, as he raised his eyebrows in mute inquiry, she said, 'It's not often a man cares about what's happened to a serving-woman.'

His mouth twitched but he didn't laugh. Instead he said, 'You've been very kind to me since I came to Greenock, Mrs Moncrieff. If I can help, I'll do so.'

She told him, being careful to omit Douglas's harsh treatment of the maid and her own shocked reaction to it.

He listened courteously enough, but when she finished said, 'These things happen, Mrs Moncrieff. Your husband has the right way of it when he says that you cannot be expected to take on the responsibility for other people's actions.'

Anger flowed in her. 'You're just like my husband, Captain Brenner. So sure of yourself, with no understanding of what it's like to be alone and helpless.'

Colour rose beneath his tan. 'I don't mean to be heartless, ma'am, but I believe that you yourself have never been alone either.'

'It's possible to be alone and even frightened although there's a roof over one's head and other people about,' Annis said bleakly, recalling the loneliest moments of her childhood when her father and Olivia had been so wrapped up in one another that she had wondered in a panicky way if she was real or just imaginary.

'Mrs Moncrieff . . . ?' She wrenched herself away from her memories to see that Gideon Brenner was looking intently at her, a perplexed frown between his green eyes.

'Forgive me, Captain. Perhaps it's only women who know about loneliness and the fears that it can bring with it.'

'Where do this girl's parents live?'

'East Quay Lane.'

'Would you like me to call on them to find out if Jane is there? It might set your mind at rest.'

'Janet,' she corrected him crisply, then, as an idea struck her, she added, 'What I'd like is for you to accompany me there. It's not an area I'd care to visit alone.'

'When?'

'This very afternoon would suit me well enough.' She glanced at the mantel clock. Tib wouldn't be back for another hour. Now that the thought had come to her she was impatient to turn it into action. 'I can be there and back in that time.'

'Are you quite certain that . . .'

'Quite certain, Captain. We can take a cab . . . that way there'll be less chance of me being seen.' She was on her feet, on her way to the hall to fetch her cloak, when she stopped and turned to him, reluctant to admit even to herself that the sudden plan had two motives: to make sure that Janet was all right, but also to savour the thrill of a small adventure with Gideon Brenner by her side. 'Will you help me?'

'It seems,' said Gideon wryly, 'that I have no option.'

An empty hire cab came rattling by when they had covered a short distance; Gideon Brenner hailed it and helped Annis into its dusty interior. She leaned well back against the shabby cushion as the vehicle reached the busy part of the town, fearful that Douglas might see her. Brenner watched her, a frown tucked between his brows.

'I'm certain your husband wouldn't approve of this, Mrs Moncrieff. You should have let me deal with it on my own.'

He was quite right, of course. She knew that she was deliberately going against Douglas's wishes and a sudden wave of guilt made her voice tart. 'We all do things that others don't approve of, sir. I understand that you've taken Adeline Fraser into your house.'

His eyes widened, then swung away from hers. A touch of colour brushed his tanned cheekbones.

'Now that I've taken rooms I need a house-keeper. The woman suits me well enough.'

'I'm glad to hear that.' She heard the dryness in her own voice, and knew from the swift glance that was thrown her way that he too had noted it.

She had seen Adeline Fraser sailing around the shops, a basket on her arm, with the smug air of a woman well pleased with life. Gone were the lowered lids and demure expression; when they met in the street nowadays Adeline lifted her head and stared Annis in the eye, a self-satisfied smile playing round her lips. She didn't have the look of a mere house-keeper, in Annis's opinion.

But the relationship between Gideon Brenner and Adeline Fraser was none of her business and almost immediately she was angry with herself for having stooped so low and snapped at the man who was helping her.

'Jem tells me that you've been on at him to make use of the schooner he's building, instead of selling it,' she said in an attempt to clear the air between them. His voice was chilly when he answered.

'I'm quite sure that your cousin would make a tidy profit if he found a crew for the boat and traded along the coast. Why should he always build boats in order that others can make money?'

'Jem's a builder, not a merchant. And a man with few ambitions. I admire him very much.'

The anger suddenly left him and he gave her a brilliant smile that bathed her in its warmth and made her heart beat a little faster. 'So do I, ma'am. Jem Moncrieff is a good and honest man, a man with deep love for his craft. He reminds me strongly of my own father. I think it harsh,' he added carefully, 'that you and Robert must always visit him in secret, without your husband's knowledge.'

'So do I, Captain Brenner, but there it is . . . and I trust that you will keep our secret.'

'Of course.' There was silence, then he said, 'I suggested recently to your husband that the *Grace and Charity* should perhaps go to Australia. The wool trade's worth entering into, and it would no doubt ease your mind if I was to see your sister and bring back first-hand news of her.'

She leaned forward eagerly on the seat − then settled back again and said dryly, 'It would indeed.' It would be good to hear first-hand news of her sister, but drat the man . . . there he was, thinking about Olivia again. When would he realize that she was gone, and he might as well put her out of his head? Hard on the heels of that thought came another . . . if Gideon accepted that Olivia was lost to him he would have no reason to see Annis again. The idea numbed her.

The cab lurched to a standstill and the driver grunted over his shoulder, 'We're here.'

'Wait for us.' Gideon tossed him a coin, then jumped down and reached up for Annis. His hands were firm and strong, clasping hers closely then releasing them as soon as her feet had touched the muddy stones. She looked down the length of the lane, a narrow tunnel with ancient, vermin-ridden warrens on either side, and was glad that she wasn't alone.

'Which house?'

'About half-way down, I think.' Annis gathered her skirts up in one hand and began to walk down the lane. Gideon immediately put a protective hand beneath her elbow.

'Stay close to the walls, Mrs Moncrieff, and you'll avoid the worst of the refuse.'

East Quay Lane was the most convenient route between the railway station and the harbour. People arriving in Greenock by rail on their way to board a ship were obliged to walk down its insanitary, smelly length; there had been a number of suggestions as to an alternative route or the improvement of the lane itself, but as yet nothing had been done.

Ragged children played in the gutters and women leaned out of the windows overhead, shouting to each other and watching the people passing below.

Two men lounged at the entrance to the close where Janet's parents lived. Their eyes devoured Annis as she approached, and at first she thought that they were going to refuse to move to let the visitors through. But a look at her companion's face changed their minds. Reluctantly they shuffled to one side and Annis and Gideon walked into the dark passageway.

Gideon uttered a small exclamation as the smell of the place struck them and his free hand whipped a handkerchief from his pocket. Annis, who had heard what the place was like, had taken a deep breath just before entering; she let the air out of her lungs slowly so that she wouldn't have to inhale. The American, seeing that she was apparently unmoved by the stench, replaced his handkerchief and suffered in grim silence as they mounted the hollowed, slimy stone stairs.

As they gained the first landing a little girl came out of a doorway directly in front of them. Annis had to ask twice before the child, scratching at a tousled head, pointed with her free hand at one of the other doors.

Gideon knocked on it, then knocked again. After a long wait it opened slowly, just wide enough for an eye to be put at the crack. The room behind smelled as though it had never known a breath of fresh air.

'Janet?'

The eye widened, then the door opened a little more. Janet, frowsy and rumpled, no longer the neat little maidservant who had worked so willingly at the house in Low Gourock Road, stared at her former mistress, then at Gideon.

'Whit are you doin' here?' Her accent, like her appearance, had changed.

'I came to see how you were. Janet . . . ' Annis said hurriedly as the door began to close again, 'I can't do anything to help you just now, but after the child's born . . . '

'You couldnae dae nothin' for me before and ye'll dae nothin' for me after,' the girl said flatly.

'I will, I promise. Here . . . ' Annis fumbled in the bag that dangled from one wrist and held out some coins. As the girl snatched at them a voice cawed from inside the room. At once Janet dropped the coins into the depths of her shabby blouse.

Then she was pushed aside and a scrawny woman twisted with rheumatism took her place. She reeked of stale drink and her toothless mouth was sunken.

'Whit d'ye want?'

'It's Mrs Moncrieff, mam,' Janet said from behind the door and the woman's eyes narrowed.

'Mistress Moncrieff, is it? The fine lady that pit my lassie oot of her house an' oot o' work . . . an' me a poor invalid wi' no' a penny to bless mysel.'

'My husband . . .'

'Oh aye, we all ken whit a fine upright man Douglas Moncrieff is,' the woman sneered. 'For a' I ken he's the yin that did it tae my poor lassie. The gentry can dae whit they —'

'That's enough!' Brenner's voice cut across the mumblings decisively. 'You've seen that the girl's with her family, Mrs Moncrieff. I'll take you back home.'

'Hoo am I tae manage wi' anither twa mooths tae feed and nae siller comin' in?' the woman screeched hurriedly.

'If you stayed out of the public houses you'd manage a sight better.' Gideon was unmoved by the plea, but Annis fumbled in her bag again and dropped a coin into the dirty hand held out for it. Then she turned and stumbled back down the staircase, glad of the American's supporting hand, her stomach beginning to rebel at the stink of the place.

Out in the street she drew in a long breath of sour air that seemed fresh by comparison with the interior of the building, then said shakily, 'How can folk be expected to live in such a place?'

'It's the way of the world. You shouldn't have given money to that old witch.' Gideon's voice was tight with disapproval. 'She'll only drink it away.'

'Money was all I had to give.'

'Sometimes,' Gideon Brenner said as he steered her towards the waiting cab, 'I don't understand the way women's minds work.'

Jem Moncrieff's small boatyard lay to the east of Greenock, between Custom House Quay and Garvel Point. Fortunately, Annis thought as she hurried along, head down against a chill easterly wind, it was too far along for Douglas to take much heed of it. Otherwise he might well have seen his wife and his nephew calling on Jem. Of late, as Douglas's temper grew shorter, both Robert and Annis had become more inclined to seek shelter with Jem. She slipped in through the gates, casting a guilty backward glance along the street. The small yard echoed to the sound of hammers and saws. Two men were working on the small 'shipyard' schooner, one of a series of small ships that Jem kept on the stocks so that between orders his men had work to do: a brigantine, almost ready for launching, was on the stocks in the main area. Three men, in thin jackets despite the cold January wind, balanced easily on the narrow scaffolding that surrounded her.

Jem and Robert were nowhere to be seen. Annis, glad to be out of the wind's reach, went into the large shed and gathered her skirts into one hand before beginning the climb to the loft above. All about her as she ascended the wooden staircase was a rich mixture of smells . . . the timber that was stacked on the ground floor of the building, glue, tar, chalk and canvas. Used to the continuous aroma of beeswax and dust and washing soda and cooking, she breathed the boatyard air deeply into her lungs and felt the better for it.

Jem and Robert were in the loft with another two men. Jem was on his knees tracing out a design on chalk on the great expanse of floor. Robert stood by his side, his pencil flying over a sketchbook balanced between the crook of his left elbow and his hand. At a long rough table at one end of the loft a half-model had been propped against the wall. Beside it were several large sheets of paper covered, Annis knew from experience, with details of a new design. The other two men were nailing narrow battens into the loft floor, following the chalk lines.

Annis hesitated at the top of the stairs, unwilling to disturb the men at their work.

'If he'd just agree to this . . . and this . . . ' Robert was saying earnestly. 'D'you see what I mean?'

He stooped down to his kinsman. Jem looked carefully at the sketches and nodded.

'I see just what you mean, lad, but I doubt if Mr Grieve'll see it. You're cutting back on space in his holds.'

'But giving him a faster ship . . . and a safer one,' Robert protested just as Jem looked up and saw Annis. A smile swept the frown of concentration from his face. He got to his feet, dusting chalk from his trousers with a few casual sweeps of his big capable hands, and came over to her, followed by Robert. The other two men went on working without looking up.

'I'm late home,' Robert said in swift, guilty apology as he reached his aunt.

'You are that. It's getting dark and your Uncle Douglas will be back within the hour, expecting to find you studying in your room.'

'I wanted to show Jem these alterations to the new ship.'

'You've got another commission?' Annis asked with pleasure, smiling at the older man. She knew that Jem had been worried about the lack of orders recently.

'Aye.' Neither Jem nor Robert looked cheerful about it.

'What's amiss?'

'The design's terrible,' Robert burst out. 'The man doesnae know what he's about at all!'

'Does not know,' Annis corrected him without thinking, and could have bitten her tongue off when he turned scarlet and shot an embarrassed glance at Jem.

'Tell me about it,' she said to atone for her blunder.

'He's a merchant in one of the big houses on the hill. A man by the name of Grieve.'

'He's not long in the area,' Jem chimed in. 'He's commissioned a ship to trade between here and America. But I'm not happy about it, and neither was Robert when I asked him to have a look at the plans.'

Annis was pleased to see that the man-to-man reference brought another blush, this time of pleasure, to the boy's cheeks.

'Why not?'

Jem frowned and ran a hand over his greying beard. 'To my mind his designer's given more thought to the size of the holds than to the lines of the vessel. Robert agrees with me, but not a blind bit of notice will Grieve pay to what I have to say. These men,' said Jem bitterly, 'never go to sea themselves, so they have no knowledge of what it takes to sail a ship from one end of the world to the other.'

'They sit on the land, safe and sound.' Robert's voice

was scathing. 'And all they can think of is the added profits they'll make on every extra pound of cargo they can squeeze aboard.'

She couldn't help but smile at the boy's worldly air and as Jem took over the tale Annis was struck by the family resemblance between them and, more than that, the way they seemed to fit together. She had never noticed that with Douglas and Robert — with them, physical similarities appeared to be coincidental.

'He plans to take goods to America and ship cotton back here. A gross of cotton takes up a hundred cubic feet of space in the holds. As he sees it, the larger the holds, the more cotton he'll be able to ship back in one voyage.'

'If you think his design's bad, refuse to do it.'

Jem gave her a bleak smile and for a moment his resemblance to Douglas was strong. 'That's what's sticking in my throat. I disapprove, but I cannae afford to turn him down, lassie. In my own way I'm selling myself for money just as he's selling the lives of seamen.'

For a moment the three of them stood locked in glum thought, then Annis recalled her reason for hurrying along to the boatyard. 'Robert, you must get back home before your uncle arrives.'

The boy nodded and thrust his sketchbook into Jem's hands. 'I'll leave this with you. It's safer here.'

'I'll follow you in a few minutes. You can make better time on your own.'

Robert hesitated at the top of the stairs, frowning. 'It's getting dark . . .'

'Oh tush! I'll be fine walking back on my own. Get along with you now!'

As the clatter of the boy's boots echoed on the wooden

stairs, Jem led Annis into the tiny boarded-off corner that he used as an office. There was just room for a small table, a plain wooden chair, and a three-legged stool. Every surface was piled with papers and notebooks, and more papers hung on nails hammered into the walls.

He cleared the chair, adding its contents to the pile on the table, and placed it for Annis with all the style and grace of a gentleman. Then he perched himself on a free corner of the table.

'You know, Annis, Robert's ideas for the new vessel are sound. He's got the makings of a fine designer.'

'Douglas is determined to take him into the office when he finishes his schooling in the summer.'

Jem's arms spread out as far as they could in the little cubby-hole where they sat, to indicate the loft and the yard below. 'This is the work he wants to do. And he'd be good at it, far better than I ever was. He'd make a success of it, I'm certain of that. It's cruel to force another human being to bend to your will.'

'I know that, but what can I do about it? I wish,' said Annis impulsively, 'that Douglas was more like you.' As soon as the words were out of her mouth she regretted them. No wife should speak against her husband, especially to another man, and his kinsman to boot.

But Jem, instead of being shocked or surprised, only laughed. 'Never say that. Douglas is a successful man with a fine house. You'd surely not want him to be a struggling boat-builder living in lodgings?'

She had meant that she wished Douglas had his cousin's gentleness, his understanding and quiet, affectionate courtesy. Both had the long Moncrieff face and brown, heavy-lidded eyes — and yet they were so unlike each other in temperament. Where Douglas was aloof, Jem was open and easy. His eyes sparkled with life and his shoulders were square and ready to carry the weight of the world, while Douglas's back was stooped with desk-work. Jem was filled with vitality, Douglas with self-respect.

'If only you and Douglas could be friends, perhaps he'd listen to you.'

Jem shrugged. 'Men change as they get older, Annis. For now Robert must just do as his uncle wants, and perhaps one day when he's grown to manhood he'll be able to follow his own inclinations.'

For a moment there was silence in the little office. The sound of men's voices carried from the other side of the wooden partition. A gust of wind made the building shake and groan and some papers rose lazily from the desk and eddied round the room, riding on a current of air. They both hurried to collect them.

'God protect the men at sea tonight,' Annis said as the wind moaned outside.

'If it's the *Grace and Charity* you have in mind I'm thinking that there's no need to fear. Brenner'll bring her home safely.' He stacked the wayward papers and anchored them with a hammer. 'Did you know that our Yankee friend's trying to get Douglas to let him take the *Grace and Charity* to Australia?'

'Do you think Douglas should agree?'

'I do. Brenner's right when he says that the clipper was built for longer voyages than she's doing now. Not that he's only thinking of Douglas's pocket,' he added shrewdly. 'Your sister's in Australia, isn't she? I gather Gideon likes the cut of her jib.'

Pain stabbed through Annis, but she forced a smile to her face and said flippantly, 'He does . . . and she

164

set all sails for Australia when she heard about it.'

Jem's weather-beaten face cracked into a broad grin, and then a laugh that was so infectious that Annis had to join in. But after a moment the laughter drained from her. 'But he's found consolation with Adeline Fraser.'

'Aye.' Jem, too, sobered. 'He'll have to watch her, for she's a hard-mouthed trouble-maker, that one. The sight of you always makes me wish I'd married again after I lost Kirsty . . . but the sight of Adeline always makes me glad I'm single,' he added, and teased a smile back to her face.

'Why didn't you marry again, Jem?' Annis had long wondered why such a gentle man had never found a second wife.

'Och . . . I just never seemed to get round to it. I was never good at courting. Besides, I'd my work to keep me busy.'

'I wish Douglas had commissioned his new ship from you, Jem. Then you'd not have to build ships you disapprove of, like this new one.'

He covered her hand with his in a warm, comforting clasp. 'Never fret yourself about me, lassie. I'll manage fine. And Douglas made a good purchase . . . the *Grace and Charity*'s a bonny vessel. It's a pleasure to watch her going by the yard.'

'Gideon — Captain Brenner — tells me he's been trying to get you to sail your schooner when it's completed, instead of selling it.'

'He's got almost as good a sense of money as your husband. But och, what would I want with a ship at sea? I'm a builder, not a merchant.'

One of the men tapped apologetically on the wall of the office and as Jem went to solve a problem that had arisen Annis hurried down the staircase and out into the night. The darkening sky was ominous and beyond the yard angry white-capped waves hurried one after another towards the mouth of the Firth.

Annis, grateful for her thick, warm jacket, went quickly towards home. As she walked, she recalled the pain she had felt when Jem mentioned Gideon's continued love for Olivia. Slowly, reluctantly, she was being forced to acknowledge her resentment against her sister, who still held the American in thrall, even though she was at the other end of the world.

Had she herself been wooed by Gideon Brenner, Annis thought, she would have considered herself a fortunate woman. Nothing would have torn her from his side.

She stopped short on the footpath, dismayed, reaching out for the thought of Douglas and holding it close for comfort. But there was no comfort there, not any more. Gradually, without her being aware of it, her love for Douglas had loosened its grip and begun to fade, spurred on by his behaviour towards Janet two months earlier. It was Gideon who had gone with her to see the girl, not Douglas, she thought drearily as she started walking again. Gideon — who thought only of Olivia.

Enveloped in confusion and misery she reached the house in time to take off her outdoor clothes and smooth her hair before Douglas arrived. When he came in she lifted her face for his kiss, as usual, and knew that it no longer meant anything to her.

By the time the *Grace and Charity* returned to Greenock Annis had more to worry her than the way her emotions were torn between her husband and his shipmaster. The clipper sailed in on a March morning when the clouds hung so low that their full grey-clad bosoms almost rested on the folded arms of the sullen, restless sea. The small town of Helensburgh on the far shore had been hidden from sight for most of the day, but in the afternoon a slice of brightness came into the west between sea and sky, and within an hour the dark clouds had begun to roll back towards the east.

The sea calmed, and its slate grey took on a broad gleaming band of pewter as the sun, still hidden behind clouds, managed to make its presence felt. Another thirty minutes and the sun was through, the pewter band turning to sparkling silver, then gold as the last of the lowering clouds moved off to torment someone else, somewhere else.

Annis stood at the window of her bedroom, Olivia's latest letter in her hand, and waited for Gideon's visit. He would come as soon as he was free, seeking news of her sister. She knew beyond all doubt that he would come, and wished with all her heart that this time he would stay away so that she would never have to say the words that would break his heart.

But come he did, hurrying along the pavement with his long stride, skimming lightly up the steps, not looking up to where she stood at the window. She sighed and left the room, meeting the maid on the stairs.

Gideon's presence, as always, filled and brightened the parlour. The scent of fresh salty air clung to his broad shoulders and crisply curling hair. He looked strong and heart-stoppingly handsome, but this time Annis took no pleasure in his company.

He knew from one look at her face that she had bad news for him. His eyes darkened.

'Olivia . . .'

Annis wondered if Douglas would look so stricken on her behalf. 'Perhaps there's a more gentle way of telling you, Captain Brenner, but for the life of me I can't think of it. Olivia is married.'

He stared at her, a hard, cold emerald stare. His lips parted, closed, parted again. 'Married, you say? But how could this happen so quickly?'

'She met her . . . husband . . . at her employer's house and they were married within two weeks. His home is in New South Wales, in sheep-farming country.'

'I see,' Gideon Brenner said carefully, formally. He walked to the fireplace and stood staring into the flames for a moment. Annis had to fight the impulse to go to him, just as she had had to fight it the day he heard that Olivia had left Greenock. Finally he turned and said, as though speaking through numbed lips, 'I trust that she's happy?'

'She seems to be. Her husband's family own a great deal of land. They're very wealthy. Here . . .' She held out the letter. 'Read this, if you wish.'

'They would be wealthy,' he said with a hard note in his voice. 'When next you write perhaps you would convey my congratulations to your sister.'

'Captain Brenner, I'm very sorry.'

'No need to be sorry, ma'am.' He looked as though someone had lashed him across the face with a whip, but his eyes, after the first blaze of shock and incomprehension, were now hooded, his shoulders squared. He didn't seek sympathy, certainly not from Olivia's sister.

'You'll take some tea?' she said foolishly, in a vain bid to keep him with her for a little longer.

'No, thank you. I'll trouble you no further,' he said

abruptly, and left, striding out of the house and down the steps without a backward glance. Following him, standing helplessly on the top step, she saw him brush with only a muttered greeting past Douglas, who was coming in the gate.

'What did you say to Brenner to put that fierce look on his face?' Douglas wanted to know when he joined his wife.

'He came seeking news of Olivia.'

'And you told him that she had found herself a suitable husband. Perhaps he'll stop calling on you now that she's out of his reach.'

'He cares very much for Olivia,' Annis protested. 'It was a great blow to him . . .'

'He'll survive.' Douglas's voice held no sympathy. 'Come inside before you catch a chill.'

Gideon Brenner had disappeared into the dusk, walking on the road, covering the ground with long strong strides. Annis turned and did as Douglas bid, closing the stained-glass door behind her, hating Olivia with a fierce, fiery hatred.

Now there was no longer any reason for the shipmaster to visit her. At that thought the loneliness that was never far away came back, welling up in her until the pain was almost too much to bear.

'Your supper's spoiled,' Adeline Fraser informed her employer when he stepped into the comfortable tenement flat he had rented in Bank Street. 'I expected you back a good two hours since. Where have you been?'

'Mind your own business,' he snapped at her. 'Just bring the food. And a jug of ale.'

When she did as she was told, clattering the plate and

jug down on the wooden table, he was standing before the fire, staring at the opposite wall without seeing it.

He had walked up into the hills after leaving Douglas Moncrieff's house, climbing over drystone dykes, pushing his way through ferns and bushes, oblivious of everything but the news he had just heard.

Finally, when the lights of the houses below and the ships on the river twinkled up at him through the darkness, he had made his way back home, for there was nowhere else for him to go.

Briefly, he felt a desire to visit Annis Moncrieff again, to talk to her about Olivia. But her dark-browed husband and that shrew of a sister of his would be home now, and Gideon, no fool, had begun to realize that Douglas Moncrieff didn't welcome social visits from his employees.

'You've torn your coat,' Adeline said as he moved towards the table. 'Take if off and I'll stitch it for you.' Gideon said nothing. 'You'll have been visiting Mistress Moncrieff?' Adeline added slyly as she helped him out of his coat.

'What's that to you?'

'You'll have heard that Miss Olivia's found herself a fine rich man in Australia? She'll be happy at last. Money's all that one ever wanted.'

'Women,' said Gideon roughly, 'are all alike. Why don't you get to bed.'

She paused by the door, one hand on her hip. 'And which bed am I to sleep in tonight . . . sir?'

The thought of sharing a bed with her that night, with Olivia so strongly in his mind, was repellant. 'Your own,' he growled at her, and she flounced out of the room.

On the way down from the hills he had been hungry.

Left alone, he filled his glass from the jug and ate only a little of the food before pushing the plate away. Adeline was an indifferent cook, but like every other seaman Gideon Brenner had developed a strong stomach and the ability to eat almost anything. Tonight, though, the stale meal was more than he could cope with. He retired to his chair by the fire with the jug and glass and stayed there, staring into the flames, until the jug was empty. He opened his mouth to yell for Adeline to run and fetch more ale, then remembered that she had long since retired. Slowly, he got to his feet and poked at the dying fire. The embers collapsed and retreated, rattling down through the bars and into the ash-pan below. Gideon put out the lamp and went to his room.

At the door he hesitated, then let his hand drop from the handle. He moved further along the passage to his house-keeper's bedroom, opened it, and stepped inside to where she waited for him.

9

The horse-drawn buggy halted at the top of the slope and John Mundy pointed with his whip.

'There it is. That's Vanduara.'

Olivia, every bone aching from the uncomfortable night spent in a sheepman's hut and from the jolting she had endured since dawn, waved the persistent flies away and looked down into the valley below.

Her eyes widened; all at once her exhaustion vanished and the terrible journey from Melbourne was worthwhile.

'But that's a small town!'

'No, it's all the one station.'

'You mean it all belongs to you?'

'To my father.'

He clicked his tongue and the horses began to make their way down into the valley. The wagon that had been sent out to meet them at the final stage-coach station lumbered along at the back, carrying their luggage.

Defying the hot dry country surrounding it, Vanduara, the Mundy sheep station, sprawled around a large lake that shimmered red-gold beneath the setting sun. There was a vast matchstick clutter of sheep pens near the lake and wooden buildings of varying sizes were scattered over a wide area.

On a low bluff on the other side of the lake, almost

opposite the cart that was now half-way down the hill into the valley, stood a fine verandahed house, its windows catching and reflecting the sun. A neat garden lay before the house; behind it Olivia could make out a large square courtyard bordered with rows of wooden buildings.

As the cart approached the station a knot of black-skinned people came running to stare. Olivia knew from the little John had told her of the station that unlike many white landowners Jeremiah Mundy had a good relationship with the local aborigine tribe. They lived on the station and in return for their labour — the men with the sheep, the women in the big house and its garden — Mundy looked after them with the benevolence of a local squire. She liked the idea of being part of the squire's family.

As they skirted the lake the black driver of the wagon called out shrilly to the group that awaited them. The women and children retreated in a giggling mass as the buggy reached them, but the men held their ground. One of them stepped forward and took hold of the horse as the buggy came to a standstill. Olivia recognized him as a man who had met them at their overnight stop and ridden ahead that morning. He had terrified her when he first stepped into the glow of their camp-fire, his black skin gleaming, his eyes flashing. She had screamed and John had laughed.

'G'day, Luke,' he said now, cheerfully, 'The old man in the house?'

Luke nodded, his dark eyes on Olivia, his teeth gleaming in a broad grin. She flushed, convinced that there was mockery in his face.

John jumped down and helped her to the ground. Her

joints seemed to have seized up and to her embarrassment she had to cling to him for a moment. She had endured a terrible journey from Melbourne, first by train, then stage-coach.

She was heartily tired of sleeping at rough little wayside stations, and to her horror, being on Mundy land, they had had to spend the previous night in a hut built for the sheepmen, sleeping on grass mattresses placed over wooden boards.

'We'd better go and pay our respects.'

'No! I can't let anyone see me like this!'

'You look fine to me,' said John and she glared at him.

'I'm covered with dust, I'm hot, my hair's a mess . . .'

'Nonsense. He'll be waiting,' said her husband, and she had no option but to walk to the house by his side, trying hard not to hobble like an old woman.

Perspiration trickled and tickled between her breasts as she began to climb the broad flight of wooden stairs to the verandah. It was a relief to reach the top step and gain the shade offered by the roof overhead.

Before Olivia had the opportunity to look about her, Jeremiah Mundy appeared through the double doors that led from the house.

'You've arrived, then,' he said briefly to his son. 'Luke told me you'd found yourself a wife. This her?'

Olivia drew herself up, straightened her back and advanced on her father-in-law, a gloved hand outstretched. 'How do you do, Mr Mundy?'

The man before her was about her own height, not as tall as John, but stockier. Although his hair was grey and his face lined, there was an impression of great strength about him — strength of mind as well as body.

He took time to study Olivia before responding to her

greeting. Determined not to let him see her nervousness she stood still, hand out — like a stranger approaching a suspicious dog, she suddenly thought — and waited while his cool brown eyes moved from the crown of her little blue feathered hat, over her face and the crumpled blue travelling dress she had been wearing for the past twenty-four hours to the dusty tips of her shoes then back again to her face.

'How d'ye do?' he said at last and took her hand in a firm grip for a moment. Then he released it and said to his son, 'You can put your things in the room at the back for the moment. We'll eat in an hour.'

Without another word to either of them he turned away and stumped down the stairs to the garden.

Five minutes later Olivia's annoyance at her father-in-law's abrupt welcome faded as she inspected the pleasant, comfortable room assigned to them.

'It's perfect,' she said with relief, taking in the plain sturdy furniture, the lace curtains at the windows, the wide, comfortable-looking bed with the mosquito net looped above it. As they had travelled deeper into the outback she had begun to worry about the sort of place she was going to. But this was very civilized indeed.

'It's all right.' John, watching her move about the room, sounded awkward.

'It'll do very well. It was kind of your father to give us such a pleasant room,' she reprimanded him, surprised by his ingratitude. But he didn't meet her eyes, turning instead with relief to a shy, giggling aborigine woman who had just come into the room.

'This is Betta, one of the maids.'

'Tub ready for new missis,' the woman mumbled and disappeared on a musical trill of laughter, leaving John to lead his wife to a small apartment where a filled hip-bath waited.

Bathed and dressed in a fresh gown, her hair well brushed and pinned up, happy in the knowledge that that night she would sleep in a proper bed, Olivia walked confidently by her husband's side to the large dining room where Jeremiah, in a fresh white linen shirt, waited for them. As soon as his son and daughter-in-law came in he unlocked the rolled top of a writing bureau that stood against one wall. Then he beckoned.

'What d'ye think of this?'

Olivia moved to stand by his side, and caught her breath in involuntary astonishment. The interior of the bureau held two rows of small boxes lined in white or black silk. Each box held a piece of jewellery or a stone on its own mounting. In the semi-gloom of the bureau most of the gems sparkled with hidden fire. Even the few that were white had an elusive silvery glow to their depths, with tiny pinpoints of colour.

'Opals,' Jeremiah Mundy said with satisfaction. 'The finest found in this part of Australia, and all from my land. And this is the best of the lot.'

His broad calloused hand lifted the largest precious stone from its box. The last of the day's sunlight, spilling into the room, glittered on the fine gold chain that the opal was suspended from. Then the light caught the opal itself and it was as though the stone had suddenly burst into fire.

Mundy supported it on the palm of his free hand, moving it gently to show how the colours hidden in the depths of the stone — blues and greens and yellows, but mainly crimson, appeared and disappeared in a tantalizing instant, gone before they could be seen properly, then reappearing.

'Let me see it on her.'

John took the pendant from his father and fastened it round Olivia's neck. As soon as his hands had fallen away she went to the nearest mirror and looked into it.

It was fortunate that she had chosen to put on a low-necked gown of pale yellow silk and lace. The opal pendant, resting on the white skin just below the hollow at the base of her throat, was shown to its best advantage. As Olivia's bosom rose and fell the stone sparkled like a small blazing fire against her smooth skin.

'It's a harlequin opal, the most widely prized of the opals found so far in Australia and a fine specimen. And it was found right here, on Vanduara land. I had it polished and mounted by the best craftsmen in New South Wales. Worth a fortune.'

He studied her in silence for a moment, then to her disappointment said, 'You can take it off now.'

Olivia bowed her head and put a hand to the stone, holding it in place until the thin gold chain was loosened. When she opened her fingers the opal flashed at her from the palm of her hand.

Reluctantly she held it out to Mundy, who placed it in its box, arranging it carefully against the white satin. Then he lifted a ring from a smaller box to one side of the bureau. 'This is for you, if it fits. Try it on her, John.'

John, obviously used to obeying his father without question, took his wife's left hand in his and slid the ring over the plain gold band he had put on her third finger the day they were married. This stone was disappointingly small; it was a milky white opal, but as Olivia moved her hand tiny pinpoints of blue and green and red and silver flashed up at her from the heart of the stone. The ring fitted well, and Jeremiah Mundy nodded with approval when she mutely held her slender white hand out for his inspection.

'Thank you, it's beautiful.'

'Take care of it. Opals are soft, they scratch easily. You can have that one . . . for as long as you might be married to my son,' he said.

Before she had more than a moment to wonder why he had said such a strange thing, the door leading into the dining room from the hall was thrown open and a tall, rangy man with a handsome face framed by thick black hair strode in.

'You're late, Matthew,' Jeremiah Mundy barked irritably.

'I was back later than I expected. And I had to take time to change; I knew you'd not take kindly to me appearing at the table in my riding clothes.'

The newcomer, casually elegant in a snowy white shirt and black trousers and jacket, nodded at John, then turned to survey Olivia with open curiosity. His face was broader than John's, and stronger, though lacking John's humour. He wore a moustache, but his chin was clean-shaven and his mouth hard. She knew from one look at his dark eyes, which had his father's coolness and arrogance, that he was Jeremiah's older son, Matthew.

'So . . .' he drawled, 'you've found yourself a wife at last, Johnny.'

'I have, Matt.' There was an edge to John's voice that Olivia had never heard before. Obviously there was little love lost between the Mundy brothers. 'And unlike you, I intend to keep her.'

Sudden anger flared into Matthew Mundy's eyes and

Olivia was reminded of the sparks of red fire that had blazed from the heart of his father's most treasured opal.

'Hold your tongues, the pair of you!' Jeremiah said impatiently, seating himself at the head of the long table and ringing a small handbell. 'I've waited long enough for my food. Matthew, greet your brother's wife properly and be done with it!'

Like his father's, Matthew's handshake was brief but firm; he released her fingers almost at once and seated himself in his chair as the door opened and Betta brought in the first course.

The food was delicious but Olivia found herself too tired to do it justice. The men talked around her as one course followed another, the initial burst of anger between John and his brother apparently forgotten as he narrated the results of his business visit to Melbourne and his father and older brother gave him news of what had happened on the station during his absence.

A change had come over John since his return to his home. His air of awkwardness had gone; as the meal went on he sprawled back in his chair talking and listening, occasionally laughing, paying scant attention to Olivia. Once or twice she looked up from her plate to see Matthew Mundy's sharp eyes studying her. Each time he met her gaze calmly and stared her down.

Apart from proudly telling her that he had the best Chinese cook in New South Wales, Jeremiah behaved as though she wasn't there at all, and she was left to her own thoughts. After some difficulty she placed Jeremiah's accent as somewhere between the Australian drawl and southern Irish, and realized that although his sons had been born in Australia he himself must have begun life at the other side of the world.

A burst of loud laughter startled her and made her shift suddenly in her chair. To her embarrassment she realized that she had fallen into a light doze.

'Take your wife to her room, John, before she falls asleep altogether,' Jeremiah said, impatiently adding, 'and you can fetch a bottle of the new port, Matthew. I've a mind to sample it.'

The bed had been turned down and the mosquito netting released to hang all round it. Having done his duty and escorted his wife from the table, John left her alone to undress and fall thankfully on to the soft mattress.

For a while she fought sleep, aware of the bulk of the large comfortable house around her, comparing it with the smaller house she and John had stayed in during the night before they drove on to Mundy land.

The house, wooden and verandahed like Vanduara, but much plainer, belonged to Albert Platt, owner of a small sheep station. His wife Drina had made her guests welcome, finding room for them despite the size of the house and the fact that she had three teenage sons, and inundating Olivia with questions about her past while the men were outside.

'You have to excuse the curiosity,' she had said at last with a broad smile. 'We see visitors so rarely that I can't stop talking and asking questions when we do.' Then she added cautiously, 'I expect John's told you all about his family?'

'Of course,' Olivia had lied. 'I believe that Mr Mundy's the largest landowner in the district.'

'My word, he is! He sold us this land, and it was like a drop in the bucket as far as he's concerned.'

Olivia had looked around the room they sat in,

181

spotlessly clean but plain, with little furniture. 'Have you seen his house?'

'Sure. We drive over there now and again, when Albert has business with the old man. It's beautiful . . . I hear that it was completely rebuilt when Mr Mundy began to make his money. Maybe one day . . .' She looked round her own small home, shrugged and sighed, then said, 'It'll be nice to have a woman at Vanduara again. There's not been one for . . . for a while.'

'You must come and visit us,' Olivia said graciously, taking her place as the hostess of the big house at Vanduara.

Drina had given her a doubtful look, then changed the subject.

She would invite Drina Platt over soon, Olivia decided now as sleep rolled over her like a soft dark cushion. She knew nothing more until John came to bed some time later, slipping under the mosquito net to join her, waking her with his hands and mouth and urgent body. Remembering that they weren't alone in the house she drew back. 'Your father and brother . . . they might hear us.'

'I want them to,' said John, and pulled her close.

When he finally turned away from her, sated, she realized that the small opal ring had turned on her finger. She shifted her position to straighten it.

'What happened to Matthew's wife?' she asked into the darkness.

'Took off with a sheepman going back to Sidney. She couldn't take any more of Matt.' There was sleepy satisfaction in his voice.

'Did he follow her?'

He gave a snort of laughter. 'Not him. He'd not beg any woman to come back to him.'

'What was she like?'

There was a pause, then he said, as though remembering after a long time, 'Red hair. Like a sunset. Green eyes. And a temper that would have made the devil cringe. The old man liked her fire, though.'

'Did she ever wear the opal pendant?'

'Sometimes, when the old man was in a good mood. He gave her a brooch, just as he gave you the ring. He was sorry afterwards, though, because she took it with her when she went off.'

'The pendant's beautiful.'

'It looked good on you,' John said, remembering. He reached out to circle the spot where the pendant had rested with the tip of one finger. 'If he takes to you the way he took to her he might let you wear it now and again.'

He gave a huge yawn and fell asleep, his hand cupping her breast possessively. Olivia, suddenly wakeful, lay staring at the grey oblongs of window for a while, her mind busy.

She wanted that opal more than she had wanted anything for a long time. She must be pleasant to Jeremiah Mundy. And she must write to Annis the very next day, describing the big house where she now lived and the fiery gemstones found on Vanduara land.

Douglas and Tib, she reflected with a smile, would be beside themselves with envy.

John twitched in his sleep and his hand closed convulsively on her breast. The nipple tautened in response and despite the heat Olivia turned over to snuggle against his lithe naked body. She had made a better marriage than Annis had, in every way.

*   *   *

John woke her on the following morning, shaking her out of a pleasant dreamless sleep.

'Time to get up if you want any tucker. Chang's got the men's noonday meal to cook.'

He was dressed in a rough checked shirt, open-necked, with his trousers tucked into high riding boots. It was the first time she had seen him in his usual attire, and the first time he had looked at ease.

She groaned and buried her head in the pillow. The bedsheet was unceremoniously hauled from her curled body. 'I've been working outside for three hours. We rise early on Vanduara, it's something you'll have to get used to.' He smacked her lightly on the rump.

'John!' She shot upright in bed, her hair tangled about her furious face. His eyes moved to her bare breasts and the tip of his tongue moistened his lips, then he shrugged and said blithely, 'Ten minutes. There's water in the basin there,' then swung out of the room.

Her first instinct was to burrow back into the bed again, then she remembered her decision to be particularly pleasant to Jeremiah Mundy and realised that an appearance at the breakfast table would be to her credit.

Just under ten minutes later, wearing a sprigged muslin gown with a demure high neck, she walked into the dining room and said cheerfully, 'Good morning!'

The four men at the table looked up. One of them, a slightly built man with greying brown hair, got to his feet, while Jeremiah, John and Matthew Mundy stayed where they were.

'Too near to noon to be morning,' said Jeremiah abruptly. 'Half the work on the station's done by this time of day. Thought we'd let you loll in bed this once.

This is Lawrie Borland. He keeps an eye on the opal miners. John's wife Olivia.'

'How do you do, Mrs Mundy?' Borland's handshake was firm, his accent English. The men had all eaten, and their plates and empty cups were pushed aside. Spread on the table before Jeremiah were a few pieces of dull grey stone. As she took her seat Olivia glanced at them and glimpsed a sudden unexpected flash of colour.

'Are these opals?'

'That's right. I've just brought them in,' Borland told her smilingly, then turned back to Jeremiah, who was examining one of the lumps of stone. 'I reckon that one'll fetch a fair amount. The new seam's good . . . I told you it would be.'

'Hm. That nose of yours never lets you down, does it?'

'Your own nose does well enough. I've never found anything like the harlequin.'

'And never will. There's not likely to be two stones like that in the whole of the station.'

Betta set a covered dish before Olivia, then poured tea from the pot already on the table and shyly retired.

Olivia lifted the cover and found herself looking at two large fried potato cakes, each topped with a poached egg. Her stomach, used to a little toast first thing in the morning, gave an alarmed lurch. It gave a second lurch when she looked at the tea, which was strong and black. She pushed the plate and cup away and asked, 'Could you ring the bell, please?'

The men stopped talking and stared at her, Matthew with amusement and John with faint irritation. 'Eh?' said Jeremiah.

'I wondered if you could ring the bell and ask the serving-girl to bring me some toast and weak tea.'

The old man's face tightened. 'Listen to me, woman — in this house you'll eat and drink what you get and be grateful for it. My cook has thirty men to tend. He's not got time to prepare fancy snacks for you.'

Olivia looked at John for support, and found none. She got to her feet.

'Then please direct me to the kitchen and I'll attend to my own breakfast.'

A mirthless smile curled Matthew's mouth. He leaned back in his chair, his sharp eyes studying his father and his sister-in-law as they faced each other.

Like John and Jeremiah, he wore a casual shirt and trousers, and he managed to wear them as elegantly as he had worn his formal clothes the evening before.

'You'll not start taking over my kitchen and upsetting my servants, girl. You can do what you want once you're in your own house, but not in mine.'

'My own . . .' Olivia stared at the old man, bewildered. 'Surely John and I will be living here, under your roof.'

Jeremiah snorted. 'Indeed you won't. Once my sons get themselves wives they get out from under my roof. And since the food here's not to your liking the sooner you move out the better.'

He swept the rough opals into the palm of one hand and put them into one of the bureau drawers, saying over his shoulder as he did so, 'It's time you men were back at your work. Not you, John — best see to settling in. But finish with it as soon as you can. There's plenty to be done.'

He stumped out, followed by Matthew and Lawrie Borland, who shot a sympathetic smile at Olivia as he left.

'I don't understand,' she said feebly. 'I thought that the room we used last night was to be ours.'

John shuffled his booted feet. 'I should've told you yesterday . . . that was just for last night. The old man refuses to have women running his house and changing things. When Matt married he was given a place on the station. The same goes for us.'

'I thought that your brother lived here, in this house?'

'He does now. Not when he had a wife.'

Olivia saw her dreams of living in luxury in the big house crumble and die. 'Where . . .?'

'I'll show you,' said John, picking up a broad-brimmed felt hat from the sideboard. 'Better put something on your head and bring that parasol of yours. I'll bring the buggy to the steps.'

The sun was high in the sky and leaving the shaded verandah was like walking into an oven. As she went down the stairs to the waiting buggy the glint of sunlight from the lake's surface seared Olivia's eyes and she tilted the parasol to shade them, then shook it irritably to chase the flies that at once surrounded her.

'That was all paddock when Matthew and I were small,' John said proudly as they drove along the water's edge, skirting groups of aborigine children squatting in the mud, playing happily. 'Father drilled down until he hit water. There must be an underground ocean down there. It's the reason why the station's done so well. He's bored wells all over the place . . . and found opals in the area that was no use for sheep. He stakes the miners who come in and in return they give him a share of the stones they find. Lawrie sees fair play. Over there,' he pointed to a huge open-sided building, 'is the shearing shed. That's the kitchen, kept separate from the house in case of fire. The men eat in the kitchen annexe. This is the buggy shed — the pig pens are over there, and the chooks we keep for their eggs have a place at the back of the house. That's the stable, and the smithy beside it . . .'

Olivia sat stiffly by his side, uninterested in his attempt to give her a guided tour. With each turn of the wheels taking her further away from the big house on the bluff her inner agitation increased.

The lake was almost a mile long, longer than she had first thought. The sheer size of the surrounding terrain had dwarfed everything when she first saw Vanduara from the slope above. The main house was situated at one end of the lake. At the far end John stopped and said 'This is it.'

'Where?' Olivia shaded her eyes again. All she could see on a slight rise before her was a cluster of trees partially sheltering a small, sad-looking little shack, a windmill marking the site of a well, and a building that was all roof right down to the ground.

'There.' John swung himself down from the buggy and raised his arms to her. Stunned, she allowed him to lift her down and lead her to the shack.

It was built of planking, with a roof of wooden shingles and a wide shady verandah on every side. Because it stood on a slope the front was raised on piles and a short flight of sagging wooden stairs led up to the verandah. Someone had had a garden once; a few plants and bushes still clung to the dry ground and a small fence had been put up to set the area apart from the rest of the land.

John pushed the door open and Olivia followed him into a medium-sized room that had once been a home, but had been neglected for some time. Faded curtains hung at the windows, there were shelves and cupboards round the walls and a rag rug on the floor by the big iron range that took up one side of the wall. A cushioned rocking chair stood on either side of the rug, pots and a skillet waited forlornly on the cold range and there was a plain wooden table with two chairs by it.

'This is the bedroom.' John opened the door to a second room, smaller than the first. It was dominated by a vast iron bedstead, but there was room for two cupboards and another rocking chair.

'The privy's out at the back and there's a windmill and well there. That,' he pointed out of the window at the roof squatting on the ground, 'is the half-cellar. You go to Chang and tell him what you want from the stores and he'll have it taken there. It keeps the food cool.'

'I'm not living here.' She glared at him implacably.

This time he met her gaze squarely. There was a hard set to his jawline.

'You are. We are.'

'It's . . . it's a hovel!'

'It's a damned sight better than some of the folk in this part of the world have to live in.'

Olivia stormed back into the living room and tugged at the curtains on one window. They came away in her hand with a dry ripping noise. A cloud of dust enveloped her.

'Look at the place, John!'

'It needs cleaning up, that's all. Nobody's lived in it since Matthew's wife left. There's bedding in the stores, and bolts of cloth that you can make up into curtains. There are brooms and dusters and soap and buckets for water . . .'

She fisted her hands on her hips and glared at him. 'I am not going to clean this place.'

He bit his lip then said levelly, 'Suit yourself. I'll not be here during the day, it doesn't bother me.'

'Take me back to Melbourne at once!'

'There won't be another visit to Melbourne for at least six months and I'm sure as hell,' said John, 'not going to make that journey just for you.'

'Then I'll go by myself.'

'Don't be a fool. You'd not last twelve hours on your own in the outback. Besides, the rains are due soon and if the creek beds fill you'll drown. We lost more than a hundred sheep and one man in a flash flood a few years back.'

'You deceived me! You told me that your family had money—'

'They do. But the old man had to work his way up and he reckons his sons should do the same. I see no reason to argue with that.'

'I do! Tell him that we have to stay in the main house.'

John rubbed a hand slowly over his jaw. 'If there's one thing my father taught me and Matt, it's to do as he says.'

'If you've not got the courage I'll do it for you!'

As she started to sweep past him he caught her arm in a tight grip. His face was hard, his voice quiet and intense. 'Listen to me, Olivia Mundy. You'll do as my father says and you'll hold your tongue. I'll not have the whole station laughing at me because my wife hasn't got the sense she was born with. And I'll not have Matt sneering.'

She was taken aback by the vehemence of his reply but she managed to snap back an answer. 'You can't make me stay here!'

He released her and stepped aside to give her access to the front door. 'You can walk out any time you like. But I've warned you what will happen if you try.' Then as she said nothing he moved to the door himself. 'I'll get bedding sent down from the main house. And your trunks. You can sort out what you want to wear and the rest can be sent back to the house for storage. You know how to cook, I suppose.'

'I've never had to cook. I'm used to having servants.'

'Not,' said John with amusement, 'in this house. Once the old man gets to know you – if he likes you well enough – we might be invited to move back in with him and Matt. In the meantime you'll be expected to cook for the two of us.'

He brushed past her to the range, where he took a thick exercise book out of a tin box.

'It was my mother's. She was a damned good cook, and she wrote all her recipes down.'

'I'm not going to cook!'

He shrugged. 'I can eat with the other men in the annexe. They'd not like a woman there, though. If you don't want to make meals you're going to go hungry.'

He went out and she heard him cross the verandah. Looking through the dirty window she saw him climb on to the buggy and lift the reins, turning the horse in the direction of the big house on the bluff.

Olivia let her rage go in a great scream of fury and threw the tin box across the room. It struck one wall and fell to the floor.

There was an answering chorus of shrieks from outside and she flew to the open door in a panic, ready to slam it shut. Beyond it she saw a flock of galahs, startled from the trees by her scream, wheeling against the blue sky and heading out over the lake. She had seen the white-backed birds on her way to Vanduara, had admired the display of their pink breasts when they were in flight. But today she was in no mood to take in the beauty of the shifting white and rose pattern against the sky as the birds launched themselves away from the house. Instead she slammed the door and ran to throw herself down on the bed, which gave out a great twanging of springs.

'Be quiet!' Olivia screamed, slamming a fist on the bed, which only twanged again. Then she burst into tears of rage and self-pity.

10

The *Grace and Charity* swung idly at anchor, her very
sails drugged by the South American heat.

On deck, seeking what shelter they could, members of
her crew either sprawled asleep, limbless as cats at rest,
or talked in low slow voices, some washing their clothes
in bucketsful of water scooped from the smooth blue-
green sea that dandled the clipper on its placid breast.

There were other sailing ships to keep the *Grace and
Charity* company; a string of them waiting to collect their
cargoes before taking up anchor and turning homewards.
On the shoreline not far away the huts and trees seemed
to tremble and waver in the heat rising from the ground.
The only movement to be seen was the slow steady
passage of a dinghy from land towards the waiting
vessels.

Gideon Brenner lowered his telescope and swept
perspiration from his brow. 'Fifteen days! Confound it,
we could rot here for all these people care!'

The mate spat into the water and stretched brawny
arms.

'The cargo'll be brought to the beach in time. They
know we can do nothing but wait.'

'I'm damned if I'll spend another day here.' Gideon
said shortly, his eyes fixed on the oncoming boat. 'If we

don't up anchor and head back to Scotland soon I'll have Douglas Moncrieff to answer to.'

Somebody in the well of the ship struck up a jaunty tune on an accordion. The music drifted pleasantly on the air, but Gideon, irritated beyond bearing with the heat and the waiting, was in no mind to enjoy it. He was waiting impatiently when his second mate scrambled aboard from the dinghy.

'Well?'

'No sign of the copper yet, Captain,' the man reported. 'They say it might be here tomorrow . . .'

'We've already waited for fifteen tomorrows!' Gideon spun away from him and strode to and fro, teeth gnawing his lower lip.

Then he closeted himself in the charthouse for a while before coming out and ordering, 'Set the sails, Mr Brown. We'll take the trade winds along the coast and aim for North America. We can pick up some cargo there and perhaps by the time we come back to Iquiqua they'll have produced the copper ore.'

The mate's mouth opened, then closed again. On board every sailing vessel the captain's word was law, and on any ship where Gideon Brenner was the master that rule was written in invisible letters of fire that hung over every man's head.

'Aye aye, sir,' he said and turned to yell, 'Man the yards! Stand by the capstan!'

The well-trained crew obeyed at once. Bare feet used to all weathers scudded over burning hot planks without noticing the heat. Gideon watched critically as the sails were trimmed and the headyards backed to act as a brake once the ship began to answer to the wind.

'Heave short!'

The men on the capstan bent their naked backs over the handle and started plodding round, bringing in as much cable as possible without dislodging the great anchor.

'Hove short, sir!' Brown shouted.

'Set the tops'ls,' Gideon thundered, exhilaration flooding him as he felt the ship begin to move beneath his feet.

Men and lads burned brown by exposure to the hot sun and just as happy as he was to be turning towards the open sea again swarmed up the rigging and swung themselves along the booms. The topsails, loosened from their ties, fluttered in the catspaw of wind then began to fill out, tugging at the ship far below like impatient dogs on a leash.

Another order and the anchor came up, freeing the *Grace and Charity*.

She eased herself out of the line of waiting ships and began to pivot eagerly away from the coast. The helmsmen hurried to take the big wheel as the backed foreyards swung the clipper about until she was facing the right direction. The anchor was secured temporarily at the cathead and the men who had been on the capstan ran to haul the foreyards round and set sail to catch the breeze as the ship moved seawards.

The sudden activity aboard the ship hadn't gone unnoticed. As she began to slide past her anchored companions one of the captains, a man Gideon knew well from Greenock, roared through cupped hands, 'Where away?'

'San Francisco, mebbe. There'll be a cargo for us there.'

'Moncrieff'll no like that.'

'He'd not like us sitting here doing nothing,' Gideon shouted back, and turned away, setting his face towards the sea, where the *Grace and Charity* belonged.

When word of his captain's activities reached him by way of a vessel that put into Greenock ahead of the *Grace and Charity*, Douglas Moncrieff was not at all pleased.

'That man thinks he can do whatever he may please!' he fumed to Annis when he returned home that evening.

'As the captain —'

'As the captain he's responsible to the owner. To me!' Douglas paced the parlour, too angry to sit down. 'Just because he brought the clipper over from America he thinks he can do as he pleases with her.'

'He's a good shipmaster. You said so yourself.'

Douglas eyed his wife suspiciously. 'You're awful anxious to speak up for the man. Is it because he's wormed his way into your affections?'

Annis felt hot colour rise into her face. 'How can you say that to your own wife! You know very well that I'd never . . .'

Douglas's face darkened. 'Sometimes women don't have the choice. A man as travelled and practised as Gideon Brenner knows how to get the better of an inexperienced child like yourself.'

'I'm not an inexperienced child, I'm a married woman with all her wits about her,' Annis snapped back, then bit her lip as he stared at her, brows raised.

'And a woman with an over-sharp tongue in her head, it seems.'

'I'm sorry, Douglas. But it vexed me to think that you could believe . . . ' She stopped.

'You know that that Fraser woman's living under his roof?'

The thought that for a man who frowned on gossip Douglas was well informed came unbidden to Annis's mind and was suppressed. 'As far as I know she's his house-keeper.'

'Humph! An unmarried man living on his own would've been well advised to find a house-keeper twice her age with warts or a hare lip if he wanted to avoid gossip. But Captain Brenner seems to thrive on notoriety. He's not the sort of man I care to have calling on my wife!'

Annis prudently held her tongue, though it wasn't easy. After a moment Douglas came across the room to take her in his arms.

'I'm sorry, lassie,' he said against her hair. 'I'd no right to voice my doubts about you and him. But it's always displeased me to know that he's made free of this house when I'm not in it.'

She rested her head on his chest, feeling the beginnings of a headache gripping at her temples. 'Captain Brenner only visited to hear news of Olivia, Douglas. He's not set foot in this house since he heard of her marriage.'

'And if he's wise, he'll not set foot in it again, unless it's by my invitation.'

'Douglas!' She tried to draw back but he wouldn't release her. 'There was never any question of wrong-doing, on his part or on mine. D'you think so little of my loyalty, let alone my common sense, as to believe that there could be?'

In answer Douglas bent his head and his lips nuzzled at her neck. 'I couldn't bear to lose you, Annis.' His voice was husky, unsure of itself. 'You mean everything to me.'

His sudden vulnerability caught at her heart and awakened the old fondness that he had almost driven out. 'You'll not lose me . . . you'll never lose me.' Then, when he had kissed her, she took advantage of the tender moment between them to say, 'I'd not want to lose you either, Douglas. Can you not see that that's why I want to have your child?'

His hands dropped from her shoulders and he turned away. 'I keep telling you that there's plenty of time for that yet.'

'But what if there's something wrong with me?' She voiced the anxiety that had been gnawing at her, burrowing deeper with each monthly bleeding. 'We've been wed for almost eighteen months now. What if I can't give you children, ever?'

'I'd not complain about that. Robert will take over the business from me when my time's over. We've no need for children, Annis.'

'But I want a child!' Then she said timidly into the silence, 'D'you think I should speak to Doctor Warwick?'

'Certainly not!' Colour jumped into his pale cheeks. 'I'll not have any man, doctor or no . . . I'll not hear any more of this nonsense, Annis!'

Afraid of a quarrel, she said no more. She must just go on waiting and hoping for the child she still so desperately wanted . . . more desperately than ever, now that she had lost both Olivia and Gideon. Robert was close to the age when he would leave school . . . another few years and he would be old enough to break free, as he still insisted he would. When that happened, Annis knew, she would be completely alone. If she could only have Douglas's child by then, life would be bearable.

But after the evening meal when she was sitting at the

parlour table writing a letter to Olivia, one of the phrases Douglas had used came back to trouble her. 'I'd no right to voice my doubts about you and him,' he had said, which meant that he had already been linking her name to Gideon Brenner's in his mind.

The pen stilled on the paper. She glanced at Douglas, who was studying the newspaper in his favourite fireside chair. Tib was at her sewing in the other fireside chair as usual, while Robert, under orders from his uncle, was studying in his bedroom as usual. Douglas's head was bent over the newspaper and the shadows cast by the gaslight on the wall above his chair deepened the lines on his face, making them look harsh and uncompromising. His mouth was pursed, with a distinct downturn at the corners.

He had aged since their marriage. The happiness that had tugged at the corners of his mouth and given a sparkle to his eyes had gone, and there was no denying that he had become harder on her and on Robert, always wanting to know where they were or what they had been doing if they were out. She had no reason to believe that he loved either of them any less, but recently, she realized with an uneasy shiver, his love had begun to take on a possessive edge, a desire to control those he cared for most.

God willing, Robert would be able to escape if he wished, when he was old enough to make his own way in life. But for herself there would be no escape.

As though feeling her eyes on him Douglas glanced up briefly and smiled at her. She realized with a start that her wayward thoughts were leading her astray, deceiving her into thinking of her marriage to this good man who only had her best interests at heart as a prison sentence.

She smiled back, turned to the letter, looked at the words, 'Dear Olivia', followed by a neat, brisk description of the weather, and wished that her sister was still in Greenock. It would have been comforting to have someone, another woman, to talk to sometimes. Now there was only Tib, and she was quite unapproachable.

She could, of course, tell Olivia in her letters of her anxiety over her childlessness, her loneliness, the bouts of panicky claustrophobia that had started with Janet's dismissal and made her long to hurry out of the house into the open air where she could draw breath. But Olivia, happy in her marriage to a man wealthy enough to give her everything she had ever wanted, would scorn such letters. And words written down could not be denied. They were there for all to see.

Annis tightened her lips and bent over the paper again.

'Life continues along the usual lines here,' she wrote, 'and as always I have so much to be thankful for . . .'

When the *Grace and Charity* sailed up the Clyde and arrived safely in Greenock, her holds filled with copper ore and timber, with more timber stacked on every available corner of her deck, Gideon Brenner and Douglas Moncrieff found themselves locked in a bitter quarrel.

Douglas's passion for Annis and its accompanying fear of losing her had gradually grown until he was tormented by jealousy. He had no illusions about his looks and he knew from his mirror that he had become old before his time. Normally this wouldn't have troubled him, but he had started to fret over Annis's opinions. She was so young, a mere child in his eyes: could she come to see him as old and dull? He had drawn back from going so far as to order Brenner not to visit his home during his absence because to do so would be to make Annis feel that he didn't trust her. He did, and yet each time he saw Gideon the man's undeniably good looks and his youthful confidence made Douglas feel a little older, a little slower. Surely someone as lovely and as innocent as Annis must be attracted to the shipmaster, even against her own better judgement?

The American's complete confidence in his own ability as a shipmaster, his unspoken refusal to bow to his employer's decision in all things, even his affection for the *Grace and Charity*, which he had known long before Douglas ever heard of the clipper, had begun to rankle. When the ship came back to Greenock, Douglas, beset by his jealousy and furious because everyone knew by that time that Brenner had flouted his orders, had made up his mind to give the shipmaster a sound dressing-down and be done with it. The young rip needed to learn a lesson. But to his surprise he found that Gideon, who had had a hazardous journey back to Scotland in poor weather, was in no mood to take criticism from a man who sat safely in his office and sent others to face danger so that he might make profits.

'The last time I had to cool my heels off the South American coast,' he reminded his employer crisply, his eyes green and cold as the icebergs that had threatened the *Grace and Charity* on her struggle back round Cape Horn, 'you told me that I should have gone further up the coast to take on timber. This time I did — and brought it back through seas that swept the cargo from the decks of other vessels — and again I find myself in the wrong.'

'I had a buyer for all the copper ore that you could ship back!'

'Is your buyer still eager?' Gideon asked, and Douglas flushed angrily.

'No sir, he is not! And why? Because other vessels brought ore in and he bought from them.'

'I wonder if you could have sold an entire cargo in any case? There were two other ships from this port lying at Iquiqua while I was there, all of us playing with our thumbs and broiling in the heat and wasting time.'

'It was your clear and bounden duty —'

'I'd no mind to lie there until the sun fried my crew's brains in their skulls, then race the others back. If the *Grace and Charity* had lost that race you'd have had a full load of ore and no buyer. As it is,' Gideon pointed out, heartily tired of the whole business of dancing to a merchant's tune, 'you've enough ore to sell and a good load of timber that you'll have no trouble in clearing.'

Douglas thumped his fist on the table. 'Do you presume to tell me how to run my business, sir?'

'Since you presume to tell me how to run my ship.'

'The *Grace and Charity* is my ship!'

'Not,' said Gideon coldly, 'while she's at sea. We were doing no good lying at anchor, waiting for those confounded shore-weasels to bring us the cargoes we'd been promised day after day. The decision to up anchor and search for other cargo was mine and mine alone. It was the right decision.'

'So you think that I should fill my ship's hold once more and send you off with no notion of when you'll choose to come back, or what you'll bring with you?'

A flash of anger crossed Gideon's face. 'I know my duty sir. I have never let you down and I never shall. But I ask you again, don't waste the *Grace and Charity* on the South American run. She was built for longer, faster

202

journeys. It's too late to make for China — the tea season's almost on us and the clippers will be waiting in Fouchow and Whampoa already. But Australia now . . . There's a fortune to be made in the wool trade, and I'm confident that the *Grace and Charity* could get there and back in record time.'

'It's not the first time you've urged that. You seem very eager to make the Australian run, Mr Brenner. Tell me, what benefit will such a journey bring to you?'

The sarcastic tones brought colour to the shipmaster's face. 'I'm thinking only of what's best for the clipper — and for you. Send me to Australia to seek your fortune, and I'll do it gladly.'

But Douglas Moncrieff was beyond rational thinking. Gideon's impertinence in answering him back instead of taking his punishment meekly had driven his employer to the brink of caution.

'Send you to Australia so that you can seek my wife's sister, you mean. You have the impertinence to think that I would do that, with the whole town already tattling about the woman you keep in your house? Not to mention,' he said, the bitter words forced from between his teeth, 'your persistent and unwanted visits to my own house, to my own wife.'

The colour drained from Brenner's face. The bones seemed to stand out beneath the skin, and his eyes blazed.

'Not only do you insult me, Mr Moncrieff, but you do your wife a great injustice,' he said at last, his voice so quiet that it could only just be heard. 'There seems little sense in continuing this . . . brawl. I bid you good day. Perhaps we can discuss our business some other time.'

'No other time.' Douglas's voice stopped him as he

reached the door. 'We have no further business, you and I. I intend to find a new shipmaster for the *Grace and Charity*; a man who knows how to do his employer's bidding and mind his tongue. If you care to call tomorrow my clerk will give you the moneys due to you.'

Gideon's hand, about to take hold of the door-handle, clenched into a fist, then slowly uncurled. He walked out of the office without another glance at Douglas Moncrieff, strode past the staring clerks, who must have heard their employer's final words and possibly some of his earlier ravings as well, and left the building.

His first thought was to go to Annis, to give her his apologies for any embarrassment that his visits may have caused. Then he realized that that was out of the question. It would only compromise her further in her husband's eyes.

He started to walk towards the harbour, then stopped. It was his custom and his duty to keep an eye on the unloading, but he didn't want to face his crew — his former crew, he reminded himself savagely — while such a white-hot rage simmered inside him. He would wait until the holds were empty and the crew had dispersed before he collected his belongings from the master's cabin.

Instead he swung round and made for Bank Street and home, turning into the street and striding up the hill past the old Bridewell and Sheriffs' Court, now vacated and forlorn in favour of new buildings in Nelson Street, without taking his eyes from the ground.

The house was silent, and at first when he let himself in he presumed that Adeline, who must know by this time that the clipper had arrived, had gone out to buy food for his evening meal. Then hearing a thump and a muffled exclamation from his own bedchamber he threw the door open and stood surveying the couple who had tumbled from the untidy bed and begun hurriedly, guiltily, to scramble into their clothes.

He had seen the man before; it was Sam McNair, the shifty-eyed dock rat who had caused so much trouble on the *Grace and Charity*'s voyage from Boston.

'Get out of my house,' Gideon said quietly, but with such contempt and soft menace in his voice that the two in the room flinched back.

'Cap'n . . .' McNair whined ingratiatingly, 'You know how a man can be tempted —'

'Shut your mouth, Sam McNair,' Adeline screeched, hauling her gown over her bare shanks, in too much of a hurry to put her drawers and her grimy petticoat on first. 'It was you wanted it, not me. I swear, sir, that he pestered me until —'

'Out, I said!' Gideon stepped to one side, leaving the doorway clear. The man, shirt unbuttoned and trousers held up in one hand, snatched at his ragged jacket and scurried out of the room, cringing away from the shipmaster as he passed.

'Wait!' Gideon's voice stopped him as he reached the front door. The shipmaster clamped a hand on Adeline's shoulder as she made to leave the room, her underwear bundled in her arms, and pushed her into the narrow hallway. She stumbled and almost fell against McNair, who was forced to catch and hold her.

'You forgot to take your doxy with you,' Brenner said.

'But . . . you'd not throw me out!'

For answer he walked past her into the tiny room that had been hers. In a moment he re-appeared, his arms filled with her dresses and shawls.

He thrust them at her and opened the door leading to the common stairway. 'Get out of my sight, the pair of you. And don't ever let me get within arm's reach of you again.'

Sam McNair went gladly, bolting on to the landing like a rabbit that had just escaped the claws of an eagle. Adeline, clutching her few belongings, whined, 'Sir . . . where can I go if you put me out of my home?'

'Go with him.' Brenner jerked his head towards McNair, who was already on his way downstairs. 'Go to the devil for all I care. But don't ever come back to me!'

She saw that he meant every word. Her expression changed, the pleading eyes narrowed into slits, the thin mouth hardening. 'Damn you, Gideon Brenner! I'll make you pay for this . . . I promise you I will!'

He shut the door in her face and walked back into his bedchamber, where he ripped the soiled linen from his bed and carried it to her room. He tossed it into a corner and added the sheets and blankets torn from the narrow cot there. Then he went back into the little parlour, reached for the brandy bottle, and changed his mind. He had seen too many men turn to drink to find the answers to their problems.

He walked to the window, noting when he got there that the panes were dull and dusty. Below, Sam McNair crossed the narrow cobbled street, head down and hands thrust into his pockets. He was followed by Adeline. On the far footpath Sam stopped and spat some words at her. Adeline dropped the clothes she was carrying and flew at him, her clawed hands fastening themselves into his lank sandy-coloured hair.

Gideon could hear her angry screeches and the man's howl of pain as he pushed her violently away. She aimed a kick at his shins and he skipped aside, then scuttled out of reach, making towards the nearest howff and possible safety.

Adeline scooped up her scattered clothes. When she straightened she looked up at the little window and for a long moment she and Gideon Brenner stared into each other's eyes. He saw her lips writhing and had a good idea of the foul things she was saying. Then she turned and hurried after McNair.

Gideon stood where he was, his eyes fixed unseeingly on the empty footpath opposite. He was sick with self-loathing. Adeline Fraser had made a fool out of him: Jem had tried to warn him, but stupidly, arrogantly, he had paid no heed because the woman's body had helped him to forget his longing for Olivia Kerr. He turned from the window, almost stumbling over a chair, kicking out at it and sending it spinning noisily across the floor. He had made a fool of himself over Olivia Kerr too . . . The Scottish air must have addled his brain, he told himself savagely. Olivia was gone, married to someone else, and that was an end of it. Unable to accept the truth until now, he had hung around her sister's house, almost begging for news of Olivia just as a homeless cur might beg for food. And what was the result of that? As well as embarrassing Annis Moncrieff, something he deeply regretted, he had alienated her husband, his employer. And then he had allowed that same man to goad him into a quarrel that had deprived him of the only thing he had left — the *Grace and Charity*. He cursed the arrogance he had inherited from his mother, even though at the same time he recognized it as an integral part of his being. Without it he would still be in America, living on an heiress wife's money or working on board a steam kettle.

He sank into a chair and glared at the empty grate for an hour before the black mood began to lift and he started making plans for the future. He must find another house-keeper — a docile elderly widow-woman this time. He must find employment. The thought of going home crossed his mind briefly and, as before, was rejected. He liked Greenock well enough and there was more work for him here than there was in his own country.

But before anything else he must try to right the wrong he had unwittingly done Annis Moncrieff. Jem could be trusted to deliver a letter to her the next time she scurried along on one of her secret visits.

He fetched paper and pen and the silver inkwell his parents had given him when he first went to sea, and sat down at the small wooden table in the parlour.

For a moment he stared thoughtfully at the wall, then he began to write. By the time he had finished the letter his spirits were rising and an idea had begun to form in his mind.

When Jem handed the letter to Annis three days later she turned it over in her fingers, staring down at her own name, written in an unfamiliar hand. 'How is he?'

'He's fine,' Jem said cheerfully. 'He's been taken on as master of a schooner that plies between the Clyde and England and Ireland.'

'That's not the right sort of work for Captain Brenner!'

'It is not, but he says it'll suffice until he decides what he wants to do.'

'If only Douglas . . . ' Annis burst out, then stopped herself just in time and said instead, 'I wish Douglas had given more thought to the matter instead of dismissing Captain Brenner for disobeying his orders.'

'Aye. But it was Douglas's decision, and his right.' Jem, who knew exactly what had been said in Douglas Moncrieff's office and was inwardly furious with his kinsman, had no intention of letting Annis know how pig-headed her husband had been. Instead he said, 'You'll have heard that he dismissed Adeline Fraser?'

'No.'

'Found out for himself that she was a sleekit besom not fit to live under his roof.' Jem winked. 'He's got a respectable widow body for a house-keeper now.'

Annis slipped the letter into her pocket and took it out again after she had returned home and was in the privacy of her bedchamber. Tib was in the kitchen and Douglas still at Cathcart Square, so she had no fear of interruption. With the tip of one finger she traced the outline of her name, written in Gideon Brenner's flowing, confident hand, then opened the letter.

It was brief, the few words pouring themselves across the page in that clear strong script that reminded her of the sea itself with its sweeping curves and its power.

As she read them she drew in her breath in a tiny hiss of dismay. It was clear from what Gideon Brenner said that he was under the impression that she had been embarrassed and offended by his visits.

'I meant only to show my gratitude for your hospitality towards me when I first arrived in Greenock,' he had written. 'If I unwittingly intruded then I can ask you to attribute my poor manners to the fact that I am a stranger to your country and have not yet grasped its etiquette. I apologize and assure you that I will never again disconcert you in this way . . .'

The letter fell from her hand and she looked up to see in the mirror before her that her eyes were bright and her colour high with anger. Douglas must have given the shipmaster the impression that she had been upset by his visits. Who else but Douglas could have done such a thing?

'How dare he?' she said aloud, and knew, helplessly, that he dared because she was his wife and therefore his possession. There was nothing she could do about it, for she certainly couldn't confront Douglas.

If he knew that Gideon Brenner had written to her there was no telling what he might do. He was powerful enough to ruin the young shipmaster's future in Greenock and drive him away. And that, Annis realized, was not what she wanted. She wanted Gideon to stay in Greenock, so that she could at least see him occasionally, even if she couldn't talk to him.

The thought of his going was more than she could bear. In fact — she got up suddenly from the dressing table and walked to the window with short, agitated steps, her hands clasped tightly — it was so unbearable that it had to be the answer. Suddenly it was clear that Douglas's fears were not as unjustified as she had thought — at least, as far as she was concerned. It was wrong for a married woman to care so much for another man. Meeting the young American, Annis thought wretchedly, was the worst thing that had ever happened to her. But she couldn't help feeling that it was also the best thing.

She went back to where the letter lay and picked it up.

The words danced over the page, blurred by tears that quite unexpectedly filled her eyes. She let them flow for a few self-pitying moments, then made herself stop. There was no sense in weeping and wailing like a spoiled child. Gideon Brenner cared for nobody but Olivia, who had found herself a husband in Australia. Annis herself was married to Douglas and would remain married to him for the rest of her life. It was all a sorry mess, with only Olivia, happy with her wealthy husband, free from heartache.

Trying to divert herself from further self-pitying thoughts Annis wondered how many other people going about their everyday lives with outward serenity had secrets such as hers. A picture of her butcher came into her mind, and the thought of him harbouring a secret longing for some woman he could never have brought a sudden giggle to her lips.

It made her feel better, and able to dry her eyes and consider the situation. She could never say anything to Douglas about her anger with him because then he would know that Gideon had been in contact with her. And, worse still, he might find out that Jem had acted as go-between.

But she could write to Gideon, and she would. Douglas kept writing materials in a drawer in the bedroom as well as in the writing bureau in the parlour; Annis found all that she needed and cleared a space on the dressing table.

'It seems from your letter that my husband has mistakenly given you the wrong impression of my reaction to your visits,' she wrote in her neat, childish script. 'I enjoyed and appreciated our conversations, and I regret that they must come to an end. I wish you every success in your future life.'

She signed and sealed it, and the next time she was in the town she took it to his rented rooms, having first ascertained from Jem that Gideon was at sea.

A plump white-haired woman opened the door. 'Captain Brenner's not at home, ma'am.'

'I know that. I only called to deliver this message.'

Annis handed over the letter then escaped, thankful that the woman was a stranger to her and probably didn't know who she was. It had been foolish of her to deliver it in person, she scolded herself as she hurried back down Bank Street towards the safety of the shops. She could have found a child willing to deliver it for a penny.

But she had wanted just one moment of adventure and daring, had wanted to see for herself the building where he lived, the stone staircase he trod, the door that he opened. She had wanted to see and experience it all just once, and lock it away among the small memories of him that would have to sustain her throughout the rest of her life.

That summer Robert left school and began to work in the Moncrieff shipping office in Cathcart Street. Only Annis and Jem knew how much he hated the work and how determined he was to give it up as soon as he could.

'I'll thole it while I must,' he told Jem, his voice deepening into manhood, 'and I'll learn all I can, for that's what Uncle Douglas wants. It'll mebbe stand me in good stead one day, but as soon as I'm old enough to make my own decisions I'm leaving, no matter what he says.'

'We all have to make our own way in life, laddie. I think you'll make a good job of it when the time comes.' Jem paused, then said diffidently, 'Gideon's been on at me again about that wee schooner. He's offered to sail it for me if I decide to keep it.'

'Does he mean it?'

'I think so.' The shipbuilder scratched his head. 'I told him I'd think it over. What do you think of the matter?'

Robert's face flushed with pride at being consulted.

'Do it, Jem. There's good money to be had from trading up and down the coast.'

'You think so?' Jem jammed his cap back on to his greying hair, then said, 'Ach, it'll be a while before the schooner's ready anyway, and by that time he'll have found himself something else. Gideon's a fine shipmaster, he'll have no trouble getting a good ship again.'

He was wrong. After making a few short trips to England and Ireland Gideon formally proposed that he and Jem should set up a partnership.

'She's got fine lines . . .' He nodded at the small schooner that had just come off the shipyard stocks. 'She'd be a good vessel to handle. I've not got enough money to buy her, but if you were of a mind to do some trading I could put in half the money to buy a cargo, and half the crew's wages.'

Jem's brows shot up. 'Man, you'd not make enough to live on with cargo to buy and men to pay.'

'It wouldn't take many men to handle a ship that size,' Gideon argued. 'And as long as I got my food and enough to pay my lodgings and my house-keeper I'd be willing to do without profit for the first few trips. I'd take her down the English coast, delivering cargo on the way and filling her holds with anything that's on offer. With the right cargoes my guess is that we'd begin to get our money back and a bit over by the fourth or fifth time out. Within the year the cost of the vessel would be made up and we'd still have her to trade with. What d'you say?'

Jem chewed on his lower lip. 'I've never thought of going into trading before. I've always been content enough to build and sell.'

Robert, on a stolen visit to the yard, could hold his tongue no longer.

'Do it, Jem. Gideon's right . . . you could be in profit within the year.'

'Listen to the man who knows it all after only a few weeks as a shipping clerk,' Jem teased affectionately. The boy reddened, but persisted.

'My uncle does well with the wee ship that plies along the west coast, up among the crofting communities and the islands. I don't know why he doesn't send one of his vessels south, but he won't. I know that what Gideon says makes sense.'

'You see?' Brenner clapped a friendly hand on the boy's shoulder. 'Robert knows what I mean. Use the schooner while you're building another. If I'm wrong you can always sell. If I'm right . . . you might end up building a fleet for yourself as well as commissioned vessels for other people.'

'I wish you could.' Robert cast a dark look at the new ship taking shape on the main stocks. 'Then you wouldn't have to build ugly floating holds like that one, just because you need the money.'

Jem laughed, then shrugged and held out a hand to Gideon. 'Since Robert agrees with you and I trust his judgement it seems that I'd be a fool not to try the new venture. The schooner's yours.'

'Ours,' Brenner corrected him. 'I'll have papers drawn up so that everything's the way it should be. I tell you, Jem, you'll not regret it!'

Robert gave Annis the news of the new partnership as soon as he got home.

'It'll not please Douglas, Captain Brenner throwing in his lot with Jem,' was her cautious response.

'Ach, it's his own fault for letting Gideon go,' the boy

said blithely. 'He's one of the best shipmasters in Greenock, and I'm sure Jem'll do well by the new agreement. Mebbe one day I'll buy a partnership there for myself.' Mischief sparkled in his eyes. 'I wonder what Uncle Douglas'll have to say about it?' Then he added casually, 'Gideon was asking after you. He sends his regards.'

'Indeed?' Annis bent her head over the table she was polishing for fear that Robert would see her sudden startled pleasure.

'Aye. I told him you were well enough. He was asking if you'd heard from Olivia and I said that she seemed to be fine too,' said Robert, and sauntered from the room, completely unaware of the turmoil he had set up in his young aunt's heart.

There was no telling when Douglas found out about the new partnership between Jem and Gideon. He said nothing to Annis, even when a small wooden hut was erected just within the gates of Jem's yard with a bright, freshly painted signboard above it that read 'Moncrieff and Brenner, Shipping Merchants.'

Douglas had found a master for the *Grace and Charity*, and the clipper continued to ply between the Clyde and South America. Robert, who kept his eyes lowered but his ears open in the office, reported in confidence that after the new man's first voyage, which took longer than any of the voyages under Gideon's command, several crew members had declined to sign on for the next trip.

Then the new master had a difference of opinion with the agent at Iquiqua and as a result the *Grace and Charity* returned from her next trip with her holds only half-filled, thus cutting Douglas's profit. He was more often than not in a bad mood these days, and life in his household grew even gloomier. It was a wet, colourless autumn, and the stripped dripping trees in the garden echoed the depression within the house.

The ship that Jem Moncrieff was building for Charles Grieve, the ship that had been designed for the carrying of large cargoes rather than for speed or safety, was almost completed when Douglas finally decided that the South American run was no longer for him and began to investigate the possibility of stretching his net as far as Australia.

'You've no need to send a ship all that way,' Tib said sharply when he first mentioned it. 'Father didn't, and our brother didn't. Why should you?'

Douglas rubbed a hand thoughtfully over his beard. 'Things are changing, Tib, and a man must change as well if his business is to prosper. The South American run's all very well, but a clipper like the *Grace and Charity* was built for longer runs. Mebbe it's time to try her on the Australian trade. I've been making serious inquiries, and there's a good market for Australian wool.'

'You'd have to go to the trouble of finding an agent over there.'

'I was wondering if that family Olivia's married into would be interested in letting me bring their wool over here. I'd have to go over there, of course, to speak to the people myself.'

Excitement flowered in Annis. She dropped her knitting needles. 'When would you expect to go?'

'I've not made up my mind to it yet. But if I do it'll have to be before the end of the year. Otherwise it'll be March at least before anything can be done.'

'Can I come with you?' The thought of getting far away from Tib and the dark house that seemed, at times, to be the centre of her web, was breathtaking. Not to mention the chance to spend time on board the clipper, to visit Australia, to see Olivia.

'It's no sort of journey for a young woman,' Tib said, but to Annis's delight Douglas contradicted his sister.

'I see no reason why not. The *Grace and Charity*'s a strong ship, well able for the Australian run. And I'd like to keep Annis by me.'

His eyes rested on her and all at once she knew what he meant. Now that Gideon was on short voyages and in Greenock more often, Douglas was afraid to leave her behind while he sailed to the other side of the world. She felt herself flush with anger, but held her tongue. What did Douglas's silly jealousy matter now? She was going to get away from Greenock and Tib for a while. She was going to see Olivia!

'You've dropped a stitch,' Tib pointed out critically.

Annis gave her a radiant smile and picked up her knitting. Douglas opened his newspaper and Tib bent her head over her sewing.

Robert winked at his aunt. She winked back, then made herself get on with her knitting, when what she really wanted to do was to run out into the garden and whirl in giddy, joyful circles.

11

John Mundy was very proud of the wash-board he had provided for his wife's use. It was made of glass set in a solid wooden frame, and it had been brought to Vanduara from Melbourne by his brother Matthew as a gift for his own wife.

'Lucky for you she didn't take it with her when she ran off,' he said when he first showed the wash-board to Olivia. 'Wooden boards wear down, and tin cracks. Glass is the best. I'll wager you've got the finest washing board outside Melbourne. It'll last for years.'

'Why can't one of the aborigine women wash the clothes?' she wanted to know. 'What do you call them . . . libraries?'

'Lubras.' He chuckled at her mistake, but as Olivia remained stony-faced his amusement died down and he asked, 'Why should they?'

'They wash your father's clothes. And your brother's. I've seen them at the lake.'

He settled himself more comfortably in his chair on the verandah, puffing gently at his pipe. 'They haven't got a woman of their own to wash their clothes. I have.'

She glared down at him. 'I am not your woman!'

'What are you then?'

'I'm your wife. Not your servant.'

'Wives,' said John calmly, 'should know how to wash and cook and keep house. One of those days the old man might tell some of the lubras to come down here and give you a hand. Until he does they'll not set foot near this place. The abos around here do what he tells 'em.'

'They're not the only ones who do as they're told,' she sneered. 'I thought I'd married a man, not a dog that runs to heel all the time!'

A flash of anger, as red as one of the points of light in the depths of the milk opal ring that was kept carefully tucked away in a drawer, came and went in his eyes. But when he finally spoke his voice was as calm as ever.

'He knows what he's talking about . . . and anyway, it doesn't pay to disobey.'

'How do you know?'

'I've tried it. So has Matt. It's not worth it. He owns the place and he's got the right to say what goes.'

'And after he's gone?'

John took the pipe from his mouth and gazed across the stretch of open land before the house. Night was coming down and the first stars were high overhead. The faint breeze riffling the surface of the lake carried the smell of cooking from the men's quarters.

'We'll think about that when the time comes, Matt and me,' he said, and refused to be drawn into further discussion about the future.

In any case, there was no arguing with John. The reins of power at Vanduara were held firm in Jeremiah Mundy's hands. He was the man Olivia must challenge.

When John had left for work the next morning she put on her yellow silk. As there was no form of transport she set out to walk to the main house, with a small white fringed parasol as her only protection against the sun.

She knew from what John had said the previous night that Jeremiah, who was often out working alongside his sons and the hired men, would be at home today.

He was on the verandah, seated at a table, going through papers. As Olivia, hot and tired, climbed the steps he looked up without surprise.

'I want to talk to you.'

'You'll need to take a seat then,' said the old man. 'Betta!'

An aborigine woman, bare-footed and dressed in a bright cotton gown, came from the house. 'Uh-huh, boss?'

'Lemonade,' he said, and went back to the paper he was studying.

When the lemonade arrived, freshly made and deliciously tart, he poured two glasses. Olivia sipped, then gave in to her dust-parched throat and drank thirstily. Jeremiah refilled her glass before sitting back in his chair.

'So, what do you want to talk about?'

'About that — that hovel you expect us to live in.'

'It was good enough for me, once. It was good enough for Matt and his wife.'

'She ran away.'

'She couldn't take the life.'

'We're entitled to something better than that shack at the other end of the lake!'

'Johnny hasn't complained.'

'That,' said Olivia icily, 'is because he's afraid of you. But I'm not. I'm John's wife, and I'll not have you treating him like a hired hand.'

His brown eyes were like polished pebbles. 'If my son's got a complaint let him come to me himself.'

Olivia had taken another sip of lemonade. She banged

the glass down. 'You know he'd not do that. He's afraid of you. But I'm not. I want my husband to be treated on equal terms with his brother.'

'Johnny's the younger, and Matt's the smarter. Matt's my heir and Johnny knows it, girl. It was all settled between the three of us years ago. Johnny accepts it, and so should you.'

'But John's married now . . . he and I are entitled to more consideration!'

He leaned forward and said slowly and distinctly, 'I own Vanduara. If you don't like the way I handle things here, Missy, you can clear out, as the other woman did.'

She stared into his gaze, unflinching. 'That's what you want me to do, isn't it? You want me to run back to Melbourne.'

'Neither of 'em could choose the right woman,' Jeremiah Mundy said. 'Neither of 'em. Matt at least had an excuse. He thought he'd fallen in love, poor stupid bastard. But there's no excuse for Johnny. He only brought you here to taunt his brother.'

Olivia opened her mouth, then closed it. The old man, watching her closely, chuckled.

'Don't like the truth, do you girl?'

'You're lying!'

'No need for me to lie. Johnny's always been envious of his brother. All he wanted was to show Matt that he could get himself a woman too. Wants to show that he can hold on to her longer'n Matt could as well, but I don't think he will. You don't belong here and you'll be no good to John, so you might as well go away. D'you want my help?'

'The way you helped Matthew's wife to leave?' She stood up, shaking with rage. 'I'd not ask you for help if you were my last chance!' she said, and made for the steps.

At the top she turned. He was still watching her, a mocking smile curving his lips.

'I'm going to stay,' Olivia said. 'I'm going to stay, despite you, Jeremiah Mundy!'

It wasn't until she was half-way back to the shack that she realized what she had done. In her anger at the old man she had committed herself to Vanduara, to a life that she hated with a man she cared little for.

She gritted her teeth and strode on. She would stay. She wasn't like Annis, meek and mild and submissive. She was made of stronger stuff, as Jeremiah Mundy would soon find out. One day John would be wealthy, and as his wife she was entitled to share in that wealth.

A warm breeze brushed her cheek. In her rage she had covered most of the distance to the wooden house without noticing the heat or the flies, but as she skirted the end of the lake she stopped and sheltered her eyes with one hand, staring out over the red-earth plain, dotted here and there by low pale-green spinifex. Something was moving out there, dancing to and fro, rising towards the blue sky then shrinking, coming closer all the time.

Olivia suddenly realized that this must be a willy-willy, one of the whirlwinds that came skimming across the plains, gathering up dust and debris as they went. 'If you see one coming,' John had warned, 'close all the doors and windows if you want to keep the dust out.'

The willy-willy was positively speeding towards Olivia now. It was almost as though it had spotted her and was challenging her to a race. With a small yelp of dismay she gathered up her skirt in one hand and began to run towards the shelter of the house.

She had almost reached it when the willy-willy caught her and whirled around her, filling her mouth and eyes with fine grains of soil. The parasol was whipped from her hand as her skirts tightened against her legs, making it impossible for her to run. She stumbled, blinded and choking, lashed by small twigs and leaves, then her outstretched hands grasped and clutched at the wooden railing of the stairs leading up to the verandah.

The willy-willy, tiring of the game, left her there and whirled on, through the open windows at the front of the house and out the other side.

Coughing, spitting dust and leaves, Olivia climbed the stairs and went into the house. Every surface was covered with a fine red dust. When she took her hat off more dust showered down from her hair. Her dress was covered with it and there was a small tear in one sleeve.

She picked up a cloth, wet it in the bucket of water standing by the stove, and rubbed at her face, then looked into the mirror that hung on one wall. As the cloth itself was covered with dust and there was a scum of it on the surface of the water, she had only succeeded in smearing the stuff over her face. She looked like a painted heathen.

Tears welled into her eyes and ran down her cheeks, cutting white tracks in the smeared ochre that covered her face. Slowly, she went back outside into the heat. Her abandoned parasol lay like a wounded bird on the ground several yards from the house. Olivia picked it up, and saw that one of the spokes had snapped.

It was the last straw, and yet in a strange way it was the opening move in the challenge Jeremiah Mundy had thrown down before her. In that moment, she found it easy to believe that the old man sitting comfortably on his verandah at the other end of the lake had deliberately sent the willy-willy to torment her.

Olivia tightened her grip on the battered parasol and lifted her smeared, tear-streaked face to the calm blue sky. 'Damn you, Jeremiah Mundy,' she screamed. Several brightly coloured birds, cawing their fright, rose from the trees and took wing. Olivia had no eyes for their rainbow flight overhead. 'Damn you to hell! You'll not defeat me! I'll survive! I'll not be beaten!'

John came home in a rage, slithering from the saddle and bounding into the house, leaving his horse, for the moment, to its own devices.

'What the hell d'you mean by going to see the old man and telling him off?' he wanted to know, throwing the door open.

Olivia, who had been nursing her own anger all afternoon, stared at him, taken aback for a moment. Then she rallied. 'I did what you should have done — I told him what I thought of the way he's treating you — us!'

John threw his hat down on the table. A puff of red dust rose from it. 'I'm not going to tell you again to mind your own business, Livvy. If anything has to be said to him in future I'll do it . . . not you. You're my wife, and wives keep their place.'

'According to your father,' said Olivia icily, 'I'm only your wife because you wanted to gloat over your brother. Is that true?'

'What the hell did the old fool tell you that for?'

'Is it true?' Then as he said nothing she flew at him, beating his chest with her fists. 'It is! You married me because you wanted to show Matt you could bring a wife to Vanduara!'

John seized her wrists and held her back without effort. 'And what about you? You married me because you were broke, with nowhere to go. You'd heard about Vanduara and you wanted a wealthy husband.'

'Did your father tell you that?'

'Is it true, Livvy?'

'My name is Olivia! Why shouldn't I want a wealthy husband? D'you think I wanted to work as a governess all my life, at the beck and call of someone like Jean Stobo? Though right now,' Olivia said bitterly, 'I'd trade my life at Yarra for my life here without a thought!'

There was a short angry silence, then he said quietly, 'Too bad you can't. You're stuck here so you might as well make the most of it.'

From that moment, as far as Olivia was concerned, her marriage turned into a battle. Each attempt at outright rebellion met with indifference from John.

After she had made it clear that she wouldn't cook or clean the shack he rode the boundaries by day with Matthew and the other men, and ate in the main cookhouse with the others while Olivia sat alone, getting hungrier and hungrier. He only came back at nights, walking into the bare, comfortless house without seeming to notice that nothing had been done in his absence, sleeping on the unmade bed and rising early in the morning to go back to work.

When she tried announcing that she would sleep alone until he came to his senses, he calmly lifted her from the bed, dumped her into a chair, and left her there while he stretched out on the bed.

'I've to work all day. You just sit around here feeling sorry for yourself. You can sleep when I'm out,' he said.

She endured three miserable aching hours before he got up, came to her in the darkness, and took her to bed, where he made love to her with a rough hunger that, despite her determination to be aloof, brought her to panting, vocal response. Afterwards, taking advantage of the tenderness between them, she tried to reason with him, only to discover that he was sound asleep. From then on, they shared the unmade bed.

Ten hungry, lonely days later Olivia was finally forced to realize that there was little point in rebelling when nobody was there to see the rebellion. The only person she was hurting was herself.

Slowly, she set about putting the wooden shack to rights and cooking meals, watching John from beneath lowered lids when he came home; determined, if he showed any signs of crowing over her, to go back to her mulish suffering.

But he had the good sense to say nothing, even when she made a complete mess of her first attempts at making bread. She had worked hard at it, but when it was cut she discovered that it was yellowy and chewy, with a sour taste to it. After his first bite into it John's jaw stopped moving for a moment, then got back to work. Methodically, he and Olivia, at opposite ends of the table, worked their way through a slice each. Then John pushed his chair back and wandered thoughtfully out to the verandah, picking up his pipe and tobacco pouch on the way.

Olivia, feeling as though she had swallowed a stone, washed the dishes. At that moment she would have given anything to have Annis there, with her practical knowledge of housewifery. Annis, she thought miserably as she scrubbed at a pan, would probably have taken to this sort of life like a duck to water. But she was living in comfort far away in Greenock, with servants to do all her work for her if she so wished, while Olivia, who had been born to have servants, had to slave away in this godforsaken corner of the world. A self-pitying tear dripped into the bowl of water and she blinked hard, determined not to let John see her weeping.

The next day Chang, the stout Chinese cook, came smilingly to her door, carrying a tray of eggs, and announced that it was time that he showed Missus John how 'we Australians' make bread.

'Did Mister John put you up to this?' she asked suspiciously, and the cook's dark eyes opened as wide as they could.

'No, missus! I always show how to make bread. I make best bread in whole New South Wales. I bet you always buy bread, huh?'

While talking he had eased his way in and put the eggs down. Before she quite knew what was happening Olivia found herself fetching and carrying, stirring and kneading at his command.

'See? Simple, huh?' said Chang when two light, fragrant loaves were cooling on the table. 'Now I look at your cellar an' see what needs to be sent down from my kitchen. You want, you ask, missus. I got ev'thing in my store.'

Gradually Olivia conformed. There was nothing else she could do . . . for the moment. In her letters to Annis she wrote about the main house and her life there with servants to obey her every whim and a husband who was devoted to her. Her sister's answering letters, filled with admiration for Olivia's success, helped in a small way to make her life more bearable.

But she never came to terms with the hated wash-board. John might have been proud of it, but to her it represented everything she loathed about her new life. As she laboured in the yard behind the house a year after her arrival at Vanduara, Olivia was convinced, as she was every washing day, that she would wear down long before the wash-board.

She gave a bedsheet one more drubbing on the board before lifting it from the tub of hot soapy water and dousing it in the tub of clear rinsing water. She pushed it under again and again until the soap had floated clear then hauled the wet, dripping mess of cloth out and began to wring it. A wisp of pale grey smoke floated from the dying fire under the copper a few yards away and tickled her eyes. She shook her head impatiently, not having a hand free to wave it and the flies away.

The 'wet' had come and gone, bringing very little rain this year, and the hot weather was back. The creeks, where in past years, John told her, whole tree trunks had been carried along in the foaming waters, had half-filled and were already empty again.

Thinking, as she toiled over the washing, of John's calm acceptance of this intolerable life-style, Olivia began to twist the sheet viciously. In her mind the heavy stretch of wet linen became a Mundy neck — any Mundy neck. She didn't care whether it was John's, Matthew's, or old Jeremiah's.

Water poured from it, then the torrent became a thin trickle that finally stopped. She shook it out, cracking it in the warm air, and went across to the rope stretched between the house gable and a tree. Within an hour it would be dry and ready for ironing. There was one thing to be said for anger — it helped on washing day.

By the time Olivia's thoughts had travelled over the past year and returned reluctantly to the present, the clothes and sheets had been scrubbed and rinsed and wrung and hung on the line. She straightened her back, took off the broad-brimmed straw hat she wore as protection against the sun, and pushed damp strands of hair back into place. Then she tied her hat on again and picking up a wooden bucket, dipped it into the tub that held the soapy water, and started round the front of the house.

She had demanded plants for a front garden and John had dutifully brought them down from the main house. Olivia, working more from instinct than knowledge, had carefully tucked them into the dry red earth. Every day she trickled a little water round each one and today as she emptied her bucket a faint sharp sound reached her. She straightened and shielded her eyes with one hand to stare out over the plain, away from the lake.

At first it seemed as though a tiny insect was crawling along its surface. Then the shimmering waves of heat that distorted everything and made distances hard to fathom moved and Olivia realized that she was looking at a small buggy. The sound she had heard came from the whip, its thong decorated with a small barrel of rolled silk to make it crack like a pistol.

The buggy dissolved, then came back into focus as she blinked and narrowed her eyes. There seemed to be two people in it, one of them wearing a dress and bonnet. Suddenly Olivia gave a yelp of horror as she realized that the buggy was heading towards her, and carrying Albert and Drina Platt. The last time Drina had called, a few months after Olivia's arrival at Vanduara, she had run and hidden herself among the trees, cowering there until the woman climbed back aboard the buggy and left. She couldn't hide again!

She dropped the bucket and sped into the house, tearing off her sacking apron as she went. Because there was little room in the shack and because there was no occasion to wear the fine gowns she had brought with her, the trunks containing most of her clothes had been put into the store rooms adjacent to the main house. Olivia made do with two blouses and two skirts, which were usually covered by large aprons made from flour sacks, and a change of underwear.

Fortunately she had retained one dress, the yellow silk dusted with sprays of green leaves which she had planned to wear in the evenings. But usually by then she was too tired to do more than take off her apron and tidy her hair.

With fingers that trembled in their haste she ripped off her skirt and blouse, splashed water into a bowl from the jug by the door, and washed her face and neck and hands. As she snatched the silk gown from the doorless wooden cupboard in the little bedroom she heard the whip crack again. Whimpering to herself in her panic, she managed to slip every tiny button of the bodice into its buttonhole, fastened the cuffs, then snatched up a brush and attacked her long dark hair.

As the rattle of the buggy and the jingle of the horse's livery came clearly to her through the open door, she twisted her hair into a knot, pinned it at the back of her head, fetched the opal ring from the drawer where it spent most of its time, carefully wrapped in a handkerchief, and cast a glance round the room. She snatched a book from a shelf, opened it at random and closed it again, with one finger keeping an imaginary place, before going to the door.

'G'day, Mrs Moncrieff,' Albert Platt called from his seat on the buggy, which was rolling to a halt before the verandah steps.

'Mr Platt . . .' She smiled graciously, noting how he stayed where he was while his wife scrambled down from the bench as best she could. Drina Platt reached up to lift a covered basket down, then came up the steps, beaming, as the buggy moved on towards the main house.

'Albert's got to go to see old Jeremiah so I asked him to bring me along so's I could visit you whilst they do their business.'

'How kind of you,' Olivia said graciously. 'Won't you come in?'

'You've got it all very nice,' Drina said when she had stepped into the living quarters and looked around with a swift glance that missed nothing. 'The last time I called you were out.'

'What a pity I missed you,' Olivia said. From her hiding place in the trees she had watched the other woman peering in through the windows and noting the drab neglected appearance of the place. There was some pleasure, now, in knowing that the interior of the shack had completely changed since that day.

'We'll sit out on the verandah − it's cooler out there,' she said when her visitor had had time to take everything in. By the time she had set cups on the table Drina Platt had taken her bonnet off and seated herself.

'My word but it's hot! I'll be glad when the cooler months come. Not that they're much cooler out here.' She burrowed into her basket. 'I brought some scones over in case you hadn't got the hang of baking on an open fire yet. Got a plate?'

Before Olivia could respond she jumped to her feet and

disappeared into the shack, reappearing in a moment. 'Here's one. Albert brought back a big drum of treacle last time he was in Melbourne. My word, he loves treacle!'

The scones were plump and brown and floury. It made Olivia's mouth water just to look at them. Her own scones looked anaemic and flat beside them, but her visitor seized one with enthusiasm and bit into it.

'I like your biscuits,' she said, and Olivia, pouring tea, was too humiliated to correct her.

'Well now — how are you getting along with old Jeremiah? He's a character, isn't he? I thought when I met you that he might have had you and John living at the house, you being such a lady. But I suppose Jeremiah breaks his rules for no one.'

'Have some more tea, Mrs Platt.'

'Call me Drina.' She held out her cup. 'The dust gets into your throat, doesn't it? Oh . . .' she plunged a hand into her bag again and handed over a large jar. 'I thought you might be able to use this. It's cream for your face and hands. The sun goes for 'em. Too late for me . . .' She indicated her brown, weathered face and laughed. 'But then I never was much of a beauty. But you are. You want to keep your skin nice.'

Olivia, turning the jar over in her hands, was touched by the woman's generosity. 'Thank you, Mrs . . . Drina. It's kind of you.'

'That's what neighbours are for. And the good Lord knows we all need our neighbours in this part of the country. I'll give you the recipe if you want, before I go. Then you can make it for yourself. The cook'll have all the ingredients in that big store.'

She sighed, then took another of Olivia's flat buns. 'I

wish our cook was as good as Vanduara's. Half the time ours is drunk and I've to turn to and make all the meals myself. Trust Jeremiah to get the best cook in the territory. You know all about Jeremiah, of course?'

Her eyes were bright with unshed secrets. When Olivia said a trifle sharply, 'I only know that he owns a lot of land and keeps everyone round here under his thumb,' the woman leaned forward in her chair, lowering her voice, though there was nobody around to hear her.

'He was a convict.'

'What?'

'Shipped out from Ireland when he was a slip of a lad. The Lord knows what he had done, for Jeremiah's never said a word to anyone. Or if he has, they've kept quiet about it. Anyway, he escaped and made his way to New South Wales. The Lord knows' — it was clearly one of Drina Platt's favourite sayings — 'how he survived, but survive he did, and arrived here, on Vanduara. Not that it was half as large then as it is now. It was owned by a squatter and by all accounts he was a right brute of a man.'

Despite her distaste for gossip, Olivia was following the story closely. She hadn't realized just how much she had been missing the sound of another woman's voice.

Drina went on. 'Jeremiah worked here for a while, and he was treated like dirt. Everyone on Vanduara was, including the man's poor wife. When he took over the land the squatter had treated the aborigines badly and those that worked for him were terrified of him. Seemingly Jeremiah hated him, but once the man found out that he was an escaped convict he had all the power he needed over the lad. And Jeremiah was a good worker with a quick brain.'

A few yards away a kookaburra gave its maniacal, irritating laugh, and was ignored by the two women bent over the wooden table.

'What happened to the squatter?'

Drina Platt shrugged, her face alight with the pleasure of telling the story. 'He dropped his bundle. He died,' she explained to her hostess's mystified face. 'A hunting accident, his widow said. But his abos went walkabout on the very day the body was found out by the border fence, and when they came back there was a lot more of 'em. It seems that the ones who ran away because of his cruelty came home again. Jeremiah and the abos had been real friendly from the start, sort of getting together to console each other for the way the old man treated 'em.'

The kookaburra laughed again, derisively.

'The widow hired Jeremiah as the leading hand after that. Within six months he'd married her, then fathered two sons on her, even though she was a good twelve years older than he was. From the time he took it in hand Vanduara's flourished and expanded, and the abos here are treated better than anywhere else. Folks reckon it's 'cause Jeremiah owes them an' they owe him. Then opals were found on the property and now Jeremiah Mundy's the richest man in the territory. And the hardest, though you can't blame him when you think of what he's been through in his life. . .' Drina's voice trailed off. She waved away the flies then said briskly, her voice normal again, 'You want to try some carbolic acid on a hot shovel to keep those flies out of the house. Or boil up some linseed oil and ground resin and spread it on some heavy paper so's they stick to it.'

When her husband came back for her two hours later

he brought with him an invitation to Olivia to dine at the main house. By the time she arrived there with the Platts the sun was down and the air slightly cooler than during the day. Matt and John were already at the house, the worst of the day's dust brushed from their clothes, and Lawrie Borland had ridden in from the mines to collect some letters the Platts had brought with them.

As always happened when visitors arrived in the outback, there was a festive air about the table. Chang had surpassed himself, serving up cream of potato soup, a baked glazed ham with potatoes and a light vegetable soufflé, then a spicy sponge pudding thickly studded with raisins.

As the talk flowed across the table Olivia looked around her at the good solid furniture and the comfort of the room. It was wrong that she, a woman raised to enjoy fine things in life, should have to live in a wooden shack while Jeremiah Mundy, a convict and almost certainly a murderer, had this handsome, spacious house.

She caught Jeremiah's eye and was certain, when she saw the amused irony in his look, that he knew what she was thinking. She lifted her chin and stared back at him.

The party broke up early, for everyone had to be up and about before dawn. The Platts were staying the night and setting out for their own station at first light.

Before she and John left, Jeremiah handed Olivia a packet of letters. The top envelope was addressed in Annis's neat hand.

'Platt brought me a letter from your brother-in-law,' he said casually.

She gaped at him. 'From Douglas?'

'Seems that he's interested in shipping our wool back

to Scotland. He's coming out to Australia to talk about it.'

Olivia's blood ran cold. 'He's coming to Vanduara?'

'To Melbourne. We'll meet there . . . or I'll send one of the boys in my place. Seems to be a shrewd businessman, Douglas Moncrieff. I'll be interested to hear what he's got to offer. Your sister's travelling with him. So you'll want to go to Melbourne too, I suppose.' His eyes met and held hers. 'You'll want to enjoy some city life.'

She knew well enough what he meant. Now was her chance to get back to Melbourne and stay there, leaving him in peace with his two sons. Since the day she had tried to talk to him about John's rights, Jeremiah Mundy's dislike for her had been as obvious as the overpowering smell of sweat that clung persistently to the man's working clothes. He cared little for women, John had told her, trying to dismiss her complaints about his father's attitude, but she knew that Mundy disliked her in particular because, unlike everyone else on the godforsaken station, she had refused to accept his word as law.

As one of the house servants drove Olivia and John back along the side of the lake to their own house, with John's horse trotting along behind them on a tether, her mind was occupied by the news she had just heard. She did want to go to Melbourne, but she'd come back to Vanduara afterwards. Jeremiah wasn't going to get rid of her as easily as that.

He couldn't live forever. One day he would die, and then Olivia would reap the harvest she was sowing at the moment. She could wait . . . she must wait.

At least Annis and Douglas weren't coming out to

Vanduara. It was still possible, with John's connivance, to let them go on thinking that all was well.

When they reached home John stripped off her clothes, then his own, and took her to bed, his breath sour with the beer that he and the other men had been drinking during the evening. Afterwards he fell at once into a sound sleep.

'Did you know how your father came to own Vanduara?' Olivia asked in the morning. John stopped in the middle of pulling on one boot and looked up at her. His face was closed, his eyes carefully blank.

'Drina Platt's been tattling, has she? Yes, I knew. He's never made a secret of it.'

'You should have told me.'

'Would it have made any difference? All that mattered to you,' said John shrewdly, 'was that he had money. And he came by that honestly, so his past's of no importance. In Australia we count a man — and a woman — by what they make of their lives, not their past,' he said, pulling on the other boot.

He stood up, stamped his feet to settle the boots, and picked up his hat. 'See you tonight.' Then he went down the steps without a backward glance.

When she was alone Olivia took the packet of letters she had received on to the verandah, turning her back on the work that needed her attention. They followed the pattern she had become used to: Annis faithfully described the weather, the little gossip she had heard, and reported on the health of the Moncrieff household.

Her letters, as always, sounded contented, as well they might, Olivia thought, staring out over the hot red land before her. Annis had servants, shops to visit, dressmakers near at hand. Annis had everything whereas she, Olivia, had nothing.

A wave of nostalgia gripped her. Sitting in the frightening vastness of Australia, she longed for the sting of cold rain on her face, the sound of it gurgling along the street gutters, the sight of white-capped waves and the low hills on the other side of the Firth of Clyde shrouded in mist. She shivered, then shook off the misery that had gripped her and opened the final letter, the letter that bubbled with Annis's pleasure at coming out to Australia and meeting her sister again.

'We have so much to talk about,' Annis wrote. 'So much has happened — to you rather than to me. I look forward to meeting your husband and hearing all your news.'

Olivia chewed her lower lip. Not only was she living like a skivvy, but she was at the mercy of a man who had been — and still was, for he had not served his time or been pardoned — a mere convict.

How Douglas would gloat if he ever found out! She shuddered at the thought, determined he never would.

12

By the end of November the *Grace and Charity*'s master cabin had been refitted and was suitable for the owner's wife. It was a mild winter and Douglas, impatient to start for Australia now that his mind was made up, decided to set sail.

But two days before the clipper was due to leave her master was struck by a carriage while crossing the road near the harbour, and broke his leg. Douglas brought the news home, storming into the house in a raging temper.

Annis swallowed her disappointment down and asked patiently, 'How long will it be before he's well enough to sail?'

'God knows. A month at least, perhaps never. It depends on whether or not the bone will knit. Either way he's of no use to me. This clement weather surely won't last until January. If we don't sail within a week we could find ourselves waiting for another three months.'

'What about your other shipmasters?' Tib asked, and was regarded with a withering look.

'Neither of them has the way of a clipper the size of the *Grace and Charity*. Nor do they know much about travelling half-way round the world and rounding the Cape of Good Hope. It takes an experienced man to guide a ship safely in these waters.'

Douglas tugged on his beard, scowling at his womenfolk. 'My chief clerk's out now seeking a shipmaster who's able for the task. I've already sent word to Mundy that I'll meet him or his representatives in Melbourne in three months . . . I can't afford to waste time!'

For the next two days the house was tense with his irritation. Tib, already irked by the upheaval, the plans to be made and the trunks dragged from the attic and standing now in the front hall, getting in everyone's way, took on her brother's black mood with ease, and Annis and Robert found themselves having to tread carefully.

Annis was terrified in case Douglas changed his mind and cancelled the entire voyage. The need to get out of the house and away from Greenock, the yearning to see Olivia again and talk to her, almost consumed her.

'He'll not decide against it,' Robert assured her when she fled to him for comfort. The two of them were in his bedroom with Robert, as usual, busy at his sketch-book as he talked. 'When Uncle Douglas gets an idea in his mind he doesn't let go.' He sighed, and his own cheerful face darkened. 'I just wish I was coming with you.'

'I know.' Guilt wrapped itself about her as she realized that Robert would be left alone with Tib. 'Your turn will come.'

'I hope so.' His eyes held hers. 'You promise to write down every single thing that you see, both during the voyage and in Australia?'

He had given her a lined exercise book so that she could keep a record of the entire journey for his benefit.

'I promise. And it won't be long before we're back.'

'It'll take forever,' he said gloomily. For him, it would.

But for herself, Annis knew, the time would rush past. She would be back in Greenock long before she was ready to return. And her memories of the trip to Australia would have to last her for the rest of her life. The words she planned to write in the exercise book would be for herself as well as Robert.

'You'll have Jem to talk to when things are too . . .'

The front door opened and shut with unnecessary force, signalling Douglas's return home. Annis went to the door at once. 'I must go.'

'Jem asked me to give you a message,' Robert remembered guiltily. 'It's about Janet. She's in the Poorhouse.'

'Oh, Robert!'

The Poorhouse was a grim, damp, crumbling building on Captain Street, a place that even the most poverty-stricken avoided unless it was absolutely necessary. There had been a time, after her father's death, when Annis had almost been out of her mind with fear that she and Olivia might end up inside its walls. Ever since then the very mention of the place made her shudder.

'I must go to her.'

'You can't bring her back here, and she'd not thank you for reminding her of what she's lost,' he pointed out.

'There must be something I can do!'

'What?' Robert asked flatly. 'You've got no money to give her. Better stay away until you can be of more help.'

'I can't just leave her there without a friend in the world.'

'Mebbe when you come back from Australia you can find someone who'll give her work and let her keep the child by her, but until then . . .'

They stared at each other, numbed by the knowledge of their own helplessness.

Gideon had once thought he would never walk into Douglas Moncrieff's office again. When he did, it was with the bold stride of a man convinced of his own value.

'Tell Mr Moncrieff I'm here.'

Beaton, the chief clerk, gaped. Robert looked up from his small desk in the corner and grinned at his friend.

'I'm not certain if . . .' the chief clerk began, but Gideon cut across the fumbled words.

'Confound it, man, will you tell him I'm here or will I do it myself?'

'I'll tell him,' Robert said, willingly.

'You'll do no such thing!' Beaton snapped, leaping to his feet.

He scurried to the inner door, tapped on it, and disappeared inside. Gideon winked at Robert as they listened to the rumble of voices, Douglas's incredulous, the clerk's low and hurried.

The man came out again almost at once. 'Mr Moncrieff will see you.'

Brenner nodded and stepped through the door leading to Douglas's office. He closed it gently behind him and said without wasting any time, 'I understand that you need a shipmaster for the *Grace and Charity*. I'm applying for the position.'

Moncrieff's face purpled. 'You?'

'You'll not find a better man. I know the vessel.'

'I thought' — there was a sneer in Douglas's voice — 'that you were too busy working in partnership with my cousin to go looking for employment elsewhere.'

Gideon Brenner refused to be drawn. 'The partnership

can manage well enough without me for a while. I've a mind to put in another long voyage. What d'you say?'

Douglas got to his feet and began to move round his desk. 'I say, sir, that I'd let the *Grace and Charity* rot at the pier-head before I'd allow you to board her again.'

Unabashed, Brenner shrugged. 'As you wish. But the offer remains open — for a day or two. You'll not find a better shipmaster.'

At the door he turned. 'I thought that a man of your business reputation would have more sense than to let a former quarrel stand in the way of gain,' he said, and walked out.

'Well?' Jem wanted to know when his partner arrived back at the shipyard.

The American grinned. 'His temper almost burst him in two, but I think he might take up my offer. Time's running out for him. The *Grace and Charity*'s costing him money, lying at anchor when she should be at sea.'

Jem shook his head. 'You must be eager to set eyes on Olivia again.'

The smile faded from Gideon's eyes, though it lingered about the mouth. 'I want to make certain that she's contented,' he said, then added, 'but I'm even more eager to feel the deck of the *Grace and Charity* beneath my feet again.'

A day passed, then another, and Moncrieff's clerk was unable to find a suitable master for the clipper. On the third day Douglas Moncrieff knew that he must either withdraw from the proposed voyage to Australia or take up Gideon's offer.

'It sticks in my craw, taking the man on after his impertinence in the past,' he grunted to his clerk.

'He's a good shipmaster, sir.'

'I know that!' Douglas knew, too, that for himself he could swallow his pride and sail with Gideon. But there was something he couldn't tell his clerk.

He had decided to take Annis to Australia with him because he couldn't bear the thought of leaving her in Greenock, where she might see the American. On board ship, with him, she would have been safe. But if Brenner was on board as well . . .

He deliberated while the clerk watched him, waiting for a decision. He could leave Annis behind, but he needed her with him. No, the voyage must go ahead as planned with the only suitable shipmaster available. He would just have to watch over his wife and keep her safe from harm.

'Very well,' he said at last. 'Send word to Brenner that I want to see him. The *Grace and Charity* sails as soon as her cargo's aboard.'

Gideon stood on the poop deck of the *Grace and Charity*, the slight movement of the moored ship beneath his feet as familiar to him as the fit of his boots, and felt as though he had come home. They had grown up together, for he had watched the clipper being built in his father's yard during the year that he himself was changing from boy to man. Every timber that made up the *Grace and Charity* reminded him keenly of that New England yard, the salty tang of the air, the sun on his skin, the feeling of belonging. Above all the ship reminded him of his father, a greying, bulkily muscled man, weather-beaten and laughter-lined — a man capable of great love for his ships and his family, a man of wisdom and foresight and compassion. Gideon had taken to Jem Moncrieff from the first moment they met because, despite his Moncrieff features, Jem reminded him of his father. They had the same good qualities: one day, he thought, he must take Jem to New England to meet his family.

He gave a sigh of satisfaction and looked up into the rigging, then along the length of the deck to the forecastle. He and the *Grace and Charity* had sailed together, they had come to Scotland together, they belonged together. Although his mind roved, his keen eyes were alert for the slightest discrepancy, but found none. The cargo was stowed snugly below, the hatches battened down. A plume of black smoke curling above the forward bulwarks marked the presence of the tug that waited at the bows. With the owner and his wife on board, the clipper was to be towed to open water to minimize the risk of collision in the crowded river.

Aloft, the main and mizzen were trimmed and the loosened sails held by a few gaskets only. The vessel was ready to sail as soon as the Moncrieffs arrived. Their luggage had been delivered by a carter a good half-hour since, and was stored in the master's cabin, which had been refurbished for Annis Moncrieff's comfort.

Gideon recalled Jem's words, 'You must be eager to set eyes on Olivia again,' and his own reply. He knew deep within his heart that Olivia was a part of his past now, and the clipper ship meant more to him than she did. Perhaps it meant more to him than Olivia ever had. She had given herself to another man, and she was beyond his reach. He wanted to know that she was happy. But more than that he wanted to sail the *Grace and Charity* once more, to take her on a long journey more worthy of her abilities than the comparatively short voyages to South America that had irritated him beyond endurance and driven him, finally, to fall foul of her arrogant owner.

Brenner's lips tightened. It was wrong that a man as blinkered as Douglas Moncrieff should own a lovely vessel like this.

The prospect of sailing with the owner on board made him uneasy, for even in the short time he had known the man Gideon had sensed a change in him, a narrowing of his attitude, a withdrawal to some dark place within Moncrieff's own self. He felt sorry for the man's wife. Remembering the way she came to life when he spoke to her about his time at sea, he made up his mind to see that she enjoyed the voyage. She had spirit . . . far more spirit than her husband.

A carriage turned on to the quay, passed the imposing pillared entrance of the large Custom House, and halted opposite the gangway.

'Our passengers are arriving, Mr Brown,' Gideon warned the mate, and cast one final glance below to make certain that all was in order for the owner's arrival.

Then his hands gripped the polished wooden railing before him as he noted a crewman working on the deck below, a man with limp, dirty fair hair that fell over his forehead. He stared so hard that the man glanced up, then let his eyes slide away again, crouching over his work as though trying to make himself invisible.

'Mr Brown!'

'Aye, sir?'

Gideon pointed. 'That man. Who signed him aboard?'

The mate glanced down at the deck. 'Mr Moncrieff's clerk, sir.'

Gideon was already on his way down the steps to the deck. 'You, come here!'

The man looked up, then left his work and came reluctantly to stand before the shipmaster. There was insolence in the pale blue eyes that met Brenner's. This was the man he had trouble with on the clipper's first voyage to Greenock, the scoundrel he had found in his bed with Adeline Fraser and thrown out of his house. Bile rose in Gideon's throat.

'Get off my ship.'

'But—'

'Get ashore!' In his anger Brenner seized him by the shoulder and the man twisted away, his raddled face sullen.

'I signed on for the voyage,' he whined.

'Not on my ship!'

In his anger Gideon had forgotten the arrival of the vessel's owner. When a cool voice asked abruptly, 'What's the meaning of this?' he turned and glared at Douglas.

'I'll not have this man in my crew!'

'Beaton?' Moncrieff turned to his clerk, who hovered by his elbow.

'I signed him on, sir. I saw no reason to turn him away when he applied. He's had experience of such ships.'

'And what's your objection to him, Captain Brenner?' the merchant wanted to know

'He's a trouble-maker. I have the right to decide who sails on board a ship that's under my command. It's my view that this man is not suitable.'

'Beaton?'

'He seems quite suitable to me, sir.'

'Then he stays.'

'Mr Moncrieff, might I remind you that I am the master of this ship?'

249

'And I,' countered Douglas silkily, 'am the owner.' For himself, he didn't care whether the man stayed or went; but he was going to show Gideon Brenner that he was not going to get his own way.

There was a brief, angry pause. Sam McNair cowered in the midst of the group, sidling nearer to Douglas as though in search of protection. He had the air of a whipped cur, not a man, Gideon thought with disgust. He shrugged. 'Since it's your wish, Mr Moncrieff. But if this — this creature give short measure in any way . . .'

'You'll be at liberty to punish him as you would punish any member of the crew,' Moncrieff said impatiently. 'You hear what I say, McNair?'

'Aye, sir.'

'Get about your business. Now,' Moncrieff went on as the man scuttled off, 'can we set sail or do you have further objection as to the crew my clerk has signed on? God knows I've had hindrances enough!'

Gideon turned to Annis, who had been standing silently beside her husband during the angry altercation, watching both men with wide grey eyes. At one point, he had noticed, she had put out a hand to Moncrieff's arm and opened her mouth to speak — on his behalf, Gideon thought. Then she had drawn back. Prudently, in his opinion. If she had sided with him it would only have angered her husband further.

'Mrs Moncrieff, welcome aboard.' He bowed and gave her an apologetic smile. She answered it with a radiant beaming smile of her own.

'Boy!'

A red-haired lad who had been hovering a few yards away came darting forward.

'This lad will tend to the cabin and see to your needs

while we're at sea, ma'am. Take Mrs Moncrieff down to inspect the cabin,' Gideon ordered the boy, who did as he was told, strutting before Annis with excited self-importance.

When she had gone Gideon turned to Douglas. 'Once your clerk is ashore, sir, we'll set sail,' he said tersely, then returned to the poop deck, scowling as he went.

It made him uneasy to have Adeline Fraser's sly-eyed lover aboard. But there was nothing he could do about it. If the man proved to be as useless as Gideon suspected, the fault would lie with Moncrieff. Though he doubted if Moncrieff would be man enough to admit that, if the occasion should arise.

The *Grace and Charity*'s saloon had been converted into a comfortable drawing room for Annis's benefit. A blue chenille table-cloth covered the long table along one side of the cabin; a red plush wall-bench served the table on one side, and there were chairs with red plush seats on the other.

By the enclosed coal-burning stove with its neat mantel-shelf stood two comfortable oval-backed chairs and there was a dresser and a few rugs on the floor. The wood and brass of the apartment and that of the small night-cabin adjoining shone, and curtains were hung at the square windows.

Annis surveyed her new home with delight. It was more comfortable than she had expected — and better still, it had no Tib.

'Is there anything else, ma'am?'

'What's your name?'

'Callum, ma'am.'

'Thank you, Callum. Nothing else at the moment.'

When the lad had gone she peered out of one of the small square windows and found herself looking at the busy river from close to. Fascinated, she watched a tug go by, towing a four-master barque up-river, possibly all the way to Glasgow; then a string of shouted orders and a sudden scurry of calloused bare feet on the deck timbers above sent her out into the companionway and up to the poop deck where Douglas stood by his shipmaster's side.

Annis checked her impetuous move towards the two men. Douglas had made it quite plain that she would be expected to remain below for most of the journey, explaining that the deck could be a dangerous place for anyone unused to shipboard life. If he saw her now he might send her below. So she stayed where she was, well out of the way of the seamen who swarmed over the deck and the yards, but able to see everything.

The tug's heaving-line had come aboard and the hawser it dragged behind had been slipped into place, linking the two ships for the journey down river.

The mooring ropes were cast off and slowly, smoothly, the clipper eased away from the quay, following the little puffer, her head swinging out into the river and into the wind. The helmsman stood with legs braced and hands gentle on the wheel, his eyes watchful on the plume of smoke that indicated the tug's position.

As the stretch of water between ship and harbour widened, Annis let her breath out in a long sigh of relief. She had wanted to go on this trip so badly that she had been plagued by the fear that Douglas might change his mind at the last minute. At the news that Gideon Brenner was to be the shipmaster for the voyage she had sensed a flood of happiness that almost took the feet from under her. She hadn't set eyes on the American since he had been dismissed by Douglas: not even in Jem's yard, though each time she slipped through the gates she hoped that Gideon might be there. The prospect of not only seeing him again, but seeing him at work as the master of the *Grace and Charity* meant that she had scarcely slept for several nights and had passed away the dark hours mouthing prayers that consisted in the main of 'Please, please, let me go to Melbourne . . . please!' while Douglas, a man and therefore master of his own fate, slumbered by her side. Now, for the first time in weeks, she felt herself relaxing as the clipper moved out into the river.

Although he couldn't have heard her sigh of relief Gideon cast a glance over his shoulder. He gave her a smile — brief, almost absent-minded, but sufficient to banish the misery that had been in her heart since they had last met — then turned back to the business in hand.

She stayed where she was, entranced, as they moved down past the town. On the other side of the river, some distance away because the firth was wide at Greenock, lay sloping green hills and the small houses of Roseneath and Helensburgh. On the near side Gourock soon appeared, hard by Greenock, then they eased past the islands of Bute and Cumbraes before slipping between Arran, its range of mountains outlining the form of a huge helmeted sleeping warrior, and the green mainland with its towns and villages nestled all along the water's edge. The ensign at the peak of the mizzen-gaff and the Moncrieff house flag on the mainmast streamed out in the stiff wind.

'Ma'am?' Callum arrived by Annis's side with a chair. She thanked him, smiling, but found that no sooner had she seated herself than she was on her feet again. There was so much to see . . . an inlet sliding by close to the clipper, a fishing boat, low in the water, making for home, another sailing ship, also low in the water, her holds filled with goods from a foreign land, being towed up river to her port.

Because of the wind that blew in from the open sea and the bustle of water-borne vessels of all sizes, it took some time for the *Grace and Charity* to reach the Mull of Galloway where the mouth of the firth opened into the Irish sea. But at last the land began to fall back on either side then drop away astern as the tug ahead pitched and climbed the next wave to pitch again, and the clipper began to lift and curtsey to the first great swells of the open sea. Men ran to loosen the tow-rope and put it over the side.

'Set top'sls!' Gideon roared to the sailors already high in the yards, strung out along the arms like beads on a necklace. The sails overhead began to flap and fill as the wind caught them. The clipper, sensing freedom, gave a little skittish movement like a ripple of excitement and began to move forward under her own wind-power.

As the tug veered away and gathered in the loosened hawser, Annis ventured down the steps to the main deck, where she could see the tug more clearly.

The clipper began to pivot round, then as the great sails above bellied out and the helmsman settled his feet into the wooden deck planks and tightened his grip on the wheel she started to move forward, eagerly dipping her bows into the water. The tug gave a brisk toot of farewell and turned back towards the river. The crew raised a cheer and Annis saw Gideon wave acknowledgement to the captain of the sturdy little steam-ship. Then the *Grace and Charity* was on her way, moving confidently forward beneath the great white wings of her own sails.

As Annis turned to mount the steps to the poop deck again, she bumped against one of the seamen. The man caught hold of her and steadied her. The hands lingered a little longer than they needed to and she saw his pale blue eyes drop as though meekly avoiding her gaze. Instead, they rested on her body, burrowing beneath the demure high-necked brown woollen dress, taking in curves and contours with a quick hot gaze that brought colour to her face. It was the man who had caused the brief skirmish between Douglas and Gideon Brenner just before the ship sailed.

'Sorry – ma'am.' There was the faintest of pauses between the two words. Suddenly Annis knew beyond question that this man had no time for women other than as objects to be used. She twisted away abruptly, breaking his hold on her.

'Annis!' Douglas had just noticed her. As she made her way back to the poop deck, fighting against an impulse to brush the touch of Sam McNair's hands from her clothes, he came to meet her, his face dark.

'You should be in your cabin.'

'I wanted to be on deck for the departure, Douglas,' she said reasonably.

'I don't see why. There are windows below deck.' He put a hand on her arm and led her to the cabin. She went submissively, catching a swift glance of sympathy from Gideon.

When Douglas had returned to the deck and she was alone in the cabin she took off the gown she had been wearing and washed herself, scrubbing her upper arms where Sam McNair had touched her until the skin was red and tingling. Then she selected a blue skirt and cream-coloured bodice from her trunk and put them on.

The gown she had been wearing was hung up in the little wooden cupboard in the night-cabin. Putting it away, she thought with a little shiver of distaste that she might never wear it again.

Douglas's attempts to impose his will on their little floating world caused friction between himself, his wife, and his shipmaster from the beginning of the voyage. To his annoyance the crew, careful to avoid him whenever possible, ignored any orders he tried to give them and Gideon finally asked him outright to refrain from questioning or commanding the men. 'I pay their wages,' Douglas retorted. 'I shall certainly reprimand them when I find them skylarking and laughing instead of working.'

Gideon had lingered after the midday meal, which he and the two mates ate in the saloon with the Moncrieffs. 'You may pay their wages, sir, but at sea the master is in sole command of the ship. If you have any complaints or questions you address them to me, not to my men.'

'You're being impertinent!'

Gideon's face was impassive. 'Should the ship ever be at risk our lives might depend on the men knowing who to obey without question. I'll not have them ordered about by anyone other than myself or my officers. And I see nothing wrong with them skylarking, as you put it, in their own time, when their work has been done, and done well.'

Douglas's face was almost purple with anger. Annis put a restraining hand on his arm as he took a step towards the shipmaster, and to her relief he subsided.

'Your behaviour will be noted, Captain Brenner!'

'Yours, sir, already has been,' said Gideon tightly, and left the saloon.

Douglas whirled on his wife, dragging his arm from beneath her hand.

'I'll see that man never finds another command out of Greenock!'

'Douglas, he's right when he says that he must be in control. He's a good master. You've told me that yourself.'

He glared at her. 'He's arrogant, and he'll never set foot on the *Grace and Charity* again once this voyage is over. I wish to God that I had called the whole thing off and let the ship lie in the harbour.'

Then, as she prudently said nothing, he added, 'Keep out of his way, Annis. Keep to your cabin. I don't want you to have anything to do with him.'

'But —'

'D'you hear me?'

'Yes, Douglas,' she said, 'I hear you.'

When he had gone on deck and she was alone she blinked back the angry, bewildered tears that threatened to overflow. She had looked forward so much to the voyage and Douglas was doing all he could to ruin it for her.

He wasn't the man she had married, Annis thought wretchedly. She had no doubt that he still loved her, for he told her over and over again, but his love was beginning to frighten her. She felt as caged as the penned chickens and pigs which they carried for fresh food.

She longed to ask Olivia's advice about how best to cope with Douglas and his moodiness and jealousies. There was no reason . . . She suddenly sank on to a chair and stared at the opposite wall, where a painting of some pastoral scene hung. But there *was* reason, she thought, stunned. She cared for Gideon Brenner, cared a great deal. Annis put a hand to her mouth and noticed that her fingers were trembling. Her whole body was trembling. She cared for Gideon Brenner more than she had admitted to herself before then. More, to be truthful, than she cared for Douglas. Then she amended that to caring in a different way. For Douglas there had been gratitude, so much gratitude that in her foolishness she had mistaken it for love. Had Gideon Brenner not come into her life — how could she have borne that, she wondered with a painful catch of breath, then told herself sensibly that she could scarcely have missed somebody she didn't know — and had Douglas not changed in the past year, she would still be under the impression that gratitude and love were the same thing.

She lowered her hand and folded it firmly on her lap with the other hand. Gideon Brenner cared nothing for her, which was just as well considering that she was a married woman. Nothing could come of her feelings for him, and she must learn to overcome them, for she had no right at all to be thinking in this way of another man. She was Douglas's wife and would remain so. He loved her, and on her part gratitude must be enough.

She wondered if she could be entirely truthful with Olivia. Now that she herself was well-married there would be no more resentment on her sister's part. They would surely be able to meet and talk as adults, form a new and more precious relationship.

Callum's bare feet slapped along the passageway outside. His red head appeared at the cabin door.

'Can I clear the dishes away, ma'am?'

'Yes, Callum,' she said, then picked up her embroidery and sat down by the stove to work on it, wishing that she could be on deck.

258

* * *

Eight days after slipping out into the North Atlantic the *Grace and Charity* ran into bad weather. Green water cascaded over the sides on to the decks and before the sails could be hauled in, two of them shredded with a noise that sounded as though the sky itself had been torn apart. The men aloft clung grimly to the yards, using one hand for themselves and one for the ship as the wind and rain beat on their backs.

In the saloon and night-cabin Annis staggered to and fro, clinging to any handhold she could find, gathering up books and needlework that had been tossed to the floor with the pitching of the ship. She was not yet used to a room where anything laid casually down on a level shelf was apt to be pitched to the floor at the whim of a wave.

Douglas went on deck to stand by the shipmaster, and was helped below by young Callum two hours later and laid in his bunk, groaning and shivering. Annis, who felt no trace of sea-sickness, was filled with compassion at the sight of his pale green face.

Working as best they could in the rolling cabin, she and Callum heated bricks and put them at Douglas's feet, then bound his stomach in a flannel cholera belt to comfort it. They coaxed him to sip a little brandy and tucked the blankets tightly around him.

For a while Annis sat by the bed, Douglas's hand in hers. By the time he fell asleep, the jerky plunging movement of the clipper seemed to have eased. Douglas twitched and muttered in his sleep, then subsided. Watching him, Annis was struck by how lined his face was. He looked older, with a stern double-line impressed deeply between his brows and a petulant droop to his mouth. She wondered if that was how he would look in a few years' time, and if they would both still be in the Greenock house then, with Tib, also older but as sour as usual, in her usual chair. And Annis herself, lines running from the corners of her mouth to her chin, the life gone from her eyes. . .

The sensation of unreality that she had first experienced on the night Janet was ordered from the house came over her and she started gasping for breath. Douglas twitched again, and his grip on her hand tightened spasmodically. Annis jerked her hand free, fortunately without waking him, and scrambled to her feet, backing away from the bed, her heart pounding so loudly that she was sure he must hear it. The cabin walls started shrinking in on her and she blundered out into the saloon. But the breathlessness persisted, and she snatched an oilskin cape from the clothes cupboard and ventured on deck, clambering frantically up the narrow companionway, her lungs labouring at each breath.

The sky overhead was leaden and grey and cold rain still sluiced the decks, but the horizon had lightened and the wind that had been screaming through the shrouds earlier had quietened to a querulous moan, sounding something like Douglas before sleep overtook him. Annis emerged on to the poop and stood clutching at the railing for a moment, sucking in the cold fresh air, listening to her heart slow down. Several minutes had passed before the panic that had seized her eased, the trembling faded away, and she was able to look around.

Gideon Brenner stood by the wheel, his wet black hair flat against his skull, rain running down the strong planes of his face. His oilskin coat was open and the shirt beneath it soaked and clinging to his chest. Even so, his eyes were sparkling, his mood buoyant. He was where he belonged. He looked, thought Annis, strong and confident, so unlike Douglas. She had never in her life seen anyone so . . . so beautiful. Annis started trembling again, but this time Brenner himself was the reason, not the foolish claustrophobic attack that had caught her in its grip.

'Mrs Moncrieff . . . ' He gave her a broad grin, running the fingers of one hand through his hair to push it free of his eyes. 'How's your husband?'

'Asleep.' She wondered if the tremor could be heard in her voice. 'And likely to recover.'

His green eyes studied her with approval. 'I hope you weren't afraid, ma'am. The storm's almost over and we should find ourselves in pleasant weather once we drop below the mouth of Biscay.'

'There was no reason to be afraid, Captain Brenner. I have complete faith in you and in the *Grace and Charity*.' She had managed to bring the trembling under control, which was just as well. She could scarcely travel all the way to Australia in a constant tremor, she told herself severely as she looked around for a quiet corner. 'Where can I stand without bothering anyone?'

'Over there. Stay clear of the rail. If the ship should roll heavily it's easy enough to go over the side.'

He pointed, and she moved to the spot, in the shelter of the small deckhouse behind the helmsman. From there she watched Gideon Brenner, and was struck again by the way the man seemed to be part of the ship. He and the *Grace and Charity* belonged together.

She could see his love for the clipper in the very way his hands rested on the railing before him, the confident tilt of his head as he watched the men swarming back into the yards to release the sails and bend on new sails to replace those blown away.

When the ship was once more hissing through the water under full sail he came over to stand beside her.

'Captain Brenner, you may find my husband a rather . . . exacting person.'

'I already have, Mrs Moncrieff.' His voice was dry.

'He has an unfortunate manner at times, but he means no —'

'Mrs Moncrieff, your husband doesn't like me and I don't like him. I'd rather not have him on board, but as the owner he has the right to be here. As long as he accepts my rights as master I doubt if we'll come to blows.'

Then he added, his voice softening a little, 'But I respect you, and I regret any embarrassment that our animosity may cause you. Am I right in thinking that he's told you not to speak to me?'

She nodded and looked down at her hands. Although the rain was almost off and the skies ahead clearing by the minute, her face was still wet. Even so, she felt the warmth of sudden colour.

'Douglas sometimes asks too much of me.'

'Mrs Moncrieff . . .' he moved to stand before her, his sturdy body blocking the rest of the ship from her sight, '. . . it's best for your sake if we comply with his wishes.'

'It's so unfair!'

'Men have different ways of showing love.'

'You have more compassion for him than he deserves,' said Annis boldly, made dizzy by his nearness.

'As I said, ma'am, I respect you. I've no wish to compromise you in your husband's eyes.' Then his voice became matter-of-fact as he stepped back from her. 'I shall have a shelter set up in this corner so that you can come on deck whenever you please. I shall see to it that you are undisturbed — at all times.'

'Thank you, Captain.' She looked up into his green eyes, then beyond him to where men who had been aloft were slipping easily down the rigging, apparently impervious to the strong wind that buffeted them.

One of the sailors was Sam McNair. As she recognized him his head turned towards her. Although he was some distance away, and still moving towards the deck, she felt that she was being studied.

The unease she had felt earlier with his hands on her shoulders drifted over her again.

13

When Douglas regained his sea legs and tried to insist on his wife remaining in her cabin instead of spending most of her time on deck, she shocked him with her defiance.

'You've changed,' he said, altering his approach, his voice taking on a hurt tone. 'You've become hard, Annis. Perhaps I was wrong to bring you on this voyage.' Then, his eyes narrowing, he added, 'Is Brenner behind this new insolence of yours?'

'I'm not being insolent, Douglas, and this conversation has nothing to do with Captain Brenner.' Annis tried to keep her voice level. 'I don't think it's unreasonable to want to spend more time in the fresh air. I have to sit indoors at home. Why should I sit indoors at sea instead of enjoying the good air?'

Faced with her new determination he finally gave in. But when she was on deck he hovered near her, eyeing Gideon suspiciously if the shipmaster happened to be in the vicinity.

Apart from wishing her a brisk, civil good day each morning, Gideon left her to her own devices, although once or twice when their eyes happened to meet she was vexed to see the sympathy in his look. She didn't want this man's pity, she wanted . . . but each time her thoughts ranged in that direction she halted them. It was safer that way.

She tried, when she and Douglas were alone together at night in their tiny cabin, to demonstrate her affection for him, to show him that as her husband he had no need to fear any other man, no reason to be jealous.

In answer he clutched at her and held her so tightly that her ribs creaked. He poured protestations of love into her ear . . . and the next day his glares at Brenner or any other man who came near her, even the young cabin boy Callum, were as black as ever.

Annis realized with despair that the feelings she had had for him were being destroyed by the unreasonable force of his own demanding love. She still felt affection towards him, as well as gratitude for all he had done for herself and Olivia. But as they forged through the sea towards Australia she knew that at last she was growing up, and in doing so, growing away from Douglas, who persisted in treating her as a child.

The strength of her feeling for Gideon Brenner was surely, she thought, the way a woman loved a man. She had never cared for Douglas in that way. She had married him under false pretences, but he didn't know that, and nor did she at the time. He must never know it. He deserved her loyalty, at least, but in giving it, she had also given herself unwittingly into a loveless marriage.

Annis fretted as the sails above her bellied out and the clipper hissed through the water, for she could see no answer to the dilemma she now found herself in.

The weather cleared and the sun shone as they made good progress down the coast of Africa. Then the clipper sailed out of reach of the trade winds and into the Doldrums, that stretch of water with no trade winds of its own. The sails emptied and hung limply from the yardarms and the *Grace and Charity* idled on a flat, glittering expanse of water, her decks so hot that the tar began to bubble between the planking.

Gideon took advantage of the lull to prepare for the hard journey before them, round the Cape of Good Hope. The sails were overhauled and new canvas bent on the yards in place of any canvas showing signs of weakness.

The pigs and chicken pens were cleaned out and refurbished with fresh straw. The animals were allowed out to roam free while the ship was still and the decks safe for them. The deck timbers were sluiced down with sea-water and scrubbed, and the crew were put to scraping the masts and oiling them with linseed, and overhauling the standing and running rig.

From her shaded spot on the poop deck Annis watched the sail-makers sitting cross-legged on the hatches, stitching away at great lengths of canvas, patching old sails and making new ones. All the men were barefoot and stripped to the waist in the heat, their torsos gleaming like mahogany in the sun. She eased the neck of her muslin gown away from her damp skin with one finger and envied them the freedom to go about clad only in light trousers. She pinned her curly hair, shot through with glowing red under the sun's caress, on top of her head so that her neck was free of its weight and warmth.

Douglas was driven by the heat to shave off his beard and after the initial shock Annis was struck by the way he seemed to have shaved years from his age as well. Now that his mouth and chin were exposed he looked almost boyish, certainly much nearer his true age. But as the sun tanned his face to an even brown it also highlighted the deep lines about his mouth and the youthful look soon disappeared.

Once Gideon was satisfied with the clipper's condition, the men, other than those on watch, were free to do as they wished. They hauled up buckets of sea-water and took the opportunity to scrub their clothing, which dried almost immediately. Then they sprawled wherever they could find shade, talking and laughing, some of them carving pieces of wood and one playing the accordion he had brought aboard.

Gideon discarded his jacket and stood by the wheel in shirt and waistcoat, ever alert for the merest catspaw of a breeze. Whenever he sensed its motion through the air he barked out a crisp order and the lounging men leapt to their feet to haul the yardarms around so that the sails could catch the wind. Then for a short while the *Grace and Charity* came to life, surging forward then slowing and stopping as the puff of wind passed her by and left her becalmed once more.

It amazed Annis that such a slight breeze could move a large heavy vessel through the water.

'It's the way she's been designed, and the breadth of sail on her,' Callum explained proudly when she asked him about it. 'A good shipmaster moves his ship whenever he can through the Doldrums, even if it's only a matter of yards at a time. And Captain Brenner's a good shipmaster,' he added, his round face glowing with hero-worship.

Annis smiled at him. Callum reminded her in many ways of Robert, although there was no physical similarity. Knowing how much he would have enjoyed this voyage, she thought of Robert often, and missed him.

For his part, Douglas fretted at the enforced delay, and seemed inclined to blame Gideon for the weather. Even a visit from the captain of another becalmed clipper, who had himself rowed over the glassy water from his own vessel to exchange news and take a glass of Madeira in the saloon, failed to convince him that no shipmaster, however good, could take his ship through the Doldrums without losing time.

'We use the winds and the tides, sir,' the visitor explained cheerfully. 'And we can't complain if at times they grow tired of our impudence and leave us to our own devices to teach us a lesson. The skill lies in making the most of the good sailing weather when we have it, and learning to cultivate patience when necessary.'

Annis took advantage of his arrival to write the last of a series of letters to Robert, for the visiting captain was on his way back to the Thames and would pass any packages entrusted to his care on to a ship bound for the Clyde once he reached his own destination. She had done as her husband's nephew asked; every part of the voyage had been described as fully as possible, and what had started out as a chore had become a pleasure as she discovered an aptitude within herself for words. As a result, the packet she handed to their visitor was quite substantial. Douglas wrote a short note to Tib and a longer letter to his chief clerk.

Two days later the sails flapped, collapsed, then began to flap and fill again. Every head lifted alertly, then the men cheered as a welcome breeze swept across the deck and the surface of the sea wavered, then broke up into ripples.

Gideon, who had been in his small cabin below, appeared on deck at once, shouting to the mate as he reached the top of the companionway. Men rushed to round up the pigs and hens, the birds fluttering and squawking their irritation as they were shooed back into their pens.

This time a steadier wind came up, with sufficient strength in it to carry them, with careful manoeuvring on Gideon's part, out of the Doldrums and on to the south-east trade winds, where they set out to challenge the Cape of Good Hope, well named the Cape of Storms by the Portuguese when they first encountered it. With each day from then on the skies began to fill with heavy threatening clouds. The winds strengthened and the temperature dropped as the *Grace and Charity*, with all sails set, forced her way through high white-spumed seas. The tops of the masts arced across the grey skies with the roll of the vessel, and the men on deck and up aloft were constantly soaked by rain and spray.

Douglas managed to stay on his feet this time, but he became increasingly concerned about the safety of his ship as they battled further into bad weather, and began to urge Gideon to reef the sails and run for shelter.

'There is no shelter, sir,' the shipmaster told him with barely concealed irritation, having been torn away from deck to hear Moncrieff's demands. 'We must press on and round the Cape.'

'Surely you're risking us all by keeping all sails set? Furl them, man, and leave only what we need.'

The ship suddenly seemed to fall away to one side and Annis had to grasp the arms of her chair to prevent herself from being thrown across the cabin into her husband's arms. Douglas, panic fleeting across his face, staggered a few steps, then caught at the edge of the mantelshelf. The pipe that he had just placed on the shelf spun across the room and landed at Gideon's feet. Brenner bent and retrieved it, stamped out the glowing embers that had fallen from it on to a shifting rug, and handed it back. He alone was unperturbed by the violent motion of the clipper, planting his booted feet firmly on the carpet and letting his body swing to the movement of the ship.

'Not long ago you were urging speed, Mr Moncrieff. I know the *Grace and Charity*, and I know the Cape. I'll not shorten sail until I feel that it's necessary. The sooner we round the Cape the better and in this latitude the weather won't improve however long we wait.'

On the way out he turned and said with a faint smile, 'My apologies, Mrs Moncrieff, for the discomfort you must be suffering. I'll endeavour to bring us to calm waters as soon as possible.'

'My only regret,' said Annis, clinging to her chair for dear life, 'is that neither you nor my husband will allow me to go on deck and see the storms. As for myself, I have complete faith in the *Grace and Charity*.'

Responding to Annis's faith, the clipper fought her way round the Cape, with every inch of the way a struggle. But at last the skies began to clear again, the sea calmed, and the torrential rain that had lashed the decks ceased. The ship emerged into the Indian Ocean and Annis was able to return to her corner on the poop deck.

It was then that Sam McNair took to his bunk, claiming that he was too ill to work. Ordered by the second mate to get on deck, he refused and Gideon was told.

'Is the man malingering?' His clear voice carried to where Annis was sitting writing another long letter to Robert.

'I'd say so, Captain. He's a whining, miserable creature.

271

He's not pulled his weight since we left Greenock,' the second mate said with an uncomfortable glance in Douglas's direction. Annis glanced at her husband, who stood impassively nearby, his eyes on the horizon, apparently disinterested in what the men were saying.

'Mr Brown,' Gideon said tersely, 'See to him. Get him aloft.'

The mate shinned down the companionway to the deck, only to return a short time later.

'Well? Is he ill?'

'Not in my opinion, sir. But he refuses to turn out.'

Gideon muttered an oath under his breath then turned to Douglas. 'Since your clerk signed the man on board, sir, perhaps you would care to deal with this matter?' he asked with exaggerated politeness.

Douglas's face flushed. 'As you continually remind me, Captain Brenner, you are the master on board this ship.'

Gideon shrugged, then left the poop deck, throwing himself down the steps and storming across the main deck. Annis rose and moved quietly to a position where she could see the door to the crew's quarters under the forecastle.

It banged shut behind Gideon. A few minutes passed, then it opened again and Sam McNair, in shirt and trousers, erupted from it and went sprawling on the scrubbed white deck planking.

After him came Gideon. Even from a distance Annis could see the rage in his handsome face. He picked McNair up by the collar of his shirt and shook him as though he was a rag doll.

'Mr Brown!' His voice rang out. 'Tie this man up in the ratlines. That might teach him to guard his tongue and obey orders!'

'Aye, sir!' There was an approving gleam in the mate's eyes as he hurried down to the deck and beckoned to one of the hands. Annis watched, appalled, as the two men hoisted McNair up the rigging and lashed him to it by his wrists and ankles about a third of the way up. Leaving him spreadeagled there they came back down to the deck where Gideon stood, hands on hips, watching.

'You'll stay there until I decide otherwise, McNair,' he called up. 'It's dock rats like you that make me regret that flogging is no longer permissible.'

'Captain . . .' Forgetting Douglas's orders for the moment Annis stepped forward as the shipmaster returned to his customary place on the poop deck. 'You can't leave the man hanging there!'

Gideon glared at her. 'I can, ma'am, and I will, for as long as I deem necessary.' It was hard to remember, at that moment, how his handsome face could light up with laughter and compassion. It was set in hard uncompromising lines, his eyes as merciless as the heavy seas she had seen at the Cape of Good Hope. And as dangerous, too, she realized.

'Douglas . . .'

Her husband looked indifferently at the poor wretch hanging in the rigging. 'It's entirely up to the captain, my dear,' he said, and turned his back on her.

Annis, unable to watch McNair's misery, went below to the saloon. She had heard that the officers aboard the crack American clippers were more ruthless than their British counterparts, and now she was seeing a little of that ruthlessness.

'Have you taken the man down from the rigging?' she asked eagerly when Douglas and Gideon and the two mates arrived in the saloon for their evening meal several hours later.

Gideon was still hard-faced. 'I have not, ma'am.'

'Surely he's been punished enough.'

'Not,' said Gideon, passing the bread plate along the table, 'in my opinion.'

'Is this a fair penalty for malingering?' she appealed to the mates, but they shifted uneasily in their seats, eyes lowered, and left it to their commander to answer.

'If it had only been that, Mrs Moncrieff, I would have set the wretch to work until he dropped and left it at that. He's in the rigging because of his insolence.'

'What did he say to you?'

Gideon merely looked at her, then bent his head over his plate, shutting her out of his sight and his thoughts as firmly as if he had walked from the cabin.

They sailed through a short heavy squall during the night. Annis lay awake beside Douglas, who was sleeping the sleep of the self-righteous, and listened to the rain hurling itself against the windows. She couldn't get McNair out of her head. She didn't like the man, but she couldn't bear to see him – or any man, for that matter – punished so severely. He was still there in the morning, hanging limply against the ratlines, his head drooping. The minutes dragged by until finally, when the midday sun high overhead must have been an unbearable torment to McNair, Gideon ordered him brought down.

Annis watched, her fingers white-knuckled on the deck railing, as the limp body was lowered to the deck. A bucket of sea-water was hauled inboard and thrown over him. He coughed and shook his head, then gulped greedily at the pitcher of fresh water the boatswain held to his lips. After a moment he was hauled to his feet and helped towards the crew's quarters.

'You see, ma'am?' Gideon's voice said coolly from just behind Annis. 'He's none the worse, and a deal wiser, I hope.'

She turned, saw his lifted eyebrow and faintly mocking eyes, and walked back to her corner without answering. She was shaking, but with disgust and anger this time, not emotion. Gideon's deliberate cruelty towards McNair had appalled her, shown him in a different light. She had longed to see him at the wheel of a ship, but now she had seen enough. She swallowed hard, staring out over the moving ocean without seeing it, hating Gideon Brenner for what he had done.

By that afternoon Sam McNair was back at work. But two days later Callum slipped into the cabin when Annis was alone and said hesitantly, 'Ma'am, d'you mind the seaman that the captain punished?'

'Yes?'

'He's sick,' said the boy. 'Real sick this time. But if the captain finds out he'll only think he's pretending the way he was before.'

His clear blue eyes met hers and she saw honest concern in them. 'None of us likes him, Mrs Moncrieff, for he's a trouble-maker and a whiner. But it wouldn't be right if he was to be punished this time.'

'Where is he?'

'In his hammock. His watch'll be called out soon and I don't see him being able to go aloft, not the way he is.'

'If the man's really ill Captain Brenner will surely see that for himself.'

Callum's fingers twisted together nervously. 'You'd

think so, ma'am, but the captain has a down on Sam for some reason only the two of 'em knows and—'

'Take me to the crew's quarters.'

'You couldn't go there, ma'am,' the boy said in horror. 'I just thought that you might speak to the captain before he sees Sam.'

'I'll have to see him for myself before I speak to the captain,' Annis informed him. 'Come on now . . . I'll make sure that nobody blames you.'

The crew slept and ate in an apartment below the forecastle deck. A long table with fixed benches on either side took up one wall; above it, and all along the opposite wall, there were lockers where the men could store their belongings. The ceiling was studded with hammock hooks and the hammocks themselves, when not in use, were neatly rolled and stacked against a third wall.

The place was only dimly lit by daylight filtering in through the small ports. It smelled sourly of damp clothes and human habitation. As Annis stepped in, the men lounging at the table looked up in astonishment. The drone of conversation stopped at once as the sailors scrambled to their feet, clearly horrified by this intrusion.

Ignoring them, Annis went at once to the single hammock slung from the roof. She recognized Sam McNair, even in the gloom. His lined face was flushed and sunken and in the sudden silence his breath sounded harsh.

She put a hand on his forehead. It was burning hot.

'Is nobody looking after this man?' she asked quietly.

There was an uncomfortable shifting of feet. It was left to Callum to whisper, 'They're afraid, ma'am, lest . . .'

Lest they incur the shipmaster's wrath, Annis thought grimly.

'D'you have a medicine chest on board?'

Someone brought it to her, together with a copy of *The Ship Master's Medical Guide*. Someone else, when she asked, brought her a lamp, for although the sun was shining outside it was quite dark in the crew's quarters. As she sifted through the medicine chest and selected the items she needed a voice outside roared an order and the men melted away, leaving her alone with Callum and McNair.

A moment later a figure darkened the doorway and Gideon Brenner's voice said, 'What's going on here?'

Annis turned to face him. 'This man is ill.'

He stepped to the hammock and glanced at its occupant. 'Get up, McNair!'

'For pity's sake, man, have you no sense at all?' Annis caught his hand, lifted it to McNair's face. 'He's got a fever!'

Gideon pulled his fingers free of hers. His face was hard as he looked down at her. 'Perhaps he has, this time. But that's no reason why you should be in the crew's quarters, Mrs Moncrieff. Allow me to escort you back to your own cabin.'

'What will happen to him?'

Gideon didn't look at McNair. 'He'll get better, or he'll die.'

'What if his fever spreads to the others?'

'We're not far from Australia now. We've a fair chance of reaching land while most of the crew are still able to man the ship.'

'And then you'll bury your dead and find another crew to take the vessel home?' She laced her voice with the anger and contempt she felt for him at that moment.

'If necessary,' he said, his own voice level. 'But I doubt

277

that it'll come to that. In the meantime the crew's quarters are no place for a passenger.'

'In that case, Captain, please have this man removed to a place where I can look after him.'

'Madam,' his voice took a cutting edge, 'I have already had occasion to point out to your husband that on board this ship there is only one master.'

'If I defy you, Captain Brenner, what do you intend to do with me? Hang me from the ratlines as you did with this poor man? Go ahead and do it if you wish. I will not leave him here to die alone and without help.'

Anger almost crackled in the air between them. Annis could feel Callum's tension as he tried to shrink back into the shadows, afraid to go without permission, yet afraid to stay. Finally Gideon said tightly, 'Mrs Moncrieff, there is no need—'

'There is every need,' Annis interrupted. She was furious enough now to move Sam McNair on her own if need be. 'In my view you've treated this man badly, and as a result he has a fever. Somebody must see to him. If you refuse to move him then I'll care for him here.'

McNair groaned and his head thrashed from side to side. Even in the dimness Annis could see Gideon's face set into stormy lines. For the first time they faced each other as enemies; then after a moment he said stiffly, 'Very well, ma'am, since you will not do as I ask I shall have the man moved to the wheelhouse aft.'

She gave him a stiff little nod. 'Thank you, Captain Brenner. Callum, come with me . . . and bring the medicine chest with you,' she commanded and swept out on to the deck, where she drew in deep draughts of fresh air.

For once shipmaster and ship-owner were united in

their views, but like Brenner, Douglas found that Annis was deaf to appeals or orders.

'If the man has something catching you'll give it to us all, having him brought to this part of the ship,' Douglas raged.

'Better to remove him from the rest of the crew. If they fall sick, you and I will be of little help to Captain Brenner,' his wife retorted. 'He can do well enough without us.'

'Have you no thought to your own safety, or mine?'

'I don't intend that either of us will sicken or die, Douglas. If the man's taken out of that miserable hole he lies in now and nursed in isolation there's a very good chance that nobody else will fall ill.'

'I wish,' said Douglas bitterly, 'that I had not given in to the temptation to keep you by my side. You were never as rebellious as this in Greenock!'

Once McNair was settled in a bunk in the wheelhouse Annis set Callum to bathing his body with vinegar and water. She knotted her brows over the *Medical Guide* and the well-stocked box which held laudanum, mercury, quinine, carbolic acid lotion and gentian violet, as well as purging pills and various patent medicines. When Callum pointed out that the only person on board who knew something of the box's contents was the ship's master she told him curtly that she could manage. She would not turn to Gideon Brenner for advice, not after the way he had treated McNair. Carefully she mixed up one of the powders with water and coaxed it into the man's mouth, drop by drop. Then she spooned a weak mixture of brandy and water into him at frequent intervals.

He babbled in his delirium, broken sentences that Annis didn't understand. The little she did grasp did nothing to endear her to the man. Clearly he was an unscrupulous rogue, and she wished that Douglas hadn't insisted on his staying on board as part of the crew.

Douglas kept well away from the deckhouse and insisted on Annis washing thoroughly and changing clothes before going near him, in case of contagion. Gideon looked in from time to time, his face and voice noncommittal when he asked after his crewman and after her own health. He was furious with her for defying him on board the ship he commanded, she realized that, but she was equally angry, and their brief cold exchange of words each time he appeared showed that neither of them was prepared to back down.

Within a few days McNair's fever had broken and he was clear-eyed. Annis added raw eggs from the few chickens that hadn't been eaten during the long journey to his brandy and water, and went down to the crowded little galley to make some soup to tempt his appetite. Propped up against the bulkhead, McNair obediently took the soup from the spoon in her hand, his eyes fixed on hers with a disconcerting stare. She kept her own gaze firmly on the spoon, and jumped when his dry, rough hand suddenly clamped itself about her wrist. A few drops from the spoon fell to the coverlet.

'I'll not forget what you done for me, missus,' he said. His voice, though weak, held the ingratiating whine that seemed an integral part of it.

'It was nothing.'

'I'd have died without you,' he insisted, adding with a venomous look towards the open door. 'He'd've let me die and been glad to throw me over the side.'

'I doubt that. Captain Brenner's a just man.'

'Not when he bears a grudge. An' he bears me one, though only him an' me knows the truth of it . . .'

He seemed set to tell her more, but to her relief Gideon himself came into the deckhouse at that moment. At once McNair's hand fell away from Annis, his eyes closed and he sagged back against the bulkhead, his breathing roughening.

Gideon selected a chart from the table, then stepped to the bunk. 'How's your patient this morning, ma'am?'

She ignored the thread of sarcasm in his voice. She had not forgiven the heartless way he had behaved.

'Doing well, Captain. I think he'll be ready to return to his own quarters tomorrow.'

'Good,' he said, then, 'And yourself, Mrs Moncrieff? Are you well?'

'Perfectly well, thank you.' She lifted her eyes to his, then let them drop again. Angry though she was, his clear straight gaze set her heart thumping.

'But somewhat pale. You should walk on deck more and get good fresh air.' His voice, though formal, had a rough kindness in it.

When Gideon had gone McNair's eyes snapped open to look at her reproachfully.

'I doubt I'll be well enough by tomorrow, missus.'

'I think you will,' she told him crisply. She had just seen evidence for herself of the man's willingness to malinger, and she wanted no part of it. The grip on her wrist had been surprisingly strong, and now that he was no longer weak and helpless her former uneasiness had returned.

Two days later Sam McNair was back on watch, though confined, at Annis's request, to doing only light

281

duties. Her life on board returned to normal now that she no longer had a patient, but the former warmth between herself and Gideon Brenner had gone. For her own part, Annis told herself, she was glad about it. Disliking him made for an easier and less guilt-ridden life than caring for him. She nursed her anger and took solace from it.

As the *Grace and Charity*, named for two sisters who had let pride turn them into strangers, winged her way like a huge white bird towards Melbourne, Annis was free again to look forward to her meeting with Olivia.

14

'The best is what he wanted, and the best is what he's getting. But I still think that Grieve made a mistake with the designer he chose.' Jem Moncrieff stood at the door of the building that acted as store, sail and design loft, and office, and glowered at the great hulk of the vessel in the stocks before him.

The ship was to be launched on 2 February, and at that moment some of Moncrieff's men were busy checking the retaining supports and placing the great anchors firmly into gravel so that their chains would slow and stop the vessel's rush into the water once the cradle beams let her go.

'You can't stop men making fools of themselves if they're bent on it,' Robert Moncrieff said with a wisdom beyond his years. Although he was well wrapped up against the winter cold, his straight Moncrieff nose was bright red. 'But it's sad to think that if we're right she'll have more chance than most of going to the bottom.'

'Bad enough to lose a good ship that's had craftsmen's work put into her, but worse to think of the lives she might take with her,' Jem agreed.

There was silence for a moment, then Robert, deciding that the sleety smirr that blew in on them from the river made the day gloomy enough without adding to it, slapped his kinsman on the back. 'Cheer up, Jem . . . once she's gone you'll be able to start on the new brigantine.'

Jem caught the boy's change of mood and followed it. 'I will – and it looks as though my luck's changing. Gideon was right when he said that I'd be wise to use one of my own ships. That wee schooner's almost earned her own keep already. I think I'll keep that one too . . .' He nodded to the half-built vessel on the smaller stocks. 'There's no shortage of seamen to sail in her, and by the time she's seaworthy Gideon'll be back to take command. I near forgot – there's a parcel of letters from the *Grace and Charity* in my office. The schooner captain brought them in yesterday from a vessel in the Thames.'

Robert followed him upstairs, glad to get out of the wind, and eagerly thumbed through the letters, stuffing the first two into his pocket. His face lit up when he came to the last and thickest one.

'It's for me, from Annis. The others are for Mr Beaton and Aunt Tib.' He fingered the package, then asked diffidently, 'D'you want to hear what she has to say?'

Jem did, very much, but he could tell by the boy's eyes that he wanted the first precious read to be in private so that he could savour every word.

'I've got too much to do today. Why don't you tell me about it later?' he suggested, and Robert nodded his relief as the bulky package was stowed carefully in an inner pocket where Tib's sharp eyes wouldn't spot it.

'You'll be coming to the launch tomorrow?' Jem asked as they went back downstairs and out into the yard.

'I will that. I'm going to take the time off no matter whether old Beaton tells Aunt Tib on me or not. Jem, can I go on board for the launch?'

'You cannot. There'll be enough people on board, what with some of the owner's friends and the workmen who have to be there.'

'I've never been on a ship during a launch,' Robert persisted. 'I'd stay well out of the way, I promise you. Please, Jem?'

The older man surveyed him sternly for a moment then said grudgingly, 'Very well. But you'll keep aft, for she'll smack hard into the water and I don't want anything happening to you.'

'Thank you, Jem!' Glowing, Robert seized Jem's hand and shook it hard. Then he turned and took one last look at the ship towering above them.

'I'll try to bring you some good luck, *Venturer*,' he promised.

'God's teeth, has the man gone and told everyone what her name's to be?'

'I heard it in the office this morning.' Robert tugged his coat collar up around his ears.

Jem's brows were furrowed. Used to being outdoors, he was impervious to the wind that made Robert's eyes water. 'She'll need the luck you mean to bring her, then, for it's not good to let folk know a ship's name before the launching. What's the point in me keeping my tongue between my teeth if the owner goes mouthing the name to anyone who cares to ask him?'

'Ach, mebbe it's all superstition,' Robert said lightly, and went off through the yard gates with a farewell wave.

Jem watched him go. He loved Robert dearly, far more than the boy realized, and often railed helplessly in secret at the way Douglas and Tib had raised the boy, doing their best to break his spirit and make him conform. He shouldn't have agreed to let the lad go on board the new

285

vessel for the launching, but he felt even sorrier than usual for him. Robert wasn't one to complain, but from the little he let slip Jem gathered that Tib Moncrieff and the clerks in the office were taking advantage of Douglas's absence and giving him a hard time. With Annis away from home he had no one to confide in, so he came to the yard whenever he could. Busy though he was, Jem always made him welcome.

There was one consolation, Jem thought as he turned back to his own work. Robert was made of better and stronger stuff than Douglas Moncrieff, and one day it would come to the fore. When that happened, when Douglas no longer had the power of guardianship over the boy, Jem would be able to show his pride openly. Until then, all he could do was to create pockets of happiness and security in the rocky road that Robert had to walk.

'You'd think,' Jem muttered to himself, 'that Douglas might have taken the trouble to write a word or two in his own hand to the laddie!'

Although his ship was built in a small yard, Charles Grieve had decided to make an occasion of the launching. Mercifully the wintry showers cleared in time for the occasion, although the sky was low and grey and the wind still keen when Robert arrived at the yard the next day.

The place was bedecked with flags, long tables had been set up in the loft to accommodate the official revellers afterwards, and a brewer's dray was drawn up in the cobbled street outside, the horse occupied with a nosebag while the driver and his assistant carried barrels and crates up the shaky wooden stairs.

On the launching platform someone was trying to wrap

coloured ribbon round the rails and supports, fighting the wind every inch of the way.

Jem was overseeing the placing of baulks of timber along the line of the anchor chains. If the anchors digging into gravel dragged after the ship once she reached the water some strong men would be ready to use the timber to wedge the anchors in place. Otherwise, the newly-launched ship would charge across the river out of control, colliding with any craft in her way.

'Best whisky for this launch,' he said with a grin when Robert joined him. He looked unlike himself in a formal dark jacket with a white shirt and a neat cravat. His beard and hair had been trimmed. 'It seems a shame to me to give it all to a ship.'

'There'll be plenty more afterwards, from what I can see.' Robert was pleased to see that his kinsman's mood had improved overnight. A launch was a launch, and no matter how much he might disapprove of the ship's design Jem was now as caught up as everyone else in the excitement of the day.

Together they walked round the ship, checking that everything was in readiness. As they went, Robert gave Jem a swift résumé of Annis's long letter, ending, with a grin, 'I'll admit that I'm pleased it was Uncle Douglas that fell seasick and not her.'

'Aye, he'd be black affronted at being shown up by a slip of a lass, would Douglas. They'll be close to Australia now, all going well.'

'It will be with Gideon in command.' Robert turned his head as a carriage swept in at the gate. 'Here's your owner and his wife. I'll leave you to greet him.'

'You'll come up to the loft afterwards?'

'Mebbe,' Robert said non-commitally. 'And mebbe I'll

just stay on board a while before I go back to the office. I'll be interested to see how she rides the water.'

When Jem had gone, he wandered back around the ship, then walked to a spot some distance away and studied her, lips pursed. Taking a small pad of paper and a pencil out of his pocket, he sketched her lines roughly, then went over them again, this time in more detail, fining her down, drawing her as he still thought she should have been designed.

He was so caught up in his work that he almost missed his hard-won chance to go on board for the launch. Seeing the workmen shinning up the scaffolding like monkeys and the désigner and other guests, all snugly wrapped in furs and good broadcloth, being helped up the ladders that had been placed for them, he pushed paper and pencil into his pocket and ran, reaching the scaffolding and climbing it as nimbly as any shipwright's apprentice.

On board he looked with satisfaction about the great expanse of deck, clear as yet of masts and rigging. These would be fitted later, when the ship was towed to another wharf. At the moment the pitch-pine decks were laid bare to delight the eye. The companionways and skylights and other deck fittings were made of solid teak which would eventually be finished off with copal varnish to give it a look of mahogany. Robert ran his fingers round the edge of a hatch cover and experienced the pure pleasure of touching a beautiful piece of wood. Jem was a master at his craft and Robert, straightening up to gaze once more about the deck, resolved again to work with his kinsman when he was a full-grown man.

Most of the people on board were lining the decks, peering down past those gathered below. As he had promised, Robert made his way aft and found a quiet spot by the rails, too far away to look down on the launching party or hear Mrs Grieve's short speech, delivered in a fluting voice that was, for the most part, snatched from her lips by the wind and carried inland. Instead he peered down at the water's edge, where those shipwrights who had no duties to perform waited with their apprentices.

Robert grinned and congratulated himself on gaining a place on board, when he might have been left to stand beside the wrights. It was their custom to 'blood' new apprentices at a launch; once the ship went in the apprentices would be picked up and hurled into the great wave it set up. The lucky ones would only get one ducking; those who didn't run fast enough when they scrambled out were usually thrown in again. Today the water was icy, and Robert well knew that 'prentice or no 'prentice, he would probably have been hurled in with the other lads in the excitement of the moment. The apprentices who had already received their blooding were on board, gathered forward in a tight group, ready to haul in the bottle once it had been smashed on the bows.

Robert yawned and stretched and wished that the people down below would get on with it. And as though he had bawled the words down at them, they obeyed. He heard the smash of broken glass, then the howls of the apprentices as they fought over the line. One lad emerged the victor, and as he stood up and brandished a handful of bright ribbons over his head Robert heard the dull thudding of mallets as the dog shores holding the cradle were knocked loose far below.

The *Venturer* shivered, stilled, shivered again. Robert turned to look out over the river, gripping the rail and pushing hard against it as though his puny strength could shift the great mass beneath his feet.

'Come on, lass . . . come on!' he whispered between gritted teeth, then gave a whoop of delight as he felt her quiver again, then start to move.

With a resounding clatter of wooden blocks and the rattling of huge links of chain, the ship slid down the aisle carefully greased for her, gathering momentum as she went.

Everyone on deck cheered, a cheer that was echoed again and again from the yard below. Although he had found a sheltered spot, Robert's hair was lifted from his head by the wind generated by her increasing speed; together he and the *Venturer* skimmed towards the river, and into it.

It was the most exciting moment he had ever known. Since babyhood he had been captivated by the graceful curtsey of a ship entering water for the first time. Now he was part of that dip and rise, and below him white spray rose and flew to either side as the *Venturer* tasted the river for the first time. Behind him the deck rose so that the knot of apprentices, still over dry land, were uphill of him, hanging on to the rails to stop themselves from sliding down the deck. Then the whole length of the *Venturer* took to the water and the stern bounced up beneath Robert as the deck levelled off.

In the yard Jem watched anxiously as the chain cables ran out. He swore and jumped anxiously forward as one of them snapped, but his men knew their business and none of them were hit by the loose chain as it lashed viciously through the air, then collapsed well clear of the crowd.

At the water's edge the first of the new apprentices was

being thrown into the great wave that was sent crashing inland by the shock of the *Venturer*'s arrival. The others were taking to their heels with burly wrights in hot pursuit.

Now that one of the cables had gone it was up to the anchors to stop the vessel's headlong rush into the river. One of them held firm but the other dragged through the gravel. Three or four men were waiting; the first huge timber baulk thrust into the jaws of the anchor stopped its rush and secured it.

Jem gave a sigh of relief. Every launch, no matter how carefully planned, had its risks. But this one, he thought, was a success.

A gasping cry from the crowd snapped his head round towards the river. The *Venturer* had slowed to a standstill; for a moment she had floated there, but now, slowly, slowly, before the horrified eyes of the onlookers she began to heel to starboard.

For a moment Jem stood still, then he began to run towards the water's edge.

'Robert!' he screamed. 'Robert!'

When he felt the slight movement to starboard Robert thought at first that he was imagining it. But when he looked across at the far shore and saw it tilting he realized that the *Venturer* was indeed beginning to list.

There were cries of alarm from other people on the deck. As he turned to look down the length of the ship he saw some who had been at the port rail slithering down the tilting planks. As the list quickly became more noticeable Robert let go of the rails and began to run awkwardly, arms held out for balance, making for the dipping rail with the intention of diving off it and swimming clear if he had to.

It seemed impossible that the *Venturer* could heel right over, but there was no sign as yet of her righting herself. She lurched, and Robert staggered and almost fell. He regained his balance and ran on down the wooden hill that was growing steeper by the moment.

He wasn't afraid, but he knew now that he had to get into the water as quickly as he could, before the bulk of the capsizing ship rolled on to him. As he ran he tore off his jacket and threw it aside, dimly registering the thought that Aunt Tib would be furious if he lost it.

Aunt Tib, he thought with bleak despair as he reached the rail and stopped to pull his shoes off, would be furious anyway. There would be no way now of hiding today's disobedience from her, no way of pretending that he had gone to the office as usual.

The port rail was thronged with men and boys now, some of them screaming for help, some silent. Some, like Robert, were preparing to dive into the water, directly below them but still some distance away.

'Jump!' he shouted at a well-dressed, elderly man who huddled against the rail, ashen-faced and motionless. 'Jump for your life!'

The man looked at him and Robert saw the fear of death in his eyes. He thought of trying to lift him and push him over the rail, but the ship gave another shuddering lurch just then and he knew that there was no time. He planted one stockinged foot on the rail, then dived.

The water was like liquid ice, but the dive had been a good one and he surfaced without any trouble. There were a few people in the water besides him, all trying, as he must try, to swim clear.

He took a few strokes, but his limbs were already

numbed and weakened by cold, and he registered with dim surprise that the ship's undertow was strong enough to pull him back. He looked up and saw that the *Venturer* was heeling over fast now, descending on him and the other swimmers like a box lid closing on a set of toy soldiers. At that point he knew there was no time to swim clear of the great smothering weight, or the whirlpool of sucking water it would create when it went down to settle on the river-bed.

'We were right,' he thought. 'We were right, Jem and I. That design was all wrong.'

Then the *Venturer* completed her roll and there was no more time, in the great confusion of rushing water and crushing timber, to reflect any further on the folly of the ship's design.

15

The *Grace and Charity*, making excellent time in spite of the Doldrums and the struggle round the Cape, docked in Melbourne a full week before its expected date.

Leaving Gideon to see to the unloading of cargo and the loading of new cargo, which had been arranged in advance, the Moncrieffs drove into the city and booked rooms at a comfortable hotel in Bourke Street, where they settled down more happily than they had been on board ship. The stimulus of being so far from home and in a continent entirely new to him brought about a change in Douglas. He became relaxed and enthusiastic, much easier to be with. For her part Annis was relieved to be away from Gideon, for the tension between them since their disagreement over Sam McNair's treatment had destroyed all the pleasure she had known during the earlier part of the voyage. Now, as was only right, she was free to devote her time and attention to her husband.

Impressed and delighted by the size and sophistication of Melbourne, they spent a few happy days exploring its parks and shops and suburbs while waiting for Olivia and her husband to arrive. Douglas took a delight in spoiling his wife, showering her with gifts as they went from one shop to another.

'I've no need of any more gifts,' she protested,

laughing, as the two of them emerged from a jewellers' eight days after their arrival.

Douglas patted his pocket, where a gold and pearl necklace lay snugly in its velvet-lined case. 'You'll wear it beautifully, and that's all that I ask,' he said, and drew her on to the next shop to study the silk gloves laid out on display.

They returned to the hotel to find a letter waiting for them. Douglas scanned it swiftly. 'At last! Your sister has arrived in Melbourne, my dear. She and her brother-in-law are staying at the Oriental Hotel in Collins Street.'

'Her brother-in-law? But why hasn't her husband come with her?'

'I've no more idea of that than you have,' Douglas pointed out. 'They ask us to dine there with them, at eight o'clock this evening.'

As she dressed for the appointment Annis felt quite sick with excitement. Her hands trembled as she donned the blue silk gown that Douglas had bought for her the day before. She was wearing it at his wish, though she would have preferred to wear something more mature. The sky-blue silk, with its demure lace-edged neckline and slightly trained skirt, made her look like a child.

Douglas came into the room at that moment. 'Let me look at you.' He nodded his satisfaction as she revolved obediently before him. 'You look beautiful, my darling. Come here . . .'

He opened the box in his hands and brought out the new necklace, fastening it carefully, then kissing the nape of her neck.

'I'm quite certain that Olivia cannot better you for elegance,' he said with satisfaction, and some of Annis's excitement in the meeting ahead ebbed away. She felt like a doll dressed up to be put on show.

Douglas turned her to face the mirror and stood by her side so that they were both reflected. He himself was stylish in a dark blue suit with snowy white shirt and a black bow tie.

'I think,' he said, 'that we make a most handsome couple, my dear. Shall we go?'

Olivia was even more nervous than Annis, but determined not to show it. In the past few weeks she had used up all Drina Platt's skin cream, then raided the store at the main house for glycerine and honey which she had whipped up into a lotion. Each night she brushed her hair until it crackled and shone. Each morning when John had gone she rubbed fat into her hands and put on gloves to protect her skin from the rigours of housework. She also beat up the whites of eggs and smeared them over her face, grateful for once that the hut was so isolated. At first sight of anyone approaching she flew to tear her gloves off and wash her face before her secret was discovered.

She was put out when she heard that Matthew, not John, was going to Melbourne to meet Douglas Moncrieff. At her urging John might have presented himself well enough to the Moncrieffs, but she doubted her control over his brother. From the first moment they met in his father's house she had been aware of Matthew Mundy's antagonism. He wanted her out of Vanduara just as much as Jeremiah did. He had managed to make it obvious with a word here and there, a raised eyebrow and a sneering curve of the lips when she spoke. He had failed in his own marriage, and he and Jeremiah wanted no more women on Vanduara. But they had met their match in Olivia, she was quite sure of that. Her husband was joint heir to the Mundy money and she would be by his side when he inherited it. The Lord knew that she had earned it already, living in that pitiful shack, putting up with the sun and the flies and the hated wash-board and everything else Australia threw at her.

'Why won't your father send you?'

John shrugged. 'I was there the last time. And Matt's the oldest.'

'How can I travel with him?' Olivia wailed.

'Stay home then,' said John. 'Stay with me.'

But she would rather have travelled with the devil than missed seeing Annis.

'I'll go to Melbourne,' she said through tight lips. She raided the trunk stored at the main house and chose three of her finest gowns, thankful that because of Douglas Moncrieff's need to hurry back to Scotland she would only need sufficient clothes for a few days.

'You're surely not taking all that,' Matthew protested when he saw the luggage John was loading on to the buggy.

'Yes I am,' Olivia snapped, and pulled on her be-ribboned wide-brimmed bonnet. As John helped her up into the buggy, Matthew, already on the bench, gave her a sly sidelong look which she ignored. She knew that the hat was out of place at Vanduara, but it wouldn't be in Melbourne. Besides, she must protect her skin from the sun.

As the buggy drew away from the station she twisted in her seat to see John standing there, watching her. Glad though she was to visit Melbourne again, she felt a strange twinge of loss as his tall spare figure wavered in the heat waves, then disappeared. She wondered if he would miss her, and wished that he had been by her side, not Matt.

Because of the sheer size of Vanduara they had to spend one night under the stars. On her way into the station as John's bride Olivia had been horrified at the prospect. Now, she was not only hardened to suffering, she would not for the world complain to Matthew, whose eyes held the same sardonic glint as his father's.

On her way in, she and John had stayed in a sheepman's hut, but this time the dry creek bed was running and they had to turn away from where the shack stood on the opposite bank in order to find a crossing, the horses plunging through yellow water while Olivia held her skirts as high as modesty allowed to keep them from getting splashed. That night she had to sleep as best she could on a pile of soft leaves in a bower Matthew made for her by pulling branches down and tying them into place. Their second night was spent in greater comfort at the Platt homestead, where Olivia passed a few pleasant hours showing Drina her lovely gowns and basking in the other woman's admiration. When they set off on their way to the stage-coach the next day, three jars of Drina's face-cream had been added to her luggage together with a list of items to buy in Melbourne so that she could make up her own preparations.

They had endured the long and bumpy stage-coach ride with its stops at wayside inns and were in the train, close to Melbourne itself, before Olivia plucked up the courage to ask Matthew the favour that had been trembling on her lips since the moment he had driven her away from John and Vanduara.

He was staring intently out of the train window,

studying the sheep in the pastures and pens as they passed, when she cleared her throat and, with a confidence she didn't feel, said, 'Matthew, I would appreciate it if you would not talk to my sister or her husband about the living conditions John and I have to endure.'

'Hmm?' He dragged his eyes reluctantly from the window. For a moment he looked perplexed, then his brows rose in that maddening superior way that he had. 'Ahh! Am I take it, my dear Livvy, that you've been less than truthful with your sister?'

Angry colour rose to her face. 'My sister — and her husband — would be most annoyed if they knew that John and I were expected to live in such a hovel.'

'I found it comfortable enough.'

'You Australians are used to primitive conditions,' she snapped, and the grin that had been hovering round his mouth broadened.

'You've let them think that you live in the main house, haven't you?'

Humiliated, angry enough now to attack him, she linked her hands tightly in her lap and said nothing.

'Would your family really think the less of you if they knew the truth? After all, John's the son of a rich man and one day you really will live in the big house. Won't you, Livvy?'

'You're hoping I'll run first . . . like your wife,' she snapped at him, driven to it by his tormenting. The jibe hit home. His smile faded and for a moment his eyes were icy. She instantly regretted what she had said. He would never agree to help her now. He would ridicule her in front of Annis and Douglas, she knew it. To her horror she felt her eyes fill with sudden tears.

She blinked rapidly, then bent her head as a few of

them refused to be banished and threatened to overflow down her carefully creamed face.

Matthew didn't say another word. When she looked up again he was gazing out of the window once more, and it was as though the conversation had never taken place.

He had arranged rooms for them at the hotel where she and John had stayed for the few days before their marriage and spent their wedding night. As soon as they arrived Matthew went off to find out if there was any news of the *Grace and Charity*. Olivia unpacked her clothes and took a long hot bath in one of the hip-baths provided for hotel guests. Afterwards she took her time over dressing then went downstairs and ordered tea. She had no interest in going out; she just wanted to surround herself with the sheer luxury of the place, the carpets underfoot, the servants, the air of opulence.

It was a world away from Vanduara and the wooden shack. The thought of going back there was unbearable now, and she wondered, as she sipped her tea and nibbled on some sweet biscuits, if she should tell Annis the truth after all. Even Douglas would be shocked to learn about the life she was forced to lead now. Surely he and Annis would insist on taking her back to Scotland with them. Not — Olivia shuddered at the thought — to live in that dreadful house again with that dreadful sister of Douglas's. No, she would never do that. But there were other places: Glasgow, Edinburgh, even London. Places where she could find a good position and ultimately make a better marriage than the first, she was sure of it.

Matthew arrived while she was still thinking about it. 'They've been in Melbourne for the past week,' he reported, dropping into a chair by her side and reaching for a biscuit. She was annoyed to see that he was not in the least awed by the splendour of the hotel; Matthew Mundy, it seemed, had enough arrogance to be at home anywhere.

'You saw Annis?'

'No, but I spoke to the shipmaster. She and her husband are staying in one of the Bourke Street hotels. They were out, so I left a message inviting them to dine with us here this evening. Brenner said that the clipper's almost ready for the return passage and Moncrieff wants to be off as soon as he can, so we'll not be delayed here for long ourselves.'

Olivia was jolted by the news. 'Brenner? Gideon Brenner? I understood that he had left my brother-in-law's employment some time ago.'

'I don't know about that,' Matthew said carelessly, helping himself to another biscuit, quite unaware of the turmoil he had caused. 'I only know that he's the shipmaster. An American, to judge by his drawl.'

She dressed very carefully for the dinner party, choosing a gown she had bought in Scotland and never had occasion to wear. It was a deep red taffeta dress trimmed with black silk ruffles. The bodice was low-necked and tight-fitting, showing off her figure to perfection. Studying herself in the mirror, running her hands over her breasts and waist and hips, Olivia thought how fortunate she was to have such a good body. Beside her, Annis would always look immature.

She piled her hair on top of her head, allowing a few ringlets to cascade down her neck, then slipped the opal ring on to her finger and turned to the mirror again. She looked every inch the wife of a rich and successful man.

Matthew, she saw as soon as they met in the private

dining room put aside for their use, looked every inch the son of a rich and successful man. He had chosen a black jacket and grey trousers with a white shirt and a multi-coloured silk waistcoat. His hair had been well brushed and his nails, she could swear, had been professionally manicured. There was no trace now of the casually dressed boundary rider who spent his days in the saddle beneath the blazing sun. She wished with vexation that John had his brother's way with clothes as well as his brother's hold on his father. John's lean, rangy body looked good in the casual shirts, trousers and riding boots he wore at Vanduara, but in more formal clothes he looked ill at ease.

Matthew's dark eyes travelled over her slowly with a masculine appreciation that was both offensive and flattering. 'You look beautiful, Livvy,' he said lifting the glass of wine in his hand in a toast. 'Beautiful enough to turn any man's head.'

'But scarcely yours, Matthew.'

He filled a glass and handed it to her, letting his fingers brush against hers. 'You think so? Here we are, far from Vanduara, far from John . . .'

He paused, watched her with bright eyes. A wave of anger swept over Olivia as she realized what he meant. How dare this man who had done all he could to make her feel unwelcome in her husband's home make advances to her when it suited him? How dare he think that he was a better man than John?

'Unlike you, Matthew, your brother married a woman who believes in the vows she took,' she said, her voice biting. 'But I expect you'll find some women less able to resist your charms here in the Melbourne streets. Such females ply their trade in all cities, I believe.'

His brown face flushed to brick red. He laughed, but the sound was strangled and mechanical. 'Quite the lady of the big house, aren't you, Livvy — when you dress the part.'

She managed to smile at the jibe and sipped her wine, in need of its strengthening properties. Ignoring the fact that she still stood, Matthew threw himself down in a chair, gnawing at a finger. It suddenly occurred to Olivia that he may well take revenge by telling Annis and Douglas the truth about her life in Vanduara. For a moment she felt as though an icy hand had touched her, then she shrugged and took another mouthful of wine. Let him say what he wanted — nothing would be worse than submitting to him in order to buy his silence.

She looked down on his dark head and thought that John may have his faults, but he was easily twice the man Matthew was. Then the door opened and Annis and Douglas were ushered in.

Matthew leapt to his feet, the anger smoothed from his face. Although Douglas put a restraining hand on his wife's arm, Annis ignored it, running across the room to throw her arms about her sister.

'Olivia! I thought I'd never see you again!'

It was the first time the Kerr sisters had ever hugged each other with genuine warmth. For a moment everything was all right for Olivia, close in Annis's loving arms. If they had been alone at this first meeting her pleasure in seeing her sister might well have stayed, leading them both into the confidences they longed for. But when Olivia looked beyond Annis's shoulder she saw Douglas, dour and unchanged, and her heart fell. Then she heard Matthew's voice, saw the two men she so disliked advance and shake hands. Just then Annis drew back, laughing, and Olivia's eyes fell on the beautiful necklace that circled her sister's slim throat. She had a good idea of how much it had cost, and in that moment the old envy blazed up in her. It was for jewels such as these that she had come all the way to Australia, only to see them decorating a girl who could never appreciate them as she herself would.

She knew then that she could never tell her sister the truth about her life at Vanduara. She could never bring herself to seek Annis's sympathy and help.

'You look very well, Annis.' Her voice was friendly, yet distant, as though she was speaking to an acquaintance rather than the sister she had been longing to see again. 'Did you have a pleasant voyage?'

Annis immediately felt that nothing had changed. She was still the younger sister, the one who could do nothing to please. Her fingers nervously smoothed the folds of her skirt as Olivia offered a hand to Douglas, then introduced Matthew and Annis. The Australian held Annis's hand for just a second too long, in Olivia's opinion. She stood by, a smile pinned firmly to her lips, certain that he was trying to annoy her by paying attention to her sister.

Wine was poured, the first course brought in. Olivia seated them all at the small table, Douglas and Matthew facing each other, Annis opposite her.

The men were of one accord; time was short and they had a great deal to discuss. During the meal they launched into talk of wool prices, the cost of shipping bales to Britain, the market there.

As she gazed across the table at her sister, Annis knew that she should never have allowed Douglas to persuade her to wear the blue silk. Olivia glowed in her red taffeta gown. She was beautiful, and even the gold and pearl necklace, which Olivia had glanced at without interest and then ignored, suddenly felt like a mistake.

Olivia wore no ornaments with her gown except two rings, one of them a wedding ring. The other was very unusual, a white stone that suddenly flashed with unexpected colour as Olivia reached for some bread.

'May I see?' Annis asked, eager to engage her sister in conversation.

Olivia slipped it off and handed it across the table. 'It was a gift from John's father.'

'It's beautiful! Look, Douglas . . . see how the colours jump to the surface, then vanish again.'

Annis, entranced, turned the ring this way and that to catch the light, then handed it to her husband, who examined it before returning it to her waiting palm.

'It's a milk opal, Mrs Moncrieff,' Matthew Mundy told her. 'Mined on Vanduara. We've found a selection of fine stones there.'

As Annis toyed with the ring, fascinated by the moving pinpoints of colour, he told her how opals of varying sizes and colours could be found near the surface of the ground.

'I've seen it for myself. A shallow underground tunnel and the miner chipping away at the walls with his handpick. And suddenly' — he spread one hand in a graceful gesture — 'there it is. A sparkling band of colour. A fine piece of opal to be eased out of its resting place and cut and polished, ready to grace a lady's throat or fingers.'

'Of much value?' Douglas wanted to know.

'Indeed yes. The Vanduara mines have produced some of the finest opals in Australia. But the best are not for sale. My father prefers to keep them,' said Matthew casually, his eyes still on Annis.

When the meal had been cleared away the men moved to the window so that they could look out on Collins Street while they talked. Olivia and Annis sat on a plush sofa and Annis, delving into her memory for something that would interest her worldly sister, chattered on about Greenock.

'I understand that Gideon Brenner is here?' Olivia interrupted the flow of meaningless words. 'I thought you told me that he and Douglas . . .'

'Yes,' Annis interrupted hastily with a swift glance at Douglas. 'But the new shipmaster was unable to sail on this voyage, and there was nobody else but Gid — Captain Brenner.' She gave her sister a sidelong look. 'Perhaps you'll meet him before we sail.'

'I have no wish to meet him.' Olivia's voice was curt and dismissive. Her expression gave Annis no clue as to her thoughts.

'It's a great pity that your husband was unable to accompany you.'

'His father needed him on the sheep station. Matthew could be spared more easily.' Now it was Olivia's turn to glance guiltily at the men.

'Is he as handsome and charming as his brother?'

'Indeed,' said Olivia, 'or I wouldn't have married him.'

'What's Vanduara like? I wish we could visit it for ourselves,' said Annis, quite unaware how appalled Olivia was by the very thought, 'but Douglas is impatient to get back, so I can only learn about it from you.'

Olivia was well launched into a description of the big house with its shady verandahs, its fine furniture, its garden and cool rooms and servants, when the men turned from the window.

'My dear, it's getting late. We must get back to our hotel,' said Douglas, moving towards them.

Matthew, catching the drift of their conversation, smiled down on Annis. 'Is Olivia telling you all about her life on Vanduara? I can't think how we managed before she came to run the house for us,' he said silkily.

Olivia's head turned swiftly towards him. He met her glance, held it until she turned away again. There was a slight smile on his lips. He wasn't going to give her away, she realized. Not yet, at any rate. It pleased him more to keep her waiting, wondering when the blow might fall.

Back in her hotel room Annis took off the gold and pearl necklace and put it into its box. Compared to Olivia's beauty, offset by the opal ring, the necklace looked like a bauble. She had started the day in such high spirits, and she was ending it in a great depression. It seemed clear that Olivia's fine and successful marriage, instead of bringing them closer, had driven them even further apart.

'He's an astute man, Matthew Mundy.' Douglas, emerging from the small dressing room that led off the bedroom, was in a good mood. 'I believe he took a liking to you, my dear.'

'I don't think so.'

'He could scarcely take his eyes from you during dinner,' Douglas disagreed smugly. 'Be pleasant to him when we meet . . . it could well help to oil the wheels of business.'

She stared at him, and saw that he was quite serious. Apparently the imagined attentions he disapproved of in

Gideon Brenner were to be encouraged in Matthew Mundy because they suited Douglas's purpose.

Annis bit her lip to keep hurt, angry words back, and felt all her pleasure in being in Australia drain away. The idyllic days they had spent alone together in Melbourne were over. Now that Douglas was involved with business again, her life was slowly, inexorably, slipping back into its old rut. Back into the well of loneliness that, assisted by the realization that Olivia, like Douglas, hadn't changed, had already started to draw her into its depths. Later, in bed, she had to fight hard against a panic-stricken impulse to push her husband away when he reached for her in the dark.

The sisters were in each other's company frequently during the next few days, but to Annis's disappointment they only talked of superficial matters. Any attempt on her part to talk about themselves was carefully and coolly turned aside by Olivia, who took it upon herself to act as hostess and guide, showing her sister the city with a bored, worldly air.

Together they visited the museum, where Olivia stood by, fidgeting with her gloves, while Annis hovered over the exhibitions of the wool and leather and timber that illustrated the products of Victoria. They visited the shops, where Annis bought small gifts for Robert.

'Don't you want to buy anything?' she asked, and Olivia gave her a condescending smile.

'We want for nothing at Vanduara. Besides, most of the shops cater for empty-headed visitors looking for trinkets to prove that they've visited Australia.'

'Oh . . .' said Annis, and replaced the beautiful blush-pink shell she had been about to purchase.

On the day before the *Grace and Charity* was due to set sail for Scotland, Gideon was summoned from the harbour to give his views on the best way to pack and store wool for a long sea-voyage.

When Annis returned to her hotel room to change for the evening after a final day's sight-seeing with her sister, Douglas, already there, said irritably, 'Brenner's joining us for dinner and attending the concert with us.'

'Indeed?' She felt a little flurry of pleasure ripple through her, closely followed by a sense of unease at the thought of Gideon and Olivia meeting again.

'It was Mundy's idea, not mine. And since he's our host for the evening I had no choice but to agree.' Douglas's voice was sour.

Gideon dressed carefully for his appointment in a well-cut brown tail-coat, grey trousers, fawn waistcoat, white shirt and dark red cravat.

When he arrived at the restaurant in Collins Street, near the imposing Treasury, the rest of the party were waiting for him. At first he saw nobody but Olivia.

'Mrs Mundy . . .' He took her hand in his, taking in every detail of her in one glance. She was as lovely as he had remembered her to be, in a gown of vivid green that brought out the emerald lights in her hazel eyes. 'I'm delighted to see you looking so well, ma'am.'

She looked back at him coldly. 'Mr Brenner . . .' Her voice was flat and formal. She inclined her head and withdrew her fingers from his, turning away from him at once.

During the meal that followed Gideon sensed any feeling that he still harboured for Olivia withering and dying. Watching her across the table he began to wonder why he had ever allowed himself to be enslaved by her beauty. Behind it, he thought incredulously to himself, there was nothing — no warmth, no reality.

He glanced at her sister, who sat beside her, and saw that although Annis Moncrieff might live for ever in the shadow of Olivia's beauty, she was by far the better woman. There was fire in Annis's eyes, laughter in the curve of her mouth. He remembered the way she had defied both him and her husband over the business of Sam McNair, and how she had nursed the wastrel back to health with no thought for her own safety. And she had coped so well with shipboard life. She was worth six of Olivia, and ten of that shallow fool of a husband of hers. Poor woman, to be married to Douglas Moncrieff.

He turned from his study of Olivia and began talking easily to Matthew Mundy, including Douglas and Annis now and again, ignoring Olivia as she had ignored him. As he had said to Jem, there had been a need to see Olivia again. Now he had, and now he knew that the infatuation he had felt for her could never have bound them together. He felt whole again, alive and free.

After the meal they attended a musical concert in the Town Hall. Once or twice, during the evening, Annis stole a glance along the row at Gideon Brenner's profile, uplifted to the stage, and wondered what thoughts lay behind the calm mouth and hooded eyes.

At the end of the concert the Town Hall foyer was filled with people. Matthew Mundy shepherded his guests into a corner and left them there while he went in search of their carriage.

Annis, watching the crowd, saw a man and woman nearby, the man clearly impatient to be out of the crush, the plump woman's head turning this way and that, her eyes greedily devouring details of hair-styles, jewellery, gowns and cloaks. Suddenly the woman halted and gaped openly at Olivia, one hand twitching at the man's sleeve. He turned. A smile broke across his face and he bowed as best he could in the crowd. For a moment it looked as though he was going to join the group, but he faltered and stepped back, flushing, as Olivia, as she had done on meeting Gideon, turned her back on him.

The woman's face turned an ugly, angry red and she battled her way past, suddenly as anxious as her escort had been to get out onto the street.

'Who was that?'

'Nobody of any note,' Olivia said shortly. 'Just John's banker and his wife.'

'You must all come back to our hotel,' Annis suggested impetuously when they stood on the Town Hall steps. 'Since we leave tomorrow please allow us to return your hospitality before the evening ends, Mr Mundy.'

'We'd be delighted, Mrs Moncrieff,' Mundy said at once, without looking at Olivia.

'And you must come too, Captain Brenner.' She wanted to make amends for Olivia's rudeness.

Gideon hesitated, and for a moment she thought that he was going to make his excuses and return to his beloved clipper. Then he said formally, 'Thank you, ma'am, I would be delighted.'

As the carriage would have been crowded by five of them he elected to walk to the hotel, assuring Annis that he needed to stretch his legs.

'I can't think why you included Captain Brenner in your invitation, my dear,' Douglas said reprovingly as their party trundled back to the hotel.

'It would have been churlish not to.'

'It's going to be bad enough spending three more months in his company on the passage home without socializing with him as well.'

'I like the fellow,' Matthew Mundy announced.

'Probably because the Americans and the Australians, being colonists, have much in common,' Olivia said sharply. 'It's a different matter entirely for the British.'

'Olivia, how can you be so − so insensitive!' This time Annis didn't try to keep the anger from her voice. Her sister shrugged, and Matthew Mundy laughed.

'Please don't concern yourself, my dear Mrs Moncrieff. Your sister's outspoken views are a constant delight to my father and myself, I can assure you.'

Olivia said nothing, but Annis, seeing her sister's white teeth catch at her lower lip, had the feeling that she had just seen Olivia bested in some quarrel between these two that she knew nothing about.

Because the crush of people travelling homeward from Melbourne's various theatres was so great, the carriage took some time to reach the hotel and Gideon was already waiting for them in the private room that had been set aside for the Moncrieffs' use during their stay. Douglas saw to it that his wife and sister-in-law were supplied with glasses of cool lemonade, then turned to Matthew. 'You'll have a glass of the whisky I brought with me?'

'It would be a pleasure, sir.'

'Brenner?' Douglas asked stiffly.

Gideon was as impervious to his employer's coolness as he was to Olivia's. 'Thank you, sir,' he said cheerfully.

'You had no right to invite him,' Olivia muttered beneath her breath and Annis abruptly rose and crossed to the window where she fiddled with the curtains and

313

wondered how on earth she had ever thought of confiding in Olivia. Marriage and money had done nothing to mellow her sister.

'I hope that now that our families are to be partners in business we'll meet again, Mrs Moncrieff,' Matthew Mundy said by her side.

She turned, startled, and smiled at him. 'I hope so, Mr Mundy.'

'Next time I must give you one of our opals, as a gift. Do you know,' he went on smoothly, 'that your eyes are like opals, Mrs Moncrieff? Tonight, when you're happy, they're blue. When you're thoughtful, they're grey.'

'A toast to the success and prosperity of your business venture,' Gideon said at that moment. 'And to the *Grace and Charity*. May she serve you both well.'

Annis moved to the centre of the room, Matthew Mundy trailing after her. 'May I propose a toast to you in turn, Captain Brenner. To your own prosperity.'

Surprise, then appreciation ran across his features. Deliberately, aware that Douglas and Olivia were hesitating, she raised her glass to him and drank just as someone tapped at the door.

Douglas put down his drink quickly, the toast unacknowledged, and strode to the door. After a whispered consultation he turned to the shipmaster, an impatient frown knotting his brows. 'Someone from the *Grace and Charity* wants to talk to you urgently. I hope it's not some problem that's going to delay our departure.'

'I'll try to make certain that that won't happen, Mr Moncrieff.' The American put his own glass down and went from the room.

They were discussing the departure plans when he

returned, coming into the room so quietly that they weren't aware of him until the click of the door closing. Annis turned, and knew after one brief glance at his face that the news he brought was bad.

'Well?' Douglas demanded, 'What was so urgent that they had to seek you out here?'

The chattering in the room fell silent.

'A fast ship that came into the harbour today brought news from Scotland,' Gideon's voice was low but steady. 'Mrs Moncrieff . . .'

'Has something happened to the business?'

'It's not the business,' Annis heard herself saying. 'It's far worse than that, isn't it?'

'Yes, it is, ma'am. It's about Robert . . . ' said Gideon, his gaze, as it rested on her face, filled with compassion.

16

As the *Grace and Charity* sailed out of Port Philip Bay
on her homeward journey, Douglas stayed in the saloon
with a case of whisky for companionship. When the
shipmaster and two mates came below for meals he retired
to the night cabin where he ate alone, emerging into the
larger, more comfortable apartment only after everyone
had left.

At first Annis sat in the stuffy cabin, pretending to read
or sew, just wanting to be there in case Douglas needed
someone to talk to, and longing, herself, to speak about
Robert and release her own anguish. But he was silent,
emptying and refilling his glass at intervals, staring at the
floor. When she ventured a comment he either ignored
it or raised his head for a moment and looked at her as
though she was a stranger. He had aged in a few days.
The shock of Robert's death had put everything else from
Annis's mind — Gideon, Olivia, the pleasure of being
away from the house in Greenock. All she wanted was
to be able to comfort her husband in his grief, share it
with him, be close to him with a closeness that they had
not known for some time. But now Douglas, that
possessive man who had always wanted her by his side
at every available moment, rejected her.

At first, just after hearing the news, he had demanded

to know why Robert was in Jem Moncrieff's yard. Without thinking, Annis had said, 'I don't know, Douglas,' then caught Gideon's eye and wished that she had had the courage to tell her husband the truth.

But it was too late, for the lie was spoken. She tried to tell herself that she had wanted to spare Douglas further anguish, but sitting by his side, silently and helplessly watching him drink whisky and stare into space and remove himself further from her, she hated herself for her cowardice. He should have been told the truth. By the time they reached Greenock, she resolved, he must be told the truth.

Eventually, realizing that he wanted only to be left alone, she gave up her vigil and went on deck, thankful to be in the fresh, warm, salt-laden air.

For the first few days on deck Gideon left her alone. She was free to watch the glittering, sun-kissed sea and let it soothe the ache inside her. As the clipper raced for home under a press of billowing sail, a good wind on her starboard bow, flying fish drew rainbows of sudden colour in the air, and once a playful school of porpoises raced alongside, tumbling over and through the waves. Annis watched and thought only of how much Robert would have enjoyed the sight. Once or twice she picked up the exercise book he had given her, only to put it down again, remembering that there was no point in writing in it now that Robert wouldn't be there to read it.

Gideon watched and waited, and chose his time to go and stand by her side, pointing out to the horizon.

'Look there, Mrs Moncrieff.'

She followed his gaze and saw a silvery spray of water arc into the air like a fountain.

'A whale!' The sight of the glittering spray broke through her misery for a moment.

'A large one,' he said, smiling for the first time in days. Then the smile faded and one of his brown, strong hands came to rest on the rail near hers.

'I'm truly sorry, Mrs Moncrieff,' he said quietly. 'I know that you cared very much for the boy. And he worshipped you. He talked about you a great deal each time we met at the yard.'

'Did he?' She realized that she was hungry for news of Robert. She needed desperately to talk about him.

'Indeed, I feel that through him, you and I are close friends.' The shipmaster smiled wryly. 'I came to know you well through Robert . . . and to like what I knew,' he added, gazing away from her towards the horizon.

Being with him provided the comfort Douglas could not give her. This time his nearness didn't set up confusion within her, because Robert was dead long before his proper time, and loving and wanting had gone from Annis's life, perhaps for all time. Instead, she craved only friendship, and the shipmaster, somehow knowing her need, was filling it.

'He would have been . . . he was,' she corrected herself firmly, 'a fine young man.'

'Indeed he was,' Brenner agreed wholeheartedly, and the icy pain that had gripped her since hearing of Robert's death began to ease.

Grateful, at least, for that, she wanted to do something for him. 'Captain Brenner, my sister's attitude when you met her in Melbourne —'

'Brought me to my senses,' he finished the sentence crisply. 'I realized when I saw her that there had never been any future for us.'

319

She listened carefully, but was too numb with grief to take in the meaning of the words. 'I'm sorry,' she said, without quite knowing why she was sorry.

'I'm not,' he said, then went on to a subject that troubled him far more than Olivia. 'I'm concerned about your husband, ma'am. It's not good for a man to shut himself away and brood. Nor is it good for a man to find solace in drink.'

She flushed, wakened from her misery, immediately on the defensive. 'Robert was the only child of my husband's brother. He loved both of them dearly.'

'I didn't see much evidence of his love when the boy was alive. Not did Robert himself.'

'You're too outspoken, Captain Brenner!'

'I'm being honest, Mrs Moncrieff. No shipmaster likes to see too much drink taken aboard his ship. It can lead to trouble. I think you're intelligent enough to understand what I'm saying.'

The mate called him and he left her without waiting for an answer, As the breeze slowly cooled the angry heat from her face, Annis turned his words over in her mind and knew that they were true. In Douglas's eyes Robert had represented his dead father, a man Douglas had worshipped, from all accounts. It might even be that at that moment, below deck, Douglas was mourning the father rather than the son.

The macabre thought made her shiver. All at once she was eager to be home, even though it would mean incarceration once again in that gloomy house, this time without Robert for companionship. But her concern for Douglas outweighed personal feelings. He was making himself ill. Perhaps he would come to terms with his loss once they were in Greenock. The sooner they got there the better.

They could have retraced their steps and sailed eastwards, going back round the Cape of Good Hope, but Gideon opted for the westward route, south of Tasmania and the Campbell Islands, set like rich jewels in the seas that lapped their shores, then past the most southern point of New Zealand and into the South Pacific, going round Cape Horn. As the winds lost their strength Gideon nursed the clipper along, his men working hard to turn the great sails so that they caught every puff of wind. They sailed through drizzling rain and forged through warm dense fog that blanketed the sails overhead and muffled the mates' voices as they yelled their orders. Then they picked up the westerly winds once more and the ship became a winged bird again, scudding along with her forefoot biting deep into the water and sending it creaming along her smooth flanks.

And still Douglas remained closeted in the cabin, refusing to come on deck, refusing to talk about Robert, totally uninterested in the running of the ship, which must, Annis realized, at least be a blessing to the shipmaster.

As the clipper nosed southward in preparation for rounding Cape Horn the weather began to get colder and Annis was glad to replace her light plain dresses with warmer woollen gowns and a thick cloak to wear when she was on deck. The flying fish and porpoises disappeared, though the occasional whale could still be seen, either spouting or coming up to the surface for air, then diving again with a great shower of spray as the big tail slapped the water with a booming noise that could be heard a considerable distance away.

Once they glimpsed an iceberg far to the south, glinting colours like a prism when the sun touched its flanks.

Annis strained her eyes to watch it, wishing passionately that she could have climbed into the rigging to see it more clearly. She would never see such a wonder again, she knew it.

As though he had only waited for the bad weather to begin, as though he needed it as a backdrop, Douglas came out of his silence one night when the ship was ploughing and wallowing through a high sea, her decks sluiced with rain and half her sails furled against a hungry wind that would have torn them to shreds. Above the sea ragged clouds raced across the sky, only allowing occasional glimpses of moon and stars. The men on duty worked the ship with one hand, using the other to anchor themselves firmly to the lines that had been put out for that purpose. Annis, banished from the deck by Gideon because of the danger, retired to the saloon, finding Douglas in his usual chair, a bottle near at hand. The case of whisky he had brought with him from Greenock was almost finished: she hoped with all her heart that once it was gone he would become his old self again.

As she went into the saloon the ship lurched and she had to catch hold of the sides of the door for a moment. Douglas's scrabbling fingers, reaching for the whisky bottle, knocked against it, toppling it to the floor. Fortunately it was stoppered and the golden liquid inside didn't escape as it rolled to Annis's feet. She picked it up as the clipper levelled and the floor returned to horizontal.

Her husband watched blearily, then held out his glass. 'Fill it.'

Instead, she put the bottle down on the mantelshelf, then knelt by his chair. 'Douglas, I want to talk to you about Robert.'

'Nothing to talk about.' His tongue moistened his lips. She was close enough to see the stubble of beard on his chin now that he had stopped shaving, smell the whisky on his breath.

'I loved Robert too. I need to talk about him, and so do you. We need to mourn him together.' She tried to take his hands, but he pushed them aside and stumbled to his feet, almost knocking her over, reaching for the whisky bottle. He filled his glass and drank, watching Annis get to her feet.

'Love, woman . . . what are you talking about? Love! That boy was my heir, my brother's only child. And Jem Moncrieff killed him.'

'Jem didn't kill him! He wouldn't have harmed a hair on that boy's head, I know it.' Douglas's head jerked round, his hand, reaching for the bottle again, fell to his side. His bloodshot eyes narrowed, but Annis, although she saw the danger signals, failed to recognize them in time. 'Robert . . . and others . . . died when a ship capsized during its launching. If the fault lies with anybody it lies with the owner and the designer. Jem and Robert both said —' She stopped, suddenly realizing where her tongue was leading her.

Drunk though he was, Douglas was still able to take in what she had just said. 'Jem and Robert both said what?' he wanted to know.

She got to her feet, running the tip of her tongue round lips that had gone suddenly dry.

'Jem and Robert said what? Damn you, woman, answer me!'

'They said . . . that the new ship was unwieldy.' The words were thick and awkward and had to be forced out. 'The owner wanted more room in the holds than . . .'

323

'How do you know that, Annis? How could you know, without being there?' His face purpled and for a moment she thought that the empty glass was going to break in his clenched hand. He put it down and reached for her as the ship lurched again, sending her into his grasp. His fingers gripped her shoulders painfully. 'Will you tell me the truth, woman!'

'Douglas . . .'

He shook her until her head flopped helplessly on her neck. She heard pins, loosened from her hair, which had been allowed to grow longer than ever before, tinkle against the stove. Soft tendrils of hair swung against her face as Douglas gave her one final shake. 'Tell me! You and Robert defied me, isn't that right? You saw Jem Moncrieff against my wishes, didn't you? Didn't you?'

His face was inches from hers. His lips were drawn back from his teeth and a vein throbbed thickly in one temple. The smell of whisky almost took away what little breath she had left. The sound of the storm outside, the shrill shrieking of the wind, the creak of timbers and thump of water against the ship, seemed to fade into the background, puny in comparison with Douglas Moncrieff's terrible anger.

'Jem's a g — good man, Douglas. Robert was always interested in design and Jem — let him visit the yard to watch the ships being b — built . . . ' The muscles in her jaw seemed to have locked with fear.

'And you,' said Douglas softly, 'are you interested in shipbuilding, Annis? Or were you just interested in Jem Moncrieff?'

'No!' A surge of anger gave her the strength to pull away from him, drawing herself upright. 'How can you say that, Douglas! You have no right to —'

'I've every right,' said Douglas, his voice thick and uneven with rage. 'I have the right to seek out Jem Moncrieff, my nephew's murderer, and see that he's rightly punished for what he's done. I have the right to . . . ' He stopped suddenly, then said, 'Get in there!'

The unlatched door of the night cabin had been swinging and banging against its frame. Annis was caught by the shoulders again and spun around, then pushed towards the door. She resisted but a savage thrust delivered just when the ship heeled over sent her staggering through the doorway. She tripped on the raised sill and fell, dimly aware that her head had narrowly missed the corner of the bed.

Douglas, following close behind, dragged her to her feet. 'I've got work for you to do, my dear,' he said breathlessly as his fingers moved to her neck. For a panic-stricken moment she thought that he intended to choke the life from her, but instead he caught the opening of her gown and wrenched the material apart. As the hairpins had done a few minutes earlier, buttons cascaded to the floor. Annis could hear them rattling into the corners as the *Grace and Charity* rolled to the erratic pattern of the waves.

'Please, Douglas . . .'

He knocked her hands aside as she tried to protect herself. 'You want a child, don't you? You've been whining on at me about a bairn of you own and now you'll have one. You let Robert die, so you'll give me an heir to take his place.'

'I do want your – child, Douglas, you know I do . . .' She tried to take him into her arms, but he caught her wrists and held them, pinioning her. 'But I want him to be conceived with love . . .'

325

The sentence ended in a gasp as Douglas wrenched her wrists cruelly, driving her to her knees. 'With love, is it? You think I could ever again love the woman who sent Robert to his death? Tib was right. I should have listened to her from the beginning and let you and your arrogant bitch of a sister rot in the gutter.'

The words poured from his slack mouth. Saliva gleamed on his chin and she realized, terrified, that he had gone far beyond reason. 'But I'll get something out of it yet. I'll get my son and heir!'

He picked her up and tossed her on to the bed, then followed her down, tearing at her clothes. When she tried to push him away he caught her wrists again, pinning them above her head while his mouth covered hers in a hard, angry kiss that bruised her lips against her teeth and almost suffocated her.

She sucked air into her lungs when his head finally lifted. Douglas, mistaking the intake of breath for the beginnings of a scream, said swiftly, 'Don't call out, Annis. No man can deny me my rights. You'll only make yourself the laughing stock of the whole damned ship.'

She had had no intention of screaming for help. She knew as well as he did that it would be useless, and she didn't want any of the men above to know what drink had done to her husband.

She tried, as his fingers pulled impatiently at her clothes, to lie still, reminding herself that she had indeed wanted Douglas's child, that the hot-eyed, panting man astride her was the husband she cared for, temporarily changed by grief. But as his hands found her soft flesh and began to crush and bruise it, fear began to take over. This was no marital intimacy, this was assault. God only knew what he might do next.

Douglas relaxed his grip on her wrists to wrench impatiently at his own clothes and Annis lunged upwards and managed to catch him off balance, a half-formed idea of escaping into the saloon and barring the door until he slept off his drunken rage running through her head.

With a yelp of startled surprise Douglas fell on to his side, and Annis rolled from the bed, landed on the floor, scrambled to her feet, gained the door, and slammed it shut.

There was no catch on the saloon side. She caught at the handle of the trunk that held her clothes and began to drag it across the doorway but before she had properly begun the task the door was forced open.

'Annis!' Douglas pushed hard and to Annis's horror the trunk began to slip to one side. She released it, and backed to the door leading to the corridor and the upper deck. To her surprise it opened as she reached it, and Gideon Brenner, wind-blown and with water streaming from his hair and shoulders, came into the saloon.

His eyes fell first on Douglas Moncrieff, purple-faced, his shirt half off, emerging from the night cabin, cursing as he stumbled over the trunk. Then, following his employer's furious glare, Brenner turned and saw Annis crouched by the door, trying in vain to pull her tattered clothing together.

'What's going on here?'

'Mind your own business, sir,' Douglas growled at him. 'Get back on deck!'

'Everything that happens on board this ship is my business, Mr Moncrieff. Allow me, ma'am . . . ' Gideon stepped into the cabin, took Annis's warm cloak from the hook where it always hung, and held it out to her. As she wrapped herself in it he said to Douglas in a tone

327

of casual common sense, 'Perhaps you'd care to come on deck, sir. Your wife would be the better for a while on her own.'

'Don't you tell me how to treat my own wife, you Yankee upstart!' Douglas took a step forward and Gideon moved very slightly, but enough to bring his body between husband and wife.

Douglas halted, blinking to take stock of the situation. The ship rolled and he staggered as Gideon reached behind him with one hand to support Annis.

'Get out of here,' Douglas said, slowly and distinctly.

'If Mrs Moncrieff wishes me to leave, I will.'

'Annis, tell the impertinent scoundrel to go!'

'Please . . .' She caught Brenner by the arm, terrified in case Douglas got his way. 'Please stay, Captain Brenner.'

'I've no intention of going, ma'am, I assure you.'

'So,' Douglas grunted, his gaze shifting from one to the other. 'I was right about the two of you. Damn you, Brenner, I'm going to stop this ship; I'm going to lower a boat and have you thrown into it. I'll not have you on board my vessel a minute longer!'

'Don't be a fool, Moncrieff!' For the first time Gideon's voice had an undertone of anger in it.

Without answering, Douglas pushed roughly past Gideon Brenner and went out into the passageway, cursing and catching at the doorway as the *Grace and Charity* lurched and staggered under the onslaught of a heavy sea. They heard him stumbling up the companionway to the poop deck, roaring oaths Annis had never heard on his lips before as the clipper pitched and his feet slipped and slithered on the narrow stairs.

'Follow him . . .' She released her hold on Brenner's

arm and pushed him towards the door. 'Don't let him harm himself!'

'I'm more concerned with the harm he could do to you, or to my ship,' Brenner said grimly. 'Owner or not, he's going to be locked into the deckhouse until he sobers up. Wait here until I come back.'

Annis was shaking violently from head to foot. Slowly, fighting against her own weakness as much as the roll of the ship, she managed to make her way across the saloon and into the night cabin. Averting her eyes from the tumbled bed, she took off the torn remnants of her gown and put on a grey and red checked dress. Her fingers were all thumbs but she managed to fasten most of the buttons.

On the deck above someone screamed something in an urgent voice that rose above the wind's banshee howling. An army of bare feet pounded across the timbers as the clipper seemed to slew round, then exchange its forward motion for a tossing corkscrew lurch. Forgetting Gideon's orders, Annis ran across the saloon and into the passageway, then clambered up the companionway, clinging tightly to the hand ropes on each side as the ship rolled.

The moon appeared briefly as she reached the poop deck, then disappeared again. The wind caught at her loosened hair and tugged at the roots hard enough to bring tears to her eyes, rain sweeping out of the darkness to pierce her skin with tiny icy pinpoints.

The moon came out once more, allowing her to look around the deck. The helm had been jammed into position and the helmsman, together with Gideon and the second mate, was leaning over the side of the ship. Annis knew enough about sailing by now to recognize that the great mainyards had been backed to hold the ship stationary against the screaming wind.

Unnoticed, she reached the men at the rail and followed the line of their gaze. The seas were high, but not as mountainous as they had been earlier. Something flashed on the crest of a wave, then vanished. Annis watched for its re-appearance and realized that one of the ship's boats had been lowered and was already some distance from the clipper, battling through the water. It hesitated on the crest of the next wave and for a terrible moment she thought that it was going to slew over, spilling the men into the ocean's hungry mouth. But it steadied and plunged into the deep trough of the wave, out of her sight again.

Someone on the main deck set off one of the flares carried by sailing ships to warn off steam-ships that might get too near at night, when the sailing ships were lit only by red and green lamps to port and starboard. The picture revealed by the vivid white light lasted for only a few seconds but it seared deeply into her mind, so that for the rest of her life she was able to recall it with ease. The flare illuminated every single part of the ship and her intricate rigging, turning the great sails that were still spread into huge cliffs looming above the hull and the deck. The light froze the sea in a moment of time so that the spume on the crests of the waves was crystallized into ice and the troughs became black, menacing caves. It picked out the ship's boat, visible again and in the act of sliding down into one of these troughs. There were seven men aboard, six of them pulling desperately on the oars, the seventh, the mate, on the steering sweep, peering into the darkness.

Nearer to hand the brilliant glare sculpted the planes

and hollows of Gideon Brenner's face, turning the raindrops caught in his black hair into a thousand diamonds, highlighting a huge bruise and a glossy trickle of blood at the corner of his mouth.

The flare went out, but not before its hard brilliance had alerted Gideon to Annis herself. His head turned sharply in her direction and he left his post and hurried across to catch her arm.

'I told you to stay below!' He hustled her back to the companionway.

Her skirt twisted round her legs: the wind tried to whip the cloak from her shoulders and she had to hold it tightly round herself. 'What's happening? Where's Douglas?'

'Get below and stay there until I come to you!' he roared and almost pushed her down the companionway. She caught at the hand-lines to steady herself, then obeyed him, the realization slowly dawning that the small boat tossing in the waves was searching for her husband.

In the cabin she huddled in the chair Douglas had used only a short hour ago, fingers pressed tightly to her mouth, and waited. Thoughts fled through her mind in a confused jumble that made no sense. When she heard, or thought she heard, the ship's boat being hauled inboard again, she looked towards the door, but stayed where she was.

She didn't want to go up on deck, didn't want to know what had happened. All she wanted was to be able to turn time back to a happier time, the time before Olivia went to Australia and everything began to go wrong.

Feet scampered across the deck again, then the movement of the clipper changed and she guessed that the helm had been released and the mainyards swung back to their original positions to allow the ship to make her way forward again. When Gideon came to her at last, his face drawn with exhaustion and dark with the news that he had to bring.

'Did they find him?' she asked before he could speak. Then, when he shook his head, 'What happened?' Her mouth felt strange, as though the words didn't fit.

He looked dazed and his voice was unnaturally subdued. 'I tried to reason with him, but the drink had taken control of him entirely. He was shouting orders at the men and I took hold of his arm and tried to lead him into the deckhouse. He swung his fist at me' — he touched a finger to the corner of his mouth, where the blood had crusted — 'then pulled away from me just as the vessel rolled. He . . . he went over the side before I could get to him.'

'Poor Gideon,' Annis heard herself say, 'That's twice you've had to be the bearer of bad news.' Then the realization that Douglas was gone for ever — Douglas, not the drink-fuddled, grief-stricken stranger who had so terrified her, but the man who had rescued her and cared for her, the man she had married — came to her and the tears spilled over and started flooding down her cheeks.

Blindly, she got up from the chair and stumbled across the saloon. Gideon Brenner met her half-way, folding her into his arms and holding her while she wept into his rain-soaked jacket.

Later he knelt by her chair, coaxing her to drink some whisky that Callum had mixed with hot water and sugar. At first she tried to resist, not wanting to taste the spirits that had changed and destroyed Douglas, but Brenner insisted until she emptied the glass.

'It was my doing,' she said as he took it from her

fingers. 'My doing. I told him about . . . that Robert and I had visited Jem. My fault!'

'He had to know.' Gideon eased her to her feet and helped her into the night cabin, which had been tidied by a wide-eyed, silent Callum on the shipmaster's orders.

'My doing . . .'

He sat her on the edge of the bed and she looked down at his wet black hair as he knelt to pull off her shoes. 'Annis . . . Mrs Moncrieff, your husband, God rest him, was not an easy man to obey. Nobody should lay down rules without a reason. Nobody, least of all you, is to blame for what happened.'

He eased her on to the mattress and drew the blankets up around her neck. 'Sleep now,' he commanded with rough gentleness. He blew the lamp out and through a blur of weariness she saw his broad shoulders silhouetted against the light from the saloon. Then he closed the door and she was in darkness.

As the *Grace and Charity* fought its way round Cape Horn with safety nets strung to the height of six feet above the bulwarks to prevent men being swept overboard, Annis stayed below, scarcely aware of the clipper's struggle or the danger they all shared.

With Robert and Douglas lost to her, she didn't care whether the ship survived or foundered. While the sea broke green over the gunwales and swept from rail to rail across the main deck, she lived deep within her grief, unable to tell the difference between the storms that raged outside and the storms in her own heart and mind.

She saw little of Gideon, for he had no time to spare from his duties. When he did come into the saloon she was aware of the concern in his gaze and grateful for it in a numbed, bewildered way.

The clipper had rounded the Horn and reached the Doldrums before Annis came to herself one morning and looked out to see the sun sparkling on flat, calm water. She gazed into a mirror and was appalled to see a dull-eyed old woman staring at her. Her face was drawn, her grey eyes hollowed and blank, more like pebbles than the opals Matthew Mundy had likened them to. The sun's golden touch and the vitality that the outward-bound journey had given her were all gone.

Something deep inside stirred; the dead were beyond recall, but part of her at least was still alive, and still young. She had been sick with sorrow, but she knew now that she would survive. She sent Callum for food and some hot water, and ate hungrily before bathing herself and washing her hair.

Throughout the voyage home, in mourning first for Robert and then for Douglas, she had worn the few dark clothes she had with her. Now she put them aside and dressed in a green blouse and tawny-coloured skirt, then combed the tangles out of her damp hair and pinched at her cheeks to bring the colour into them, remembering with a pang how she used to do that after a day spent in the house in Low Gourock Road.

Suddenly hungry for fresh air and a sight of the sea and sky, she scooped up all the clothes that needed washing and asked Callum to set up a tub for her under her usual shelter by the deckhouse.

The sun's heat enfolded her as soon as she stepped on to the scrubbed white deck. The warmth sent a shiver through her body, followed by a sudden wonderful sensation of well-being. She knew now how a butterfly must feel as it wrenched itself free of the chrysalis that had held it. She knew, too, that she was too young to mourn for ever. Years, perhaps more than she had already lived, stretched before her, and she must face their challenge.

The lower courses and upper topsails were set, with enough of a breeze in them to draw the clipper through a sea that was only slightly ruffled. Sam McNair was at the helm, with Gideon beside him. The shipmaster's eyes were fixed steadily on the clews at the bottom of the sails to make certain that the ship wasn't steering too close to the wind or too far from it, but as Annis emerged on deck and advanced with determination on the tub that Callum was filling, McNair's gaze slid in her direction and once again she felt a chill, damp sensation creep along her spine.

The man lifted his top lip in a strange snarling grin, and she had the disquieting feeling that he knew just how he affected her, knew of that feeling that started between her shoulder blades and followed her backbone all the way down at the mere sight of him. Ignoring him, she rolled the sleeves of her blouse up and plunged a dress into the tub.

It was good to be doing something again and to be out on deck, breathing good fresh air. Gideon had the sense to leave her alone, and for a while she worked hard, lifting the soapy clothes from the tub into another of clear water, then wringing them out and hanging them up on the line that Callum had rigged up for her. The water splashes she made on the deck dried almost at once and Annis's mind began to lighten as the sun poured its healing warmth on her.

'Mind your helm, man,' Brenner suddenly snapped,

and the helmsman, alerted, shifted his feet on the hot planks and eased the great wheel round. The sails, which had started shaking, steadied again, and took back the wind they had begun to lose.

Gideon barked an order and another seaman, his naked brown back gleaming like a chestnut in the sunlight, came scurrying from the main deck, the sailmaker's needle still strapped to the palm of his hand.

Under the shipmaster's scowling gaze the two men changed places, the newcomer taking over the wheel while Sam McNair, with a martyred air, strapped the needle on to his own hand and went down to the maindeck, where several men were working on a great stretch of new canvas.

'A bad helmsman can lose a good ship,' Gideon said, crossing over to Annis once the change-over had been made. 'That man's a fool. I trust you'll never allow him to set foot on the *Grace and Charity* again.'

She straightened her back and wiped her forehead with a forearm. 'I?'

His green eyes swept her face in a brief glance that still seemed to find time to study every feature carefully. 'The clipper belongs to you now, I should imagine. The business too.'

She stared at him. 'I hadn't thought of that.'

'You've had other things to think of. But with respect, ma'am, the time's come for you to consider your future. If you leave it until you arrive in Greenock, Miss Moncrieff may have made up your mind for you. I sent a message by a steam-ship that we met up with a few days back,' he added as he met her questioning gaze. 'If it doesn't burst its boilers in the stormy weather round Biscay or run out of coal, it may well reach port ahead of us. I thought that it would be best to spare you the task of telling Miss Moncrieff about her brother.'

'Thank you, Captain.' She hadn't given Tib a thought, but it was a relief to know that she would not have to be the one to break the news to the woman. She gave a sudden shiver.

'What's wrong?'

Annis bit her lip. 'I hadn't thought of having to go back to that house alone – to her.'

'Then buy a house of your own,' he said crisply, adding when she gaped up at him, 'You'll be able to afford it, I should imagine, unless there's another heir somewhere to inherit the business. If not, I expect it will be yours.'

'No . . . no other heir.' The sun was in her eyes, and she looked down into the soapy tub, where the bubbles were all the colours of the rainbow.

'Will you keep it?'

'Yes, of course,' she said at once, then checked herself and said slowly, 'That is . . . I don't know, as yet. I suppose I must. It's what D –' She swallowed, then said clearly, 'It's what Douglas would want.'

'You think you can run it?'

'If there's nobody else to do it then I must.'

'I believe you will. And yet with your hair loose like that you look little more than a child yourself.'

She returned his smile with a faint upward curve that felt good on her mouth again. 'You're very outspoken, Captain Brenner.'

'You've told me that before. It's a failing we Americans have, ma'am.'

'A good failing, perhaps. We . . . the Scots . . . never seem to say what we think.'

337

'I've noticed,' said Brenner enigmatically, and left her. Watching him stride back to the wheel, she felt another tremor run through her re-awakening body. Shocked, she quelled it and turned her attention to the washing.

17

Thanks to Brenner's skilful handling they only spent four days idling through the Doldrums before picking up the trade winds and pressing ahead, all sails set.

The weather began to cool again as they stormed north, and once or twice heavy rain lashed the decks, forcing Annis below again. This time she refused to allow herself to brood, but worked busily on some embroidery and put her mind to the future. Brenner's remark about buying a house of her own occupied her thoughts. The more she thought of it the more she liked it. A home of her own, where she would be free of Tib . . . her mind raced on as her fingers worked. She could take Janet to be her maid, give the girl and her child a home. Let Tib rail and sulk as much as she liked. She would keep the business on because that was what Douglas would have wanted.

Early one morning four weeks after his death she woke to a slow, heavy swell. It was early, just past daybreak, but she felt alert and alive, too restless to stay in bed. She dressed quickly and went on deck to find the second mate on duty.

He nodded a greeting as she went to lean on the rail. The sky was low, with a great cluster of heavy clouds massed on the horizon. The wind whipped across her cheeks and she shivered. There was something threatening about the very air she breathed, a stillness in spite of the wind, menace in the way the waves rolled and heaved with none of their usual cresting.

The purple mass on the horizon grew rapidly until it towered into the grey sky, the two colours meeting and mingling in a dirty violet shade. The second mate's forehead creased uncertainly as he watched. The sails flapped like big lazy birds. Suddenly Gideon erupted from the companionway, startling everyone on deck, dragging a jacket over his shirt as he came. His hair was rumpled as though he had just awakened from sleep, but his eyes were as clear and alert as ever.

'Haul in the royals!' His voice rang the length of the ship and men ran to obey. 'Hard down with the helm,' he ordered. 'All hands on deck to pull her round! Why didn't you wake me?'

'I . . . I didn't think it necessary . . .' the second mate faltered.

Gideon cupped his hands to his mouth. 'Bring the mainsail round! You might not have seen clouds like these,' he added to the man, 'but I have. Couldn't you feel the wind dying away?'

Annis lifted her face and found that he was right. The brisk breeze had dropped unnoticed, and the purple clouds, looming high above the ship now, were marching forward to fill the entire sky.

The helmsman dragged the ship round as the men on deck fought to swing the yards and turn the huge sails. The squall racing across the sea towards them struck with snake-like speed before the clipper was round far enough to take it on the quarter. Annis staggered as the wind hit her and only just saved herself from falling headlong by clutching at the rail. There was a tremendous crack, like thunder, and she looked up to see that the mainsail had been ripped to pieces by the sudden assault. The main mast arced crazily against the purpling sky, leaning over further and further towards the boiling sea as the ship, temporarily out of control, began to lie down before the storm's sudden onslaught.

Annis lost her grip on the railing and staggered helplessly down the slope of the deck until she collided with Gideon. He gave a muffled curse and wrapped a long arm about her, using his free hand to grasp at hand-holds as he fought his way to the stairs that led below decks.

'Get down to the saloon,' he ordered, his mouth against her ear so that he could make himself heard against the screaming wind and the frantic booming of the sails. 'Find a good hand-hold and stay there until I come to you.'

'Are we going to drown?' During the tempestuous voyage round the Horn she had been so steeped in misery that she had not cared whether they foundered. But now she knew that she wanted to live.

His white teeth showed in a grin and his eyes sparkled at her. Beyond his shoulder she could see the mainmast, still canting over at a crazy angle, the ribboned remains of the mainsail flapping furiously.

'I was born with a caul,' he shouted. 'The sea can't take me . . . and I'll not let it take you either. Now get below and stay there!'

He pushed her and she slithered down the steps in a boneless, awkward fashion to collapse in a heap at the bottom as the door at the top of the companionway slammed shut. She heard the bolt being shot as she crawled, bumping painfully off the wooden panelling as she went, into the saloon.

The room was slanting over at a frightening angle. Everything that had been loose was gathered at one side, against the door leading to the night cabin. Even below decks Annis could hear the sails cracking and booming like cannon, the howling wind and the solid thump of water against the hull as the *Grace and Charity*, almost lying on her side, some of her sails still set, skidded through the turbulent sea.

She began to haul herself up on to the padded bench that ran the length of the table. The angle of the ship created a corner where she might be able to wedge herself to wait out the storm. She had almost gained the bench when the room gave a frightening lurch and Annis was thrown about like a rag doll, her hands reaching out without success for something stable to grasp.

She thought, when the ship steadied again, that she was lying on the floor, but when she opened her eyes and began to pull herself on to her hands and knees she was puzzled to see what she at first took to be a mirror in front of her face. She peered into its depths and saw only blackness. She blinked, then recoiled with a gasp of horror as a thin line of bubbles drifted across her vision and she realized that she was in fact lying on the ship's side and looking through a window at the sea, which was pressing against the glass.

Crab-like, she backed into a corner enclosed by the now-upright table and curled in a tight whimpering ball. Something hard jabbed into her backside; she shifted, explored with one hand, and found one of the whisky bottles that had belonged to Douglas. About to throw it aside, she paused, then managed to wrench the top off.

She drank, then choked and spluttered as the raw liquid burned its way down her throat. But when it reached her stomach it brought with it a slight lessening of the terror.

She took another swallow, then another. Squeezed into a small space as she was, she was much less aware of the violent motion of the clipper.

The bottle almost slipped from her grasp and she stoppered it, afraid that it might spill. Comforted by the spirit's warmth, she let her eyes close and her head droop to her knees, closely tucked in to her body. Exhaustion and whisky overcame her fear, and she slept.

When Gideon Brenner finally unbolted the door from the poop deck and came down to the saloon, cushions and books and clothes lay everywhere. At first he couldn't see Annis; then, stooping, he found her still wedged into the corner, still asleep, rolled up like a hedgehog, the whisky bottle held close in her arms.

He looked again and permitted himself an amused grin. Then he straightened his face and said, 'Mrs Moncrieff . . .'

She snapped awake and stared around. Her grey, sleep-misted eyes blinked, cleared, and focused on him. She smiled, a smile of such happiness that he stared back, disconcerted for a moment.

'We're not dead!'

He started to laugh. 'Not quite. I trust that we both have many years ahead of us, ma'am.'

Annis, suddenly realizing that she was crouched beneath the table, wriggled free, disregarding the hand he held out to her, rising stiffly to her feet. Her hair had long since come loose and was curling about her shoulders in a mass of auburn tendrils.

'The storm . . .'

'. . . is over.' Brenner's own hair, wind-whipped and

343

lashed by rain and spray, stood out in a halo about a face drawn with weariness. His clothes were damp and there was a long tear in one jacket sleeve. A vivid red welt ran along his left cheekbone.

She discovered to her embarrassment that she still clutched the bottle of spirits. 'I . . . I found this. Would you like some?'

There was an amused glint in his eyes as he took the bottle from her and put it on to the table, which was now upright again. 'Thank you, no.'

To hide her confusion Annis began to put the cabin to rights. Brenner helped her as he talked.

'It would take more than a squall to finish the *Grace and Charity*. If I'd been on deck sooner . . . but I wasn't and the weather hit us too quickly. Before I could bring her round we lost control of the helm. She lay down before the wind and it just carried her along.'

'I saw the water — through that window.' Annis remembered with a shiver.

'Her mainmast was almost in the sea, but she weathered it. She's a fine ship,' he said, love in his voice. 'We lost some sails but they can be replaced. And your cabin boy was hurt, I'm afraid.'

'Callum? How bad is it? Where is he?' She would have pushed past him to the door, but he stopped her with a hand on her arm.

'It was only a dislocated shoulder. He was helping the helmsman and the wheel kicked. The lad's too slight and inexperienced for the job but there was nobody else to do it at the time. He's got the makings of a fine seaman. His shoulder's been put back and bound, and he's asleep just now. You need some sleep yourself, Mrs Moncrieff.'

344

'So do you.' She reached up and touched the weal gently. His face was cool from the outside air, and firm to the touch. 'Let me see to that for you.'

'No need.' Then he said, without moving from beneath her fingers, 'You're a very brave woman, ma'am. Most females would have been screaming and carrying on if they had been through a storm like that.'

'I'd faith in you, Captain. You said you'd not let me drown.'

'I'd never let that happen to you,' he said quietly, then to Annis's horror the cabin and the man standing before her seemed to dissolve and swim out of focus. She blinked, and they returned to normal. Deep inside, she felt a tremor that took a hold and spread.

'I think,' she said, 'that I will rest, as you s – suggest.'

She began to walk towards the night cabin door but all at once her legs refused to obey her. The trembling grew and she saw that her hands were shaking. Her knees seemed to turn into hot butter, and if Gideon Brenner hadn't caught her she would have fallen to the floor at his feet.

He lifted her into his arms and managed to ease himself through the narrow door into the night cabin. When he seated her on the side of the bed Annis clung to him, mortally afraid that the trembling that gripped her would shake her to pieces if he let go.

He held her, her face pressed tightly against his shoulder, her hair tumbling over his chest. Slowly, slowly, the violent trembling began to ease, and at last her convulsive grip on his arm loosened and she lifted her head to the face that was bent over her.

'You must think I'm a very weak woman, C – Captain,' she said shakily.

His eyes searched her features as though he had never seen her before and had a need to study every single inch and angle. 'I think you're a very courageous woman, Annis Moncrieff,' he said slowly, his whole heart in his voice. 'I'm the fool, knowing you for all those months yet not knowing you at all.'

She sensed, even before his lips found hers, that they would be hard and hungry and gentle all at the same time. She had been waiting for his kiss, his touch, all her life. Everything that had happened to her before that moment fell away as Gideon's mouth teased her own lips apart. A yearning she had never known before, or ever dreamed of, caught hold of her, sending her hands to tangle themselves in his hair, arching her body against his, teaching her, in an instant, how to return his kisses with a matching passion that carried them onwards without a pause for thought or speech.

In a moment the bed was soft beneath her back and Gideon's hands deftly, tenderly, easing the gown from her shoulders while her own hands, greedy for him, slid beneath his jacket and the half-opened shirt beneath to caress his smooth, spray-damp chest.

Never, in all the nights she had spent with Douglas, had she known that the touch of a man's hands on her breasts could be so exquisite. The fire that raged within became concentrated in the centre of her being, a blazing ember that tormented her and set her tossing and moaning beneath Gideon. She wanted to devour him, to be devoured by him, to meld her body with his so that they would be one and the same for ever.

They struggled deliciously together; half-naked now, she gasped at his touch, then gasped again, this time in shock and pain, as he moved astride her, then plunged down, entering her and piercing her to the very place where the fire raged most fiercely.

The pain was more intense than the fire. She squirmed in agony, tried to draw away from the intrusion into her body, gave a breathless protest.

Gideon answered her cry with one of his own, a cry of triumph and pleasure. He braced himself with his arms on either side of her head, his own head arched back. Then he gave a great shiver and she felt that part of him that was inside slacken as he fell forward, his sweat-streaked body collapsing on to hers.

He rolled off her, to one side, and put an arm about her. His face, on the pillow beside hers, was softened, his eyes were happy. 'Annis . . .' The fire had gone but the pain was still there, though muted. Confused, she sat up and looked down at herself, then got off the bed and quickly snatched at the robe hanging on the back of the door, wrapping it closely about her body to hide the blood running down the inside of her thighs.

Gideon sat up. 'Annis . . .' he began, then stopped short. 'Good God, Annis!'

She followed his gaze and saw that there was tell-tale blood on the sheet where she had been lying.

'You hurt me,' she said, backing away from the bed. The happiness was gone, vanished in the dawning horror in his gaze. 'You hurt me.'

'But surely your husband . . .' The words hung in the air, demanding to be answered. Annis tried to run a hand through her hair but the tangles defeated her.

'Not like that. Never like that, to hurt me.'

In one movement Gideon was on his feet, ignoring his own nakedness. 'Never like what, Annis? Tell me,' he insisted, his fingers biting into her shoulders.

'Never like . . . that,' she repeated, aware that there was something terribly wrong. The passion that had been between them was soured, gone. 'Never . . . inside. Not hurting.'

There was a silence, then, 'Dear God,' said Gideon Brenner, his voice thick, 'You were a virgin!'

'No! I was Douglas's wife!'

The green eyes looking down on her now were dark with a mixture of pity and loathing. 'But not a proper wife. Don't you know anything about what goes on between a man and a woman?'

She glared back at him, frightened without knowing what frightened her. 'My husband taught me.'

'He taught you what it suited him to teach you, Annis!' Gideon gave her a little shake, then turned away and began to drag his clothes on, his voice shaking as he went on; 'God only knows what his purpose was, but you were never a proper wife to him and he was never a proper husband.'

'That's not true!' She hugged her body tightly; her tingling, glowing, hurting, shameful body. 'It's not true!'

'It is. It must be. And now I've . . .' He turned to face her, throwing his hands out helplessly. 'If I had known I wouldn't have touched you.'

She clutched the neck of the robe close, shame burning her face. 'Am I so repugnant, then?'

'Repugnant?' Under the tan his face, drained of blood, was yellowish. The livid bruise on his cheekbone stood out. 'You could never be repugnant. The fault was mine for taking your virginity. Annis . . .'

He tried, too late, to take her back into his arms, but she pulled away. A few moments ago she would have gone to him gladly, but not now. Not now that he had discovered and exposed the shame she had never known was hers.

'Leave me, Gideon.'

'Mrs Moncrieff. . .'

That was the most hurtful of all. She turned on him like a wild cat, her eyes blazing. 'I said leave me be . . . Captain Brenner!'

He hesitated, then picked up his jacket and went past her, out of the room.

Alone, Annis huddled into one of the button-backed chairs in the saloon — not the chair Douglas had always favoured. She would never sit in that chair again.

She remembered Olivia's scornful refusal to tell her anything about the secrets of married life, and Douglas's pleasure when he discovered that she was a complete innocent. She recalled his love-making, when his seed was spilled on her belly while she lay submissively beneath him. She thought of the way he had treated her like a little girl, and the times he had brushed aside her anxiety because there was never any sign of a child. His child, their child.

Knowing, as he did, that there could never be a child because his wife was a virgin.

She had to face the truth and, slowly, she began to understand. Douglas had never wanted a real wife. He had had no need of one. Robert, his beloved brother's son, was the heir to the business and any children that Annis might bear would only get in the way of that inheritance.

But Robert had died, and on the night of his own death, out of his mind with grief and rage, Douglas had tried to force himself on his wife, to father on her the heir that was now needed.

Memories of Gideon's horror, bewilderment, and — worst of all — his pity, came to the fore, and again she burned with humiliation. To think that she had been deceived for so long, and that this man of all men should be the one to find out. She had wanted his love, but never his pity. Whatever there might have been between them both was dead, killed at the very moment of its beginning by Douglas's cruelty.

There was no other word for it. For two years and two months she had been his wife, trusting in him. And knowingly, deliberately, he had betrayed her.

She washed in cold water, then dressed herself and brushed out her hair. The face that looked back at her in the mirror was calm and closed. She no longer mourned Douglas. She hated him now, hated him for the way he had used her innocence and trust.

Dead though he was, she wanted to find a way to hurt him as he had hurt her.

18

Jeremiah Mundy's bedroom was large and almost totally unfurnished apart from a bed, a wardrobe, and a chest of drawers, which meant that Olivia had had to have a comfortable chair brought in and placed by the window for her own use.

The room was cool and the screens over the windows ensured that it was free of flies. Much more comfortable than the hovel she and John lived in, she thought bitterly, and looked up from her book at the man lying on the bed.

The mosquito net had been drawn back. Jeremiah lay propped up on a pile of pillows, his eyes closed and his breathing loud, but without the frightening rasping undertone it had had the day before.

Olivia and Chang had disagreed over whether or not the invalid should be lying flat or half-raised. Eventually Olivia, reminding the Chinaman acidly that she was after all Mundy's daughter-in-law, had won the day. Being raised up had certainly eased the old man's breathing, but Olivia, who knew nothing about nursing, was worried about him. It was wrong of John and Matthew to be away, somewhere on the far boundaries of the Mundy land. One of them should have been here to shoulder the burden when Jeremiah collapsed.

But neither of them was at hand, and it was to Olivia

that the aborigine woman Betta had come, jumping from the seat of the little buggy, pounding up the steps of the hut and bursting into the main room without stopping to knock at the door. 'Boss he fall down,' she'd panted. 'Chang say for you to come longa me, missus!'

And so Olivia found herself back in the main house, where Jeremiah Mundy, having terrified his servants by suddenly crashing from his chair on to the verandah, lay helplessly in his bed, his face twisted down one side.

What if he should die? The thought kept chasing itself through Olivia's mind, superimposing itself between her eyes and the book she was trying to read. She didn't care a jot for the man, but she had no wish to be left with a corpse on her hands. If only John would come!

Riders had been sent out to find Jeremiah's sons, but nobody knew for certain where they might be and it might take days before they got back. And Olivia wanted John here, now. She needed his quiet strength, the reassurance of his presence. For the first time she recognized her growing dependence on him, then pushed the realization away, refusing to think of it.

After a moment she gave up all pretence of reading and began to pace the room restlessly. The slightly trained skirt of her russet gown whispered across the wooden floor. Now that she was living in the big house to be near the sick man at all times, she had opened the trunks stored there and chosen a gown she couldn't possibly have worn while working round the shack.

Suddenly the old man's breathing pattern altered. He grunted, flailed the air with his right arm, then opened his eyes. 'Huh?'

Olivia went swiftly to the bed. Slowly, his brown eyes moved from the ceiling until they found her face. They narrowed, blinked, opened again. He tried to move and she put a firm hand on his chest. 'Lie still.'

'Wha' . . . ' The tip of his tongue moistened his lips and he tried again, the words difficult to shape because the left side of his mouth was stiff. 'Wha' 'appened?'

'You fell . . . yesterday. You've had some sort of seizure.'

A low angry growl rumbled in his throat. He tried again to move, to lift his left hand to his face. The fingers twitched but the arm wouldn't obey him. Instead, he touched the twisted part of his face with his right hand.

'A 'plexy.'

'Yes. But I think you'll recover.'

'Dam' sure I will,' he growled, his voice stronger already. 'Wa'er!'

She filled a glass from the jug by the bed, put a towel under his chin to catch the drips, and raised his head so he could drink. Noisily he managed to slurp half the contents of the tumbler down before closing his eyes peevishly to demonstrate his refusal of more. Olivia wiped his mouth and chin, then dipped a cloth into a basin of water and used it to cool his forehead.

He slept, a more natural sleep than before, and when he woke he allowed her to spoon some food into a mouth that was slack and dribbling at one side; then he set to work grimly to unlock his stubborn muscles.

Grudgingly, she admired him. The man's determination was impressive; she could see evidence of the grit and courage that had led him, as a youth, to escape imprisonment and stoically suffer the cruelties of the man who had owned Vanduara before him. The same determination, if Drina Platt's story was true, that led him to kill his tormentor and then build Vanduara into the successful sheep station it was now. And that was something Olivia couldn't help but respect.

Three days after his seizure Jeremiah had regained control over his facial muscles. His speech was still slow, with pauses as though he was shaping the phrases in his mind, but his voice was strong.

'Thought you'd have . . . stayed in Melbourne while you had the . . . chance,' he said suddenly while Olivia was tidying his bed.

'Why should I?'

The right side of his mouth twisted up in a smile while the left side remained grim.

'Thought . . . hated the place.'

She straightened, looked down on him. 'I'm John's wife.'

'Love him?' There was derision in the grunted words. When she ignored the jibe he tried another tack. 'Or is it . . . my money?'

Exasperation made her throw caution to the winds. 'John's your son just as much as Matthew is. But he's not as hard as you two, is he? You'll both do him out of his rights if you can. I'm going to make sure you don't get the chance.'

He managed to squeeze out a husky laugh. Then he said, 'Fetch my robe. I'm getting up.'

'No you're not.'

He glared. 'Hold your tongue and do as . . . say!'

Olivia shrugged. It was no business of hers if he killed himself.

With the help of two of the servants he made his way slowly to the verandah and sat in the shade, his eyes fixed on the land that stretched to the shimmering horizon. His land. The aborigines gathered in front of the house, eyes shining and teeth gleaming in wide grins of pleasure at seeing the master recovering. In the pens nearby, sheep bleated. Jeremiah gave a sigh of contentment.

He slept soundly that night and Olivia was able to retire to her own room, the room she and John had stayed in when they first came to Vanduara. Lying in the large bed, she recalled that first night and, tired though she was, she tossed and turned for a long time, wondering where John was at that moment, if he had had news of his father, if he was on his way back. She was tired of looking after the old man on her own, she told herself, thumping her pillow. It was time his sons were back to take over the responsibility which was rightfully theirs. But even as she shaped the words in her mind, she knew that she wanted John back for her own sake, not his father's.

Despite her fears, Jeremiah Mundy was stronger in the morning, and by mid-afternoon he was fully dressed and sitting out on the verandah again.

'Tell Chang to make . . . good dinner for two tonight,' he said unexpectedly as the afternoon sun arced across the blue sky. 'And put on something . . . pretty.' His speech was slow and indistinct still, but her ear had become attuned to it.

'Why?'

'I've got a mind to . . . celebrate. Dammit, woman, I've been snatched from the . . . jaws of death. Suppose I've got you . . . to thank . . . in part, at any rate. Go on!'

Chang beamed at the thought of making a special dinner, and launched himself at once into a frenzy of cooking, oblivious to the suffocating heat of the kitchen. Jeremiah was persuaded to rest and Olivia, excited despite herself, searched through the trunks and brought out her finest dress, a deep rose silk trimmed with ivory ribbons.

To her surprise Jeremiah also dressed carefully for the occasion. He came slowly into the dining room, leaning on Betta's arm, handsome in old-fashioned formal evening wear, and gave a nod of approval when he saw her. The rose silk glowed against her golden skin and emphasized the hazel lights in her eyes. She had put her hair up and twined scarlet ribbons through it. Gold studs in her ears and a gold necklace completed the outfit.

Jeremiah's gaze lingered on the necklace and he scowled lopsidedly. 'Take that off,' he ordered, and motioned Betta over to the case where the opals lay.

Instinctively, the woman knew what he wanted, and lifted out the opal pendant.

'Wear that . . . tonight,' Jeremiah said gruffly. Betta opened the catch and Olivia felt the black fingers, warm and deft, on the nape of her neck.

'Mighty pretty, missus,' Betta said, standing back. 'Huh, boss?'

Jeremiah surveyed his daughter-in-law with satisfaction. 'Like to see . . . the pendant in a good . . . setting,' he said, then with a sudden change of mood, 'Damn that cook, where's . . . the food?'

They ate in state at either end of the long dining table, which had been set with the best china and a snowy tablecloth. Chang himself brought in each course, chuckling his delight at the sight of the master and Missus John eating like gentry for once.

Each time she turned slightly, Olivia could see herself reflected in a mirror on the side wall and, as darkness fell outside, the fabulous opal resting on her breast burned in the candlelight with a thousand fires. She was aware of Jeremiah's eyes on her throughout the meal. He was enjoying himself, dining in style with a beautiful woman. Now, she told herself, was the time to work on John's behalf — and on her own.

Olivia put a hand briefly to the opal and felt its smooth cool surface beneath her fingers. One day it would be hers, in her jewel case instead of under glass with the other opals. When that happened she would take it to Scotland on a visit to show her sister and brother-in-law how well she had done. But she had to act soon.

Chang served coffee in the living room, then withdrew, his full, beaming face peering at them round the closing door until the last moment. When they were alone Jeremiah demanded a glass of brandy, but Olivia only poured a little into the glass, firmly announcing that she would water it well.

'You like being . . . in charge, don't you?' the old man grumbled, accepting the glass and looking at its contents with distaste.

She seated herself opposite him and poured coffee, aware that the folds of her skirts were draped to perfection about her chair, and that the opal pendant flashed myriad colours against her smooth, warm skin each time she moved. 'I don't want you to make yourself ill again. You should see a physician.'

'Don't . . . trust 'em.' He took a sip from his glass, watching her over the rim. 'You've got too much pride in you, girl, but you've got the . . . ability to change, if you've a mind to. Young Johnny's made a better . . . choice of woman than I first thought.' She smiled faintly, and he gave her a crooked grin. 'You've got guts. And you're right . . . he needs someone to . . . push him on.'

357

'That doesn't make him less able than Matthew,' Olivia pointed out swiftly. 'If John had been the older, he'd have been your favourite, wouldn't he?'

'I have no . . . favourites,' Jeremiah's voice was cold.

'Prove it,' she challenged. 'Treat them alike. Leave the land to them both.'

'And have them . . . quarrelling over it?'

'They wouldn't quarrel.'

'And you'd not . . . come between 'em?'

She flushed and bit her lip. Then she said, 'If John had his fair share of the place I'd not have to come between them, would I?'

There was a long silence. Olivia moved restlessly, longing to say more but afraid to say too much. The movement set the pendant sparkling.

'You reckon that . . . I owe you,' Jeremiah said at last, slowly.

'Yes, you do.'

There was another silence, then he said. 'P'raps you've got the . . . right way of it.'

He held out his glass for more brandy and this time she didn't add water. Jeremiah gave her a lopsided grin as he took it, and lifted it to her in a toast before draining it.

She was about to press for a move from the shack to the big house when Betta came bursting into the room, her face wreathed in smiles. 'They's comin', boss! Mister Matt an' Mister John, coming in past the sheep pens!'

Ten minutes later both Jeremiah's sons were in the house, covered from head to foot with dust from a long hard ride back home, tired and hungry and thirsty, gaping in disbelief at the sight of their father and Olivia in their finest clothes. Olivia, who not long ago had been praying for John's return, glared as he came into the room.

Half an hour more with Jeremiah and she would have had his firm promise in writing. His sons could scarcely have chosen a worse moment to interrupt. If Matthew found out about it he would be sure to try to change his father's mind again. She would have to content herself with that verbal assurance, for Jeremiah Mundy was known as a man who never went back on his word.

Chang came at the run with trays of food and bottles of beer and she was pushed aside in the noisy reunion between father and sons, the news of the boundary fences and the sheep out to pasture far away, and questions about Jeremiah's sudden illness.

'You look fine,' Matthew kept saying as though sheer determination was enough to keep his father alive and well.

'Tired, though,' John chimed in, his eyes on Olivia now that he had assured himself that his father was going to survive. She read the growing hunger in them and her body tingled in response. His lean face was drawn with fatigue, his clothes powdered with red dust from the long ride back to the station, but even so, anticipation uncurled itself slowly in her belly. Before her marriage Olivia had thought of her body as a way of binding a man to her: she hadn't realized, until now, that men could have the same physical hold over a woman.

'Reckon you ought to get in a good night's sleep,' John was saying, 'and we'll finish jawing tomorrow.'

Jeremiah was visibly tiring. 'You're right, Johnny. Plenty of time . . . tomorrow.' Then he said, 'Just put the pendant back in . . . its place first . . .'

Reluctantly, Olivia unfastened it and returned it to the

case, giving it a final pat when she had arranged it properly. One day it would be hers . . . she was sure of that now. One day nobody would be able to take it back.

When they had retired for the night she responded fiercely to John's love-making, her appetite sharpened by his absence and satisfaction with the progress that she herself had made.

'Since the old man's on the mend and Matt's here to look after him we'll get back to our own place tomorrow,' he mumbled sleepily into her shoulder afterwards.

She stroked his hair. 'Are you in such a hurry to get back there?'

'It's ours, and it's away from the rest of 'em.'

'We'll be back here soon enough.'

He raised himself on his elbow. Moonlight shining into the room gave his naked shoulders and chest a bronze sheen. 'What have you been up to, Livvy?'

'Your father and I have got to know each other better since I've been nursing him. He's realized how foolish he's been, favouring Matthew over you.'

'You reckon?' Then, suddenly suspicious, he asked, 'You didn't go putting your oar in again, did you?'

'I did not. He just told me that he realized that you were worth a fair share of Vanduara. He's going to make you and Matt equal partners, he told me so himself.'

'Mebbe him taking badly wasn't a bad thing after all, Livvy. It's given the two of you a chance to get to know each other.' He bent and kissed her. 'I was right, Livvy. I knew from the first moment I saw you that we could be good for each other.'

He slept then, but Olivia lay awake for some time, planning her future. She and Jeremiah would get along well from now on. In a way they were two of a kind.

*   *   *

Jeremiah Mundy gathered the reins back into his own hands with stubborn persistence as his strength steadily returned. He was soon able to get about the house with the aid of a stick, and his speech improved with every day that passed.

A swagman calling in at Vanduara for a meal on his way across to Kalgoorlie delivered a letter from Annis, an uncharacteristically short note passed from the *Grace and Charity* to an Australian-bound clipper.

Olivia read it, then read it again, unable to take in the news of Douglas Moncrieff's death, the fact of Annis being a widow. She walked on to the verandah and stared across at the lake, sparkling as ever beneath the sun, as a new thought came to her. Annis would be a *rich* widow. Little mouselike Annis would surely inherit everything Douglas left now that Robert, too, was dead. And Annis was still young and wealthy enough to attract another husband, a better husband than Douglas, perhaps a better husband than John. She slammed her hand on the verandah post, the good humour which had followed from her dinner with Jeremiah seeping rapidly away.

A lizard had run out from beneath the shelter of her carefully watered rose bushes. Half-way across the path it stopped as Olivia's sudden movement caught its attention, and turned its scaly head towards her. The hooded eyes surveyed her, the grotesquely blue-lined mouth opened wide to reveal a flickering pink tongue as the reptile hissed. The first time she had seen one of those harmless creatures she had rushed screaming into John's arms. This time she picked up a tin bowl that lay on a rickety table nearby and threw it viciously at the reptile with all her anger behind it.

With a flick of its tail the creature disappeared. The bowl landed a fair distance away from where it had been and rocked to a standstill, reflecting sunlight back into her eyes.

When Jeremiah heard of Douglas Moncrieff's death he decided that one of his sons should make the trip to Greenock to talk to Annis and to the men who would buy Vanduara wool when the Moncrieff clipper took it to Scotland. Olivia's heart almost stopped when John brought the news. She went on with the ironing, smoothing the same blouse sleeve over and over again.

'Why?'

'We have to know if your sister intends to continue with the business. If not, we'll find someone else to take our wool.' John's normally serious face was alight with interest. 'Don't you see, Livvy, that it's a fine chance for us? You can see your home again and I can meet your sister.'

'I thought your father would want to send Matthew.'

'He hasn't decided yet. But why let Matt go? It's my turn.'

She looked back at him, her mind racing. It was too soon. Now that Annis was wealthy in her own right she didn't want to go to Greenock with John . . . at least, not until they themselves could match her wealth. John was too quiet, too easy-going. He would be awkward there, out of place. He was too honest, likely to say the wrong thing. Her sister would quickly realize that this wasn't the man she had described in her letters.

'But if Matthew goes you'll be your father's right-hand man here. You'll get the chance to show him what you can do without your brother always being around!'

John's face darkened. 'I don't need to prove myself in Matt's absence. The old man knows me well enough.'

'Does he?' She set the iron down with a thump and faced him. 'As long as Matthew's around you're only second-rate in your father's eyes, John. Will you never get that into your head?'

To her astonishment he asked levelly, 'What's the matter, Livvy . . . scared that your sister will find out the truth about your life here?'

'I . . . don't know what you mean.'

'Don't you? Matt told me a thing or two while we were out bush together. But nothing I hadn't already worked out for myself. I know you, Livvy.' His eyes were hard, angry. 'Such a grand lady . . . I don't suppose you could bring yourself to tell her what being my wife is really like.' His eyes darted to the table, where her letter-pad lay. With a swift movement he snatched it up and thumbed it open to the page where she had started a letter to Annis.

With a shrill cry Olivia darted forward and tried to take the pad from him. He held on to it and they tussled like children before the page ripped and she fell back with most of it in her fingers. She crumpled it up and fisted it into her palm.

John's eyes were hard as he dropped the letter-pad back on to the table. 'Reckon you've answered my question, Livvy,' he said quietly. 'And you've made up my mind too. I'm going to Scotland and you're coming with me. It's time Annis met me. P'raps she's not as high-minded as you are. P'raps she'll accept me for what I am, not for my father's money. I'm looking forward to giving her the chance.'

He turned and walked out. By the time she reached

the door he had vaulted into the saddle and was on his way back to the main house.

A short week after he had agreed to send John to Greenock Jeremiah Mundy took another apoplectic fit and died just as Matthew, who happened to be working in the nearby sheep pens at the time, reached him.

He was buried by his wife's side in a small enclosed graveyard a mile from the house. The entire camp of station aborigines mourned as his sons, grim-faced, lowered the hastily made coffin into the ground and shovelled earth in after it. Olivia scarcely heard Matthew's level voice reading a short extract from a battered old Bible. 'Now,' she was thinking to herself, weak with the knowledge that the hardships, the humiliations, were over at last, 'now John and I can take our rightful place in Vanduara. Now I can visit Greenock and look Annis in the eye.'

Matthew closed the book, stood for a moment staring at the mound of earth that marked Jeremiah Mundy's last resting place, then turned on his heel and walked back to where his horse waited patiently beside the gig that John had driven out to the graveyard.

'Come to the house tonight for supper. We've got things to talk about,' he said abruptly when he was in the saddle.

Olivia stared resentfully at his retreating back. Both the Mundys rode as though they were part of the horse.

'To hear him speak you'd think he was the new boss instead of a partner.'

John lifted the reins and clicked his tongue at the carriage horse, and they travelled back in silence. Supper was a quiet, patchy meal. Chang, heart-broken at the death of his employer, was in no mood to cook, and John and Matthew were in no mood to eat. Olivia waited, hiding her impatience, until the meal was over and Matthew had filled two glasses with brandy.

'Livvy?'

She shook her head and poured out a cup of tea for herself as Matthew went to his father's desk and brought back a folded document. He tossed it on to the table before John, who silently unfolded it.

'Straightforward,' Matthew sat down and emptied his glass, then put it on the table with a decisive click.

Olivia watched her husband's face closely as he read the will. The excited tremor deep in her stomach faded and was replaced by an ice crystal as she saw his jawline tighten.

'What does it say?' she asked. Matthew looked at her in faint surprise, as though questioning her right to know, but John, tossing the will down, was the one to answer her, his voice harsh.

'Vanduara goes to Matt.'

She gaped foolishly for a moment. 'But it's to be an equal partnership!'

'You're wrong, Livvy. When I think the time's right I'll make John an equal partner. But not until then.' Matthew's face was tilted to hers, his eyes amused and knowing. 'That was what the three of us agreed, wasn't it, Johnny?'

John swallowed hard. His face was dark with disappointment. 'That was a long time ago, before I took myself a wife.'

'But he agreed . . . he promised me . . . ' Olivia interrupted, stumbling uncharacteristically over her words in her fury.

'Promised you what, Livvy? That John would inherit a fair share?' Matthew laughed. 'He told me that. He was only amusing himself with you.'

'No!'

'He could have changed his will any time he wanted since his first turn,' Matthew said blandly. 'But he didn't.' His finger stabbed at the document on the table. 'That's all there is and we'll stand by it. Johnny?'

John picked up his glass, emptied it, and got to his feet. 'No, Matt,' he said. 'We'll not stand by it. You know that I'm entitled to my share now. I want it.'

For a moment Matthew stared, then he too got to his feet. 'Too bad, Johnny . . . I've got every right to go by the old man's will. You read it. When I think fit . . .'

'And when's that going to be?' John Mundy's hands began to curl into fists.

'When you've got the sense not to let that wife of yours run your life for you,' said Matthew contemptuously. 'D'you think I want her living in this house, pushing her way between us all the time? Get rid of her, Johnny, and we'll . . .'

With a snarl John launched himself across the room. The small table that held Olivia's teapot went flying and Matthew, taken by surprise, reeled back under a blow to the jaw. Then he balled his fists and forged towards his brother.

Olivia, her skirts wet with hot tea from the shattered pot, ran to the door, convinced that the two men rolling and punching and gouging on the floor were out to kill each other. Before she reached it the door burst open and Chang charged in with Betta and two other women who worked in the kitchen close at his heels.

'You stop fightin' on master's ca'pet!' the big

Chinaman bellowed in a high-pitched scream, like a woman's.

In spite of his bulk he moved fast, dragging both men to their feet, managing to wrench them apart and hold them there.

'You stop!' he commanded, shaking them. Olivia could only stand staring, her fists pressed against her mouth. John's attack on his brother had surprised her just as it had surprised Matthew. She hadn't believed her husband capable of standing up for himself like that. Part of her was glad that he had finally taken matters into his own hands, but the other part was frightened by the sheer rage and hatred on his face as he glared at his brother.

'Let me go, you stupid yellow bastard,' Matthew panted, and the cook released his shoulder so promptly that he staggered. Then John was released, while Chang kept his bulk between the two men, watching them closely.

They glared at each other, sucking in air. Matthew dashed blood from his nose with the sleeve of his jacket, while John's left eye was already beginning to bruise.

'You'd better go home, Johnny,' the elder brother advised breathlessly. 'Go home and think it over. But remember that the will's on my side, not yours. If you don't like it, you can get out altogether!'

'No, Mistah Johnny,' Chang warned as John took a step towards his brother. 'You bettah go, like he say. Or I th'ow you out. No mo' fightin'.'

'Come on, Livvy.' John took his wife's arm and hustled her out of the room, past the gawping lubras.

'One other thing . . . ' Matthew's voice followed them to the door. 'I've decided that I should be the one to go to Scotland, Johnny. After all, I was the one who started the proceedings in Melbourne.'

'John . . . ' she began as they started down the verandah steps to the waiting buggy.

'Not a word, Livvy. Not a word, or so help me, I'll take my fist to you,' John promised.

They drove home in silence, John grim, Olivia sick with anger. When they were back in the shack she burst out, 'John, he promised me!'

His eye was half shut now. He poured some water into a basin, picked up a towel, soaked it, and held it to his face. 'He promised you, not me. I didn't ask you to interfere.'

'You can't mean that you're going to let Matthew get away with this?'

He looked up at her, his one good eye cold. 'I mean that I'll deal with things in my own way, in my own time. I'll not be run off Vanduara, and that's what'll happen if you interfere again. So hold your tongue, Livvy.'

'How dare you . . . !'

'I dare because you're my wife. Either get off the station or keep quiet and leave me to do as I think best,' said John; it was a new, hard John that she had never seen before.

Olivia stormed out on to the verandah. Night had fallen and the air was filled with the sounds of the insects that ventured out when the birds were asleep. Something splashed in the lake, something else rustled beneath the nearby trees. The sky was thick with stars and the air was pleasantly cool.

Olivia hugged herself, shivering, her mind bleak. She had been tricked by that evil old man. His death hadn't freed her; it had merely been a hiccup in her dreary existence.

'Livvy, come to bed,' John ordered from the doorway. She thought of defying him, but it would do no good. There was nowhere else for her to go. She was dependent on him, and they were both dependent on Matthew.

Slowly, hating John, hating Vanduara, hating Australia, she went into the house and closed the door.

Matthew rode down to the wooden shack on the day before he was due to leave for Scotland. Olivia, hoeing the garden, straightened her aching back when she heard the jingle of the horse's tack and the thud of hooves on the sun-baked ground.

'Any letters for your sister?' he asked, resting his wrists comfortably on the pommel before him.

She had been expecting him. She reached into her apron pocket and handed up the package. He took it and slipped it inside his shirt. 'You'll enjoy yourself while I'm away, Livvy. You can move into the big house for a spell and run the servants. You'll like that. But don't ruin them.'

She glared up at him and he laughed, then clicked his tongue at the horse. Turning away towards the other end of the lake, he remembered something else and reined in. 'You don't need to worry, Livvy,' he said, smiling back at her across his shoulder, 'I'll keep your secret.'

As soon as the cloud of dust that marked the buggy had merged into the heat-warped distance, Olivia closed the shack and moved into the main house.

As she walked up the steps into the shadiness of the verandah and saw Chang and Betta and the other house servants waiting at the door to welcome her, the anger that had gnawed at her since hearing about the will melted

369

away. She had six months at least in which to enjoy the house before Matthew's return.

Indoors, she walked through every room, touching the curtains and the fine furniture with loving fingers. Six months, during which there would be someone else to do the laundry and see to the garden and cook the meals. She must invite Drina Platt and her husband over and show them how a real hostess behaved.

She finished her tour of inspection in the dining room, where she went to the glass case, then stopped, frowning. She tried the lid and found it locked.

'Betta!'

The woman came running, anxious to please the new Missus.

'Where's the key to this case?'

'Mister Matt has it, missus,' Betta said. 'He carry it here . . .' She pointed to her midriff and her finger indicated a loop, like a watch-chain.

Olivia turned back to the case. It was locked and Matthew had taken the key that his father had always carried.

Not only the key. The magnificent harlequin opal pendant, the centre-piece of the Mundy collection, had gone.

19

During the final part of the *Grace and Charity*'s voyage
Annis remained in the saloon, retiring to the night cabin
when the shipmaster and mates came below for meals.
The thought of facing Gideon Brenner, the one man who
knew of her deep shame, was unbearable.

But as the clipper followed its fussing, steam-wreathed
attendant tug past the sturdy shape of the Cloch
Lighthouse to starboard, then past the neat little town
of Gourock, she made her way up to the poop deck and
stood by the rail. Smoothly the *Grace and Charity*
rounded the point and Greenock came into view, its
cluster of houses, quays and boatyards dominated by the
gracious façade of the Customs House with its high four-
pillared portico and two rows of windows, the lower
windows gracefully arched.

As befitted a widowed woman Annis was wearing
her darkest dress, a plain black silk with its pretty
cream rosettes and ribbons removed. Her curly hair
was tightly fastened back, its colour subdued beneath
black veiling.

Gideon was standing in his accustomed place, keeping
a keen eye on the men aloft. When at last he turned and
saw her, his face was a mixture of surprise and
awkwardness. She crossed the deck to stand by his side.

'Captain Brenner.'

'Ma'am?'

'I must thank you for bringing the *Grace and Charity* safely home.'

'I only wish that your husband . . .'

She cut across the words. 'It's obvious, Captain, that you care a great deal for this ship. You may have her,' she said, and turned away from the blaze of astonishment in his eyes.

He followed to where she stood by the port rail. 'What nonsense is this?' he asked, formality gone, his voice low and angry.

'I think you heard me, Captain Brenner. I've no further need of the *Grace and Charity*. I give her to you and Jem.'

'As a reward?' he asked bitingly, and hot colour flamed into her face as she realized what he meant.

'How dare you say such a thing to me!' If they had been alone she would have flown at him.

'What else am I supposed to think? This clipper is the basis of the entire Moncrieff business. You can't give her away!'

'I can, now that she's mine.'

'And the company?'

'Will be sold.' She spoke the words with grim satisfaction. This was the outcome of the time she had spent below decks, brooding over the wrong Douglas had done her. She had aged in those hours, felt herself harden with bitterness and anger. Selling Douglas's beloved family business, having done with it once and for all, was the greatest revenge she could think of.

'I thought that . . .' Gideon began, then stopped himself and said instead, stiffly, 'If you mean to sell her,

then sell her to Jem and myself. But let it all be above
board, for God's sake!'

She realized that she had behaved foolishly in offering
him the clipper in such a fashion, but she wouldn't admit
it. Instead she said haughtily, 'Very well. Call at the office
in a week's time. I'll instruct my chief clerk to agree to
whatever terms may suit you.'

'Annis.' His hand moved towards her arm, then fell
back. 'Keep the clipper. Marry me.'

'How very honourable of you, Captain.' The hurt that
Douglas had dealt was so strong in her that she needed,
wanted, to hurt others. The old Annis would have found
such a desire beyond comprehension, but the old Annis
had gone forever. 'Since you deflowered me you should
be the one to restore my good name. Is that it?'

His colour deepened until he was brick red.

'I can promise you, ma'am,' he said coldly, 'that
nobody will ever know the truth from me. But it is my
bounden duty to offer you my protection . . .'

The word hurt her far more than he would ever know.
'Your bounden duty, Captain Brenner, is to the clipper,
not to me. In the eyes of the good people of Greenock
my good name is beyond question and I intend to see that
it remains so. Without your assistance!'

She turned and went below, where she stared into the
mirror with angry eyes the colour of the sea on a cold day.

'His bounden duty!' she repeated the hurtful words
through set teeth. And her duty, no doubt, was to meekly
submit to his domination. Oh, no, Annis Moncrieff had
done with duty to others. From now on her allegiance
was only to herself and not to any man.

For the first time in her life Tib had come down to the

quay to meet the incoming boat. When Annis returned
to the deck a quarter of an hour later she saw the woman
standing there, a small black crow festooned with
mourning ribbons. Just behind her stood Beaton,
Douglas's chief clerk. Her heart sank for a moment, then
she pushed her doubts back and lifted her chin. Douglas
was dead, and Annis need fear Tib no longer.

Her sister-in-law greeted her with a cool sharp peck on
the cheek when Annis, with a nod of farewell to Gideon
Brenner, walked alone down the gangplank.

'This is a very sad day.'

'Yes,' said Annis.

The clerk, also in mourning, stepped forward. 'Mrs
Moncrieff, please allow me to express my deepest
condolences. Mr Douglas will be sadly missed, not only
by his employees, but by . . .'

She heard him out with as much patience as she could
muster. When he finished with a discreet, 'As to the
business . . .?' Tib immediately cut in.

'The solicitor will contact you in due course. In the
meantime, Beaton, you may continue to run the office
as usual.'

'I myself will be in contact with you within the next
few days, and with the solicitor,' Annis said clearly and
deliberately. 'There are a number of business matters
to be discussed. In the meantime, Mr Beaton, I would
be obliged if you would continue to run the office as
usual.'

She turned away from the surprise on his face and the
growing anger on Tib's, then turned back to add, 'If you
have any problems please come to Low Gourock Road
and ask for me.'

'I cannot think why you had to speak like that to

Beaton,' Tib said when the two of them were in a carriage and on their way to the house. 'You're in mourning. And in any case, what do you know of business?'

'I've done my mourning and I've neither the time nor the desire to prolong it.' Annis watched from the window as the carriage carried them through familiar streets. 'There are important decisions to be made.'

'I cannot see why you should be involved. Mr McWalters has been the Moncrieff family solicitor for many years. He and Beaton are quite capable of attending to things. Apart from Douglas's loss . . .' Her voice wavered, and for a moment Annis felt sorry for the woman. Then Tib gained control of herself again. '. . . life will go on as before.'

'I think not,' said Annis, 'not quite as before.'

She heard Tib's sharp intake of breath, but the woman said no more and they completed the journey in silence.

The house looked strangely small to Annis, used as she was to the vastness of the sea, to the spread of sail and stretches of holystoned decks. As she followed Tib up the stone stairs to the front door it opened and she stared as Adeline Fraser, demure in a black dress and snowy white apron, came out on to the porch.

The woman looked back at her, a tiny cold smile flickering in the depths of her deep-set blue eyes.

'Welcome home, ma'am.' She stepped back and allowed Tib and Annis to pass her. Then she followed them in and closed the door.

'Your cloak, ma'am?'

The woman's fingers slipped the cloak off, then helped Tib with her cloak. 'I'll send Celia to the parlour with the tea, Miss Moncrieff,' she said, and disappeared with the merest rustle of skirts into the back quarters.

'What is she doing here?' Annis demanded as soon as the two of them were in the parlour.

'The cook gave notice some two months ago. It was most inconvenient. I had still not recovered from the burden of overseeing Robert's funeral. Fraser applied for the post of house-keeper. She has been most helpful.' Tib settled herself in her usual chair.

Nothing had changed, Annis noticed with a slight shiver of fear. Everything was just as it had been before she left. Just as it would be for ever, if Tib had her way. For a moment the house nudged at the old Annis, at Douglas's child-bride, his good little girl. For a moment only, then she was forced back into the shadows and the new Annis spread her hands to the fire, then sat down, noting that the comfortable chair that Douglas had always used already bore the look of a shrine. His slippers were still on the hearth, his pipe-rack still within easy reach of his chair. A folded newspaper, she noticed, lay on the small table he had always used.

The maid brought in tea, her eyes sliding towards Annis as she put the tray down by Tib.

'That will do, Celia.'

'Yes'm. Mrs Moncrieff, ma'am,' the girl turned to Annis and said in a rush of words, 'Welcome home, ma'am, and I was ever so sorry to hear about . . .'

'I said that will do!' Tib's voice cracked through the room like a whiplash and the girl turned scarlet and bolted for the door.

'Thank you for your kindness, Celia,' Annis said before the maid was fully out of the room. Then she turned to Tib, ignoring the chilly anger in the woman's eyes. 'My tea, if you please, Tib.'

*   *   *

That night she felt as though the large marriage bed where she now slept alone was like an island tossing on the sea that still, after months afloat, rocked her in her sleep.

Before retiring she had folded up the large unwieldy screen in the corner and pushed it, after a struggle, against one wall. From the moment she had come into the room she had had the uncomfortable feeling that at any moment Douglas might appear from behind it, dressed in his night-shirt, his hands hungry for her.

Two days later, when the bed had settled and she had no longer felt as though the floor was moving under her feet, she found Tib standing in the parlour, an opened letter in her hand.

'What is this, Annis?'

Annis took the proffered sheet of note-paper and anger surged within her. 'This letter is addressed to me.'

'Douglas always opened any letters that came to his house.'

'Douglas is no longer here. Please don't open my letters again.'

'Why,' persisted Tib, a bright red spot in each cheek the only sign that her sister-in-law's manner had ruffled her, 'have you arranged to visit Mr McWalters?'

'Because he's the Moncrieff solicitor.'

'We can send for him to come here. The man has no right to expect us to visit his office . . .'

'I prefer to visit his office. That is why I wrote and asked for an appointment. And I wouldn't dream of asking you to go with me, Tib. I can manage fine on my own.' Annis glanced again at the letter. 'If I leave now I'll have time to call in at the shipping office first. I promised Mr Beaton that I would see him soon.'

As she walked out of the gate she knew without looking

up that Tib was watching her from behind the lace curtains in the parlour. Annis, drawing on her gloves, smiled to herself, a cold smile. In her arrogance Tib had assumed that everything would go on as before, but now she was worried. And well may she worry.

One of the first things Annis had done after coming home was to visit Robert's bedroom. Her hand stilled for a moment on the doorknob, but when she made herself go in it was to find a room devoid of its previous occupant. The bed was stripped, the cupboards empty, the books and drawings and the prized items that Gideon Brenner had given the boy were all gone. It was as though Robert had never existed.

Before coming out Annis had mentioned his name for the first time. It seemed that Tib hadn't wasted any time mourning the boy. Dry-eyed, she had at once embarked on a tirade against Jem Moncrieff, with some barbed comments thrown in about disobedience finding its own punishment. No, there was no sense in fretting about Tib's welfare, for she never worried about anyone else's.

Annis called at the shipping office first. Mr Beaton gaped when he heard that she intended to sell the *Grace and Charity* to Captain Brenner and Mr Jem Moncrieff.

'But she's a grand vessel, Mrs Moncrieff. You'll not find it easy to replace her,' he said, clearly bewildered.

'I've no plans to replace her, Mr Beaton. Captain Brenner will be calling within the next few days. Kindly arrange to sell the vessel to him for whatever sum he mentions. I don't think he'll give us an unfair price.'

The man's eyes bulged. 'Mrs Moncrieff, I must protest! In an open sale you could get . . .'

'I'm not interested in an open sale, Mr Beaton. The

clipper's already promised to Captain Brenner and Mr Moncrieff.'

There was time, when she left him, to go to the boatyard. She wanted to see Jem, but hoped that Gideon wouldn't be there. To her relief, Jem was alone in the loft. As soon as she reached the top of the stairs he came hurrying towards her, to take her hands and draw her into the little office where they could talk unheard.

He had aged considerably in the seven or eight months since she had last seen him. The heart had gone out of him, Annis could sense it immediately. Jem's face was deeply lined, his straight shoulders were stooping, and there was deep tragedy in his eyes, even when he smiled.

'Annis, I'll go to my grave seeing that damned vessel heel over.' His voice was tight and hard. 'I should never have agreed to build it — never!'

'You had to take the work. You couldn't know what was going to happen.'

He shook his head, then turned so that his back was towards her. 'God, Annis, if I could give my life for his I'd do it gladly. You've no way of knowing how gladly!'

Acting by instinct she put her arms round him. He turned blindly and they held each other close. For the first time Annis heard a man cry, and it was a terrible sound. But for the first time she herself was free to weep for Robert, for the honest, clever, golden lad who had been denied the right to grow into a fine man.

Later, when they were both calm, she told him what had been arranged with Mr Beaton.

'Brenner mentioned something of it, but he didn't think you were in earnest. Neither of us did. Annis,' said Jem with real concern in his voice, 'you can't sell the *Grace and Charity* to us. She costs more than we can afford at the moment.'

'I've arranged to sell her at whatever price you can afford.'

'But . . .'

'You need her, Jem. I've seen Captain Brenner handle her and I know that he could do well for your partnership with a ship of her calibre. You can take on the wool contract that Douglas and Matthew Mundy drew up. Gideon — ' she stopped, then corrected herself — 'Captain Brenner was there for part of the discussion. I've no doubt he knows enough about the contract to take it over.'

'But what about Moncrieff's shipping office?'

Time was getting on. Annis peered into the misty piece of mirror hanging on the little office wall and saw that her eyes were no more shadowed than one would expect of a recently bereaved widow. 'I think the shipping office can do well enough for itself without the wool contract. I've no need of it now,' she said, and left.

When she arrived home later that afternoon, Tib was almost beside herself with curiosity. Annis let her wait until after the evening meal, eaten in silence in the gloomy dining room.

Celia served them under the stern-faced supervision of Adeline Fraser. The woman was doing her best to ingratiate herself with Tib, Annis quickly realized. She herself was treated as a visitor, and Tib was given her place as head of the house. Adeline had obviously decided which of them would best repay her loyalty.

Annis cast a sidelong glance at her and shivered. There was something about Adeline that made her uneasy. They were a house of women now, with Robert and Douglas both gone, but she was anxious to be done with the place as soon as possible.

Back in the parlour Tib could contain her curiosity no longer. 'Did your interview with Mr McWalter go well?' she asked, the tension showing in her clipped tones.

'Well enough.'

'What did you discuss?'

'The shipping business. This house. Our future.'

Tib's eyes darted at her uneasily. 'Our future lies here.'

Annis drew a deep breath. The moment had come. 'Not my future, Tib. Normally everything would have gone to Robert — '

'Of course. He was Douglas's heir.'

' — but Douglas had the good sense to make provision for the — possibility — of Robert's pre-deceasing him.' She had dropped, without meaning to, into the solicitor's dry legal language. 'The house is left to you for the rest of your life, to pass to me . . .'

'After my death, or if at any time I should choose to live elsewhere,' Douglas's sister interrupted. 'I know that. I know that we'll continue to live here.'

'You may live here as long as you choose. I will find somewhere else.'

Colour flooded into the older woman's face, then faded just as quickly, leaving her skin mottled and patched. 'What?'

The smooth wooden arm-rests of Annis's chair were cool beneath her fingers. 'I don't want to live here any more. I shall find myself a smaller place. As for the business . . .' She paused for a moment, then said, 'It comes to me, and I intend to sell it.'

Tib bleated helplessly for several seconds, and even the

patches of colour left her face. It turned grey, and the veins stood out on her stringy neck. At last she found her voice. 'But . . . but . . .' She seemed to shrink back into her chair. 'It belongs to the Moncrieffs!'

'If Douglas and I had had children, it would have been passed to them,' Annis agreed. 'But we didn't. It's mine to deal with as I see fit.'

'Mr McWalter won't let you do it. I shall call on him tomorrow . . .'

'He has no option but to do as I ask.'

Spittle glistened on Tib's lower lip. Her eyes were wild, her fingers writhing on the arms of her own chair. 'If Douglas knew . . .' she said thickly. 'If my brother knew what you propose . . .'

'Douglas is no longer here, Tib,' Annis said. She rose and crossed to the chair that had been her husband's. As she seated herself in it Tib's bulging eyes followed her. The woman got to her feet and took a few steps forward.

For a moment Annis thought that Tib was going to take her by the shoulders and wrench her out of the chair by force. Her hands curled tightly over the padded arms.

Then Tib said in a faraway voice, 'I feel tired. I think I'll retire . . .' and blundered from the room.

As the door opened Annis caught sight of Adeline Fraser hovering in the hall, stepping forward with a solicitous expression as Tib went out of the parlour. Then the door closed, and if the two women outside had anything to say to each other it was blotted out by the solid varnished panels.

Alone, Annis stayed where she was, her hands gripping the arm-rests, her slight figure scarcely making any impression on the cushions that had been worn by prolonged use into the shape of Douglas's body. She had not been totally honest with Tib. The solicitor had been just as appalled as Douglas's sister at the thought of the family business being sold. He had persuaded Annis to delay her decision to sell for six months in the hope that she might change her mind.

But she had stood firm on the sale of the *Grace and Charity* to Brenner and Jem, and Mr McWalter had had to accept that, together with her request that the Moncrieff business should hire the clipper, complete with Gideon Brenner as shipmaster, during the six-month reprieve.

Tib was right. Her actions would have broken Douglas's heart, just as he had broken hers. Although he was beyond her reach now, she could still find revenge in selling off the company that had meant more to him than anything else. More than Annis herself, and her longing for her own children. In six months Moncrieff's shipping company would have ceased to exist, and Annis would have won.

During that time she had plenty to do, finding a house of her own and moving into it. She would start her search within the next week, she decided, getting up from the chair and walking briskly to the door.

It was Jem who broke the news to Annis, sending a boy with a sealed note. Ignoring Tib's open curiosity, Annis folded the single sheet of paper and pushed it into her pocket as she got to her feet. 'I must go out,' she said, scarcely glancing at her sister-in-law.

'You've not finished your breakfast yet.'

'I'm not hungry.' It was the truth; since returning home she was finding the usual Moncrieff breakfast of solid well-salted porridge less palatable than ever before. She was glad to leave the table and get out of the house.

Jem was in his yard, watching the gate. He led her to a quiet corner, not taking the time to go upstairs.

'Where is he?'

'In the Bridewell.'

'I must see him . . .'

'No, Annis. He doesnae want you to be involved in any way. He made that plain when I spoke to him this morning. Just tell me exactly what happened at the time of Douglas's death. I need to know.'

She couldn't tell him the truth. Only Gideon knew that and she was quite certain that he would never betray her secret. Slowly, carefully, she told of Douglas's grief, his continual drinking, the moody silence that erupted into a final rage.

'He went on deck and Gideon followed him. I didn't see Douglas again. I only know what Gideon told me and I've no reason to doubt that. Why would they accuse him of murder?'

'A seaman called Sam McNair was on deck at the time of their quarrel; he claims to have seen the two of them struggling and Gideon striking Douglas, then throwing him overboard.'

'No!' The cry came from her heart. 'Gideon would never do such a thing!'

'From what I hear there was no love lost between the two of them. Douglas had done his best to make the voyage difficult for Gideon.'

'But that doesn't make Gideon a murderer!'

'Whatever we may think, McNair's managed to convince the police. Gideon's to appear at the Sheriff Court and if the Sheriff thinks there's a case to answer he'll be sent to the High Court in Glasgow. It seems,' said Jem wretchedly, 'that this man McNair keeps company with Adeline Fraser. She used to be Gideon's house-keeper until he found her entertaining McNair in his absence and threw her out. To my mind the two of them have hatched this accusation by way of revenge. But whatever caused it the damage is done and Gideon'll have to answer to the Sheriff.'

When she had left him Annis went to Nelson Street and looked at the forbidding façade of the new Bridewell and Sheriff Court. Gideon was trapped in there somewhere, locked away with his very life in the balance. She swallowed back tears, resisted the impulse to march in and demand to see him, and hurried home to where Tib waited, her sharp face flushed with excitement.

'Thon American's in the jail,' she announced, opening the front door as soon as Annis reached the final flight of steps.

'I know.'

'So that's what took you hurrying out this morning.' Tib's fingers locked together, twisting. 'I knew there was badness in that man. I knew it from the first moment I saw him. Douglas should never have employed him, and now he's dead, God rest his soul, dead at the hands of that . . .'

'Tib, Gideon Brenner didn't kill Douglas.'

'How do you know? Did you see what happened?'

'No, but I believe Captain Brenner's account.'

Tib sniffed. 'More fool you to believe a murderer. At least he'll hang for it, though it won't bring my brother back to me.'

Appalled, Annis stared at her. There was a faint rustle of skirts and Adeline Fraser emerged from the gloomy shadows at the back of the hall. The house-keeper's pale face seemed to float above and behind Tib's shoulder; her mouth was twisted in a faint ugly smile and her eyes, as they rested on Annis, were alight with pleasure.

Bile rose into Annis's throat. She dragged her eyes away from the two gloating faces and stumbled up the stairs, reaching her room only just in time.

Retching miserably, she wished that she had managed to force down some porridge earlier. At least her stomach would have had something to reject. When the spasm was over she bathed her face with cold water then sank into a chair by the window, her arms wrapped tightly about her body.

It was natural to feel sick and faint after hearing such terrible news. There could be no other reason. But this was the third morning she had felt unwell. There could be one other reason. Annis stared unseeingly out of the window and prayed that she was wrong.

By the time the trial began Annis knew that she was not mistaken. She was carrying Gideon Brenner's child.

Her first thought was that her condition must be concealed for as long as possible, at least until after the trial. But she had underestimated Tib and Adeline Fraser.

'You can't appear in court,' Tib said flatly when, going against Gideon's wishes, Annis announced when the date was set that she would appear as a witness in his defence.

'I must.'

'It would be bad for you, in your condition.' Then as her sister-in-law stared at her Tib said, colour rising in her face, 'You surely didn't think to hide it from me, did you? Adeline told me a full week ago. My own brother's child, and you left me to find out for myself! We must look after you. You must stay at home and rest.'

'Tib, I'm perfectly well and quite capable of giving evidence,' retorted Annis, badly shaken by their discovery of her secret. But Tib's natural assumption that the child was Douglas's showed her the road forward. Her baby would not be born a bastard, but would have the protection of Douglas's name. That much, Annis decided in an attempt to quell the guilt she felt, he owed her.

And nothing Tib said would change her mind about the trial. 'You still mean to defend the man who struck down your husband?' her sister-in-law stormed at her on the day she was due to give evidence.

Annis smoothed her gloves carefully. 'Captain Brenner did not strike Douglas down.'

'The evidence against him says otherwise.'

'The evidence bandied about the streets, you mean. Some folks have tried him already and found him guilty. To my mind he's in sore need of someone to speak up for him and tell the truth,' Annis retorted, and left Tib to seethe on her own.

She knew from Jem that the prosecution case rested almost completely on Sam McNair's accusation. He had found another two crew members willing to testify to the treatment he had received at the shipmaster's hands on the *Grace and Charity*'s voyage to Australia, and the entire case had been built on the shaky pyramid of Gideon Brenner's ruthlessness.

Jem was waiting for her outside the court-room and nodded approval as he came forward. She had given a great deal of thought to her appearance for this important occasion, and had settled for a black skirt and jacket relieved by a white lacy high-necked blouse and a small grey hat with a black veil. She had begun to put on weight, though not sufficiently to attract attention. The top button of her skirt refused to meet the buttonhole and she had been forced to sew the two ends of the waistband together, but her buttoned jacket covered the top of her skirt.

The small Sheriff Court was filled with people, for Greenock didn't often enjoy the entertainment of a murder trial and Douglas Moncrieff had been a well-known businessman. As her name was called and she walked to the witness box Annis's courage almost failed her. She faltered, then tilted her head high and climbed the steps that led to the box. When she reached it she put her gloved hands on the rail and looked about the court, breathing deeply to calm the flutter of her heart.

Sam McNair, unusually clean and well-groomed, sat in the front row, his eyes meeting hers, then sliding away in their usual fashion. Her heart began to race again as she looked across at the dock and saw Gideon for the first time since her arrival back in Greenock.

He was smartly dressed in a russet-brown coat and trousers that became him well. His black hair, which she had so often seen blowing freely in the sea winds, was brushed into a smooth glossy cap framing a face that looked tired, but was still strong and resolute.

His eyes, as clear and sharp as ever, swept her face. She saw anger in them and in the way his mouth tightened. She looked back at him defiantly, then turned to look at the defence lawyer, who was asking her to state her name and her relationship to the deceased, a word that sent a shiver down her spine.

Calmly, clearly, she spoke of the voyage to Australia and back, of the blow of Robert's death and Douglas's grief-stricken reaction.

'Mrs Moncrieff, what did Captain Brenner tell you of

your husband's disappearance from the decks of the clipper?'

'He said that he had tried to calm my husband down. Douglas — my husband — struck him, then the clipper rolled to the waves and my husband went over the side.'

'You believed Captain Brenner?'

'I had no reason to doubt him. His mouth was bleeding and he was' — her voice shook, then recovered itself — 'he was very distressed. He did everything that he could to find my husband.'

She knew, for Jem had warned her, that the Procurator Fiscal was the man to treat with caution. It was his task to prove Gideon's guilt. His questions began softly and politely enough, but they soon began to gather impetus and weight.

'Tell the court, if you will, about the occasion when Captain Brenner punished one of the crew, a Mr Samuel McNair. I understand that you and Captain Brenner quarrelled bitterly over his harsh treatment and that Mr McNair owes his very life to you.'

'You exaggerate, sir.' Annis's hands curled about the rail before her, then relaxed with a deliberate effort as she realized that the gesture might be construed as overly nervous. 'Captain Brenner thought that Mr McNair was malingering. I went to the crew's quarters to see the man for myself and realized that on this occasion at least he was genuinely ill.'

'So . . . Captain Brenner, in a rage, would have worked and beaten an ill man if it had not been for your intervention.'

'I believe that he would have realized for himself that the man was ill. He agreed to me removing Mr McNair to the deckhouse and nursing him. Mr McNair made a full recovery and stayed with the ship for the rest of the voyage. He came to no harm.'

Her interrogator stood silent for a moment, then said abruptly, 'I understand that on arriving back in Greenock you gave your late husband's ship, the *Grace and Charity*, to Captain Brenner. A fine vessel. A very fine gift. To demonstrate your faith in the captain, no doubt?'

'I did not give the clipper to the captain. He and my husband's cousin, Mr Jem Moncrieff, have set up in business together and I knew that they were in need of a good sea-going vessel.' She realized with a wave of thankfulness that Gideon had been right in refusing the offer of the ship so angrily. What would this man standing below her have made of it if the shipmaster had accepted? The thought made her feel light-headed and she had to grip again at the railing before her.

'I sold the *Grace and Charity*, sir. I did not give her away.'

He made a pretence of glancing through the papers in his hand, then said silkily, 'Forgive me, ma'am, I see that you did indeed sell the vessel. But at a low price. You would surely have got much more for her in open auction.'

'I . . .' The face of the man before her seemed to dissolve, then reform. She swallowed hard, and heard the Sheriff say, his voice blurred, 'A chair for Mrs Moncrieff . . . and a glass of water.'

A buzz ran through the court-room as someone brought a chair into the witness box and someone else offered Annis a glass. She sipped gratefully at the cold water and the dizziness began to pass.

The Sheriff rapped on the desk before him with his gavel. 'Since the afternoon is well on, this court is dismissed until tomorrow morning . . . to give the witness time to recover fully,' he added with a kindly glance at Annis.

All too quickly the Sheriff was on his feet, the court rising as he left, and she was committed to returning in the morning to continue her ordeal. She fumed at her own weakness as she left the witness stand.

Tib was furious when she discovered that Annis had to go back. 'I shall call Doctor Warwick and tell him to refuse to allow you to return!'

'I'm bound to finish giving evidence and I shall do so. Mind your own business, Tib,' Annis said, too distracted with worry about Gideon to care about what she said to her. The older woman gave an outraged gasp, but held her tongue with an effort, letting her furious eyes do all her speaking for her.

That night, Gideon's face floated through Annis's disturbed dreams. She woke to a grey dreary day, and saw in the mirror as she dressed that her face was pale and her eyes shadowed.

Tib didn't come down for breakfast, choosing to sulk in her room. Adeline, knowing full well that her young mistress could no longer stomach food in the mornings, slapped a plate full of grey, unappetizing porridge before her. Annis pushed it away abruptly and poured herself some tea. Over the rim of the cup she watched the housekeeper's face. Jem's story about Adeline and Sam McNair came back to her mind and she realized that there had been an air of subdued excitement about the woman ever since Gideon's arrest. Adeline, Annis realized with disgust, wanted him to hang.

'What do you think of Captain Brenner, Adeline?' she

asked suddenly just as the woman, the unwanted plate of porridge in her hand, was about to leave the room.

The house-keeper turned, taken aback for a few seconds before her astonished face assumed its usual carefully blank expression.

'I have no opinions, ma'am.'

'You lived in his house for some time, did you not?'

Adeline's mouth tightened to a thin line. 'I was his house-keeper, ma'am.'

'Until he dismissed you. Something to do with Sam McNair, I believe.'

If looks could have killed Annis would have been struck dead on the spot. The woman opened her mouth, then closed it again. A shiver of fear ran cold fingers along Annis's spine. For her own reasons, this woman wanted to see Gideon Brenner on the gallows. There wasn't an ounce of mercy or decency in her.

'The tale going about is that Captain Brenner bore my husband a grudge.' Annis sipped at her tea, then said slowly, 'This whole business seems to be brought about by grudges. It's my view that the court doesn't know the whole story.'

'Whatever you say, ma'am,' Adeline Fraser said stonily. 'May I go, ma'am?'

'Hear this first. I'll not stand by and see an innocent man hanged for something he didn't do just to gratify some warped desire for revenge. Now,' said Annis after a short, tense silence, 'you may go.'

20

The scene with Adeline strengthened Annis's resolve and gave her the courage she needed to go back into court and face the Procurator Fiscal again. This time she knew what she was dealing with: there would be no more fainting fits.

Even so, his first question, 'Do you have any reason to protect Captain Brenner, Mrs Moncrieff?' took her aback.

But her response was adequate. 'Protect him? I imagine that Captain Brenner is well able to protect himself,' she said dryly and a faint ripple of amusement ran over the onlookers.

'It seems to me that the final moments of your late husband's life are somewhat vague,' the man persisted. 'You are asking us to believe that for no good reason, he flew into a rage, ran on to the deck, attacked the captain and then . . . threw himself overboard.'

'My husband did not throw himself overboard, sir. The clipper was sailing through a storm at the time, and he fell against the rail as the ship rolled. As to his rage, it concerned me, not Captain Brenner.'

'Indeed? This is something you didn't tell us yesterday, Mrs Moncrieff,' the Sheriff interrupted.

'I had hoped that it wouldn't be necessary to speak

of it.' She raised her voice, well aware of the way the entire court hung on every word. 'My husband had discovered that I knew of my nephew's visits to Mr Jem Moncrieff's yard, where he died in a tragic accident.'

She kept her eyes on the Sheriff, not daring to look over to where Jem sat. 'He started shouting at me and I was in considerable fear. He was . . . inflamed by drink. Captain Brenner came into the cabin at that moment and my husband left.'

'The captain followed him?'

'I asked him to try to calm my husband.'

'And instead they fought, and one of them died.'

'Instead, my husband struck Captain Brenner and then fell over the side when the ship rolled. I have no reason to believe that it was anything but an accident. Samuel McNair' — she turned and pointed an accusing finger at the man sitting gaping up at her — 'had a grievance against Captain Brenner because he had been punished on an earlier occasion.'

'When he was genuinely ill.'

'Before he became ill. The man was a malingerer. I know that, and so did the rest of the crew. I nursed him out of pity. I wish to God,' said Annis, her voice ringing out now, 'that I could have known what form his gratitude was going to take. If I had I would not have been so kind to him.'

This time there was a positive buzz of excitement. Sam McNair's face went white as he stared back at Annis with a malevolent scowl.

For a moment the Procurator Fiscal was taken aback, then he rallied and said to the Sheriff, 'I think, sir, that we must make allowances for Mrs Moncrieff. I understand that she is in a . . . delicate condition.'

Again the court seemed to rock about Annis's ears. As an excited murmur ran through the onlookers she had to fight against the inclination to turn and look at Gideon.

In spite of the confusion raging within her, her voice was remarkably calm as she said, 'I can assure you, sir, that there is no need to make allowances for me. I am young and in good health, and to the best of my knowledge being with child does not turn a woman into an imbecile.'

The onlookers tittered as the man's face turned red. He opened his mouth to say something further but the Sheriff intervened, putting some questions of his own, taking Annis over the events of Douglas's death again.

He spoke quietly and politely and she answered him as clearly and concisely as she could, grateful for his gentleness. When he sat back, nodding, and said, 'Do you have any further questions to put to the witness, Mr Forsyth?' the Procurator Fiscal shook his head, scowling, and Annis was free at last.

As she stepped down she stole one brief look at the dock. Gideon's eyes, still wide and brilliant with shock, looked straight into hers; asking questions, finding the answers with stunned amazement. Annis read so much into that quick penetrating glance that for a frightening moment she felt that the entire court must also see what he was thinking. Wrenching her eyes from his, she walked through a sea of staring faces and left, unable to stay in the same room as Gideon now that he knew the truth.

Jem followed her out and found her sitting on a bench, leaning against the wall for support.

'I'll take you home.'

'In a moment.'

He sat down beside her and took her hand in his. 'I didn't know that Douglas had blamed you for Robert's death. I'm sorry, Annis.'

'It's not your fault.'

'It is,' he insisted. 'If I'd had the sense to tell Robert to stay away instead of encouraging him . . . But I enjoyed the lad's company so much that I let my heart rule my head. And now he's dead, and so's Douglas, and Gideon's life's in danger. All because of my stupid selfishness!'

Annis put her free hand over the large warm fist enclosing her own fingers. 'You can't hold yourself responsible, Jem. Where will the blame ever end if we keep fuelling it?'

He nodded, his head bent, his eyes fixed on their linked hands. They sat in silence for a long moment, then Jem said suddenly, 'Let me take on responsibility for your bairn, Annis.'

'I can fend for my own child.'

'Can you? You're not much more than a child yourself, and life in that house with Tib's going to be hard . . .' There was compassion and concern in his brown eyes.

'I'm going to find somewhere else to live soon.'

'I'm glad of that at any rate, for I'd not want Tib to raise Douglas's child as she raised Robert. But the bairn'll be a Moncrieff and, as the only man left of that name, I'd be proud to give you both my protection.' He squeezed her hand until she felt the bones protest, then gave a wry, half-strangled laugh. 'Fate has strange ways of treating folk. Here's me . . . wanting to look after Douglas's son to atone for what I did to my own boy.'

The words shocked Annis out of her own thoughts.
'Robert?'

'. . . was mine,' Jem said, his voice husky. 'Nobody
knew it except me and his mother and she's long dead,
poor lass. I had it in mind to tell him one day when
he was a man, if I outlived Douglas and Tib. But that
day'll never come now.'

'If Douglas knew nothing of it, why did the two of
you quarrel?'

'That was nothing to do with it,' he said swiftly.
'Douglas died thinking his brother had fathered the lad.
Alison — Robert's mother — was by way of being a
childhood sweetheart of mine, but when it came to it
she chose James, and he was a good husband to her.
But he wanted nothing more than a son and heir, and
as time went on and no child appeared James became
more and more unhappy and Alison more worried.
Finally she turned to me.'

'And you gave her a son.'

'That was all I did. From the day she knew that she
was carrying Robert she and I were no more than
acquaintances. Fond acquaintances. James was happy
and Alison was happy, and her contentment satisfied
me. It wasn't until much later, after they had both died
and the laddie's existence in his uncle's house became
so dreary, that I began to feel responsible for him.
That's why I let him come to the yard, Annis. I was
hungry for the sight and sound of him. Then, having
given him life, I killed him.'

His voice broke and Annis said gently, 'You gave
him happiness, Jem. Never forget that. Now tell me
— what was the quarrel between you and Douglas?'

It was like drawing teeth. The story came out in short,

reluctant sentences, a story of betrayal by both James and Douglas Moncrieff, of money that Jem's dead father had sunk into the Moncrieff shipping line, money that should have assured Jem a place in the firm, of being denied by the brothers once the older Moncrieffs were dead and gone.

'There was nothing down on paper, for my father and theirs trusted each other. It was only later, round about the time that James won Alison for himself, that he and Douglas turned their faces from me.' Jem shrugged. 'But I gave up all thought of it years ago. I've done well enough with my own business, and it'll improve with Gideon's help — if, God willing, he's set free.'

Then he got to his feet. 'And that's the last we'll talk of it. Sit here until I come back. I'll fetch a cab.'

When they got home Annis felt so exhausted that he had to help her from the cab and up the long flight of steps, one arm strong and steady about her. She was little cheered when Adeline Fraser opened the door, Tib close behind her.

'What have you done to her?' Tib asked her cousin, her voice bleak and accusing.

'She'll be fine after a rest,' Jem responded stiffly. 'She's just worn out with giving evidence.' He tried to help Annis indoors but the two women moved forward and removed her deftly from his grasp.

'If you want to do something to help you can ask Dr Warwick to call as soon as he can. Then leave us in peace,' Tib snapped, and closed the door in his face.

Annis was in bed by the time the doctor arrived.

'I'm fine,' she protested as Tib ushered him into the room.

'Let me be the judge of that, Mrs Moncrieff,' he answered tartly, and subjected her to a thorough examination while Tib stood by with averted eyes.

'A few days in bed would be a good idea.'

'I hope you'll take heed of the doctor, Annis,' Tib's voice rasped. 'No more gallivanting about the town, not in your condition.'

'She seems to be a strong, healthy woman,' the doctor protested mildly, putting his instruments back into his bag. 'No reason why her confinement shouldn't be straightforward.'

'She's just been widowed. And had the strain of this trial into the bargain,' Tib snapped back at him. 'Surely you can see the need for care?'

He wilted before her stony gaze. 'Aye . . . well . . . I know that you'll look after her, Miss Moncrieff.'

'That I will.' Tib opened the door and stood aside to let the medical man pass through it before her. 'I hope that I know my duty to my poor dead brother's unborn child.'

Alone again, Annis slipped her hands beneath the bedclothes and caressed her gently rounding belly.

'I promise you,' she said softly to her baby, 'that we'll both be well away from here before you come into the world.'

Her requests for news of the trial fell on deaf ears. Tib merely said that, speaking for herself, she wasn't one to thrive on gossip, and somehow the newspapers never found their way up to the room where Annis rested.

On the second day, when she had recovered from the stress of the trial and the shock of Jem's story, Annis decided she had become bored with being an invalid.

She was fastening the belt of a blue and white checked dress and deciding that it was time to take to her needle and thread and let out some of her waistbands when the knocker thundered out in a way that refused to be denied.

Annis knew at once who it was. Her heart leapt, then began to throb; colour flooded into her face and ebbed again. She hurried out into the upper hall just as Adeline Fraser opened the stained-glass front door.

'I want to speak to Mrs Moncrieff.'

'She's not seeing visitors.'

'She'll see me. Tell her that I'm here.'

'She's not . . .' Adeline began to repeat doggedly, then her head swung round as Annis said from the top of the stairs, 'Ask the captain to come in, Adeline.'

'Miss Moncrieff said . . .'

'Captain Brenner has come to see me, not Miss Moncrieff.'

Sulkily, Adeline swung the door wide and Gideon stepped into the hall, taking his hat off as Annis reached the foot of the stairs and offered him her hand. He took it, then released it before she had time to register the pressure of his fingers. 'Will you have some tea, Captain?'

'No, thank you.'

'Then you may get back to your duties, Adeline.'

The woman bit her lip, then turned away. As the door leading to the kitchen closed behind her Annis led Gideon Brenner into the parlour, closing the heavy door firmly and moving to a seat at the opposite side of the room, so that if Adeline crept back to spy she wouldn't hear what was being said.

'You're free . . .' She tried to say it calmly when

400

she really wanted to shout the words aloud in triumph.

'Aye. And it seems that I owe my freedom to you. You impressed the Sheriff more than McNair did, whining weasel that he is. But it's a strange verdict — not proven.'

'It's singularly Scottish. It means that there was insufficient proof to send you to the High Court.' And the gallows, she thought with a twist of pain.

He ignored the seat she indicated, choosing to move to the fireplace, where he stood looking down at her, his brows knotted into a frown.

'I was worried about you,' he said abruptly. 'You knew that I didn't want you there, where you could be questioned and gawped at.'

'I don't take orders from anyone, Captain Brenner. Not any more.'

His mouth tightened, then he said, 'Not proven — it also means that they think I might have killed your husband.'

'As far as most folk are concerned a not proven verdict means not guilty.'

'And you? D'you think I killed him?'

She tilted her head back and gave him look for look. Not until the ice in his eyes began to thaw and his strongly marked brows unknotted did she say quietly, 'You heard what I said in court. You know that I was speaking the truth.'

'Ah yes. The truth.' His voice took on an edge and she knew, fearfully, that the real business between them was about to be aired. 'There was another truth spoken in that court-room, Annis Moncrieff. A truth that I should have known, but didn't.'

Her fingers fidgeted with the skirts of her gown. 'Why should I have told you?'

'Confound it, Annis, stop playing with me! It's my child.'

'*My* child!'

'And your late husband's. That's what they're saying in the town. But we know differently, you and I.' He caught her hands and pulled her to her feet. 'You turned me down before but you can't turn me down this time. You must marry me!'

His face so close to her own, his clear eyes, his very presence, set up such a turmoil in Annis that she couldn't think properly. She jerked her hands free and stepped back.

'Nobody can tell me what I must do now.'

'For God's sake, I have the right to acknowledge . . .'

'The right? First you want to marry me because you see it as your duty, and now you want to own my bairn. You scarcely flatter me, Captain Brenner!'

'Stop tormenting me! I'll admit that I'm not good with fine words. Perhaps I've put my case forward in the wrong way, but if so it's only because I do care for you. More than I realized.'

As she still said nothing, he repeated, slowly. 'I care, Annis. For you as well as for our child.'

Annis took a deep breath. 'And what about Olivia?' She watched his face closely. He had said on board the *Grace and Charity* that his obsession with her sister was over. She had seen for herself how coldly Olivia had treated him in Melbourne, but she had been just as cold to him here in Greenock and he had loved her all the same. Woman though she now was, widowed, wealthy, with child, the strong feeling of inferiority that had held Annis in its grip all her life still refused to let go.

'Olivia!' he tossed the name aside impatiently. 'The moment I saw her in Melbourne I knew that any foolish notion I may have had for her had vanished long since. She's cold and haughty. Beside her you're a flame, warm and alive and worth ten Olivias. Seeing you together I realized that getting to know you during the voyage, being in your company every day, had brought me to loving you. But you belonged to another man. You'd never have known of my feelings if your husband had lived. Now you're free, Annis, free to marry me and acknowledge me as the father of your child.'

A great cleansing joyous wave rose and broke in Annis. She knew now that he was telling her the truth, that Olivia was no longer her rival in love. Then the wave ebbed away as the realities of life pushed back into her mind, cold and hard and inescapable.

'Free to marry the man charged with murdering my husband? The man who walked from court on a not proven verdict because of my evidence? The good folk of Greenock would have enough tattle to keep them going for ever if that happened!'

'Let them think what they want . . . there are other towns we could live in, away from their tattling tongues.'

She shook her head. 'No, Gideon. I'm staying here, in Greenock. I'm going to birth my baby here and I'm going to answer to no man ever again.'

'Have some sense, woman! I know better than anyone what Douglas Moncrieff did to you, but why punish me for his foolishness? Why deny yourself love because of a man who's dead and gone?'

Then as she said nothing his face darkened. 'I've as

much pride as you have. If you refuse me twice I'll
not come begging a third time.'

'I'd not ask you —'

The parlour door swung open and Tib stormed in,
her outdoor clothes still on, her face twisted with fury.

'How dare you come to this house?' she demanded
of Gideon, her voice a low growl.

'Captain Brenner came to see me, Tib.'

'Are you out of your wits entirely, girl? D'you want
the whole town to know you're entertaining the man
who widowed you?' She swung round on the shipmaster.
'Leave this house at once!'

'I'll go when I've completed my business with Mrs
Moncrieff.'

'We have completed our business, Captain,' Annis
said steadily, and he gave her one cool emerald glance,
then picked up his hat.

'In that case I'll wish you good day, ladies.'

As he walked to the door Tib retreated before him,
putting a table between herself and his tall figure. It
would have been a comic sight, Annis thought, if her
heart had not been breaking.

'Can't you see she's not well?' Tib screeched from
her place of refuge, her face mottled and twisted. 'Not
content with killing my brother, are you bent on killing
his unborn child as well?'

For a moment Gideon's stride faltered and he turned
back. For a moment Annis thought that he had been
goaded too far. She stared at him, her hands clasped
tightly, her eyes pleading with him.

His white teeth caught and nipped his lip, then he
swung round and walked from the house without giving
a glance to Adeline Fraser who, smirking, held the front

door open for him and slammed it the moment he had stepped over the threshold.

Annis refused to restrain herself this time. 'That was a wicked thing to say, Tib!'

There was a wet gleam on the older woman's lower lip. She put up a gloved hand and wiped it away.

'It was the truth.'

'It was not!'

'What did he want?'

'That's my concern . . .' Annis began to say primly, then all at once she wondered what Tib would say if she knew, and to her astonishment her mouth quivered into a smile and then a giggle.

'Annis, you're hysterical. Adeline, bring some hot milk for Mrs Moncrieff. We must think of the child's welfare.'

Annis brushed past her and climbed the stairs to her room. By the time she got there the amusement had gone, leaving a great depression in its place.

She knew that Gideon had meant it when he said that he would not ask her to be his wife again. She had lost him. She and her baby were quite alone now.

Knuckles rapped on the door. 'Your hot milk, ma'am.'

'Take it away. I don't want it.'

The door opened and Adeline came in. She crossed to the bedside table and put the glass on it.

'Miss Moncrieff said that you must drink it,' she said, her face as expressionless as a painted doll's. 'We must look after you – and the child.'

She went out noiselessly and Annis stared at the door. She knew Adeline Fraser must go, but the thought of the struggle she would have with Tib over the matter exhausted her. If she herself was moving then there was little point in dismissing the woman. Adeline and Tib were welcome to each other.

After a while she drank the milk, which was still warm, then she lay down on her bed and fell asleep.

Annis's intention to start looking for a house for herself and her baby met with a setback when she fell victim to a heavy cold and had to take to her bed. Tib and Adeline Fraser fussed over her, refusing to let her get up until she was completely better. When she finally insisted on going out for some fresh air, Tib went with her.

Each time Annis tried to go off on her own her sister-in-law appeared at her elbow, dressed in outdoor clothes. Annis was exasperated, but slightly amused. She knew from the local newspaper, which reported the comings and goings of ships from the harbours, that the *Grace and Charity* was off to America with Gideon Brenner aboard, so there was no need for Tib to chaperon. But her energy had not fully recovered after the cold and she fell into the habit of letting day follow day without bothering too much about the search for her own house. When she tore the date from the calendar in the parlour one day and realized that it was near the end of August she was horrified to discover how time had passed. Her baby was due in a little over four months and she had a lot to do before the birth.

'Tomorrow,' she told Tib firmly, 'I shall go out on my own. I have to see Mr McWalter.'

Her sister-in-law, crocheting a shawl, looked at her sharply. 'What do you want to bother yourself with solicitors for at a time like this?'

'I must find somewhere to live, and then there's the business. The six months will soon be over.'

'You already have a perfectly good home. As to the business, now that Douglas is to have a son,' said Tib, having decided from the first that it would be a boy, 'the business must of course stay in Moncrieff hands.'

Annis eased herself in her chair and put a hand to the small of her back so that the fingers could knead away a niggling pain. 'I still intend to sell, Tib.'

The soft white wool the other woman was working on slipped on to her lap. Her thin mouth sagged open with astonishment. 'It's the child's inheritance!'

'I won't squander the money from the sale. I'll probably put it into another business. I may,' said Annis, 'take out shares in Jem Moncrieff's company.'

'You can't!' Tib's voice was sharp with alarm.

'It's a thriving business, and from what I hear Jem's more entitled to the money than I am.'

'What has he been telling you?'

'I think I'll go to bed now.' Annis stood up, clumsy enough now to have to lever herself out of the chair.

'I'll send Adeline up with some hot milk,' Tib said automatically.

'I don't care for hot milk.'

'I'll tell her to put some nutmeg into it. Hot milk is good for you, and we must safeguard the baby.'

On the following day a cold wind blew in from the sea and Annis was feeling too lethargic to face the steps down to the pavement. She stayed indoors that day, and the next, and the next. But when the doctor called he pronounced himself satisfied with her condition.

'I feel so tired all the time,' Annis complained, hearing an invalidish whine creeping into her voice.

He patted her on the shoulder. 'It's only natural, given the difficult times you've been through over the past months. Plenty of nourishing food and plenty of rest, that's the answer, Mrs Moncrieff.' He was an old man and he had been treating the Moncrieffs for many years and thought highly of them. He had brought Robert into the world. 'You're a fortunate young woman,' he added, patting Annis's shoulder again. 'So well looked after.'

Tib, standing by the door as she always did, hands folded on her apron, smirked. Tib was always there, Annis thought irritably: in the parlour, in the garden when Annis went out for a breath of fresh air, in the bedroom when the doctor called. Her sister-in-law had given up marketing, and stayed home most days while Adeline went to the shops.

When the doctor had gone Annis asked Tib to send for the solicitor, but the older woman said sharply, 'Wait until you feel better. The business is doing fine.'

'How do you know?' Annis was appalled to think of her sister-in-law's influence permeating the Moncrieff offices.

'I make it my business to know.'

'It's my concern, not yours.' Annis tried determinedly to assert herself.

'Not while you're in that condition.'

Exhausted, Annis gave up the pointless argument but she did write a note to Mr McWalter asking him to call. She gave the note to Celia when the girl came upstairs to take her dinner tray away, but the solicitor never arrived. She would have questioned Celia but on the following day was told the girl had been dismissed.

'Adeline caught her going out of the house without permission when she should have been cleaning the cutlery,' Tib said in answer to Annis's questions. 'I'll not have a dishonest servant in my house.'

Annis noticed the 'my', but let it pass. 'So we'll have to find another girl?' Suddenly she remembered Janet. What with the trip to Australia, then Douglas's death and everything that had happened since, she had quite forgotten her intention of tracing the former servant and her child.

'We can manage well enough without one,' Tib was saying blandly. 'Adeline's a hard worker.'

Janet was forgotten as Annis, who was finding thinking annoyingly fuzzy these days, concentrated on Adeline. 'I don't care for that woman. I think we should dismiss her.'

'Why, for goodness' sake?'

'She's . . .' Annis searched for the right meaning and found it in a Scots word that said just what she meant. 'She's sleekit.'

'Nonsense,' Tib's voice was crisp now. 'She's the best servant I've had in years. And she's had some experience as a midwife, she tells me. That's just what we need. We must look after the baby.'

'We must look after the baby.' It was her continual chant these days. Lying in bed on the following morning pondering the phrase, Annis was suddenly jerked out of her usual lethargy.

The baby — Douglas's baby, as Tib thought — was all that mattered. Annis herself was only cared for because until the child was born she was its only hope. After that . . .

She shivered and drew the blankets up around her neck. What would happen afterwards? It was hard to concentrate because of the continual tiredness that Tib and the doctor kept assuring her was normal. But why should it be normal? She had seen pregnant women going about town often enough, clumsy and tired-looking, but not as lethargic as she was.

She pushed back the bedclothes and got out of bed, staggering slightly as she made her way to the window. It was tightly closed because Tib had decreed that the sea air was bad for an expectant mother. With an effort Annis reached up and pulled back the catch, remembering as she did so the days when she had blithely opened the window and swung herself out on to the sill to clean the glass. Those days seemed to belong to another life.

Her feeble attempts to move the catch failed. She rested, panting with exertion, leaning her head against the cool hard glass. A carriage passed on the road below, and a messenger-boy went jogging past the house, swinging a basket filled with neatly wrapped white paper parcels, his lips pursed in a whistle that Annis couldn't hear. Her entire life seemed to be spent these days behind glass walls that separated her from the rest of the world, unseen, unheard, untouched. She longed for the dip and plunge of the *Grace and Charity*'s decks beneath her feet, the keen cold wind pulling her hair back from her face, the hiss of water as the clipper cut her way through the sea, all sails set.

And she longed for Gideon; if she had only given in to her heart he would have taken her out of this house, but instead she had spurned him and he had left without her.

She longed for Olivia who, despite her coldness, would not have allowed Tib and Adeline Fraser to dominate her sister. Olivia would have sent Adeline packing no matter what Tib had to say about it.

Annis, realizing that she was sinking into a well of self-pity, pulled herself upright and went towards the dressing table, walking slowly and carefully, leaning back to balance the weight of the growing baby.

The face that looked back at her was pale from lack of fresh air, the eyes dazed and shadowed. She found a hairbrush and did her best to smooth her curls down, then put on her wrap and opened the door.

The house was silent apart from the slow, ponderous tick of the grandfather clock in the hall below.

At the top of the stairs she clutched at the bannisters as a sudden dizziness swept over her. When it passed she began to go downstairs, taking each tread carefully. She had some thought in her head of going out into the back garden to let the fresh air clear her head, but before she had descended three steps the parlour door opened and Tib appeared in the hall below her.

'Annis! What do you think you're doing?'

'Going out.'

'Indeed you are not,' said Tib. 'Adeline!'

Adeline Fraser was by her mistress's side in seconds. She took in the situation with one glance and surged up the stairs towards Annis. 'Back to your room, Mrs Moncrieff,' she commanded.

'I want to go downstairs!' Annis struggled against the hands that descended on her shoulders and turned her about. But it was hopeless. The woman's gentle but compelling grip propelled her back along the upper hall towards her bedroom door. Annis could hear a flurry of agitated exclamations as Tib came scurrying after them.

Then they were in the bedroom, the wrap was being removed, and Annis was slotted back between the sheets, her protests ignored.

'Are you trying to kill Douglas's baby?' Tib wanted to know, bending over the bed. Her angular face loomed over Annis, her eyes were bright and cold, like slivers of ice. 'You wicked girl to do such a thing!'

'It's my baby . . .'

'For the time being,' said Tib, as Adeline tucked the bedclothes round Annis so tightly that she could scarcely move. 'That's why we must look after you until he's born. Then we can look after him properly, can't we, Adeline?'

'Yes, ma'am.' Adeline said stonily. 'Try to sleep now, Mrs Moncrieff.'

The door closed and Annis was alone. Weak, scalding tears flooded down her cheeks and into the pillow. She tried to wipe them away but Adeline had tucked her in so securely that the effort of freeing one hand was more than she could manage at that moment.

She had left her escape from the house until too late, she saw that now. She had delayed until Tib could in all honesty claim to the doctor − that old man devoted to the Moncrieffs and therefore easily manipulated − that it was in Annis's interests to stay where she was.

With a clarity born of despair the thought came to her that they had probably been giving her laudanum or something in doses mild enough to leave the baby unharmed. Just enough to keep Annis herself lethargic and easy to deal with.

'Adeline's had some experience as a midwife.' She

recalled Tib's words. 'That's just what we need. We must look after the baby.'

Adeline's experience — and God knows in what stinking hovel it had been gained — may well be sufficient for Tib to keep the doctor in ignorance when Annis's time came. After the child was safely delivered it would belong to Tib who, with a helpless, vulnerable, living part of Douglas to keep for herself, would have no more need of Annis.

'Gideon!' she thought, 'Jem! Help me! Help us!'

Then thick drowsiness crept over her and her long lashes, stuck together by frightened, helpless tears, fluttered, then dropped to her damp cheeks.

21

Gideon Brenner came home from his trip to America with the *Grace and Charity*'s holds and decks loaded down with fine timber. It had been a satisfactory voyage with no delays. The clipper had done well, and it was good to be not only her shipmaster but her owner. Life, he kept telling himself as the clipper scudded for her home port in a strong wind, was better than it had ever been. The cargo he carried would bring in more money than he and Jem had earned in half a dozen coast trips.

Yes, life was treating Gideon Brenner very well. But even as he cast his eyes over the full spread of sail above him, each stretch of canvas comfortably bellying out, he knew that he was lying to himself.

Ten times a day during this voyage he had turned to look at the sheltered spot by the deckhouse, where Annis Moncrieff's chair had stood during the last voyage. At night, when the stars were thick overhead and the ship ghosting on the surface of a moon-silver sea, he longed to know that a slight movement of his head would disclose her standing beside him, her curly brown head not much above the height of his elbow.

Lying in the night cabin he remembered the warmth of her in his arms, her passion — and the sick shame in her lovely eyes when she realized the truth about her own body. When he slept, he dreamed of her and of their child.

He was as lovesick as a half-grown fool, he told himself savagely. She had rejected him not once but twice, and he meant what he had said. He would not go back, cap in hand, a third time. Annis and her sister, like the sisters the clipper had been named for, had more pride than was good for them, but Gideon Brenner had his own share. He would not be humiliated a third time.

But he had to admit, if only to himself, that pride was no antidote for loving and wanting and needing.

The sooner he was at sea again the better, he thought as the *Grace and Charity* followed the tug back up the Clyde to Greenock. Time and good hard work would surely cure the sickness deep within him. But despite himself he scanned the quay as the clipper was eased into her place and the mooring ropes made tight. As usual, Customhouse Quay was thronged with ships and there were a lot of people on the quay itself. But Annis was not there.

He found it hard to stifle his impatience as he went through the usual formalities with the harbour master and arranged to have the clipper unloaded as quickly as possible. As soon as he could he made for the yard where Jem was in the loft, studying a half-model that his designer had just made.

'Gideon!' The boatbuilder thumped his partner on the shoulder. 'A good voyage?'

'A fine voyage. The fastest time we've ever made round the Horn. The decks were filled with green water from rail to rail at one time but we lost not one piece of timber. I've got rock maple, cedar and pine. They're unloading at this very moment. You'll have no difficulty in finding buyers for this cargo.'

'I'll have some of it for my own yard.' Jem nodded at the half-model he had laid down on a table. 'Another order, and a good one. You've brought me luck, Brenner. I could do with buying that old yard to the west there and combining it with my own if I had the money.'

'The bank would surely lend it to us.'

Jem scratched his greying head. 'I'd need a good-sized loan, and I'm not in favour of borrowing more than I have to. I must just hope that the owner doesn't put it up for sale for the moment. We might have time to make up some of the money before he does.'

'We might,' Gideon agreed, then asked abruptly, 'How's Annis?'

'I've not seen her in a while.'

Gideon's eyes narrowed. 'She's not been down to the yard at all?'

'In her condition that isn't surprising.'

'Did she find a place of her own, as she said she would?'

Jem shook his head. 'As far as I know she's still at Low Gourock Road.'

Anxiety caught at Gideon. 'For pity's sake, man, have you made no attempt to see her or find out how she is?'

Jem flushed. 'Of course I have. I've spoken with the doctor — he's an old man, but decent enough. He says she's doing fine. I've called several times but neither Tib nor that woman Fraser'll let me over the threshold, and Annis always seems to be resting when I call. At least, that's what the serving-woman says — if I'm unfortunate enough to get Tib the door's slammed in my face before I can get a word out.'

'They'll not slam the door in my face!'

'Hold on, Gideon . . .' Jem began, but the American

417

was already clattering down the wooden steps and out into the yard.

He barrelled through the busy streets, weaving in and out of the crowds, stepping off the footpath to let a stout matron surrounded with children by, then back on to the path as a cart rattled past, splashing him with muddy water.

Here and there someone shouted a greeting or a question about the success of his voyage, but Gideon wasn't in a mood to stop for anyone. He had to see Annis, had to know to his own satisfaction that she was well.

He had almost reached the gate of the Moncrieff house when a hire carriage jolted past him and stopped. Its passenger, a lean, dark, well-dressed man, alighted and tossed a coin to the driver.

'Wait here until I come back,' he said, then turned to survey his surroundings as the carriage moved on.

His eyes widened as he saw Gideon coming towards him. 'Captain Brenner?'

The arrogant brown face was familiar. So was the strange accent, English yet not English.

'We met in Melbourne.'

'Matthew Mundy!' Gideon took the proffered hand. 'I didn't expect to see you here.'

'The old man dropped his bundle,' Mundy explained. 'I'm in charge of the sheep station now. I heard about Moncrieff's death and came to see what difference it might make to our wool agreement.'

'Have you seen Annis − Mrs Moncrieff?'

The Australian shook his head. 'I've just arrived from Glasgow. My ship went further up river and I had to come here by train.'

In a few terse words Gideon explained the situation. Matthew Mundy's face hardened.

'You think this sister of Moncrieff's might harm Annis?'

'I'd not trust her, or the serving-woman they have. I want to see her for myself.'

'So do I. In here?' Mundy went through the gate without wasting another moment.

'You'd better do the talking. They'll not let me into the house if they can help it,' Gideon told him as they went up the stairs, taking them three at a time.

Mundy gained the porch and seized the door-knocker in a strong brown hand. He slammed it against the brass panel twice, then twice again, and was about to knock again when a shadow appeared behind the stained-glass upper half.

The door was opened only a few inches. Tib Moncrieff's sharp nose and one suspicious eye appeared in the space. 'What do you want?'

'G'day, ma'am,' the Australian drawled easily. 'I'm Matthew Mundy. Your late brother and I had business in Melbourne, and I'm here to see Mrs Moncrieff. I believe that she is now in charge of the company.'

'My sister-in-law isn't well.' The door began to close, but Mundy put the flat of his hand on it and prevented it from closing entirely.

'I'm sorry to hear that, ma'am. Perhaps I could pay my respects . . .'

'No!' Tib said sharply, just as Gideon, unable to wait any longer, surged into the porch and put his weight against the door.

It flew open and Tib, with an outraged squawk, fell back against the wall. By the time she had recovered,

Gideon and Matthew Mundy were in the hall, the Australian's nose wrinkling as he took in his surroundings.

The house had deteriorated since Gideon had last been in it. The hall mirror was smeared, the woodwork no longer beeswaxed to a high gloss. The air was stuffy and dusty and Tib herself had a stale, grimy look about her.

It took one second to record his impressions, and another for Tib Moncrieff to launch herself from the wall and attack him, long-nailed hands clawed, her mouth open in scream of anger.

Taken by surprise, Gideon staggered back, his hands going up to save his eyes. Small and slight though she was, the woman had strength, and if Matthew Mundy hadn't been there Gideon might have fared worse than a scratched face before managing to subdue her on his own.

As it was, Mundy caught hold of her shoulders from behind and she turned on him at once, trying to writhe round so that she could claw at him. The noise coming from her open mouth was an eerie mixture of words and a strange, terrible, outraged gasping.

'Find Annis . . . I'll deal with this one,' Mundy said breathlessly as he struggled with the woman.

Gideon threw open the doors that led off the hall and saw that the dusty rooms were all empty.

'Annis? Answer me!' He raced up the staircase and started opening each door he came to, throwing them wide so that they crashed back against the walls. A few spots of bright blood dripped from the deep scratches on his cheek on to his hand as he reached out towards the handle of the third door.

Annis was there, lying in the bed, the swell of her belly accentuating the thin pallor of her small face. Beside her on a table stood an empty glass and a small dark-brown medicine bottle. She frowned and her eyes fluttered open in protest at the noise of the door slamming open, then they blinked and tried to focus on him.

'Dear God . . . Annis!' said Gideon, appalled. As he gathered her into his arms, blankets and all, she murmured his name and one hand lifted to touch his face. When it fell back it was smeared red. Her head rolled against his shoulder and her eyes closed again.

As he carried her down the stairs Matthew Mundy stepped quickly out of the dining room and turned the key in the lock. Something smashed against the inside of the door, and by the time Gideon reached the foot of the stairs there was a frenzy of sound from inside the room — a high-pitched screaming, the crashing of glass and wood.

Matthew took a white handkerchief from his pocket and pressed it to a split lip. Then he saw the couple at the foot of the stairs and came forward quickly, his dark eyes wide with horror. 'Annis . . . ' He tried to see the face pressed against Gideon's chest. 'She looks bad.'

'Open the door, I'm taking her to a doctor. A competent doctor, not the old fool who's been treating her.'

'I'll carry her.' Mundy held his arms out and Gideon gave him a murderous glare.

'Just open the door, damn you!'

It opened as Mundy approached it and Adeline Fraser walked into the hall. Her heavy-lidded dark blue eyes swung from Mundy's face to Gideon's, then to the bundle that the shipmaster held protectively against his chest before going back to Gideon's face with a look of hatred that could have quelled an army.

It was met, matched, and surpassed.

'Get out of my way, bitch,' Gideon said in a low voice thick with menace. 'If you ever cross my path again I'll choke the life out of you!'

He shouldered his way forward and Adeline shrank back against the wall, dropping the basket she carried.

As he started down the flight of stone steps something heavy crashed against the dining-room door.

'Your mistress?' Matthew Mundy asked Adeline as he passed in his turn. 'You'd better see to her. But look out for your own safety – she's quite mad.'

He ran down the steps to where Gideon was already carefully stowing Annis into the carriage and snapping orders at the driver.

When the carriage had gone rattling and swaying along the road, Adeline Fraser pressed her ear against the dining-room door and listened for a moment to the frantic sounds from within. Then she hurried upstairs to the attic, where she slept.

Fifteen minutes later, while Tib Moncrieff's ravings continued behind the locked door, the house-keeper left the house carrying all that she possessed – and a few small but valuable items – and hurried off in the direction of the station.

On her way she passed a police officer who had been summoned by anxious Low Gourock Road householders unused to hearing such an uproar in their neighbourhood. Adeline lowered her head and hurried past the man unnoticed.

*　　*　　*

Gideon Brenner's house-keeper, the middle-aged woman Annis had met on her visit to his home in Bank Street, was discreet as well as kindly.

When her employer walked into the house with a half-conscious, pregnant woman in his arms and, laying his burden down carefully on his own bed, said tersely, 'Look after her, Ellie,' she did just that, with not a single question or comment.

Slowly the mists cleared from Annis's brain. After floating in limbo for weeks, life began to tingle through her body once more and her head and limbs lost the leaden feeling she had become used to in the Moncrieff house.

By the time she emerged fully from her stupor and began to take an interest in her surroundings again Gideon, who had removed his possessions to Jem Moncrieff's house, was back at sea, on his way to Australia with a mixed cargo in the *Grace and Charity*'s holds. With Annis ill and Tib Moncrieff raving in the cells kept in the local Poorhouse for insane people, the three men, Gideon, Jem and Matthew, had decided that for the time being the agreement struck between Matthew and Douglas Moncrieff in Melbourne would stand, and the wool from the shearing that would be going on at Vanduara at that very moment should be brought back to Greenock.

Jem, who had appointed himself Annis's guardian for the time being, visited her every day, while Matthew Mundy called at least twice a week. It was Jem who told her how Gideon and the Australian had forced their way into the house in search of her. It was Jem who told her, when he thought she was strong enough to hear the news, that Tib Moncrieff had been removed to the Poorhouse and Adeline Fraser had disappeared.

Despite the good fire in the grate and the shawl about Annis's shoulders, she shivered at the news. 'Poor Tib,' she said quietly.

'Poor Tib? The woman might have killed you. As for Adeline Fraser . . .'

Annis's hand went up to stop him. 'What's done is done, Jem. Let me look forward to birthing my bairn now.'

It was Jem, to Annis's surprise, who refused point-blank to send for the solicitor so that she could put the disposal of the Moncrieff shipping company into operation.

'I'll not stand idly by and let you do that.'

'But I don't want any part of it!'

'That's nonsense and you know it,' the ship-builder said bluntly. 'You'd be a fool to let it go just because of some bee you've got in your bonnet about Douglas and Tib. It'll be a good inheritance for your bairn.'

'I can see to my own child. The company should be yours by rights. Your father put money into it. You should have been Douglas's partner.' She almost added, 'Besides, you're his natural heir,' then remembered just in time that Jem, like everyone else, believed that she was carrying Douglas's child.

'Och, I wish you'd never dragged that old story out of me,' Jem said, exasperated. 'I'll not let you sell the family business to one of those rich folk in the big houses on the hill, or some Glasgow man who cares nothing for it but the profit it can make for him.'

She had never seen him so angry. For a moment, as he swung round from the window and looked down on her, he was very like Douglas.

'If you want it, buy it.'

'You know fine that I couldn't afford its true value, and I'd not pay less. Annis, see sense! You've let the *Grace and Charity* go, but for God's sake keep everything else intact. You've got a good brain in that pretty head of yours, lassie,' said Jem fiercely. 'Use it!'

'Then what d'you say to a partnership? The shipping business and the ship-yard combined. That way the *Grace and Charity* would be part of both businesses.'

For a moment Jem was taken aback, then he rubbed a hand over his beard, eyes narrowed in thought. 'You might have something there, lass.'

'You'd agree?'

'I'd like to talk to Gideon about it . . .'

'I'll not wait for his return. If you don't agree, it's up for sale, whatever you say.'

'Let me think about it.'

'You've got until tomorrow,' she said ruthlessly.

'Tomorrow,' Jem said with a sigh, and came back the next day to say that he agreed. 'But on one condition,' he added, fixing her with a firm eye. 'You become a working partner.'

'Me?'

'Someone needs to see to the shipping office and Gideon and I have enough to do.'

'I've not, I suppose?' she asked in astonishment. 'Me with a house to find and a child to raise!'

'You can manage that and a partnership as well. I've already told you that you've got a good brain in your noddle. You'll soon enough find time hanging heavy on your hands if you stay in the house all day.' He dropped to one knee before her, caught her hands in his, his craggy face alight with enthusiasm. 'Come in with me, Annis. We'd work well together.'

Annis thought for a moment. The chief clerk was a capable man. With his help she could learn the ways of the business. The challenge Jem had thrown down was tempting. But there was one stumbling block.

'What would Gideon say?'

'Like you, I'll not wait for his return to find out. I see no reason why he should disagree with me. What d'you say?'

She nodded, and Jem grinned broadly and kissed her on the cheek before rising to his feet. 'I'm pleased, lass. I'd not have liked to see the business go out of the family, not after all the hard work Douglas put into it. It would have broken the man's heart.'

When she was alone Annis allowed herself to think of Douglas for the first time in weeks. She would never forgive his betrayal, but the edge of her fury had dulled.

She was not keeping the business intact for Douglas's sake, but for Jem's. And in a way her revenge was complete, for Douglas would have hated to know that his despised kinsman was going to benefit from it.

Annis's child, due in the middle of January, was born prematurely on Christmas Eve.

'Not unusual for a first bairn, and not surprising considering what you've been through,' Ellie commented calmly and reassuringly when Annis, doubled up with the first pain, screamed for her to come from the kitchen.

It was a swift birthing. By the time the bells rang in Christmas Day the baby had arrived, a scrap of a thing that Annis named Rowena, partly because she had always liked the name, and partly because in Scotland rowan trees had always been looked on as protection against witches and warlocks. Tib and Adeline Fraser might be out of her life now, she thought, holding her little daughter close, but their malice and evil lingered, and the innocent baby who had almost fallen into their hands needed as much protection as she could get.

She looked down at the small sleeping face, the tiny fist that curled about her finger, and knew a surge of love so strong that it hurt. The past was past, and now the future was all that mattered.

Matthew Mundy was still in Greenock. Once Annis was recovered from her ordeal at Tib Moncrieff's hands and able to receive visitors, he called on her several times each week, spending at least an hour with her each time. He brushed aside her concern about his need to return home.

'I intend to wait until your child is safely delivered and I can make a good report to your sister. In the meantime I'm seeing something of Scotland.'

He was attentive, gentle, amusing. He had helped Gideon to take her out of the Moncrieff house, and yet Annis couldn't think of him as anything other than a polite stranger. It seemed to her that there was a coldness behind his charm, as if everything he said, every smile, was carefully calculated.

A few weeks after Rowena's birth he presented Annis with the most beautiful pendant she had ever seen.

Delighted, and slightly puzzled by his generosity, she held it up to the light and saw deep crimson fires come and go in the depths of the large, flawless stone. 'Isn't it one of the opals you told me about in Melbourne?'

'Yes, it's a harlequin opal, the best of the stones found on Vanduara so far.' He took it from her. 'Let me see you wearing it.' He fastened it carefully about her neck, his fingers cool and firm as they brushed against her skin, then nodded his satisfaction. 'I thought that it would look well on you.'

'Surely Olivia should have it.'

'I knew from the first moment I saw you that it should be yours.' He walked restlessly to the window and peered out. 'Scotland's grey in winter-time.'

'The word we use is dreich.'

'Not like Australia. Even in our wet season it's not like this. Annis,' he said suddenly, swinging round, 'come back to Australia with me, as my wife.' Then he added as she stared at him. 'I know that I'm not giving you much time to get to know me, but I must get back home soon. I've wanted you since I first saw you in Melbourne . . . when I heard that you'd been widowed I knew that I must come here and − and ask you.'

'But Rowena . . .'

'The child too. I can give her . . . both of you . . . everything you could ever want. We'd have other children . . . sons to inherit Vanduara. You and I would have fine sons, Annis. At least think about it,' he said swiftly as she began to shake her head.

'Matthew, I'm grateful to you but I'll not marry again.'

'Is it the thought of Brenner that's stopping you?' Then, as she stared at him, taken aback, he went on, 'I'm not a fool, my dear, I could see on that first day that he cared for you. But where is he now? At sea somewhere. That's where he'll always be. You need a man who −'

'Mr Mundy, you − forget yourself!' She stammered over the words in her confusion and indignation. She knew that her face had coloured, but could do nothing about it, hoping that he put it down to anger, not guilt. 'Captain Brenner is a good friend and nothing more. I simply have no intention of marrying again. None!'

He threw one hand out impatiently. He had the look of a man not used to being denied, she thought. 'You're too young to tie yourself down to a dead man!'

She almost laughed, but controlled herself. If he only knew the truth. But then he wouldn't understand. 'I want to stay here, where I belong, and raise my daughter in my own way.'

'I needn't leave for three weeks yet. You have time to think it over.'

The man was quite impossible! 'I don't need time. I know my own mind. Here . . .' She put her hands to the nape of her neck and began to unfasten the pendant, but he stopped her.

'Keep it. It was meant for you, no matter what your answer. I don't want it. Give it to the child when she becomes a woman, in memory of the life she might have enjoyed in Australia,' said Matthew Mundy, and went.

When she was alone Annis sat staring into the fire. She knew that Matthew was wealthy, that he could, as he said, give Rowena everything. And if she accepted him she would be re-united with Olivia. But his ruthlessness disturbed her. No matter how well he might hide it beneath his easy charm, it was there; not the iron-hard resolve that Gideon had . . . her cheeks warmed as she remembered how gentle the American could be . . . but something sharper, colder. She recalled how he had referred to Rowena as 'the child' and spoken of the sons he wanted, and shivered. She had been right to deny him. She must abide by her decision to remain independent.

A cry from the crib cut into her thoughts. Annis lifted the baby and carried her back to the chair. Once settled, she drew back the shawl to clear the pursed little face and flailing fists. Rowena, distracted from her hunger for a moment, stared up at her mother with large blue eyes. Her mop of black hair was the same colour as Gideon's, but Ellie, a mother and grandmother, had told Annis that most very small babies had dark hair and that it meant little.

Annis could see no similarity to Gideon or herself. To her, Rowena was already a perfect, very precious person in her own right.

The baby sneezed, then began yelling again. Annis unfastened her blouse and offered a breast which was instantly seized on. Watching her daughter suck, feeling the warmth of the little face against her body, Annis was glad that she had had a daughter and not a son. Although Tib was no longer able to dominate her, the townsfolk would have expected her to raise the child in a manner befitting Douglas's son. Gideon, too, would probably have had ideas on how to raise the child.

But a daughter was different. A daughter belonged to Annis alone. As soon as she was able she would find a home for the two of them. She would see to it that Rowena had the love and security that she herself had never known as a child. Rowena wouldn't grow up to be dependent on men as her mother had. She would stand on her own two feet; she would know the ways of the world. And if, one day, she married, it would be to a trustworthy man who wouldn't deceive her and betray her. Annis would see to that.

She touched the curve of a cheek with the tip of one finger. 'You're mine, my little love,' she whispered. 'Only mine.'

Matthew Mundy left Greenock within the week. He called on Annis on the morning of his departure to bid her a formal farewell then, to her relief, he was gone and she felt free to turn her attention to finding somewhere for herself and Rowena to live. As she regained her strength after her confinement she had become increasingly eager to move out of Gideon Brenner's home before he came back.

Each time she opened a closet where some of his clothes hung, the masculine smell of them reminded her of him. A pair of his shoes lay neatly together beneath the chair opposite when she sat by the hearth; shells and carvings and statuettes collected by him were all over the place. She had to keep reminding herself that she must be independent. It was time to move on before living in Gideon's home became a habit hard to break.

The Poorhouse, situated between Captain Street and Duncan Street, was a dreary, depressing old building. Annis had never been inside its door before, and she was grateful for Jem's reassuring presence as she sat in the Mistress's tiny drab office.

The Mistress looked at her over steel-framed spectacles and pointed out, 'McGregor's a fallen woman, Mrs Moncrieff. She's fortunate that you're willing to give house room to her and her bairn.' Then a timid hand tapped at the door and she barked out, 'Come in!'

Annis rose and turned to face the door. Jem got to his feet too, but the Mistress remained seated.

The woman who came in, nervously drying reddened, cracked hands on a sacking apron, was middle-aged. Wisps of hair hung from below a ragged cap that had once been crisp and white but was now yellowed. Her eyes were dull, her voice bleak when she said, 'You sent for me, ma'am.'

'I did, McGregor.'

Annis, certain that this slattern had come to tell them that for some reason Janet couldn't answer the summons, gasped. The woman kept her eyes on the Mistress, who said, 'Mrs Moncrieff asked to see you.'

Then, and only then, did the woman turn and look at Annis. 'Mrs . . . Moncrieff?' her voice was disbelieving.

'Janet . . . ' Annis held her hands out, but Janet took a step back, tucking her own hands into her apron. 'D'you mind me?'

There was a ghost of a smile round the pale lips. 'Aye, ma'am. I mind ye.'

If the Mistress hadn't been there, surveying the scene with dry disapproval, Annis would have wept. Instead, heedful of the need to do things the right way, she said briskly, 'I'm looking for a good serving-woman. Would you work for me again?'

There was a flash of hope in the sunken eyes, then Janet said, 'What about my bairn? I couldnae leave him.'

'You'll bring him, of course. I've a child of my own now.'

The light flashed again, then died. 'But . . . what would Miss Tib and the master say to it?'

Mention of Tib reminded Annis that Douglas's sister was within these damp crumbling walls, and would probably stay there for the rest of her life. She shivered, and Jem moved to put a protective hand on her arm.

'Mrs Moncrieff's widowed now, Janet,' he told the maidservant. 'She's bought a wee house out at the Esplanade, just for herself and her child.'

Annis got herself under control. 'You'll come back to work for me?'

For the first time the woman looked straight at them.

A smile broke over her face; a tired, creaking sort of smile.

'Aye, ma'am,' said Janet. 'Oh aye, ma'am!'

'I want Tib out of there,' Annis said as soon as the doors of the Poorhouse closed behind them. The air on Duncan Street, never worthy of note before, was like nectar after the oppressive place they had just left.

'She can't be let out, Annis. The woman's mad, you know that.'

'Could she not be set up in a wee house with a nurse to watch her? It's wrong for Douglas's sister to be shut in a place like that!'

'If you ask me,' Jem's voice was grim, 'it's what she deserves.'

'Nobody deserves that! I let poor Janet stay a prisoner in the place for far too long . . . I'm not going to have Tib on my conscience as well. She must have somewhere better than that. I'll pay whatever's necessary.'

'But . . . ' Jem began, then sighed. 'Very well, I'll see what can be done.'

It soon became apparent that there was no question of Tib Moncrieff being allowed to live in the community, even with a permanent nurse, but to Annis's relief Jem managed to find a discreet nursing home near Ayr where she could live in greater comfort than in the Poorhouse. The house Annis and Douglas had lived in was sold and with its going Annis felt as though the final link in the chain that bound her to the Moncrieffs had parted.

The *Grace and Charity* came back into harbour just as she had moved into the small comfortable house she had bought, and as soon as he was free Gideon called on her.

The house was near the old Moncrieff house, but right down at the water's edge. The bow windows at the front looked on to a pleasant road, with the firth just beyond the railings that edged the far footpath.

Annis knew from the *Greenock Herald*, which recorded the comings and goings of ships, that the *Grace and Charity* was due in harbour, and had been watching with mixed feelings for the vessel going up river towards her mooring place at Customhouse Quay. But as it happened the vessel went by while she was in town choosing the last of the furniture needed for the house, and Janet, busy caring for the two children and trying to get the kitchen in order, neglected to tell her.

It was a pleasant March day and before hanging the curtains she had made for her bedroom Annis decided to clean the windows.

'Let me do it, ma'am,' offered Janet, ever eager to be of use, but her mistress waved her away.

'I can manage.'

'Folks'll mebbe see you . . . it wouldnae be seemly!'

'What do I care what folks might think? This is my house, and I shall do as I please,' said Annis with pleasure. 'You get your kitchen put to rights and keep an eye on the bairns.'

She tied her hair in a scarf, put on an apron, and set to work. She had almost finished when she glanced down and saw a tall, lithe figure striding along the road from the direction of the town.

Her heart turned over and she almost released her grip on the window. With his hand on the gate, Gideon looked up and saw her.

'Good afternoon, Mrs Moncrieff.' He came into the small front garden to stand below her, his teeth gleaming in an amused smile. 'It is Mrs Moncrieff this time, is it not? The last time, as I recall, it turned out to be your maidservant.'

She clung to the window-frame. 'G – good afternoon Captain. If you just ring the bell Janet'll let you in. I'll be with you in a moment,' she said, and slid hurriedly into the room, almost landing on the back of a chair.

He was examining the small parlour with interest when she arrived after hurriedly rolling her sleeves down and snatching the scarf from her hair.

His green eyes took her in carefully. 'You look a deal better than when I last saw you.'

'I'm very well.' It was the truth. Since Rowena's birth her former health and vitality had returned. Now that she had no need to be meek and submissive she had all the energy that was needed to tend to her child and to the smooth running of the shipping office as well. Beaton was a competent clerk, and Jem had been right when he said that she would need more to occupy her than domestic matters. 'Did you have a successful voyage?'

'I think you'll be pleased with the cargo I've brought back for you.' He paced the room with three long strides, then turned. 'Jem tells me that the two of you agreed to a partnership in my absence.'

His voice was cool and Annis was at once on the defensive. 'I see no reason why you should find that unsatisfactory, Captain Brenner.'

One eyebrow rose swiftly, then he said, 'I have no objections, ma'am. I'm . . . glad that you didn't sell out. Life can be hard for a woman set on bringing up a child without benefit of a husband's help. I take it that that is still your intention?'

'It is.'

435

His eyes were on her throat now, where the opal pendant Matthew Mundy had given her lay warm on her skin. 'I thought that perhaps Mundy . . .'

'Mr Mundy has gone back to Australia.'

'So Jem told me. As soon as the *Grace and Charity* can fill her holds with new cargo I plan to take her back for the rest of the wool.' Then he asked, 'Am I permitted to see m . . . your daughter?'

The moment had come. 'Yes, of course. She's sleeping in the back garden. I like her to be out in the fresh air as much as possible. Some mothers think it bad for a child, but for myself . . .'

Chattering like an empty-headed fool in her nervousness, she led him through the kitchen where Janet, still too thin and pale for Annis's liking, bobbed a shy curtsey, and into the small back yard.

The clothes-line was bedecked with small clothes and Tom, Janet's son, was busy digging in a flower bed with an old spoon. At sight of the visitor he stood upright, his dark eyes huge with alarm.

'Who's this?'

'Thomas McGregor, Janet's little boy . . .' She found herself talking to the empty air. Gideon had squatted down and was holding out one hand to Tom, gently coaxing him forward. Step by step, the little boy edged towards the man, a tentative smile ghosting round the corners of his solemn mouth. At eighteen months of age his walk was still more of a roll, with both feet wide to support his body.

'You've got the gait of a seaman already, boy,' Gideon said with amusement as the child came within range. 'Let's see how you do aloft . . .'

Two long arms stretched out, two big hands caught the

boy and swung him up as Gideon straightened. For a moment sheer panic flashed across Tom's face and Annis put up a hand to stop Gideon. But the shipmaster was laughing, a deep, infectious chuckle, and almost at once the child's alarm was swept aside as his little face split into a huge grin.

'You have a way with children,' Annis said as Tom, restored to the ground once more, trotted off to show his mother the coin that had been tucked into his hand. 'He's known nothing until now except the Poorhouse, and he'll have nothing to do with strangers, especially men.'

'Children respond to kindness just as easily as they respond to injustice, poor little devils,' Gideon said, then moved towards the baby carriage under the apple tree.

With a gentle finger he turned back the coverlet just enough to see the baby's face, puckered in sleep.

Looking at the stillness of his expression as he gazed down at her daughter — their daughter — Annis felt a moment's fear. 'She'll not waken for a good two hours yet,' she said swiftly. At that moment treacherous Rowena's fists, tucked above head, swatted at the air. Her eyelashes fluttered, then lifted to reveal wide blue eyes. She turned her head on the mattress and gazed up at Gideon.

'Since she's awake . . .' he said, and scooped her deftly from the nest of blankets, gathering her into the crook of his elbow and turning so that his body kept the sun from her eyes.

For a long moment father and daughter stared at each other. Gideon put a finger into one tiny palm, and Rowena's own finger closed about it fearlessly. She gave a little yawn, then a faint, toothless smile.

Gideon's eyes were hooded, his mouth still. At last he turned and gave the baby to Annis, gently extricating his finger from the tight little grasp.

'She's very beautiful. Take good care of her,' he said.

'D'you think I'd do anything else for my own child?' she wanted to know, too sharply.

'Of course not. Good day, Annis,' said Gideon, and walked out of the garden, stopping at the corner of the house to throw one brief glance over his broad shoulder to where she stood in the grass beneath the apple tree, the child in her arms.

22

Annis and Gideon's next meeting, a few days later, was stormy.

The three partners of Moncrieff and Brenner, shipping merchants and shipbuilders, met in the office in Cathcart Square to discuss a problem that had arisen.

'It's to be expected, I suppose,' Jem said gloomily. 'There are those businessmen in the district willing to support Douglas but not happy about entrusting their cargoes to the three of us. Some of them, no doubt, recall his attitude towards me, and resent me becoming a partner in his business.'

'I think that more would resent me than you,' Annis pointed out. As the office manager she was in Douglas's chair behind the desk with Jem sitting on the other side of the desk and Gideon pacing the room as though it was his poop deck.

'Whatever the reason the result's what we have to worry about.' The shipmaster's voice was impatient. 'We have only enough cargo to fill half the holds . . . and not much chance of more, by the sound of things.'

'Beaton's done his best. Until Douglas's customers learn to trust us as they trusted him we shall have to look further afield. But that will take more time than we can afford at the moment, with the wool in warehouses in Melbourne, waiting to be uplifted.'

'You'll have to sail in ballast, Gideon. There's nothing else for it.'

'I don't like it. And there's the money we'll lose. We can't afford it, even with the holds full of wool on the way back.' Gideon's strong teeth bit into his lower lip as he paced. 'Good God . . . when I think of all the goods that Australia still needs from us it goes against the grain sailing with empty holds!'

The germ of an idea sprang into Annis's mind, put there by the mention of cost and empty holds. She swatted it away, but it returned and the men's voices, worrying over the problem like a dog with a bone, receded into the background as she sat staring at the grain of the wooden desk, her brows together.

Jem had to speak to her three times before she heard her own name and looked up.

'You were in a dream, lassie.' His voice was slightly reproving. 'What we need to think about is how to overcome this business of the *Grace and Charity*'s next cargo.'

'What about passengers?'

Gideon stopped, and swung round on his heel to stare at her. 'Passengers? She's a clipper, not a liner!'

'Steerage passengers.' Annis's voice grew stronger as the idea took hold in her active mind. 'Clippers like ours were turned into passenger ships during the gold rushes in California and Australia, weren't they?'

'Aye, but . . .'

'What would it take? Partitions, bunks, ladders . . . would it be possible?'

'It would, but there are passenger liners now built specially to carry people to Australia. Why would they want the discomfort of travelling in the holds of a clipper?'

'I think I know some that would.' Annis fisted her hands on the desk. 'You'll have heard, Jem, that the wee straw-hat factory in Tobago Street has had to close down?'

'Aye, everyone knows that.'

'There's no work for the women to go to. That factory employed almost fifty of them, as well as a hundred more doing some of the work in their homes. I've had several of the poor souls at my door looking for domestic employment.' She paused, looking at the blank faces before her and praying that the men would understand what she was going to say, 'Olivia told me in Melbourne that there's plenty of domestic work in Australia for women from this country. And in a lot of cases there's the chance of making a good marriage with the men who poured into the country during the gold rush and stayed.'

'You're talking about shipping women out to Australia from Greenock?' Gideon's voice almost cracked.

'Why not? We could turn the empty holds into long cabins and put enough food aboard. And we'd charge a deal less than the passenger ships.'

'You'd never find anyone willing to go.'

'I'll not know that until I try. I'll advertise in the *Herald*. How long would it take to do the work on the clipper?'

'Not long.' Jem was beginning to look interested. 'I could put my carpenters on to it and supply the timber too. When you reach Melbourne, Brenner, you can have the cabins dismantled and then sell the timber, then load the wool aboard and turn back for home.'

'Then you're with me, Jem?'

'I'm with you — if you can find the passengers.'

Gideon's fist crashed down on the table. 'I'll not have my ship turned into a floating lodging house!'

'She's not your ship, Captain.' Annis knew as she said it how hurtful the words must be. But they had to be spoken. She must make her mark now or retire from the business. 'She's ours, and if you refuse to take her to Melbourne, then Jem and I must find a shipmaster who will.'

'Your husband had difficulty in finding one,' he reminded her icily.

'My husband only looked in this area. I've got the time to search further afield. I'm sure that I could find one in Glasgow.'

'As a partner I refuse to agree to this nonsensical plan of yours, ma'am.'

'You're one of three partners,' she reminded him, her voice as icy as his. 'Your duty is to the *Grace and Charity*, but mine is to the financial side of the business. Even charging a fare considerably lower than the passenger ships we can recover the money lost to us by the withdrawal of cargo.'

Their eyes met, green blazing into grey, grey catching and throwing back the glare. Neither of them was prepared to back down.

'This,' said Gideon to Jem, 'is what comes of bringing a woman into business . . .'

'When you told me that you had no objections, Captain, did you really think that I would be content to sit at home and mind my own business, with perhaps the occasional visit to the office to dust the inkwells?' Annis asked sweetly.

Jem put his hand quickly to his mouth and gave a muffled cough.

'I thought, ma'am, that you would have the sense to leave the decisions to those who know best.'

'I am a partner. I intend to do my fair share of work until such time as I stop being a partner.'

Annis drew a sheet of paper towards her and picked up a pen. 'So, gentlemen . . . is it agreed that I put an advertisement into the *Herald*?'

As the door crashed shut behind Gideon, Jem said ruefully. 'You've taken him by surprise, lass.'

'But not you?' She ran her hands through her curly glowing hair, dislodging the combs that held it back.

'Wasn't it my idea to bring you in? I knew you had fire in you, though Douglas and Tib between them kept it well banked down. Mind you,' he added, getting to his feet. 'I'm not at all certain that this plan of yours will work.'

'I am,' Annis said, and he sketched her a mock bow before leaving.

The advertisement brought in a flood of applications from young women seeking a new life in Australia as well as from whole families unable to afford the price normally charged by passenger ships. Jem's carpenters at once began work on altering the *Grace and Charity*'s holds so that she could carry passengers.

Although Gideon paid several visits to his daughter before sailing for Australia, he made a point of calling when he knew that Annis was in the office. When they had to meet on business he was withdrawn and cool towards her.

She had met him on equal terms for the first time —

partners, instead of man and woman — and he hadn't cared one whit for what he saw. She had lost him.

From now on, her life, and Rowena's future, must be all that she cared about. There could be nothing, and nobody, else.

23

Olivia's hopes of a ladylike existence in the big house during Matthew Mundy's absence seemed doomed to disaster.

While she was still fretting over the missing opal pendant, John, who had infuriated her by shrugging his shoulders and pointing out that the pendant was Matt's to do with as he wished, was busy preparing for the annual shearing.

On the previous year Olivia had refused point-blank to become involved in any way with the shearing, staying close to the shack while the big house and the surrounding area was invaded by sheep and shearers. John hadn't come home to her for almost two weeks, and when he did his clothes were so filthy, with oil from the sheep mingling with sweat and red dust to cake the fibres, that it had taken many days with the hated wash-board to restore them.

This year, living as she was in the big house, there was no escape. Dismayed, she watched the sheep being driven in from every corner of the huge Vanduara station, so many of them that the ground vibrated to the thunder of their small sharp hooves and every surface in the house was covered with the red dust they threw up. It got into Olivia's mouth and her hair, it flew in little clouds from her clothes when she undressed at night, it was on the food she ate.

As well as being dusty the sheep were noisy. The air was filled with the clamour of their complaints from the shearing pens until she thought she would go mad. And still they kept coming in, driven by bronzed men on horseback, each one with a throat as dry as the surrounding land. Chang and Betta and the rest of the house staff were kept busy day and night serving gallons of beer as well as making huge meals for the drivers and shearers.

Everyone came to help with the shearing: squatters, the opal miners, swagmen who roamed the outback looking for casual labour. One man rode in on a camel, with two more roped behind. They were hobbled near the house, where they surveyed everything about them with lordly lip-curling contempt and occasionally nipped fretfully at each other. Olivia kept well away from them, and more than once was startled awake from an exhausted sleep in the night by a deep angry bellow.

Once the shearing actually started it went on from first light until dark. It turned out that Olivia was expected to help with the cooking and serving of meals. When she tried to object, John fixed her with a cold eye and said, 'You're my wife. It's your job.'

Plagued by noise, dust and flies, she worked alongside Chang in the outdoor kitchen and helped serve food at the long tables. In order to keep the shearing going the men ate in shifts, so that there was always a group at the tables, laughing and chattering and eyeing John Mundy's pretty wife with open approval as she toiled among them, her glossy dark hair coming adrift from the knot at the back of her head, her face damp with perspiration.

The bunkhouses that normally lay half-empty were filled to overflowing. Albert Platt drove his own sheep over and Drina came with him to help in the kitchen.

Because the bunkhouses were full the Platts stayed in the main house, to Drina's delight.

'It's the best house in the territory,' she said enviously. 'I reckon our room's almost the size of our own house.'

Olivia, slicing onions for a stew, tried to smile condescendingly through a positive downpour of tears, and failed. And gradually she found herself drawn into things, sharing John's excitement as together they calculated the number of bales that the Vanduara station might collect. Now that he was the boss she saw a new side to John, and without realizing it grew to admire his confidence and ability, his knack of getting the maximum amount of work out of everyone without having to raise his voice or assert his authority. A new easy understanding sprang up between them.

It took the best part of a month before the shearing was over and the wool graded and packed after being washed in large perforated buckets set in the lake, then stretched out to dry. By that time the bullockies had arrived, their wagons drawn by teams of bullocks adding their lowering to the general noise. It seemed impossible, to Olivia, that all those men and animals could be provided with food and drink, but Vanduara was a well-run station and Chang, who never lost his beaming smile, apparently kept a never-ending supply of stores. The animals' water was drawn from the lake which, being fed from underground, was still full despite the long dry months that lay behind them.

'I hope we get some good rains this time,' Drina remarked as she and Olivia worked side by side. 'We depend on the wet, and our water supply's getting low. Old Jeremiah was always generous to his neighbours, but Albert likes to manage on his own if he can.'

On the night before the bullock wagons began to take

the bales of graded, washed and packed wool on its way to Melbourne and eventually Scotland, there was a big party to mark the end of the shearing. Chang outdid himself with food and drink kept back specially for the occasion; a fiddler and an accordionist were found among the shearers, and the big back courtyard was cleared and swept for dancing.

A few farmers' wives, like Drina Platt, had come to help out, but there weren't many women available as partners: most of the men cheerfully danced with each other, or by themselves. Olivia found herself whisked from her seat again and again by calloused, determined hands and whirled about the yard. Her partners didn't speak to her and she rarely saw a face because her nose was pressed into shirts most of the time. Bottles and jugs had been passed around with abandon and all the men smelled of sweat and drink. She had never danced with John before, and when at last he claimed her he turned out to be a good partner, moving well to the music, holding her firmly whereas most of the other men had clutched her.

'It was a real good shearing,' he said as he whirled her round. 'Matt's going to be pleased. You did well, for your first time.' Then quite unexpectedly he said, 'You look beautiful.'

She stared up at him. His dark ruffled hair was haloed by a glitter of stars. 'My skin's roughened by being outside all the time, my hair needs washing . . .'

'Shut up, Livvy, and let a man compliment his own wife,' said John pulling her close, his hands warm and strong on her back. Then, as a sudden clamour of angry voices rose from a corner of the yard he released her. 'Hell – the first fight of the night.'

As he started towards the two brawny men who were

pushing each other around, Olivia caught at his sleeve. 'John — you'll get hurt!'

'Not me,' he said, then checked for a second to add, over his shoulder, 'Nice to know that you care . . .' before charging across the yard, pushing his way between dancers and spectators to step between the brawlers, a hand on each broad chest, his voice raised in a surprising bellow that outmatched them.

The next morning the shearers and packers began to drift away. Old Renny loaded his camels and unhobbled them, providing entertainment for everyone as he danced at one end of a rope with an irritated camel prancing and roaring at the other, swinging him about as though he were a matchstick man.

At last he managed to subdue the creature and climbed aboard to lead his tall, lordly animals out into the flat red land where they soon seemed to waver and break up in the shimmering heat.

The Platts departed and John and the other herdsmen mounted up and began to drive the shorn sheep back to where the grazing was best. Olivia, together with Betta and some of the other aborigine women, turned to putting the neglected house to rights, sprinkling water and sweeping the dust from the rooms and the verandah. Then the lubras started on the washing while Olivia, free at last from that hated chore, settled on the verandah with a jug of lemonade and started a letter to Annis.

'Shearing time is over,' she wrote, then chewed the end of her pen and gazed out over the plain for a moment. 'We had a most entertaining party to celebrate the event. Everyone from miles around attended . . . Vanduara's social evenings are high on every calendar here . . .'

* * *

Drina Platt's hopes were answered and the rains came early. They started with a spectacular exhibition of tropical lighting, a firework display that bathed the landscape in an eerie, flickering pink glow. A great wind sprang up from nowhere, bringing grit and dust with it, forcing Olivia and John to vacate the verandah and close the house doors.

The night was humid, with a heavy black sky lit erratically by more lightning. Then suddenly the rains came in a torrential downpour that drummed on the roof and made it impossible for voices to be heard. John, naked, got up and threw open the bedroom door to the verandah, stepping outside and leaning out over the railing so that the rain fell on his upturned face and his chest.

Olivia followed, terrified by the noise, unwilling to be left alone. Peering out into the night she could only see water — not the slants of rain she was used to at home, but a solid sheet. It was like being under the sea.

'John . . .'

He laughed, throwing his arms open wide. Lightning flickered and she saw the water glistening on his smooth brown body. 'They've come, Olivia. The rains have come! Grass for the sheep, flowers in your garden . . .'

He swept her into his arms, kissed her, then carried her back to bed and made love to her among damp tumbled sheets.

The rain had gone by the morning, and the air was humid. That afternoon there was another fierce downpour and one of the sheepmen riding in from the direction of the Platt's farm reported a flash flood in the main creek.

By the following morning the red plain stretching to the house had a faint green tinge to it. Unable to believe her eyes, Olivia walked out to look at it, and discovered thousands of tiny spears of grass, already an inch high. Within the week the grass was lush and plants from seeds that had lain dormant in the baked ground were stretching towards the sky. The garden was bright with flowers and the plain itself had become an insect's paradise, dotted with clumps of blue and yellow and red and pink blossoms.

But the rains had come back again, slanting, lancing, driving across the land, when Matthew arrived on horseback, leaving the buggy carrying his luggage to lumber along in its own good time. Rainwater poured from his dark hair and his broad shoulders as he mounted the outer stairs with the air of a king returning to his castle.

'Livvy . . .' Before she could move back he had reached out and taken her shoulders in his hands, drawing her towards him so that he could kiss her cheek.

'You look as though life in the big house suits you,' he said mockingly as he released her. 'I hope you've looked after the place for me. You'll be anxious to return to your own home now, I suppose.' Then, as she said nothing, he slipped a hand into the pocket of his coat. 'These letters are for you, from your sister.'

'How is she?'

'Very well, and so's the child. Annis makes a fine mother.'

'Annis was always domesticated.'

'Ah, but she's got a head for business too. She's decided to run her husband's business in partnership with Jem Moncrieff and Gideon Brenner. You should be proud of your sister, Livvy. She doesn't sit around and expect people to dance attendance on her just because of her good looks. Although she has those as well.'

It took all Olivia's control to keep her arms by her sides. She could tell by his broadening smile that he knew her hands had fisted themselves. Within a few moments of his return he had made it quite clear to her that she was no longer the lady of the big house, that he was the owner of the station, and that Annis had prospered while Olivia herself had not.

John, who had ridden back to the house when he heard that Matthew had been seen on his way in, seemed to see nothing of the loathing between his brother and his wife. When Matthew turned from Olivia and asked, 'How was the shearing?' he answered calmly enough, 'Good, but I'm getting worried about the wet.'

Matthew nodded and ran his fingers through his hair so that drops of water fell to his shoulders. 'I'd to ride along the big creek for more than a mile before I found a place shallow enough to cross. I hope we don't lose too many sheep to the floods.'

Olivia left the brothers and retired to her room, where she fumed angrily for a while over Matthew's attitude and her own helplessness. Then something he said about Annis and a partnership came back to her and she snatched up the little packet of letters, hurrying impatiently over the news of Tib's madness and Adeline Fraser's disappearance, paying scant attention to descriptions of her little niece and of the house Annis had bought. She found the part she was looking for in the last letter.

'Jem has persuaded me to go into partnership with himself and Gideon, rather than selling the company. It will be my duty to see to the office in Cathcart Square. It has caused quite a stir and some of Douglas's clients have gone elsewhere for ships to transport their goods, not happy about entrusting their precious business to a woman. But I intend to show them that they're quite wrong. Why shouldn't a woman be as able as a man? Our brains may be smaller but I fail to see why they should be any less sharp.'

Olivia gaped at the page in her hand. This wasn't the Annis she had known for more than twenty years. Widowhood had changed her sister.

As she unfolded the last letter a square of board fell out from among its folds. Olivia saw that it was a photograph of Annis, seated on a low chair, smiling into the camera, her mouth curved as though she was about to break into laughter. She looked fulfilled, confident and mature. Her arms were filled with a froth of white lace and silk in which the baby's tiny face floated indistinctly.

Olivia scarcely took in the small features. Her eyes were on her sister's throat, where a familiar pendant hung from a chain.

She couldn't eat any of the delicious food that Chang brought to the table that night. Every time she looked down at her hands, the small milk opal on her finger, an eighth of the size of the harlequin stone, mocked her. And since Lawrie Borland had ridden in to give his report to Matthew and stayed to eat with them, there was no opportunity for her to say anything about the harlequin opal.

The rain fell steadily throughout dinner, beating on the verandah roof like a never-ending drum roll. As soon as the meal ended and Matthew produced a bottle of port and some cigars that he had brought home with him, Olivia excused herself and went to her room. When John came in later she was sitting on the edge of the bed, the photograph in her hands.

'Matt's gone off with some of the men to bring the sheep in from the northern area. I told him they'd be safe enough there but he just can't wait to make his mark on the place again. Lawrie's gone with him.'

She thrust the photograph at him. 'Look!'

He took it. 'This your sister? She doesn't look much like you.'

'Look . . . there!' Her finger stabbed impatiently at the pendant. 'It's the harlequin opal!'

John peered, then said, 'So it is. He must have given it to her.'

'But it should be mine!'

His face darkened. 'Livvy, the opal belongs to whoever owns Vanduara. If Matt wanted to give it to your sister he has the right.'

'You're a fool!'

His hand shot out and closed painfully about her upper arm. 'Don't ever say that to me again, Livvy.'

'I never will,' she told him, her voice thick with anger. Matthew's insolence on his arrival was difficult enough to swallow, but seeing Annis wearing the pendant that belonged by right to Vanduara and therefore to Olivia, knowing that John was prepared to stand by and let that happen to his own wife, was the final straw. 'I'm leaving, John. I'm going back to Scotland. I've had enough of this place and of Matthew Mundy!'

'You don't know what you're saying.'

'I know exactly what I'm saying.'

They glared at each other while the warmth that had begun to unite them during Matthew's absence cooled and vanished as though it had never been.

'Then go,' said John at last, adding, 'But you'll have to wait until after the wet, until the water's gone down in the creeks.'

Above their angry heads the rain drummed down relentlessly on the roof of the big house.

* * *

In the middle of the night a fist began hammering at the door, vying with the rain still pounding overhead. Olivia woke to find John already out of bed and on his way to the door. He spoke briefly, then closed it and began to throw on his clothes.

'What's happening?'

He didn't take the time to look at her. 'Matt and Borland were trying to cross the creek when a flash flood came down. Lawrie was swept away but Matt managed to climb into a tree. They can't reach him.'

A rumble of thunder almost drowned out the last few words. Lightning flashed at the window.

'I'm coming with you.' Olivia began to scramble from the bed.

'Wait here; you'll just get in the way,' he said tersely, opening the door that led out to the verandah. The curtains billowed into the room and a handful of rain spattered the floor. Then the door closed and she was alone.

Olivia pulled on a blouse and skirt and found a waterproof cape and a hat of John's which she pulled down over her head as she left the room, calling for Chang.

'Tell Luke to get the buggy ready.'

The cook's eyes widened. 'Missus no go out tonight!'

'Yes she will,' Olivia said grimly.

The rain whipped at her face as she huddled on the buggy bench beside the aborigine. Water sprayed up from beneath the wheels and the horses' hooves, and once or twice, as they rocked across the plain in the direction John had taken, Olivia felt as though they were in danger of drowning.

Every now and then thunder cracked overhead and lightning imprinted the surrounding mulga scrub and low stunted trees on her mind in jet-black against brilliant silver.

She had a vague idea of the area they were going to, for once or twice John had driven her out to look at some of the Vanduara land. The creek bed was normally dry, a broad, deep gulch running across the plain with great river gums growing on either side. The trees survived the long droughts because their massive roots were able to dig deep to where there was enough subterranean water to sustain them.

John had explained to her that now and again, during excessively wet seasons, the creeks and the billabongs that led off them filled with water. If this was augmented with flood water rushing down from the far distant hills, parts of Vanduara, particularly in the area of the main creek, could become lakes. It had only happened once before in John's lifetime.

The buggy tipped suddenly at one side and she was almost thrown off. She gasped, taking in a mouthful of rain, and clutched with cold wet fingers at the narrow board at the side. The horses plunged on into the darkness.

'There . . .' Luke said after a long time. She lifted her head and swiped the rain from her eyes impatiently. The buggy had mounted a slight rise and was dropping down the other side. Through the darkness Olivia could make out lights from hand-held torches bobbing in the distance.

As they got nearer she realized that only half the lights were held by men. The rest came from ragged, torn reflections in the fast-moving creek. And she became aware of another noise above the steady drumming of the rain . . . the deep, growling rush of angry water.

The buggy slewed round in a shower of spray and halted. Olivia half-fell from the seat, her feet sinking into mud, as another sheet of lightning lit up the scene before her.

The creek had vanished, buried under a great broad stretch of angry, white-tipped water that raced along, carrying debris in its foaming jaws. An entire tree, its branches reaching up towards the lightning-bright sky, came into view then spun by helplessly. The giant gums that normally bordered the creek were deep in the water, their lower branches whipping and thrashing in protest as the torrent tried to take them along with it.

By the edge of the water huddled a group of men. As Olivia started towards them, her feet caught and held by the mud at each step, the moon freed itself from its ragged cloud covering and someone stepped forward from the middle of a small knot of men.

'Livvy! What the hell are you doing here?'

She almost overbalanced as one foot stuck, and John caught at her arm. Her foot came free with a sucking sound. 'What's happening?'

He brushed rainwater and spray out of his eyes. 'Matt tried to cross on a raft with Borland. The raft hit a tree and they were thrown into the water. Borland's gone, but Matt managed to reach a tree that's still standing.'

She clutched at him, and her fingers encountered the roughness of a rope knotted round his waist. Sudden fear lanced through her. 'John . . .!'

'I think I can get to him. Then the others can pull us clear.'

'You can't go into that!'

'I was always a better swimmer than Matt.' His voice was even, pitched as it was above the noise of the torrent behind him. 'I reckon I can manage it if anyone can.'

She clutched at him. 'I won't let you!'

He loosened her hands. 'He's my brother, Livvy.'

'But he wouldn't do this for you!'

'Mebbe not,' agreed John. 'But that's his business. Keep back from the edge, Livvy, I don't want to lose you too.'

He stooped suddenly and kissed her, a swift, fierce kiss. Then he let her go and stepped away towards the water. She tried to follow him, but Luke caught her and pulled her back.

For a moment she struggled, then stood quietly in the aborigine's grasp as John, pulling his hat off and dropping it to the ground, moved forward into the water, out of her reach.

He staggered and almost fell, but managed to regain his balance. Waist deep, he stopped, tested the rope that linked him to the land once more, then threw himself into the flood, swimming strongly, and disappeared.

'He'll be all right, missus,' Luke said into Olivia's ear. 'Mr John, he stronger than you think.' Then he added, 'Stronger than an'body think, Mr John.'

The wait was long and agonizing. The rope tied to John's waist twitched through the fingers of the men that held the other end, yawing to one side then the other at the whim of the current. They had no way of knowing whether John was still alive, or on the bed of the creek, being dashed here and there. More than once Olivia screamed at the watchers to start pulling him in, but they had had their orders and they ignored her, gazing intently into the darkness. Each time the moon flickered through the clouds, Luke said 'There . . . he's still swimmin', missus.' Each time Olivia strained her eyes but could see nothing but debris and white tumbled water. Nobody could live in that, she was sure of it. John was dead, or dying, and she was alone.

Suddenly the aborigine holding the rope gave a whoop of excitement and chattered excitedly to the others. They all gathered beside him and Olivia saw the rope running swiftly through his hands.

'What is it?' She turned to Luke, who stood protectively by her side. His teeth showed in a broad grin.

'He made it, missus. He's got Mr Matt. Now they only have to come back.'

'Only!' There had been little chance of John reaching his brother; there could be even less chance of him coming back safely. She cared nothing for Matt; it was John she wanted back, safe and sound.

Matt arrived back first, a dark sodden bundle breaking through the shallows almost at their feet, being dragged, coughing and spewing flood-water, on to the land. Black hands caught him, untied the rope, rolled him over and thumped at him to empty his lungs.

Olivia paid no heed. Her eyes were reaching into the darkness, hungry for a glimpse of a second figure. After an eternity it arrived, staggering to its feet, lurching drunkenly out of the reach of the water, throwing back a seal-like head as Olivia broke free from Luke's hand and ran to meet it.

'John!' Laughing and crying at the same time, she plunged into the water, feeling its cold clasp dragging at her ankles and calves. She threw her arms about him and together they splashed clumsily to the land, where, too heavy for her to support, he sank to his knees, coughing and choking and gasping for breath.

When he could speak he asked hoarsely, 'Matt?'

'He's all right.' She helped him up, her eyes anxiously searching his face. His eyes were deep hollows, his body trembling with exhaustion, but he was safe, he was still alive, he had come back to her. 'John . . .'

'Give me a minute, Livvy.' He put her aside and walked, putting one foot carefully in front of the other, to where Matthew had just regained his own feet.

The others fell back as the Mundy brothers, streaming water, faced each other.

'I owe you, John,' said Matt.

His younger brother ignored the proffered hand. 'Reckon you do, Matt,' he said. 'And I owe you something too.'

His fist came up slowly, with all the strength he had left behind it. The blow was weak, but strong enough to send Matthew Mundy crashing back on to the soaked earth.

'As to the rest, we'll talk about it tomorrow,' said John. He staggered, and at once Olivia was by his side. Turning away from the sight of his brother sprawling in the mud, he put an arm about her shoulders and let her help him to the buggy.

Luke drove, while John and Olivia huddled in each other's arms in the back. Rain streamed over their faces, and his hard-jawed face was icy against her neck, but he was alive, he was safe, and that was all that mattered to her at that moment. Even the memory of the punch that had sent Matthew to the ground was unimportant beside the fact that John was safe.

'Not there,' she suddenly said as the buggy slowed at the bottom of the main house steps, 'Go on to our own house, Luke.'

'Are you m – mad?' John's teeth were chattering. 'It's not b – been lived in . . .'

'I know, but it's ours. I'm not going back into that house while your brother owns it.'

The shack was dusty and neglected. While John dropped into a chair, Olivia sped about the place, kindling the fire and pouring out some brandy that was kept in a cupboard. She knelt by his side and fed it to him, then refilled the cup and drank, feeling the numbing cold that had seized her when she watched John walking away from her into the water and gradually disappearing.

He was too exhausted and too sore to undress himself. She took off his wet clothes and towelled his muscular body dry, tears in her eyes as she found each new bruise and cut and scrape.

'We'd have been more comfortable at the big house,' he said as she helped him into bed.

'I know that.' She drew the blankets over him and began to take off her own clothes. 'But I didn't want to be under the same roof as Matthew — not tonight.'

'You'll have to get used to the idea. We're going to live there from now on, Livvy. I'll see to that in the morning. Unless you still mean to leave.'

Olivia blew out the lantern, slipped into bed beside him and reached out to warm him against her own body.

'I'm staying,' she said against his neck.

In the morning the rain had stopped and the sun was shining. Stiff and sore as he was, John refused to stay at home.

'There's things to be straightened out,' he said as he dressed. 'For one thing, we'll have to look for Lawrie Borland's body. I reckon it'll be caught up in a tree not far from where we were last night.'

'You'll be careful?'

He kissed her. 'I'm always careful.'

During what had been left of the night someone had returned his horse. Olivia helped him to harness it, but before riding off to the big house he said seriously, 'Livvy, there's something you have to do.'

'What?'

'Write to your sister. Tell her the truth.'

Olivia felt a flush of panic. 'But you said yourself that we'd move to the big house and . . .'

'We will. But I'll not have my wife living a lie. Things have changed for us both, Livvy, but I need to know that you mean it. I can't have you pretending we're living a different sort of life. You've got to show me you're happy with this one.' He put a finger under her chin and lifted her face so that her eyes met his. 'Write to her — today.'

When he had gone she went back into the house and looked around. Dust lay thick on every surface and the wet clothes, hers and John's, lay in a disgusting, clammy heap at her feet. She would have to get out that detestable wash-board again. But first . . .

She found a cloth and dusted the table and a chair then brought out her letter-pad and inkwell and pen and sat down.

'Dear Annis . . .'

She put the pen down, then made herself pick it up again. 'Dear Annis,' she wrote, while a shaft of sunlight fell across the paper and the galahs quarrelled and clowned and shrieked in the trees outside. 'There is something I must tell you . . .'

24

Rowena was a happy baby, secure and confident of being loved, just the way Annis had planned.

As the months passed and she began to take an interest in her surroundings and recognize people, her dark hair lightened to a rich auburn, deeper than Annis's own curls. Her eyes, blue at birth, turned to a striking hazel, somewhere between Annis's grey and green.

Tom and Janet adored her, and in return Rowena showered love on them. Annis was able to leave her with a clear conscience on those days when she had to be at her desk in the Cathcart Square office, knowing that her precious little daughter was in good hands.

Even so, she missed the baby and as she entered the Esplanade on her way home her steps always quickened in anticipation of the moment when Rowena would hold out her plump little arms to her and beam her special smile, no longer toothless.

Life was complete, Annis told herself time and time again. She and Jem made good partners; the shipping business and the shipyard were both thriving; she herself was fulfilled and happy and she had her house and her daughter. She needed nothing more.

But on stormy nights when she lay awake listening to

the sea crashing against the wall across the road, she fretted about the *Grace and Charity*, on her way back to Scotland. She studied the maritime reports in the *Greenock Herald* every day, and she made certain of finding out if there were any sightings of the clipper from ships that put in to harbour.

She knew, for Gideon dispatched formal reports whenever he could, that the ship had made her way safely to Australia and disgorged her passengers and cargo safely. She had loaded with Mundy wool from the warehouses in Melbourne and was on her way back home. Annis diligently set about finding a market for the wool and a cargo for the next trip, and continued to tell herself how complete her life was.

Olivia's letter was delivered to her one November day at the office. As soon as she could Annis put her own work aside and opened it, anxious as always to know how her sister fared.

She read it once, twice, a third time, and didn't even hear Beaton tapping at the door. When he opened it she jumped.

'Mrs Moncrieff, Mr Ballantyne's in the office, anxious to have a word with you.'

'Ballantyne?' She mouthed the word, then as he nodded and beamed, said clearly, 'By all means, Mr Beaton. Please ask him to come in.'

Ballantyne was one of the merchants who had taken his custom elsewhere after Douglas's death. Annis hurriedly put the letter aside and folded her hands on the blotter before her, smiling with brisk friendliness as the man, hat in hand, was shown in.

'Yes, Mr Ballantyne, what can I do for you?'

'It's like this, Mrs Moncrieff.' He stood four-square

before the desk, looking down on her, his brows knotted with embarrassment. 'I'm thinking that mebbe I was a wee thing hasty when I took my business elsewhere. There's no getting away from the fact that the Moncrieff boats were aye trustworthy . . .'

'And still are, Mr Ballantyne,' she said, indicating a chair. 'And still are.'

'Ye did well tae win Ballantyne back,' Jem said a few weeks later, toasting his toes in front of the fire in Annis's small parlour. He had had a rowdy time of it with Rowena and Tom and now they had been dispatched to bed and Janet was putting the kitchen to rights before going to bed. Outside, a strong wind from the sea blew against the front of the house.

'There was little winning to it.' Annis was busy stitching a new dress for Rowena. 'It was his decision.'

'And where he goes others'll follow. The worst's over for us, lass. We're going to weather the storms.'

A gust rattled the windows and Annis's head jerked up.

'So will he, don't fret yourself about that. The *Grace and Charity*'s a fine ship and she's got the best shipmaster in the town.'

'I wasn't fretting,' she said, and he grinned and took the pipe from his mouth to point the stem at her.

'You've no secrets from me, Annis Moncrieff.'

'Have I not?'

'Well . . . mebbe one.'

His voice had changed suddenly and Annis looked up, then put the sewing down on her lap, her gaze caught by his own.

'What would that be?'

'I've noticed,' said Jem slowly, deliberately, 'that

there's a way wee Rowena looks at me sometimes that puts me in mind of . . .' He stopped, then said, 'She's no' a Moncrieff, Annis.'

'She takes after me.'

'Aye, she's very like you. But to my eyes there's the look of another.'

Her mouth trembled and she controlled it by biting down hard on her lower lip. 'You're mistaken.'

'Am I? No need to fear, lass, the whole town's so sure she's Douglas's child that I doubt if even the gossips'll ever say otherwise. You know that Gideon thinks the world of the bairn?'

'Rowena's my concern, not yours or Gideon's!'

'Mebbe you're right . . . but if I was you I'd think carefully about the future, Annis. You werenae born tae live out your life without a man, and whatever harm Douglas did you . . . and I know,' he added swiftly as she began to protest, 'that there was something or you'd not have been so anxious to sell the clipper and the company as soon as he died . . . whatever it was, he's gone and it's gone and it's wrong to punish one man for the misdeeds of another.'

For a moment the only sound in the room was the howling of the wind and the crackle of the fire in the grate. Then Jem knocked out his pipe against his heel.

'I'd made up my mind to say my piece and I've said it. I'll never mention this again. But think on what I've said. If you're punishing yourself and Gideon for something that's by, mebbe it's time for the punishment to end.'

His words, and Olivia's letter, haunted Annis as the year drew to its close with storms and snow flurries. The new life that she had carefully built up like a wall between herself and the rest of the world had begun to crumble.

Again and again, as she read the stumbling words her sister had written, she thought of the effort it must have cost proud Olivia to write them, to confess everything . . . the misery of her time with the Stobos, why John Mundy had proposed to her and why she had accepted, the shabby little shack they lived in, the way John had been treated by his father and his brother.

'We're still living in the shack,' Olivia ended her letter defiantly. 'But not for much longer. And anyway, where my husband chooses to live is home to me from this day on.' Then she had scrawled a postscript. 'I hope that you won't think the less of me for knowing the truth, Annis. If John and I are to share our life together fully there must be no more pretending, no more foolish pride.'

Annis had written back at once, a letter filled with love and assurances. But she had withheld her own confession, unable to put it on paper. One day, she told herself as she sealed the letter to Olivia. One day — but not yet. There had been a time when she would have gladly opened her heart to her sister, given the opportunity. But not now.

Each time she opened Olivia's letter, now becoming fragile from continual study, she was painfully reminded of the two American sisters, Grace and Charity, who had let pride divide them and condemn them to lonely, empty deaths. And thinking of the sisters brought Gideon to her mind and re-awakened her fears for his safety.

It seemed no time before Rowena reached her first birthday, and the old year gave way to 1876.

'A new year,' Janet said as she and Annis stood at the front door in the cold clear night, listening to the sound of the church bells and the clamour of ship's horns drift from the town and the harbours. 'A new year, and new beginnings.'

At last, in January, came word that the *Grace and Charity* lay at the mouth of the Clyde, ready to start the last short leg of her journey home.

'She's hove-to and she'll lie there until tomorrow morning so that she can come up river in daylight,' Jem reported when he called in at the office. 'The tug skipper who told me says that Gideon's determined to bring her in on his own without the help of a tow.'

Annis put a businesslike note into her voice. 'I'd best let the harbour know that she'll be ready to unload by late afternoon, then.'

'Aye,' said Jem dryly. 'Do that, Annis,' and he departed for his shipyard without another word.

As she lifted Rowena from the basin of warm water before the fire that evening and began to dry the plump little body carefully, some revellers passing by outside broke the quiet night with a burst of song. Rowena jumped slightly and her small head with the wet auburn hair plastered against the neat skull swung round towards the window.

For a moment she listened, then turned questioningly, swiftly, to her mother, bathing Annis in a hazel-green gaze that was so like Gideon's that for a moment her heart seemed to stop beating.

'Huh?' Rowena queried.

'It's all right, my wee princess, it's just some noisy lads singing,' she said automatically, concentrating her attention on drying the baby's tiny budlike toes. When she looked into the small face again Rowena, beaming back at her, was Rowena once more.

Later, when the house was quiet, Annis sat with Olivia's letter in her hand.

'Are ye no' gaun' tae yer bed?' Janet asked, popping her head round the door.

'In a wee while. You go on, Janet, I'll see to the fire before I go up.'

The woman yawned and left. Annis walked over to the oval mirror hanging on the wall and examined the closed face reflected in the glass. One hand went up to the harlequin opal at her throat. From its depths shards of crimson and blue green flashed at her. It was beautiful, but it was not for Annis Moncrieff, she thought suddenly. It rightfully belonged to Olivia. A woman who had locked herself in bitterness and pride as she, Annis, had done would look better in hard black jet.

A tear welled up in each eye as she watched herself, then slid down each cheek. She reached to the nape of her neck and unclasped the opal pendant, then carefully put it into a drawer. She would never wear it again.

Seating herself at the little writing table against one wall she drew some notepaper towards her, made a few false starts, and tossed the crumpled sheets into the basket at her feet. Now she knew how hard Olivia must have found it to write her letter. Now, briefly, she understood why these American sisters had chosen loneliness instead of finding the courage to be honest with each other.

It was never easy to swallow pride, but at times it was the only way.

'My Dear Olivia,' she wrote at last, slowly and steadily. 'Now my turn has come to tell you some truths about myself . . .'

*   *   *

The day had started well but by noon a haar, a misty drizzle of rain, had swept over the hills on the other side of the firth and crossed the water, blotting out the boats one by one, until it finally reached Greenock.

Annis, sheltering from the worst of it under the walls of the great Customs House, drew her shawl over her head with her free hand. Her other hand held an opened umbrella above the perambulator where Rowena, snugly wrapped up, lay sleeping. After posting Olivia's letter, with the harlequin opal pendant carefully tucked into the folds of paper, they had gone straight to the harbour and had been waiting there for some time.

She shifted from one foot to the other, then back again, playing childhood games to pass the time. 'By the time I count to one hundred he'll arrive,' she told herself silently. Then it was two hundred, then the alphabet forwards and backwards, then three hundred.

It happened when she reached the count of five hundred. There was a stir on the harbour and although the mist hid most of the river from her sight she knew instinctively what it meant. Hurriedly she closed the umbrella and wheeled the perambulator to a spot as near the edge of the harbour as she could without inconveniencing the men preparing to take the mooring lines. Most of them recognized her and touched their caps.

'You'll be pleased tae see the clipper safe home, ma'am,' one of them said. 'Take the wee yin ower here, where she can see better.'

When Annis had manoeuvred the perambulator to the spot he had indicated, she bent and lifted Rowena into her arms. The little girl woke and yawned hugely, then blinked at the grey damp world about her.

An order rang out from the mist and was answered by the rhythmic thud of bare feet on a wooden deck and the roar of voices singing a shanty. A long slender jib scythed through the blanketing drizzle, followed by an elegant, familiar prow close enough for Annis to pick out the names of two foolish long-dead sisters inscribed in flowing letters. Then the masts were towering high above the harbour, with the men strung out on the ratlines gathering in the wet sails.

Rowena babbled and stretched out a podgy finger to the ship as it eased into its mooring, the ropes forward then aft smacking almost into the hands outstretched to take them.

'Yes, my love, he's home. He's come back to us.' With a trembling hand Annis pulled the baby's bonnet off, then pushed back her own shawl, regardless of the rain, so that the glow of their two bright heads would act as a beacon to catch Gideon's eye. She felt as nervous and excited as a young girl.

Forgetting the need to keep out of everyone's way, she moved forward to where she could see the poop deck. He was there, just as she remembered from her first sight of him . . . both hands gripping the rail before him, his dark head tipped back as he watched his crew aloft.

'Look there . . . look, Rowena. There's your father,' she said, and the word was sweet on her lips.

As before, he gave a brief little nod of approval and turned to survey the harbour. Annis saw . . . or sensed . . . the sudden brilliance in that gaze, the tightening of his fingers on the rail as he spied her standing there waiting for him, their daughter in her arms.

Then his eyes were hooded, his mouth tightened, and he turned to say something to the mate who was standing by his side. The man nodded and hurried off to see to something while Gideon looked back at the harbour calmly, with no show of emotion.

She understood, just as she would understand everything about this man, her man, for ever. She had rejected him twice, had over-ruled him in business. It would be hard for Gideon Brenner to forget.

But like Olivia, unlike the sisters Grace and Charity, Annis had overcome her pride; eventually she would be able to convince Gideon of that. It would be hard work, she thought exultantly, but no matter. He was safe, he was home, and she was willing to wait until he was sure of her again.

She hugged Rowena to her, kissed the top of the small head. She was willing to wait. She had all the time in the world.

More Compelling Fiction from Headline:

EVELYN HOOD
THE
DAMASK DAYS

A captivating saga of Paisley weaving

Christian Knox is a girl who dreams – of a life beyond that
of a Paisley housewife, of a world of learning beyond her
Ladies' School, of possibilities her father dismisses as 'daft
ideas'. But Christian is determined and when her father
refuses to finance her education further she resolves to pay
for it herself, by working as a tambourer, embroidering
freelance for the local textile manufacturers.

Before long she's managing a group of tambouring women
on behalf of Paisley's biggest weavers, and chief amongst
her clients is Angus Fraser, a man old enough to be her
father but wise enough to appreciate her talents. Plunged
into the fascinating world of Scotland's fledgling textile
industry Christian soon finds her combination of Lowland
resolve and female flair begins to make its mark. And, in
the shape of her greatest, most fought-for inspiration, the
Paisley Shawl, it is a mark that will be remembered for
generations to come . . .

'Reminds me of Catherine Cookson' *Glasgow Evening
Times*

Also by Evelyn Hood (writing as Louise James) from Headline

Gold Round the Edges
'Bold and compassionate' *Liverpool Daily Post*

The Promise Box
'Can't put it down' *Glasgow Evening Times*

FICTION/SAGA   0 7472 3501 5

A selection of bestsellers from Headline

FICTION

ONE GOLDEN NIGHT	Elizabeth Villars	£4.99 ☐
HELL HATH NO FURY	M R O'Donnell	£4.99 ☐
CONQUEST	Elizabeth Walker	£4.99 ☐
HANNAH	Christine Thomas	£4.99 ☐
A WOMAN TO BE LOVED	James Mitchell	£4.99 ☐
GRACE	Jan Butlin	£4.99 ☐
THE STAKE	Richard Laymon	£4.99 ☐
THE RED DEFECTOR	Martin L Gross	£4.99 ☐
LIE TO ME	David Martin	£4.99 ☐
THE HORN OF ROLAND	Ellis Peters	£3.99 ☐

NON-FICTION

LITTLE GREGORY	Charles Penwarden	£4.99 ☐
PACIFIC DESTINY	Robert Elegant	£5.99 ☐

SCIENCE FICTION AND FANTASY

HERMETECH	Storm Constantine	£4.99 ☐
TARRA KHASH: HROSSAK!	Brian Lumley	£3.99 ☐
DEATH'S GREY LAND	Mike Shupp	£4.50 ☐
The Destiny Makers 4		

All Headline books are available at your local bookshop or newsagent, or can be ordered direct from the publisher. Just tick the titles you want and fill in the form below. Prices and availability subject to change without notice.

Headline Book Publishing PLC, Cash Sales Department, PO Box 11, Falmouth, Cornwall, TR10 9EN, England.

Please enclose a cheque or postal order to the value of the cover price and allow the following for postage and packing:
UK: 80p for the first book and 20p for each additional book ordered up to a maximum charge of £2.00
BFPO: 80p for the first book and 20p for each additional book
OVERSEAS & EIRE: £1.50 for the first book, £1.00 for the second book and 30p for each subsequent book.

Name ....

Address ....

....

....